AS THE SPARK FLIES UPWARD

A NOVEL BY JENNA-CLARE ALLEN

ROUND DOOR
PUBLISHING

AS THE SPARK FLIES UPWARD

by Jenna-Clare Allen

The author may be reached via the publisher:
rounddoorpublishing@gmail.com

Published by Round Door Publishing, Cleveland, Ohio

Cover Design by Heidi M. Rolf
Photography by Lauren Stonestreet, Elle Effect Photography, LLC

This is a work of fiction. Names, characters, places, and
incidents are the products of the author's imagination or
are used fictitiously. Any resemblances to actual events,
locales, or persons, living or dead, is entirely coincidental.

First printing 2011

10 9 8 7 6 5 4 3 2 1

ISBN 978-0-9844302-0-8

LCCN 2011908686

Printed in the United States of America

To my family—both the Allens and the Roberts—
you are my past, my present and my future.

To our friends, who compel me forward, pull me outside of myself,
hold me up when I can't stand, make me want to be better than I am
and never fail to make me laugh so hard that I need an inhaler.

To my son, who is my reason for waking and sleeping and
everything in between. My life was so very small until I knew you.
Now it has whole galaxies in it that I have not yet explored.

And to J, who is every hero I have ever written and will ever write.
Ninakupenda sana. Mpendwa wangu ni wangu, na mimi ni wake.

I.

My sister was dazzling. She was the brightest red star fallen from the night sky and her heat made her untouchable, fearsome, unfathomable. From the moment of her birth she seared everything she touched. Those of us who were seared were never the same. We were eternally marked, though I have never been able to tell if this marking was for better or worse.

I think that my earliest memory is of Thena's laugh. There was nothing timid about her. There was no shyness or diffidence in her, even as a tiny child. Her laugh shook the ground beneath her feet, like the laugh of a giant or a goddess.

My whole life long, I have never seen anything that could compare with her. When she left us, it tore a hole in my soul the size of the deepest crater in the deepest ocean and left me naked and alone—and yet her birth nearly ended it all before it had begun. Even the most ordinary things, Thena could not do like the rest of us. But then, she was not like the rest of us.

My mama was a tiny, delicate woman. I have never known one smaller. As a full grown adult she was just shy of four feet, seven inches. And she was still a quiet slip of a girl when she gave birth to Thena—just nineteen.

Oh! And for a mortal to give birth to a goddess: what a mighty struggle. The pains lasted four days and three nights, and the pushing lasted from sunrise to sunset on the fourth day. Just as the sun crept away, bringing in the night sky and leaving the earth to mourn its passing, so Mama was leaving us, departing from this earth with the baby still in her belly. Though, unlike the setting sun, Mama would not have returned in the morning.

The boy-doctor watched in horror as waves of Mama's blood swept over the tiny rooms of the house. He reached a hand to his face and wiped the sweat from his burning eyes. In a final act of desperation, and in a last attempt to salvage his unmade reputation, he dried the blood from his trembling hands and took up a knife. He cut a long slash across Mama's belly and lifted the baby out. Everyone stared to see the child that had come so near to ending everything. She was thin and long and howled fiercely at the doctor who had bothered her rest, angry to be awakened from her queenly slumber.

"Mama," I used to say as a girl, climbing up into her sweet-smelling lap, "tell us the story of the day Thena was born."

I would nuzzle my face against the soft skin of her neck and listen to the deep resonating sounds rumbling up from her belly as she hummed.

"Are you washed in the blood,
In the soul-cleansing blood of the Lamb?
Are your garments spotless?
Are they white as snow?"

Sixty-six years after her death, I can still hear the sound of her voice singing softly into my ear. In her voice I hear the songs of angels.

Then she would wrap her arms around me and gather up into her lap as many of her babies as she could hold.

"Thena came into the world lookin' like a queen," she would say. "*You* were born five weeks early. Without eyebrows or eyelashes or so much as a single hair on your head."

Then she would reach up with her index finger to trace my brow bone.

"You were blue and purple and so tiny that when you cried, no sound came out." She would smile at me, her eyes alight with love.

"But Thena, she looked up at that doctor with her big shinin' eyes as if she was shocked by his impert'nence. Like she just couldn't understand how anybody would have the gall to wake her from that nice nap she'd been havin' fer so long. She scowled right into his face, with her tiny fists balled up and turnin' red." Mama would smile. "And do you know what she did?"

We would shake our heads, though we had heard the story a thousand times.

"She socked him in the eye with her little red fist. It's true!" Mama would laugh. "She did, though I don't imagine she could've done it on purpose. Anyway, she must've got him pretty good, 'cause as soon as it happened, underneath his eye I could see a little red welt just the size and shape of her fist."

Then Mama would chuck Thena under her pretty chin, her expression wry.

"You don't summon a queen. It's the queen who summons you."

Thena cried long and loud and with a fury that made the doctor and my mother's sister want to leave the room. Apart from that magnificent voice, there was nothing chimerical about her. She was not the expected misshapen monster, but a perfect, beautiful specimen. She came to us and graced our humanity with her cool, untouchable majesty. If *this* was what the human race could be then, pray, never let us fade away, but preserve us from everlasting to everlasting.

Apart from her physical perfection, she was normal in every other respect—her size, her shape, the length of her arms and legs, ten fingers, ten toes, all features in their proper place and in their proper proportions. Mama used to say that she saw disappointment on the doctor's face when he lifted Thena up to the light. He seemed to be hoping for deformities or imperfections—some indication of what could have caused such horror.

Or maybe he hoped for some anomaly that would add a notch to the belt of his medical expertise.

Instead, the young doctor found only one irregularity on my sister's perfect body. Thena's fine head was covered in silken curls so black they looked purple. The day of her birth her head was covered with all the hair it would ever possess. She was not, as most newborns, given a babyish smattering, but was blessed with the gift of as much hair as any grown woman.

"From the moment she was born," Mama always said, "her hair was her crown of glory."

Her whole life long, strangers came up to touch her hair. People literally gasped when they saw her, and whenever any of us were with her we felt as if we were under the sterile scrutiny and white heat of a microscope. People didn't bother to hide their stares. Thena was openly gaped at and she knew it. And yet she was unfazed. Her beauty was never important to her and she thought anyone to whom her beauty *was* significant a fool.

"Beauty is fleeting and charm is deceptive," she used to say, winking at Mama, who could quote long passages from the scriptures and a few dozen of its books from memory.

In the midst of the black mass of Thena's hair was one peculiarity. In the front and center of her scalp, just where her widow's peak should have lain, grew one long curl of a violent red color. It was scarlet. Crimson. Blood red. It fell across her forehead like a great red bolt of lightning. This characteristic, more so than any other, made her terrifying, holy and utterly beautiful.

In spite of this striking trait, the doctor couldn't find a single thing wrong with Thena that would explain why Mama's birthing was so difficult. There was nothing about her that should have caused such a fuss. And yet...

The doctor looked her carefully over, shook his head, wiped the brown and red mess of the birth from her long, lean body and handed her to Mama. Mama once told me that she took one look at Thena and knew that her child wasn't earth-bound. She wouldn't be like other children.

I have often asked myself if it is possible to look into the face of a young child and see what destiny lies before her. Did Mama gaze into Thena's eyes and see in them all the worlds of fire and light and sorrow lying quietly at rest, waiting for their time? Maybe, but I think probably not. It seems more likely that she looked at her and thought that all the joy this world could hold was found here in this one blessed baby, and then I think she put Thena to her breast and fell asleep.

While sewing up the long gash that ran across Mama's belly, the doctor shook his head and said, "Don't have any more children."

"But I didn't listen to him," Mama would say at this point in the story, kissing all of her babies that came after. "The best moments of my life were when my babies were born. And no matter what else my life may have lacked, I've been richer than all the Rockefellers and Lindberghs combined 'cause of you."

The young doctor gathered up his bag and medical volumes and hurried away, not even staying long enough to receive his payment. Mama named her new daughter Athena on the spot, and, pagan name that it was (and good Methodist that Mama was), never called her by it again. She was Thena from the first hour of her birth. Mama used to say that anyone who saw her even from those first minutes would have seen the necessity of naming her Athena. There was no other name to which such a child would have answered.

"Your Papa was called in from the fields. He had sat in the pasture for three days with the cattle, sleepin' under the night sky to get away from the sound of my hollerin'." Mama smiled.

For the births of our older brothers, James and Theodore, Papa was present, but those had been easy births, and Mama had not once cried out. But on the day Thena was born, he returned to Mama's bedside just in time to kiss her cheek, touch his child's face, wipe the grime and tears from his spectacles and faintly smile as his wife named their baby Athena.

Mama said that he had stayed with her all of the first day, but that his sobbing was such a distraction that she couldn't concentrate on the volcanic eruptions taking place inside her belly. And so, eventually, she sent him away. My Mama always told that story with a gentle smile. She loved my Papa fiercely. She loved his tenderness, his gentlemanliness, his erudite and meticulous schoolteacher's mind and his quiet heart. Most of all, she loved the way he loved her.

II.

I recognize that life can be good. It can be complete and splendid. But there are few guarantees, because life can also be filled with pain. I guess that, for most people, it holds a fair amount of each. And though I have now considered the question for some sixty years, I have never known if our life with Mama contained more of one or the other.

I remember falling countless times as a little girl, injuring myself in my recklessness, and then later, being injured by another—the only other. Each of these times, as I sought Mama's comfort, she would gather me up in her arms and hug me hard against her tiny bird's body and promise that the pain would soon go away.

She really did believe, even with everything that would happen, that tears last only for a night and that joy comes in the morning. As a small girl, I had no idea of the meaning of those words. But I knew that they were a promise that Mama or the God to which she so often referred would use to bring about an end to my suffering, to our suffering. I believed that one or both of them would administer a curative to whatever ailed me.

This verse, a Psalm, I believe, was always instantly calming. Not because I understood its meaning or because I fully knew the Giver of the promise, but simply because my Mama said it and above all things Mama was good. She was true. If she said it, it must be.

As I grew older and came to understand the meaning of those words,

I marveled that Mama continued to say them and, what's more, that she continued to believe them. But she always did. Even until the end.

In 1927, without anyone's permission, my father left all the joys and sorrows of this world. In his death's wake remained my twenty-four year old mother and their four babies, aged six and under. Papa died of a kidney infection. This illness, which is today so easily cured, wiped my father from our lives like a smudge from a glass. Living in the day that they did, when Papa fell ill, Mama ordered medicine from the Sears, Roebuck & Co. catalog. It arrived two weeks after my father had been laid to his final rest. From dust Adam came and to dust we all return.

I remember that when she opened the package, Mama sat down at the kitchen table. She laid her head on her arms and cried. This was the only time I saw her mourn my father's death. Her mourning was short-lived, however, for she had four babies to feed and clothe. And then, not long after Papa's death, the nation was plunged into perhaps the darkest night since its beginning: the Great Depression.

How Mama came to be married to my stepfather is still a mystery to me. Oh, that she had never met him! Oh, that he had never seen her and wanted her!

As a girl, I looked at Dan Brown and wondered where that alien creature had come from and what had he to do with us. I think it must have been a hundred tiny things, all added together, that made Mama think that living with him would be better than the alternative. It seems only fair to say that my Mama, to her last day, claimed that when he was sober he was the most charming man she ever met. I was really only to know Dan sober during the final weeks of his life, and so for nearly twenty years was denied the pleasure of his charm.

Dan was handsome. He had laughing blue eyes and black hair and was as tall and well muscled as my father was small and slight. He was as laughing and jovial as my father was somber and thoughtful. In short, Mama must have figured that, as Dan was the antithesis of my father in every other conceivable way, surely he would be as hearty, hale and long living as my father had been prone to illness and fated for an untimely death.

Whatever she thought, there were children to raise and feed, and to raise and feed them with the help of a husband must have seemed better than to do it alone. I was almost three years old when my father died and had not yet turned four when Mama married Dan.

I don't remember many things from those early years. Mama later told me that Dan's drinking did not begin right away. It came later—the gift of an alcoholic father—after several years of the Depression when Dan was unable to find work.

Mama used to tell us the story of her courtship with Papa during the long nights when Dan didn't come home. I remember Papa very dimly. The fact that I cannot remember him better is one of the great sorrows of my life. I can only recall that his hair was red-gold and his eyes blue and that his laugh was soft like the sound of rain falling on summer leaves.

My Papa married his prize pupil. He loved Mama the first day she came into his classroom as a twelve-year-old girl. He was twenty years old and, as the story goes, he resolved that he would not say a word to her or anyone else of his love until she left school. He kept this promise and came to court Mama the day after she received her high school diploma. He married her three months later, and the following year, 1921, she gave birth to James.

Though Mama was smart, she married young and never learned a trade. She was simply a wife and mother. And so, because her options were limited, after she saw that Dan would not bring in an income, Mama took a job as housekeeper to Mayor Bentley and Mrs. Rachel Wilkins. They had old family money and would remain all but untouched by the Depression—untouched enough to keep servants on while the rest of the country scrambled for food.

It was unusual in those days for a white woman to work as a servant in the south. But my mother was determined to have the job, and she got it. Maybe the mayor took pity on this young girl with four children who had already buried a husband.

My mother cooked, cleaned and raised the Wilkins' child twelve hours a day, six days a week. She made twenty-four dollars a month. When Mama began to work for the mayor and his wife, I was five, Thena was six, and Mama was pregnant with her fifth baby. She took us with her to the mayor's house every day and shooed us out the back door, calling us into the kitchen twice each day—once for breakfast, once for lunch. Every other moment of our waking lives was spent in the woods and fields around our town or swimming in the muddy brown river.

Mayor Wilkins and Mrs. Rachel had one child, Reed Bentley Wilkins, who was the apple of every eye except their own. Before Reed, Mrs. Rachel had given birth to Everett Bentley Wilkins III, a baby so perfect in body, soul and spirit that he was unlike any child who had ever been born. He gave the Messiah himself a run for his money.

I used to hear the story of his short life and of his death told around the town. It seems that Rett was so caudled by his parents that he had been formed into a holy terror—*truly* unlike any other child.

Tragically, he drowned in the river at the age of four.

In spite of the kicking fits and eardrum damaging screams of the little boy, the townspeople were heartbroken. No mother should have to lose her child. No father should have his son taken from him. But such was the power of the river. People shook their heads and held their own babies closer.

Time went on, and Mayor Wilkins eventually convinced Mrs. Rachel that they could have another Everett. Four years after Rett's death, Reed was born. Mrs. Rachel and the mayor took one look at him, knew he was no Rett, and did not look at him again until they buried him not many years later.

Rett was dark haired and dark eyed like his mother. He was fat and dimpled and had the softest skin and slept night and day for his first seven months. Reed came out with his eyes open and they stayed open for nearly twenty years. He was long and thin with deep blue eyes. His hair was the color of pure gold, and even when he was born there were tiny lines around his mouth and eyes. He had been smiling in the womb.

Though the mayor and his wife never wanted Reed, everyone else surely did. Almost as if to make up for the lack of love he was given by his parents, the rest of the town lavished him extravagantly with it.

Reed was raised, without the intervention of his mother, by two women who were not biologically akin to him. In spite of the lack of blood ties, the bonds between Reed and his two mothers were thicker than blood or water.

One mother was Adda Sinclair, a middle-aged black woman who worked as seamstress and laundress to the mayor and his wife. Mrs. Rachel had once been a beauty queen and, unwilling to relinquish her title, she gave Reed over to Adda to be nursed so as to protect her Aphrodite's figure.

Adda had a son of just Reed's age. He was named Abraham Lincoln Sinclair and was always called Ham. Adda raised Reed in just the same way that she raised Ham and loved him just as much. Ham was smart and wickedly funny, and spent the early days of his boyhood doing whatever he could to infuriate his beloved mother. He doted on and worshipped Adda. But he also loved to ignite her fiery temper and was the one person who could.

"Abraham Lincoln Sinclair!" she used to yell at him as he raced through the screen door and away into the woods, carrying a still warm pie in each hand.

"You come back here or I will take you up to the mayor's office and let you explain what happened to his peach pies!"

Her voice was furious, though her eyes were laughing.

Our town was small and entertainment was scarce. Gossip was a savory morsel and few people grew weary of partaking in it. That, of course, was how I heard the story of Ham's birth. When he was born, Adda had long been a widow. She bore him at thirty-five, thirteen years after her husband, Lemuel, was mistaken for a buck and shot (drunkards make poor sportsmen).

Before he died, Lem had given her two sons—twin boys, Gad and Asher. But Ham was the son of her old age and she considered rearing him to be her greatest accomplishment.

Now, the Book says that the tongue is a fire and once the fire begins it goes on in much the way it started, growing with the wind. The townspeople wondered aloud from the beginning about the boy's father, flames of fire leaping from tongue to tongue. In fact, his identity was still a great source of speculation some years into my childhood. Many heads shook and many tongues wagged. But Adda's joy was complete, and she never revealed—even to her own sons—who Ham's father was. Perhaps, like Thetis, a god had come down and lain with her. But it mattered little to Adda. The father had left no imprint on her life except the child himself. It was as if she had erased his existence from her mind and, consequently, from the earth. God had given her Ham; no one else had.

Mama told me once that when she saw Adda's belly begin to swell and knew that she was going to have a baby, she had a pretty good idea of who had fathered it, but Adda never said a word about it, and Mama took Adda's cue.

Reed's other mother was of course, my own mama. We shared her from our earliest years. And from the shady memories of my little girl's mind, I do not remember knowing—for probably the first decade of my life—that Ham and Reed were not really my brothers. I am not sure when I finally understood this, but I am certain I was quite a grown up girl. Adda and Mama raised us all together at the Wilkins' home. As we were raised together, surely we belonged to one another, just as a brother belongs to his sister.

Even from the beginning, though, Reed belonged mostly to Thena. He belonged to her in a way that he never did to anyone else. His one great love was Thena, a year and a half his senior and in every way his equal.

It is perhaps ironic, though not surprising, that it was Thena who came to be his love. In theory, it should have been me—I was closest in age to Reed—but how could it have been? I was always plain and unextraordinary in every way. Both child and woman, I was small and bony with a flat chest and curly hair (a plus) of a mousy brown color (a minus). I have green eyes, but they are pale and mild, whereas Thena's were shot through with a thousand colors—her eyes were a symphony of green, flashing in her face like the tail of a comet.

Mama always told me that I was pretty. She never once differentiated between Thena's beauty and mine, but she didn't have to; other people did. I can still remember hearing the townspeople, as we walked through the dusty streets of our town, shaking their heads at me and saying, "And the other girl so pretty."

Perhaps if Thena had not been born, and I had been Mama's only daughter, people would have thought I was pretty. But anyone playing second fiddle to Thena would have seemed like a novice. A daisy is quite a pretty flower until you hold it next to a rose. Then it seems shabby, badly dressed, provincial. I never stood a chance next to Thena.

No one did.

Strangely enough, there was never any rivalry between us. Maybe I recognized, even as a baby, that there would be no point in trying to contend. My would-be opponent was too far out of my league. But really, I don't think so; I think it was merely adoration I felt for her, plain and simple. She was pure magic.

Thena carried all the love in the world inside herself. And all of us need love affairs. Those who cannot have them where they will must have them where they may. The light that Thena gave off was as powerful as the sun. I could not shine on my own, but I could reflect her light. And, oh, the warmth that light gave! Our eyes are drawn to the sun like a moth to a flame. It was the same with Thena—it was worth bearing the pain of her terrible heat in order to bask in the pleasure of her brightness.

III.

I think most of our days were happy ones. As Mama used to tell it they were, or at least the early ones. I think the change came when Dan, still without work and having taken to the bottle for short spells, found that Mama was pregnant again. This would be her sixth child, another son, whom she named John Michael Brown. Drunk on the evening that Mama told him, Dan seemed to think the pregnancy was her fault. It was, of course, impossible for Mama to impregnate herself, lacking the necessary equipment, but Dan did not seem to grasp this detail.

This was the first time I saw him beat Mama. I was five, and this beating is one of my earliest memories.

I remember walking that evening along the dusty road on our way toward home. Mama was singing to us as we walked through the strange half-light, her voice clear and low.

"*Swing low, sweet chariot,*" she sang.

"Mama," I asked her, "what do the words mean? I don't understand."

"Well, baby girl, I reckon it's a song about sufferin' in this life and lookin' forward to better things."

"What better things?" I asked her.

"Heaven, darlin' girl. My mama told me that the slaves is the ones that started singin' it. They didn't have nothin' on this earth that brought joy, so they sang about heaven, where there'll be only joy and goodness."

"Mama, why didn't the slaves have any joy?"

"Because they had nothin', darlin'. They didn't even own their bodies—their bodies belonged to their masters. They had no possessions, no houses, no freedom, even their children didn't belong to 'em. And 'cause they weren't allowed to read or write, even their thoughts weren't their own," she said, touching my hair. "And that made 'em look forward to heaven all the more."

She took my hand in hers. It was brown and small and the rough, work-worn skin of her palms scratched me. The night was cool and clouded and dark, though the time for sunset was still hours away. I would have felt afraid if Mama had not been with us. We walked for a long time. Her strong, sweet voice echoed out into the night as she sang one song after another.

"Sing with me, girls," she said, laughing.

But we smiled at her and shook our heads. We wanted to listen to her sing. When we passed King Farm to the west and our little house came into view, Mama's voice faltered, and then became quiet. Dan had been drunk for almost a week; she couldn't have been looking forward to going home.

Our house sat three miles outside of town on a small piece of land that had been my father's. Small and worn as it was, we loved it. We loved it because it had been his. Mama strode bravely into the yard, Thena's hands and mine clasped tightly in hers. I glanced over at Thena, wondering if maybe she couldn't feel her fingers, either.

The older boys must have been playing in the woods out back, because when we entered the house, it was dark. Mama built a fire and the room became warm and filled with soft light. Thena, Edwin and I sat down in the front room, which served as kitchen, living room and dining room. Mama began to make dinner.

After a while, Dan stumbled into the house, toting in one hand his dearest friend and most faithful companion—his talisman against all of life's unfair jibs. Dan wore his bourbon bottle as a Jew wears King

David's star; as a Christian displays the crucifix; as if he believed in its power.

The bottle shone in the faint light of the fire, its long, thin neck gleaming and amber-colored. Mama followed him into the back room, their bedroom. First, I heard her speaking softly to him, and then I heard a great cry of fury.

"What have you done, woman?" His voice shook the house.

"I got too many mouths to feed now as it is! What'm I gonn' do with another?"

"We'll make out alright, Dan," I heard Mama say softly, "I can take in extra laundry or sewin'."

Then came the sound of a blow landing on flesh and a muffled sob.

I don't remember all of it, but I am certain that the scene ended in the front yard. I remember that I was clinging tightly to Mama's neck, stroking her cheek. I wiped from her eyes a line of dark blood that ran in a stream down over her forehead and halted, drying onto her cheek.

I whispered, "Please don't cry, Mama. He won't hurt you no more. We won't let him hurt you."

Thena's face and eyes shone like flame. She held Edwin on her hip, his little body pressed fiercely against hers. She was not more than six years old. I saw a look of deepest loathing and hatred in her eyes; and that same look was there, after that night, every time she saw Dan Brown.

She sat the baby down in front of Mama, walked to where Dan sat in a stupor in the dust and slapped him as hard as she could; first with her right hand, then with her left. Thena was always strong, more powerful than any other woman that I have ever known, and her blows landed like great cries on his face. The left hand actually split his cheek. Dan's mouth fell open, his eyes bulging. He began to take off his belt. But Thena stayed just as she was, spitting once at his feet.

Then she screamed, her voice rumbling like thunder,

"Dan Brown, you go out to the shed and sober up!"

Dan made a motion to swat at her with his belt, and then passed out in the dust of the yard.

This was the first of many such scenes; to repeat them would be redundant. Something—and I have never understood just what—had defeated Dan Brown, and he was never again seen without his bourbon after that day.

I have asked myself a thousand times why Mama didn't leave him or kick him out on his head, but I can't find the answer. I don't think she ever found it herself. Maybe it was because she sometimes managed to take the few dollars he made from odd jobs from his trouser pocket before he drifted quite accidentally out of his self-inflicted fog and spent it. It might be that on these happy occasions she would be able to buy her babies one more pair of shoes, or put away a few more dollars towards Edwin's winter coat. Maybe it was because she had never known life without a man—husband or father—and she shivered to think of feeding and protecting six children alone. Maybe it was because, God help her, she loved him and she wouldn't leave him to die alone, unwanted and unknown. It could have been all of these things or none of them. But I suspect it was because Dan broke something in Mama that day that she believed could never be fixed, and that leaving him would have made no difference.

IV.

I remember very clearly the day we met Thomas Barrett. Reed, Ham and I were nine and Thena was eleven. Long before we knew "Pope" Barrett, we knew his father, Doc, and his grandparents, the Kings. The Kings were our nearest neighbors, their house about a mile from ours, though we would not come to know them well until we befriended Pope.

Doc Barrett delivered both Edwin and John. And it was during the long evening before John's birth that we first heard the story of Pope's.

"Pope was born seven weeks early," Doc told us. "I delivered him with one hand—in the backseat of my brand new black Ford—while his mama squeezed the life out of the other." He smiled at us.

"We were on our way back from DeSoto County, over in Mississippi. Nora wanted to see her sister one more time before the baby was born, and I let her talk me into it, against my better judgment. When Pope came out of his mama, I caught him. I wiped my pocket knife off on my pant leg, 'cause it was the best I could do, and cut the umbilical cord," he said, grinning with mischief.

"I was four weeks out of medical school and still wet behind the ears. I don't guess I'd delivered more than half a dozen babies back then. Anyway, I cleaned him off a little and handed him to Nora. Her face and her eyes were shining, like she'd never seen anything she liked as much. I'd never seen her look as pretty as she did that day.

"'Nora,' I said to her, 'he looks like the Pope.' Now, that made her pretty mad. But his eyes were somber and quiet and so dark and he lay there in her arms like he was watching the world. Never made a sound. He just lay there, looking up at me. His face was too thin for a baby's. I used to think he was kind of ugly back then—don't you ever tell Nora. And his eyes were too big for his face. Even from that first hour, he seemed so peaceful and adult; even stern, like a little old man. I stood there for a long time, just waiting for him to take up his scepter and pontificate."

It was because of this story that Thomas became "Pope" Barrett to everyone but his mother for the rest of his life.

Though I had often seen Pope, our school was a county school and was large enough that each grade was divided, so we had never known one another. We saw each other from across the meeting hall in Sunday School and every fall as school began.

We met one hot spring day in early June of 1935 as Reed, Thena, Ham and I raced along the banks of the river. Very often, in those days, Adda and Mama had a hard time getting us out of their hair. We liked to stay close by the two of them, waiting for something good to come out of the oven, or begging for Adda to tell us one of her stories, or for Mama to let us make ice cream in the large tin bucket. At those times Mama would very slyly suggest that we help her clean out the cellar or polish the silver or do the laundry. This would, of course, cause the lot of us to scatter like a flock of spooked geese, and on this day it worked like a charm. We scurried away with Mama calling after us,

"No, wait! I need to you to scrub these here sheets! Wait! Thena, come back here n' peel this bushel of potatoes!"

She of course would never have entrusted us with the washing of Mrs. Rachel's fine Irish linens (nor would the Wilkins have had any use for a bushel of peeled potatoes), but still we raced away from the mayor's back porch, through the trees and down toward the river with thoughts of Mrs. Rachel the slave driver following close on our heels.

"Race you to the bridge!" Thena shouted.

We ran screaming and pushing one another until we came to the bridge that crossed over onto the east bank of the river, then slowed at the sight of a large crowd of boys.

They stood on the edge of the bank, shoving a smaller boy back and forth between them. It was Pope, who, though eleven, was only Reed's size and, who, moreover, wore glasses—an unforgivable sin amongst boys of our generation. His size, scholarly looks and spectacles made him an outcast among the boys of his age group.

His tormentors—nearly naked in the bright, burning afternoon sunlight—stood pummeling the fully clothed Pope. We later learned that Pope had been sitting at the bank in the shade of a cedar tree, reading. I suppose they must have been bored; whatever the reason, the boys had begun to hound and taunt him.

We rushed forward, pushing our way in to stand at the inner fringe of the group.

"Pope Barrett's small an' purty as a gurl," one boy sang.

"Pope Barrett's a lilly-livered sissy," hissed another of the boys, spitting on Pope's glasses.

Life has a sense of humor. One day, Pope would grow to stand many inches above the tallest among them. When he came back from the war, Pope had grown to be six feet, four inches tall and weighed two hundred and thirty pounds. He would also be awarded the Congressional Medal of Honor in the fall of 1945 for bravery in battle.

Shoving one of the largest aside, Pope thundered out, in a voice surprising for a boy of his size,

"I will race any one of you across the river *and back!*"

Everything became quiet. Minutes passed. I could hear the wind racing over the leaves and the song of the crickets. It was the first week of June, just at the close of the spring rains, and the river was at its very highest. The water was still enough, though deep, at the river's edge where the boys had been swimming. But further out, at the river's center, the current was quite strong and, on a rough day, could have carried away a full-grown man. Though they taunted Pope for his prissy ways, implying their own heroism and manliness, even the older boys had the good sense not to swim all the way out. Too many children had died in years gone by. All the boys knew that their mothers would box their ears if they heard about their sons going out too far. And every boy present feared both the river and their mothers.

Pope, however, seemed to have decided that he could withstand whatever trouble he would face. But he could no longer withstand their raillery. *It would end here, today, forever,* his face seemed to say, and then he could be left in peace with his books and his dreams.

Pope stripped down to his under shorts and stood scowling at the crowd around him, waiting to see who would take up the battle cry. Several of the oldest boys of thirteen and fourteen felt that their manhood had been challenged. And, what was more, Thena Kelley stood by watching. Any boy who would fight the river-dragon, they told themselves, would be worthy of the damsel. Perhaps the victor would be rewarded with a kiss—or a punch, which was far more likely with Thena.

"*I'll* race you, an' beat you, too!" snarled a large, pale boy with a freckled body and longish red hair.

Two bony boys of about his age followed on his heels, looking like loyal, ill-fed curs. The three waded out into the water and turned back to make sure that Pope followed after. The oldest, a boy named Howard Norton, pointed at Reed and shouted,

"Yer in charge of beginnin' it!"

Reed nodded and waded a few feet into the water.

"On your mark. Git set. Go!" he shouted.

The boy-warriors took off, followed by Pope. The sun shone off their backs as they slid through the cloudy brown and green water. It seemed to go well for a while, although Pope fell a good bit behind. But as the group neared the center of the river, the current began to overpower them. The four labored against it, and the crowd moved closer to the low ledge of the river as we heard Howard let out a strangled scream of fear. For a moment he clutched at the face of the water, and then disappeared. The crowd gasped. One boy of three or four years old began to cry. Several in the group followed Reed out into the water. Reed waded up to his hips, one hand reaching to shield his eyes. I thought he looked as if he was thinking of swimming out after the boy. Then, suddenly, Howard reappeared.

His image was blurry, but he looked as if he was swimming back to us. I put both hands up to my eyes, trying to shield them from the brilliant glare of the sun on the water, and saw after several more seconds that he had indeed given up on making it all the way across. He was swimming toward home. As soon as his friends realized that the courage of the oldest and most powerful among them had failed, they, too, turned back toward the shore.

Pope never looked back. He swam further and further away until he was only a tiny shimmering dot on the horizon. Minutes, which seemed like hours, passed and I heard someone say something about going after the Doc. Thena and I waded cautiously out into the water. I felt a lump rising from my chest as I remembered Doc and the way he always talked about his son.

Then, suddenly, I saw Pope spring out of the water and up on to the other bank. A loud cheer went up from the crowd, and then a deep sigh. I realized, gasping, that I had been holding my breath for what must have been a long time. To my astonishment, Pope turned to face us, waved, and dove back in. There were several startled screams as the crowd realized that Pope meant to swim back.

"He's a durn' fool!" shouted one of the older boys.

Although it was clear that Pope was the victor, he had a point to prove. A dark vendetta had gripped his gentle heart, and it had to be satisfied. Even with my childish mind I understood that his honor had been impugned. He had been wronged, and it needed to be made right.

I have no idea if those were the thoughts that pulsated through Pope's mind; although, at the time, I thought so. But now, so many years later, knowing him as I would come to, I think it was a much simpler matter. Pope Barrett never started a thing unless he finished it. It wasn't a matter of proving a point, but rather that his task was only halfway done. He had said, "across the river *and back*." If he only swam across the river, he would have broken his word, and Pope never broke his word.

Long minutes passed and not a sound came from those on the bank. Reed stood restlessly in the river, scowling out into the water. He slowly moved further out, watching Pope as he went. We watched breathlessly as Reed waded, the water flowing first up to his chest and then up to his neck.

The next moment, just as he got to the place where the boy-warriors had stopped and headed for home, Pope went under. Everyone waited, and I think we expected him to resurface, just as Howard had done. Seconds passed. No Pope. I heard a quiet splash and saw Reed's feet as he dove. Something like a wail went up from the crowd and the rest of the group waded into the water. My eyes scanned the surface for signs of Pope, but saw nothing.

At last, Reed arrived at the point where Pope had disappeared. We saw him dive and watched as he resurfaced for air several seconds later. Again he dove and returned, and again. On his fourth dive, he came back up with Pope, who seemed limp and unmoving. Reed swam slowly back to us with Pope on his back. He held onto Pope with one hand, and as they came slowly closer I saw that Pope's face was pale and still and that his eyes were closed.

I heard a terrible roar behind me and turned to see Doc racing into the water, not pausing long enough to remove even his shoes or jacket.

"God damn you! You fools! All of you are fools!" he screamed, his voice breaking. And then he was gone.

After another moment, Doc and Reed dragged Pope onto the bank. Doc bent down to his son's chest and the color drained from his face.

"Dear God!" he sobbed, "Oh, dear God!"

Pope wasn't breathing.

I remember hearing a low, steady sound from all around me and, looking around, I realized that many of the children were crying. I reached up and felt that my face was wet with tears.

The Doc pushed on Pope's chest and breathed into his mouth. Reed lay panting on the earth, grasping at it with his fingers to steady himself. He gasped for a long time, trying to slow his breathing. Reed Wilkins' lungs, from the time of his birth, were cursed with a thick, gripping asthma, a condition that was not well understood in those days. His asthma was a curse—or, perhaps, a blessing—which would later bar him from service in World War II.

Then suddenly, with a choke and a rush of brown and yellow water from his mouth, Pope sat up. Doc gathered his only child in his arms and, sobbing, he carried him away.

From the day he swam across the river and back and nearly drowned, I never again heard an ill word spoken of Pope Barrett. He was no longer harassed by the boys, or taunted for being smart, or shoved for being "four-eyed." In fact, he was looked upon with a kind of awe, spoken of with a certain reverence, and universally loved. He had swum, through the deadly current of the river in spring, no less than one mile.

Reed, of course, was hailed as a hero—Doc Barrett's boy would have died if it hadn't been for him. He was slapped on the back by the old men, his hand was shaken until it blistered by the young men and, by the boys, Reed Wilkins was always chosen first for baseball.

As for the girls—oh, how they sighed over his blue eyes! Oh, how they longed to stroke his golden hair! Oh, how they wished to touch his smooth, brown skin! And didn't his smile make them weep? And to all of this he added their undoing—the lines around his eyes deepened when he smiled! And thus did Reed Wilkins pass on up to Olympus, where eventually his queen, his goddess, Athena, would join him.

In the bustle of so much glory was the only time I ever saw the mayor with a kind word to say for his son, though Reed would, before long, pass back into the oblivion of his mind. I was never sure what Mrs. Rachel thought about the affair, and I don't think that Reed was, either. She never spoke of it. She never spoke of anything.

It would, of course, be unnecessary to mention who was from then on Reed Wilkin's best friend, or who was Pope Barrett's, for that matter. As a result, from June of 1935 until we were separated by the war, our group expanded to include Pope in all of our doings.

Thena sallied forth, the general in every battle, with Reed and Pope her valiant colonels and humble servants. Ham and I, faithful soldiers—in spite of our inchoate capabilities—followed close in their footsteps. We were obedient to every command. Wherever Thena sent us, whether roaming through the woods or down through the town and beyond, we went scavenging, reconnoitering. We were sent out in search of unanticipated possibilities, subservient even to our General's most unreasonable caprice and faithful unto death.

During the time of the townspeople's hero-worship of Pope and Reed, it would be natural to think that Thena and I would have been drawn to the light of their glory, but their luster fell on dull eyes. This was probably for a host of reasons. One is that the sillinesses of love strike different children at different times. For me, it would be nearly a decade before I would set precious gifts before love's feet. Thena was, I believe, blinded by the light of her own radiance. I do not mean to say that there was conceit in my sister. There never was. But for Thena, the world and all that was in it was perfect—and who needs one lover, when a lover can be made of every man, woman and child on the planet? Even the shadow of Dan Brown could never block out the light of Athena.

What was more, Reed was nearly two years her junior, and what matters little at twenty-eight and thirty matters much at nine and eleven. As for Pope, well, what can be said? To me, he looked like the Pope—serious, quiet, contemplative. I often watched him with interest as he gazed off, even beyond Thena, with a far away look in his eye. Sometimes I shuddered as I watched, wondering what it was that he saw. Years later, I asked him once. Without balking or missing a beat, he said,

"The future."

And I knew that he meant it. But even the Pope, our Pope, could not hold back the tides of the future that would wash over and drown so many of us.

V.

Many of our days after we met Pope were spent on King Farm. Scores of memories flock into my mind when I think back on that place, and all of them are good. King Farm was the home of Pope's grandparents. His mother, born Elinora King, passed her early years on that land owned for so many years by her ancestors. One rainy afternoon, Pope's exasperated grandmother, Mae King (who I called by her full name my whole life) sent us to the barn, down-pasture from the house, to look for "treasures." With little hope of finding treasure, we set out after this play. After a moment in the darkness of the barn, our eyes adjusted to its dimness. We found that we were, indeed, surrounded by treasures.

The room was filled with old furniture—bed frames of all kinds piled nearly up to the low ceiling of the first floor, an old perambulator, the remains of a carriage, a brightly painted sleigh, chests of drawers wrapped in quilts (in fact, there were dozens of quilts lying everywhere), an old settee, a rotting baby bed, and half a dozen trunks. Thena flipped back the lid of the nearest chest and began to sift through its contents. The rest of us spread out and began to look for something extraordinary to arrest the attention of the others. Thena was the first to find something of interest.

"What's this?" she called out.

I turned to see what she held up and squinted at the piece of paper. It was thick and stiff, fraying around the edges, and stained.

"I think it's very old," I said with excitement.

We studied it for several minutes, but as we could only make out several words, decided to take it to Mae King to see if she could explain what it was. We took it to the kitchen, where Pope's grandmother sat shelling peas. Mae King looked it over and then, reaching for her spectacles, sat down again at the kitchen table. She sat silent for a long time.

"This paper's the deed to this farm. I didn't know such a thaing existed. It's a document statin' that this land wuz purchased in April of 1731 by James Redmond King. It also says this land wuz then called Carolina. Our family bought this farm 'fore Tennessee wuz its own state."

"Why didn't they write it in English, Mae King?" I asked her.

"They did," she said. "Child, there wuz no set way of spellin' in those days, and people spell't a word however it suited 'em to spell it."

I marveled. They had owned their farm for more than two hundred years. And, more significantly, there had been a time when children had not been graded on their ability to spell. I made a mental note to tell my teacher, Ms. Esther Thomas, about the days when children had been able to spell a word however they liked.

Then there were Pope's great-grandparents, Grandma Netta and her Campbell, who lived about three miles from King Farm and two miles from our house. Papa's house, as we always called our tiny, three room house, was situated directly across the gravel road from King Farm, at the foot of the hill where their farmhouse sat. Netta and Campbell's farm lay on the north of our house, with the King's to the south.

Netta was a tiny woman who grew smaller every time I saw her, and I do not believe that this was a trick of the mind or the imaginings of a child. She actually did, I think, diminish in height six inches or more during the years of my childhood. There were large cataracts in both of her eyes. Netta had a dozen or more cataracts removed during her sixties and seventies. Eventually, she decided that modern medicine had failed her. When the next masses appeared, she left them as they were, giving up on dreams of healthy eyes and whole vision as a lost cause. She was also almost entirely deaf, and I know that this was hard for her because she wanted very much to hear all of our childish jabberings.

In spite of these maladies, she lived without malice toward anyone or anything in the world. And because of the sweetness of her nature and the love she gave to any young person she met, my memories of time spent with her are some of the very best of my life.

More than a dozen slimy, yellow masses of old cataracts stood in jars on her mantelpiece—the products of her more patient years. It gave her living room the mildly creepy feeling of a morgue or, at the very least, a biology lab. She also collected glass birds. Had those brightly colored creatures been real, the endangered species lists (of which we all now live in such eye-blinking, blanch-faced terror) would be sublimely barren.

Her hospitality was known throughout the county and, though she was well into her eighties, the number of hours she spent on the dusty floor playing marbles with all of us could not be counted. She had stored away, whether from sentimentality or from a strong sense of the impropriety of waste, all the toys from her daughter's childhood (her daughter was by then a woman of advanced years with grandchildren of her own). Those beautiful, heavy marbles, which I was given when she died and still have today, are glorious glass pieces of the most beautiful colors, now more than a hundred and thirty years old.

In addition to the marbles were many other toys. There were china baby dolls, with feet and hands chipped away; there was a white china cat sprigged with blue flowers and tied around the neck with a blue china bow. There was another entertainment in which I took the greatest delight: a black-and-white spotted Holstein cow made of glass. It stood about a foot and a half high. When I turned it on its side, it mooed at me, its voice aggrieved.

And though her joy in being with us was very great, she took added delight in feeding us. Every time that we went (which was nearly every day in the summer), she offered us lemonade and moon pies, which we always accepted. These somehow never spoiled our appetites. Often-times, on Sundays, whole families—whole tribes of people—were invited to her house for lunch, and I cannot begin to describe the amounts of food that this one tiny person set before these vast armies.

It is well known that all people emerge from church Sunday-noon with a voracious appetite for which they are unable to account. Why does sermon-listening work up such an appetite? And yet, it does. It is a mystery that no one can explain. Netta was always prepared, more than prepared, for these emergencies.

On any given Sunday at Campbell and Netta's table there would be fried chicken, fried fish, a ham, a turkey, a chicken, pork chops, a roast, barbecued pork, potato salad, bean salad, coleslaw, hushpuppies, corn, black-eyed peas, lima beans, green beans, tomatoes, beets, sweet pickles, cantaloupe, watermelon, mashed potatoes, brown beans, white beans, homemade bread, deviled eggs (a Netta specialty), and for desert there was always peanut brittle, pineapple upside down cake, pound cake, coconut pie and chocolate pie (another Netta specialty).

The fish were caught in her pond, the chicken and turkey taken from her yard, the pork chops taken from her pigs, the roast from her cattle, and her famous pickles from her garden. Her pickles, given as Christmas gifts in glass jars wrapped with satin bows, were local treasures. The table was spread with a hundred kinds of flowers that she tended and loved year after year. All of this she offered during the years of the Depression, mind you. Had those been years of plenty instead of famine, her feasts would have still been a miracle.

I do not think that I ever met a more gifted, a more prodigious, or a more loving person. Into her nineties, Netta maintained her garden, continued her quilting and babysat her great, great-grandchildren.

I remember sitting at her table, Sunday-noon, nearly every week of the year once we became friends with Pope.

"Grace, you haven't eaten a thaing!" she would say after I had emptied my second plate.

"Netta!" I would reply, "I cleaned my plate twice!"

"That id'n enough to feed a bird!" she would say, and then she would fill my plate a third time and a fourth and I would eat, unwilling to disappoint her, until I was sick.

I visited her one summer afternoon, years after her husband, Campbell, had left us, when she was closing in on her one hundredth year of life. She sat hunched over her sewing machine, nearly blind, sewing one last quilt. She had carefully and lovingly cut Campbell's neckties into quilt pieces and was making a quilt of all their Sunday memories together. No point in wasting perfectly good neckties.

Netta's husband, Campbell, was another matter altogether. I was quite afraid of him as a small girl. It was only as a young woman that I came to love him; so beloved did he become that I sat beside his bed years later as he, surrounded by all those who loved him most, went on to better things. He was a loud and unwieldy man with a hawk nose. His eyes were small and black and they gleamed out at me from behind large, thick glasses. He talked from the first moment of his waking until his own exhausted voice somehow lulled him to sleep at night. I have never met anyone who could hold a candle to his verbosity—who could talk for so many consecutive hours without the aid of commas, and certainly without needing periods.

What was considered by the rest of us (who were, grammatically speaking, mere mortals) to be the delights of the rules of punctuation to Campbell was nothing but a hindrance. Dickens had his Conversation Kenge and we our Conversation Campbell. If there was nothing and no one to whom he could speak, Campbell was unfazed. He spoke to nothing and no one. No subject was beneath or above his notice. His views on religion, ethics, agriculture, sociology, economics, and politics—

oh, God save us, politics!—were, though perhaps somewhat crude and occasionally uninformed, absolutely limitless. What they lacked in berth, they made up in girth. Campbell was by no means an unintelligent man; but where his knowledge ended, his speech did not.

But I never knew anyone so kind, with so good a heart and who could work as hard as he could. He ran his farm entirely by himself until he was ninety-three. In the heat of the day, when the younger men had taken to their beds with heat stroke, ninety-three year old Campbell worked on without stopping for a glass of water.

I remember that he smelled of peppermint and old sweat, even though Netta insisted that he bathe every Saturday night.

"Whether I need it or not!" he would roar with a wink and a smile.

He awoke every morning at five and required that all those in his house do the same. He ate a full breakfast of a vast array of deeply fried foods every morning and died at ninety-six without ever having been sick a day in his long life. Each morning, following the consumption of his fried breakfast foods, Campbell acted out the strangest of colloquial rituals, which I can only assume must have been handed down to him by British ancestors. He poured himself a cup of cold sweet tea, added sugar and then set the mug in a saucer. Then into the mug he poured made-up powdered milk. When the mug was full he continued to pour, until the saucer too was full. Then he lifted and drank the mug of cold, sugary tea and milk. When it had been emptied, he set it aside and drank the saucer. He and Grandma Netta did this every morning of their married lives.

They had married in their seventies—a second time for both—and they were, by all accounts, the love of one another's lives. I spent many days and nights with the two of them; wherever the five of us were at sundown, there we stayed for the night. Netta and Campbell seemed happy with the company. I think my mother allowed this in order to keep us away from Dan as much as possible, but I always felt a certain pang in my stomach and a certain feeling of disloyalty whenever we slept away

from Mama. It seemed that Dan's fists were much more inhibited when
Thena and I (particularly Thena) were in the house. The truth was that
Dan Brown lived in holy terror of Thena. As a young girl, I thought him
a coward for it. But when I became older, I began to see that he ought to
have been afraid of her. Be that as it may, there were often deep cuts and
purple bruises on Mama's body after our nighttime adventures and, as
the years went by, we stayed away from the house at night less and less.

VI.

In this way we spent our days. Oddly enough, I mostly only remember the summer days. What I recall about school was that it was stifling and crowded and that I had to wear silly dresses (hand-me-downs) and pinching, scuffed shoes (also hand-me-downs). I remember that most of my teachers were cross and a few weren't. Most of my teachers weren't good at their work (and, in fact, seemed to dislike it) and a few were. I remember reading for recreation when I should have been studying. Reading when I sat in class. Reading a book inside my Bible during Sunday school. Reading when Mama asked me to do chores, reading as I cooked meals, reading right through Dan's cussing and screaming fits. I read myself right through and out of my poverty. Though I was certainly physically impoverished, my imagination held the riches of a queen.

I didn't do well in my early years of school. I was bad at math, although I will say in my defense that I suffered long years under the both uninspired and uninspiring tutelage of a series of superbly poor math teachers. I was bad at science—too much math. I was bad at penmanship—left-handed children are not known for writing with aesthetically pleasing form. I was bad at sports—too clumsy, gawky and nervous to be of any use. I could carry a tune, but was so shy that I dropped it. I could write well, but if what you have written is too illegible to be read, it doesn't count for much. And I wasn't popular. Poor children rarely are. As a result, I was all but invisible to students and teachers alike. I have to admit I was never really displeased with this arrangement.

And then there was Thena.

We live in a fickle world. Humans are a shallow lot. At most times and in most places, physical beauty is more significant than any other accomplishment. Physical perfection—which Thena had (and I do mean *perfection*)—will generally supersede moral perfection—which Thena had not, though she was by no means a wicked child.

Thena made golden everything that she touched. If she did poorly on an assignment, the teacher thought it was a mistake and set her marks high. If she failed to turn in an assignment, it was waved away with a flourish and not counted against her. If she fell down, people stumbled over themselves to help her up. If she stood, people were possessed with the strangest urge to keep their heads lower than hers. If she touched a sick classmate, the child became well. When she opened her lunch sack with five loaves and two fishes, she fed the whole schoolroom. The world was a better place because she was in it, and when she left us, the earth shook and the sky shed great, bitter tears for many days. All of this seems strange to me now; but then, as a girl, it seemed to me that Thena was given no less than she should have had, and I loved to see other people love her as I did.

People respond differently to pain and tragedy. Some people rail against the storm and curse the dark of night. Some people fight unwillingly and then beat a hasty retreat. Others stand at the edge of the cliff, cast their flimsy souls down to the rocks below and pray that the fall will bring about an end to it all. And then some of us climb quietly into our heart's resting place and roll the stone over the doorway, shutting out all the world's sorrows and all its glories, too. We have no intention of coming out again in three days time, though we secretly hope that someone will come and roll the stone away for us. We can't be our own saviors, but maybe someone else can. Still others climb to the highest point they can find, square their shoulders and flash at the world a million-watt smile and wait for it to smile back. This was Thena. And, Oh! How the world smiled back.

Consequently, school for Thena was pure joy. For me, it was mild and vaguely uncomfortable sorrow. I felt every school year, for about nine months, a certain emotional indigestion. Not actual pain, mind you; just a feeling that I would have preferred to leave and bother me no more. It is because of this that my pleasant memories are not generally of school, but of days like those we spent on King Farm. Thus, the early years of my life seem mainly to have been made up of summers.

The smells of my childhood are of hot earth, sun-struck laundry, and the river after a fresh rain. The tastes are those of strawberries taken right out of Doc's patch in Pope's back yard, and fresh, hot tomatoes plucked up and eaten with the dirt still on them, and fried fish, and homemade peach ice cream. I remember being all but entirely unencumbered by clothes during the first decade of my life, except during the drudgery of the school months. I remember one hot night, as Mama washed me in a tub of cold water, watching her pull from the pad of my foot a piece of bottle glass. My feet had become so hardened by my barefooted savagery that I had not felt it.

In this way did I pass the first years of my life. I was loved by Mama and Adda, doted on by Grandma and Grandpa King, adored by Grandma Netta and Campbell and was the soul sister of Ham, Reed, Pope and my Thena. And in this way time passed. It was through these loves that we mostly avoided thoughts of poverty, sorrow, death, and Dan Brown.

To tell the truth, for those first years of their marriage, I hardly thought of Dan. He was really beneath being thought about. What was more, the alcohol had so destroyed whatever there had once been of *him* that, had I wished to, I am not sure there would have been anything of substance to think about. He was a ghost of a man, a dream; a bad dream, yes—but a girl can always go out into the light to escape that empty darkness. Thinking back on it, I am surprised by how few memories I have of him. How could a man so wholly unremarkable have brought about such terrible things? How is it that one who meant so little to any of us could be so intertwined with the shaping of our destinies?

I remember being woken quietly by Thena one hot night as I slept on the back porch. She shook me and then stood up and motioned for me to follow. She crept down the porch stairs and out across the yard and scurried into the trees that lined the road. I followed. We stepped noiselessly, without speaking, for nearly a mile. When I was convinced that we were beyond earshot of John and Edwin, who were still sleeping on the porch, I pulled at Thena's arm.

"What are we doing? Where are you taking me?" I whispered.

I wasn't in the habit of questioning her, and she frowned at my insolence.

"We're goin' to get Reed, and then to the Doc's to find Pope."

"What are we doing?" I repeated.

It was the middle of the night and I was tired, and I knew that we should not leave Edwin and the baby alone.

Thena stopped in the thick of the tall spruce trees and turned to face me.

"We're gonna help Dan Brown remember to keep his grubby fingers away from Mama."

My eyes grew enormous. Thena's audacity was always frightening. She would do anything, without a moment's hesitation.

"What do you mean? And anyway, we cain't leave the baby. And why do we need Reed and Pope and what if Mama catches us?" The words tumbled from my mouth and my heart leapt up into my throat.

"Hush up and come o'an. The baby never wakes up. He'll be jest fine. We won't be gone an hour."

She trotted away toward town.

We hurried, eventually running. I was nervous and couldn't keep my feet from it. We knocked quietly on Reed's ground floor window. After a moment he appeared, looking sleepy and annoyed. But, seeing the General at his window, he saluted and disappeared. In a moment, he passed soundlessly out of his front door, pulling on clothes as he came.

"How's your Mama?" I whispered.

He nodded, but said nothing. Mrs. Rachel had been ill for several weeks. Mama had taken to spending most of her nights at the mayor's house to wait on her. This time spent away had been the cause of a loud and bitter diatribe delivered by the spitting, slobbering, bleary-eyed Dan, and his fury subsided only after he had punched Mama's face and kicked her ribs. In spite of Dan's anger, Mama continued to stay at night. She felt that "poor Mrs. Rachel" truly needed her. This was an epithet that no one else would have condescended to give Mrs. Rachel.

"Blessed are the poor in spirit…" Mama would whisper to herself, sighing, when anyone spoke of the mayor's Lady.

Mama truly felt compassion for her, though no one else could. Now, as I think back on it, I marvel that Mama considered Mrs. Rachel poor in spirit, but never herself. So, night after night, she stayed on to help the Lady in need, knowing full well that Dan Brown needed nothing but his bottle.

Reed followed us out into the street, without speaking and without question. We passed down Main Street, passing Kirk House on our right, and I shuddered to see its lonely silhouette on a moonless night. Kirk House had been named by its once illustrious owner, Thomas Kirk. Mr. Kirk had been a prominent and wealthy banker in our town, but had retired many years before at the unexpected and horrible death of his wife, who had lost her life to one of our worst spring floods. Maybe "retired" isn't the proper word. He had simply stopped going to work. He never resigned; he was never terminated; he just never returned.

"What happened to him, Mama?" I once asked her. "Why is he so unhappy?"

"Well, honey, I think maybe his insides died," she said quietly.

I looked up at her, without understanding.

"His wife's name was Georgia Fleming Kirk and she was one of the most beautiful women I've ever seen," she explained. "It made yer eyes hurt to look at 'er. She was the joy of his life and when she died, he lost all his joy."

After her death, several years passed and nothing was seen of Mr. Kirk. He must have left his house at times for supplies and such, but from what Mama once told me, she saw him no more than a couple of times a year.

More time passed, and his house began to look as dead as his heart. The once beautiful garden engulfed and overcame the house. Shingles and siding began to fall off, the grass grew ever higher and the paint chipped away from the surface of the house. Eventually, after much patience on the part of the townspeople, one brave soul ventured to write an editorial in the newspaper, claiming to praise the beauties of the town, but actually writing to point out the one eyesore, Kirk House.

This article was written in hopes that the once proud and industrious Mr. Kirk would wake from his grief-induced slumber and be compelled to rectify his negligence. However, it produced the opposite effect. The morning after the editorial appeared in the newspaper, Mr. Kirk stormed into the mayor's office and unleashed all the fury of his unspent emotional arsenal. His anger about his wife must have lent itself to a rage against the writer of the editorial and, indeed, the whole town. He screamed and cursed, alternately turning vermilion and purple, and threw a potted plant at the mayor's clerk. He doused the mayor's rising temper with a pitcher of water sitting on his desk. Then, seizing the mayor by his collar he screamed,

"Today will be my last day to visit this town! Today will by my last day to leave my house! And I tell you that by no means will I ever be induced to touch one board, one nail, or one shingle for the purpose of my house's maintenance. It is mine and I will do with it as I please. And, furthermore, that meddlesome travesty of an editorialist can take herself to hell!"

With those words, he rushed from the room, slammed the door, breaking its glass panes, and flew with a shout through the town and back into his house. And since that day, some fifteen years before, he had not been seen, although I was certain that he was still living—made strong by the force of his rancor—from the faint lines of smoke that lifted from his rooftop in the wintertime. The house, as we passed quickly along, certainly looked the part of a haunted house; whether or not Mrs. Georgia Fleming Kirk haunted it, Tom Kirk, though very much alive, certainly did.

We trotted on and within minutes were at Pope's house, throwing tiny rocks at his window. Finally, Pope's outline appeared for an instant and then was gone. We scampered to his back door and met him coming out. He nodded to all of us and walked to the road, no questions asked. I noticed that he carried what appeared to be several tools wrapped in a rag, but the need for quiet kept me from asking about his bundle. We jogged the three miles home without saying a word, and just before we got to the last farm lane before our house, I stopped, out of breath, and demanded an explanation. The General frowned again and said,

"I told you, we're gonna tell Dan Brown to stay away from Mama."

The lack of reverence that Thena felt for our stepfather was staggering. But Thena never really was a very reverent person. Life had accustomed her to being the one worshipped and not the worshipper.

"Now hush up and do what you're told!" she hissed.

I was unsatisfied. It was obvious to me that both Reed and Pope knew what to expect and had come prepared. I was annoyed not to have been let in on the secret.

"How come Pope and Reed knew about all this and I didn't?" I hissed back.

"Because Pope and Reed have balls and you don't."

She smiled down at me, wickedly, and did a little dance.

I gasped. I didn't exactly know what this phrase meant, but the only other time Thena had used it had been in Mama's presence. When Mama heard Thena say it she did something I had never seen before or since. She grabbed Thena by the shoulders, marched her to Mrs. Rachel's kitchen sink and washed her mouth and tongue and teeth and gums and tonsils with as much soap as Thena's mouth could hold. Afterwards, Thena had been ill. You would think such an ordeal would have taught her.

She turned back towards our house and moved on. By taking the path through the woods to the northeast of our house, our walk ended in our back yard. Thena walked to the outhouse. She quietly opened the door, whispered something to me about checking on the baby, and moved inside.

Reed and Pope followed. John was just as I left him, sleeping quietly, sweaty and soft, with his covers kicked off. I kissed his warm cheek, smoothed Edwin's hair away from his forehead and went back to the outhouse.

Inside, Pope pulled a candle from his bundle and lit it. Thena and Reed went to work. Inside the outhouse, on the far corner, was a bench-seat, a long rectangular three-sided box that covered the waste pit. In the center of the bench was a small hole, covered with a hinged, round lid. Reed and Thena worked to pry the top piece of the box entirely off, exposing the pit—while from the side, as one first stepped into the darkness, no difference could be discerned. With the help of Pope's tools and Reed's hands, Thena soon removed the bench cover and the four of us left the outhouse. She carried it behind the small building and leaned it against the back wall. Reed and Pope nodded to Thena and, walking away from the yard, headed back toward home. Without another word, Thena walked toward the porch, laid down on our mattress and, rolling away from me, immediately fell asleep.

I lay there thinking and worrying for a long time. I couldn't sleep or rest. Hours passed and I heard the loud engine of a worn out car grinding its way into our yard. I heard drunken yelling and Dan plodding across the grass. He stumbled and cursed loudly. Then he passed into view, heading for the outhouse. Thena knew her enemy, just as any great general does. My older brothers had been gone some days, hunting with two boys of a neighboring farm. Mama was at Mrs. Rachel's. John was still in diapers. Edwin slept through the night. Thena and I knew not to go to the outhouse. That left Dan as the only possible victim.

I felt somewhat guilty, but I would not go against Thena and I knew that she was right. Dan Brown was human waste—let him lay where he had made his bed. I heard him pass through the moonless night and into the safety of the outhouse, grunting and cursing and crying. I heard him stumble. A minute passed. I heard a yelp. Then nothing. Finally, I rolled over on my side, tucking one arm beneath my head and fell into an exhausted sleep.

Dan Brown passed through a night and most of the next day lying in gallons of his beloved family's shit. Thena and I never said a word.

The next morning, we dressed and took the boys to the Wilkins' without so much as a backward glance. We learned later that Grandpa King heard Dan screaming late in the afternoon as he went down to the barn to feed his horses. His barn was a little less than half a mile from our house. If the wind was right, we could hear the cattle lowing in his barnyard. At any rate, Grandpa King heard Dan bellowing, and Grandpa King alone saw him, shining in all his hung-over glory, soaking in the feces of many happy generations.

I am certain that Mama heard of our doings. She must have. The story was told behind hands all over town. But she never said a word. I have thought of that many times since then and wondered at it. It was unlike her to allow her children to misbehave.

Mama was never unkind, but she was always stern. I don't recall getting away with any mischief as a child other than that one incident; although, I never did get into that much trouble. I remember living with the strong conviction that Mama had enough trouble of her own and did not need any more from me.

Maybe she didn't talk about it because she knew that we had done it out of loyalty to her. But I doubt it. Dan wasn't much, but he was our stepfather. And Mama always taught us respect for our elders. Eventually, I decided that Mama never confronted us because it would have been impossible for her to discuss the subject without doubling over in fits of hysterical laughter. She must have felt that firm and mysterious silence was better than letting us see her laugh about it.

In the fall of my eleventh year, I began to notice a bulge in Mama's stomach again and, for reasons that I could not exactly understand, this meant that there was to be another baby. Pregnancies were not talked about in those days. It was considered ill mannered to draw attention to a woman's "state," and it would have been downright damnable to discuss what had gotten her into it. Because of this, there was in my mind a haze of confusion made up of associations between reproduction and forest creatures—birds and bees—and portions of phrases like a woman's "curse" and "the marriage bed," to which I had heard the minister refer once in a sermon. At that point in the sermon, most of the men in the room had coughed, most of the women had squirmed, and all of the teenagers of both sexes had turned red. I also saw an engaged couple, holding hands and sitting hip to hip, move a full eighteen inches away from one another.

It was on the day of that sermon that Mama found me in her bedroom, staring at her marriage bed, trying with all the powers of my childish mind to distinguish how Mama and Dan's bed differed from the bed that I shared with Thena, Edwin and John Michael. Moreover, in spite of having lived around farm animals all of my life, I was pretty sure that babies came out of a woman's belly button. In spite of my uncertainties regarding conception, I was sure of one thing: another baby meant another mouth to feed.

I worried for Mama and for all of us and I wondered if Dan had yet noticed Mama's bulge and if he would beat her again; though of course, Dan didn't generally require a special occasion to lavish his abuse on Mama's body. It seemed contradictory to me, even as a child, that Dan could not be prevailed upon to shave his face or to clean the fish that he brought home, but he still had such limitless reserves with which to greet Mama when he was in a foul mood.

When Dan returned from a day's work of sleeping and fishing by the river, he hung his fish on a rusted nail by the front door and waited for Mama to come home and clean them. They were, as often as not, eaten by cats before Mama came home, until Edwin began to do the work for his stepfather. Dan was equally indifferent to all options. He did not care whether it was his five-year-old son, his exhausted and heavily pregnant wife, or wandering cats that removed the responsibility from his shoulders.

Though I am able to write about Dan with amusement now, as a woman of more than eighty years, I must admit I was sometimes very frightened of him during my early childhood. When Dan was angry and violent toward Mama, I sat in a corner, hugging John Michael and Edwin tightly to me, weeping into their corn silk hair. Thena was almost never present when this happened. As for the older boys, I wonder now if visions of them as young men sending him to an early grave stayed his hand, but whatever the reason, he left them alone, and was never violent unless all but the youngest were out of the house.

I remember one day, as Jim came in from hunting, he saw Mama holding a blood-covered cloth against her eye. He turned white and then red and I watched in fear as he stood clenching and unclenching his fists. After a long moment of silence and dread, he pulled two shells from his pocket and began to load his rifle. Mama was immediately at his side. She laid a hand on his shoulder and tilted his face to look over into hers.

"Don't you dare. Shootin' guns don't solve problems, and violence breeds more violence. The only thaing that gun is gonna do is make more trouble for everybody."

He stared into Mama's face. A long time passed. She touched his cheek and tried to smile at him.

"'Sides, Jim," she said, "I can take good care a' myself."

She pried his fingers away from the gun and hung it over the mantle. He turned his back to her and walked out of the house. He didn't come back for four days.

VII.

On a Saturday in early fall, Thena spent the day away from home at the birthday party of a girl from her grade. It was afternoon and I was helping Mama wash the laundry. We always did this on Saturday evenings and, even with five dirty men in the house, our poverty always insured what little laundry would need doing. All of the boys, older and younger, were helping Grandpa King with the harvest, for pay, although at least John Michael and probably Edwin couldn't have been of much use.

Grandpa King had hired Dan as well, though it could only have been for Mama's sake. I realized one day, when a memory flashed through my mind, how much Grandpa King must have disliked Dan. I recalled a habit of his, which, up until that instant, I had never interpreted. Whenever Dan Brown's name was mentioned, even after his death, Grandpa King grunted and spat a long brown stream of tobacco juice at his feet.

Dan had quit work before even the youngest of the boys and returned home hungry. It was not near any mealtime and there was no food prepared.

"Fix me sumpthin', woman," he growled.

Mama nodded.

"Let me finish the boys' shirts," she said quietly.

Mama stood facing the tin tub at the kitchen table, humming as she washed.

> "I fear no foe, with Thee at hand to bless;
> Ills have no weight, and tears no bitterness.
> Where is death's sting? Where, grave, thy victory?
> I triumph still, if Thou abide with me," she sang.

Dan stood with his back to her, leaning over the stove and looking into the empty pots. When she sang this, he whirled and punched her once on the side, with all of his might, on her pregnant belly.

"I'm not waitin' 'til yer lazy ass is ready to cook. Yer gonna' cook me sumpthin' *now*."

Dan stumbled toward the back room to lie down on their marriage bed. Mama faltered and went down on her knees, cradling her belly with gentle hands and whispering to her baby. I heard something in the very center of my chest snap. I felt a shudder somewhere deep inside of me. Bile rushed into my mouth and I swallowed over and over again to keep from vomiting.

A second later, I heard the sound of my own scream from a distance. It was a terrible sound, like the sound of sinners burning alive in the fires of hell. It filled me with horror and I wanted to close my eyes and ears to protect myself from the evil of it. Then I felt my fingers wrapped around the searing heat of the kettle—I didn't bother to hold it by the handle, nor did I even feel the pain of the terrible burns until days later. I felt my cold body stumble toward the second room and, seeing Dan, eyes closed on the bed, felt my hands mercilessly forcing the scorching iron of the kettle down onto his face. My hands held it there. My body had never been so strong, even as Dan's hands batted it away.

I heard from far away the sound of his screams and the sizzling sound of his tears against the boiling kettle. My hands poured the contents of the kettle all over Dan. The water splashed on me. Then I saw Dan come up off of the bed and I realized that he was moving toward me. I did not bother to move. Maybe it was because my body had gone into shock from the terrible burns, but, at that moment, I felt that it was because he could never harm me or any of us again.

I felt one blow to my head, then another, and another. His feet hit against my calves and thighs. I faintly heard the sounds of Mama's terror. She was wailing; I saw her pulling at Dan's arms and body, trying to get him off of me, and I heard Dan's hellish curses. I felt my lip split and blood spatter onto my dress. My body began to fall and I watched the rivers of blood as they blended with the pine boards. There were more blows and my eyes began to swell shut. I heard Mama clawing at Dan and begging him to stop.

"Dan! You leave my girl alone! Dan! She's jest a baby! Dear God, stop it! Please!"

Dan stood in the doorway. I watched him move slowly across the room, rifle in hand, and then I felt my head split and a thick stream of blood flowed out. I felt it run oozing and thick from my nose. Bones began to break and flesh tore. Then I heard Thena's scream. I felt Dan's body wrenched from atop mine with a terrible force and then there was nothing.

My first sensation when I woke was pain too thick to swim through and too heavy to lift. Pain too dark to allow me to see and so loud that I couldn't think or hear. Pain so black that I could not see any light. I tried to move, to speak, to whisper to Mama that I was okay, but all I heard were strange gurgling sounds. I felt a cool, soft hand on my forehead and I heard a voice that I recognized but could not place.

"It's all gonna be alright, sweet-girl. You go ahead and sleep now, child. You're safe. Ain't nobody gonna hurt you now."

For a moment, my mind grasped about for remembrance. I had heard the sweet cadences of that voice before, but could not recall the face that went with it, and I was tired; too tired to stay awake any longer.

Mrs. Nora told me later that I slept for another four days before I would try to speak again. By that time the swelling in my face had gone down enough that I could open my eyes a little and whisper a few words at a time. She also said that it wasn't until the day when she heard me whisper that they began to think I might live. As time went by, I recognized my resting-place as Doc Barrett's house, and I realized that the voice and strong, sweet accent I had heard came from Doc's wife, Nora.

There are several types of southern accents. One is of the so-called "redneck," who not only refuses to speak properly but, in fact, speaks worse than he needs to because he relishes the idea of being one. Another is the educated southerner who speaks with a much gentler accent, who uses proper grammar and correct pronunciation, but who has had the accent become as much a part of the language as grammar and pronunciation because she has always heard it—just as a child born by the ocean can always hear the sound of the waves in her mind. Then there is the old-money, afternoon-tea-drinking-on-the-veranda, horse-breeding, mansion-owning, gin-rummy-playing, dresses-for-dinner kind of southerner. Their accents are as beautiful to listen to as a symphony at sunset and sound every bit as refined as any British butler butling at Windsor.

Mrs. Nora fell into this last category. She would, from that time forward, be my standard of beauty, grace and good breeding. In beauty she was second only to Thena, although her beauty was made of entirely different stuff than Thena's. She was short with beautiful curves and lines to her body. She had golden hair that curled in waves around her face. Her eyes were blue and she had the fairest skin I have ever seen—not one freckle. Her skin reminded me of Grandma Netta's china dolls. She always smelled like lavender and was clean and beautiful at any time of the day or night. She was fine-boned and delicate looking. She always smiled and hummed and, after the burns and wounds had healed, hugged and touched me more often than anyone else ever had. She loved me and I adored her.

Even with my slow recuperation, even with the terrible pain through which I would suffer, even with months spent in bed, this was one of the happiest times of my life and my first glimpse of a normal family.

Doc Barrett had one glass of brandy every Saturday night after dinner. Just one—and it never had a negative affect on his courteous nature. Doc and Nora, as they taught me to call them, genuinely enjoyed one another's company. They loved and respected one another. They talked for hours every night after Doc came home from evening visitations. At night, after we had all gone to bed, I could hear quiet laughter coming from their room and wondered if their marriage bed looked different from Mama and Dan's.

This was also the time when Pope and I forged a special friendship—more special than the one that he had with Thena. He came in to say goodbye every morning before he left for school and came in to talk to me every afternoon when he got home. He read to me at night. We read all kinds of books—biographies, histories and novels; books that I had never had access to before, and which I soon realized he *owned*. My family did not own more than half a dozen books. We borrowed books from our teachers or the library, but had never had extra money for buying books.

Many months later, when I was well enough to walk again, Pope took me to see his room. Along the walls from floor to ceiling were rows of bookshelves and dozens upon dozens of books. It was also during this time that I came to know Pope's greatest secret: he played the piano and was something of a prodigy. I remember one Sunday, a couple of years after I had recovered and moved back to my own house, an elderly lady squeezing Pope's shoulder and asking him why his pretty mama didn't play the piano in church on Sundays.

"Excuse me?" he said, looking startled and as if he might wrench the boards from the floor and crawl into the cellar to escape.

"I hear yer mama playin' every afternoon when I am out fer my walk. And I never heard such pretty playin'."

Pope smiled. His face looked pinched and his muscles were taut. His skin became an unnerving shade of river-water green as he said,

"I'm glad you enjoy the playing, Mrs. Shardly."

Then we raced from the church. No one but his parents, his piano teacher and I knew. I knew only out of necessity and I am sure he would have hunted me down and cut out my tongue if I had ever told.

For reasons I am still unable to understand, southern young men were not supposed to play the piano. The boys in our town had hated him for loving to read. They would have hated him more for this. Piano playing was for prissy girls in frilly pink-dresses with satin sashes and ribbons in their hair. Piano playing was for little girls who were given paper baggies of hard candies by great-uncles for playing *Für Elise*—this was, at least, Pope's way of explaining his clandestine lessons.

His piano teacher, *Ms.* Somersby (for some reason, she always emphasized the *"Ms."* when speaking of herself) was a grey-haired spinster who smelled of Oil of Olay face cream and mothballs. Ms. Somersby always came to the Barrett's house. This fostered the assumption that the lessons were for Pope's mother (as she was the only woman in the house). And, because no one ever saw Pope go into her house with his music books, no one ever suspected that the piano playing ringing out from the Barrett's house that was so good it could have been heard from a radio broadcasted Carnegie Hall concert was actually produced by that little, owlish Pope Barrett.

It must have been very difficult for Ms. Somersby to be sworn, on pain of death, to secrecy—Pope Barrett was far and away the best pupil she ever had. I mentioned this to Pope once during the time that I lived with them. He grinned and said,

"It's 'cause Daddy knows about all her girdles and corsets."

"*Wha-at?*" I asked him.

He shrugged, "Ms. Somersby's a pretty big lady, right?" he said, holding two cupped hands out from his chest.

I nodded.

"Wrong," he said, moving the cupped hands a full two feet out from his chest. "She's enormous, but nobody knows 'cause she wears so many girdles and corsets. She's Daddy's patient and I overheard Daddy whisperin' about it to Mother one night when they thought I was in bed. She never told anyone about the lessons because Daddy had her trumped. If she spilled the beans about me, he could tell all of the single men in town what her *actual* measurements were. I remember Daddy told Mother that she looked like the prow of a ship and Mother choked on her coffee from laughin' so hard."

During those months, peace and love surrounded me. The Barrett's house was lovely. It was not large, but was clean and pretty. There were several windows in every room. There were curtains at the windows and three good meals a day with enough food for seconds or thirds. Doc and Nora never looked angry, and rarely looked tired or sad. Both of Pope's parents loved him and Pope loved both of his parents. They did not fight or scream or cry; the only time I ever heard Doc curse or shout was the day that Pope was nearly drowned at the river. I lived with them all through the winter.

Mama came to see me on the afternoon that I first opened my eyes. I later learned she had been there every day since the accident, waiting for me to wake up, holding my hand and praying. That first afternoon, when she came into my pretty bedroom, I began to cry. She had not lost the baby and was bigger than ever. She said very little about Dan. I didn't feel much remorse. I was sure that I had been right to protect Mama. I was sure that if any man had ever deserved to have a kettle of boiling water thrown on him, it was Dan Brown. But somewhere inside of me I felt sad; I felt that by hurting him I had become like him.

"Dan?" I asked Mama, holding her hand.

She shrugged.

"Pretty bad, at first. We weren't sure…he'll be alright."

Pope told me a long time later that after Dan's burns had finally healed, a group of men had come to our house in the middle of the night, taken Dan out to a field and had beaten him within an inch of his life. They told him that the next time he did anything to his wife or family he wouldn't live to see the sunrise. Then they put him in a truck and, stopping to tell Mama where to find him, drove him to Doc Barrett's. Doc had taken care of him, but had refused to keep him in his home, hoping that I would never find out what had happened. This incident just nearly taught Dan Brown a lesson.

Nearly.

He left all of us alone for a long time. In fact, he disappeared for more than two years.

My recovery was slow—very slow. I had a fractured skull, a broken jaw and cheekbone, a broken nose, four broken ribs, a broken arm, all the bones in one hand crushed and both wrists broken. One femur had suffered a clean break from the force of the rifle butt. I had stitches down one side of my face and all the way down one thigh. I lost the vision in one eye, although after nearly a year I recovered most of it. For two years I walked with a cane, and have had arthritis in my legs and back and have walked with a limp ever since.

As soon as I was able, Nora and Doc helped me down the stairs each morning and positioned me in a large chair in the front room, stuffed with cushions and a snowdrift of brightly colored blankets. Nora talked to me as she worked, through the open door of the kitchen. With even my hands so badly damaged, there was very little that I could do, so I did what I had had very little time in my life to do: I sat in the sunshine, in the cool air of the fall and daydreamed out through the open window. I slept for hours every day, as if I was catching up on years of sleep. I began to realize how many nights, up until then, I had slept with body and mind half-awake, dreading Dan's drunken early-morning returns. I have never, before that time or since, slept as well as I did when I lived with the Barretts.

The Barretts had also been bestowed with the miracle of a radio. I had never had the chance to listen to one. Although the mayor and Mrs. Rachel kept one of those elegant instruments in their company parlor, we were never allowed to turn it on. It gave Mrs. Rachel "headaches." As a little girl, I once asked Mama why, if Mrs. Rachel wasn't able to listen to it, didn't she give it away to someone who could?

"It wouldn't give *me* headaches," I told her.

"Shush, child," Mama whispered, her mouth twitching with amusement.

The Barretts listened to their radio every night and often had other people over to listen to radio programs and eat desert, or to have coffee, or just to visit. Visiting was something I learned that most of the people who lived in town did nearly every night in good weather. It was at the Barrett's that I realized just how much visiting other people did, how little visiting Mama had done, and how few visitors she had received. It was probably because Mama worked too much to have time for visiting. I also suspect that people rarely came to see us because they wished to avoid Dan.

When I was finally well enough to be downstairs with visitors in the evening, people didn't seem to know how they should treat me. They looked at me sadly out of the corner of their eyes—I was sure I must have looked like a monster. Doc and Nora kindly refused to let me look in a mirror.

"It looks bad now, but we'll have that pretty face of yours back in no time," Doc would say.

Doc was the only person other than Mama who had ever called me pretty. I tried to smile at him, but it hurt too badly.

A couple of weeks after I was taken to Doc's, Thena came to see me. She looked different. She had lost weight. Her faced was pinched and bony. Her wrist bones jutted sharply from her sleeves and she had purple circles under her eyes. She looked nervous and edgy and she had a deep, heavy cough. She was very quiet; too quiet. These days are among the very few in my memory when Thena had nothing to say. She very tenderly held the hand that had not been smashed by the butt of Dan's rifle and very sweetly sang songs to me. One day she brought Edwin and John Michael to see me, but she only stayed for a moment, because when John Michael saw me he buried his head in Thena's chest and sobbed.

"Take me home, Thena," he cried, "I want my mama."

I don't think he even recognized me. The little boy was too horrified by the sight of my broken face and body. Jim and Ted came to visit me, too, and Jim talked to me about the boys and how big Mama's belly had gotten and the fish he had caught and the rabbits that he and Ted had shot, with tears running down his face. Ted sat across the room nodding, staring down at the floor, without saying a word.

One day, Thena came in with Reed and Ham. Pope appeared and we talked for hours. They took turns reading from *Little Men*—my favorite book—and they laughed and I tried to laugh, but it hurt too much. Later, Nora came in and said it was time for dinner and that they should stay. The three of them stayed until late evening, when Doc reluctantly sent them away, thinking that the excitement might be too much for me.

In the first few months, Nora tore my food into tiny pieces, added milk to it and blended it together, because my mouth and jaws did not work well enough for me to chew. I lost a lot of weight (although I had never been able to eat enough to weigh much), and it was because of the miracle of Nora's ingenuity and the determination of her love that I survived at all.

Thena came in one afternoon, smiling broadly and holding the hand of both little boys, announcing that Mama had had another baby boy. She named him Franklin Delano Brown, after our president whom Mama greatly admired. Mama and the baby were both fine. Adda was with Mama, and would stay with her for a couple of weeks to take care of her.

Thena sat down to stay a while and whispered to me the news about Adda, wide-eyed.

"Well, as it turns out, Ham ain't gonna be Adda's last child."

"What?!" I asked her, shocked.

"Yeah, she's expectin' again at forty-five."

That Thena new Adda's age was nearly as shocking to me as her pregnancy.

"And all the town tongues are flappin' again and Adda's silent as the grave and if Mama knows anything, she's not talkin'."

"Adda's expecting?" I whispered again, irrelevantly.

"Yep! She got this great, round belly and her cheeks n' eyes jest shine."

"But how?" I whispered, more softly this time, fiddling nervously with the edge of Nora's soft powder blue blanket.

Thena leaned forward, so close to my face that her nose nearly touched mine, and whispered softly,

"The same way as last time."

Then she burst out laughing. I felt my face flushing. There it was again—the mystery of the marriage bed.

She also told me about an incident that had happened with Dan nearly two weeks earlier, just as his burns were healing, and just before the men of our town paid him a visit. One morning, after Mama had left for the Wilkins', Dan had awoken greatly hung-over and had made a trip out to the outhouse wearing only his under shorts and his boots. What he had not noticed, and what Thena had not bothered to tell him—as she never spoke to him again after the day he beat me—was that the first snow of the year lay on the ground and it was bitterly cold. As he stepped outside, Thena quietly locked the door behind him. She took up the key and the boys' coats and hurried them out the front door, locking it behind her and hurried the boys across the road into the King's cornfield. After making the quick walk into town, she dropped John Michael off with Mama at the Wilkins' and then she and Edwin went on to school and left Dan Brown naked and shivering in the snow. Dan was still pretty drunk and not thinking very clearly. After pounding at the door and shouting obscenities at the cold, gray sky, he wrapped himself in a rug lying on the back porch and took refuge in the outhouse.

When he woke up at dusk many hours later, he was seized by a terrible pain. There was a strange burning in his toes, chest and fingers. He felt sure that something was wrong and trudged, in his underwear, through the town and onto Doc Barrett's front step. Doc reluctantly examined Dan and promptly sent him to the hospital. He told him, grimly, that it was frostbite and was pretty bad. October 19th was the record low for that year, 8 degrees, and it was on that day that Thena had determined to exact but a small measure of her vengeance. Dan lost two toes and the tip of his right index finger in the ordeal and swore to his dying day that Thena was a servant of the devil sent to torture him.

Tonight, as an old woman sitting before my blazing fire and covered with two woolen blankets, I still remember those words with a shiver. I am not at all sure that Thena would have bothered to deny the allegation.

She told this story with her eyes laughing and her hands dancing. Sitting on the edge of my bed as she told the story, her beautiful face shone with malice. For a second, I forgot the circles under her eyes and that her dresses had become too large for her. I was mesmerized, terrified.

She did not tell me the story of what had been done to him by the group of townsmen. But when I heard it later, I thought grimly to myself that it was not a good year for Dan Brown. He must have been convinced of the same thing, because he disappeared a few weeks later and didn't come back until after my fourteenth birthday.

Before she left me that afternoon, Thena touched my slowly-healing face and whispered,

"I'm gonna git 'im back, Grace. I promise you someday I will. There's gonna be a day of reckonin' and when there is, it'll be a bad day for Dan Brown. He'll burn for this. I'll make sure he does."

Her eyes flashed like two cold, gleaming emeralds and she held her jaw tightly clenched. She reached out a hand to hold mine and it was icy cold. I trembled inside myself, greatly afraid, and I knew as certainly as I knew that God existed in this world that she would do what she promised.

VIII.

During those months of intolerable inertia, I began to study for the first time in my life. I applied myself to learning. Maybe it was just out of sheer boredom, but more likely it was from the influence of Doc and Pope, two fascinating and brilliant men whose enthusiasm for knowledge was contagious. It wasn't long before I felt contaminated with the germs of their need to know. When I was lost in trying to understand and memorize, the long hours of the days went by more quickly.

Pope and I studied together every afternoon. He brought home a set of textbooks for me to study so that I would not get behind on my work. He sat by my bed and quizzed me on history and spelling. He taught me math. I got to be pretty good at it, but would never come to enjoy it in the way that he did. We read together for hours at a time every day. For many months, my voice was not healed enough for me to be capable of reading aloud, and my eye was still healing—slowly—so Pope read as I lay on my mountain of pillows and listened. Later, when I became stronger, we sat in Nora's front room and each read aloud, our chairs facing one another. We read in the bright golden sunshine cast down on us by the large windows. We were transported away to different centuries and continents, leading lives that we never would have otherwise led. This became a tradition with Pope and I; we read to one another for decades.

It is strange how old I seem to myself as I read what I have written. I am astonished that my weak, old eyes now require a magnifying glass in order for me to be able to read. In fact, I don't do much reading these days, as even a magnifying glass is not powerful enough to make my eyes work properly.

I am quite an old woman now with many wrinkles and I walk feebly and my voice is not strong the way it used to be. I find myself waking from naps in the strangest places without having meant to fall asleep. One afternoon, several months ago, I awoke in my armchair with my cup of tea spilt all over my lap. I had fallen asleep while drinking it. Although I am aware of these things, I assure you that inside of me I am still quite young. The body and face of that musty looking old lady in the mirror astonish me. It is the strangest sensation to feel your body growing older, while your mind feels as young and able as it did in childhood.

The other day, as I dressed to go out, I smelt on my skin the unmistakable scent of old woman. I cried for some time to find it there. I feel that, if only my body would let me, there is a great deal more living that I should like to do. My mind and heart are as young today as that girl who sat in the sunshine and read with her Pope.

Together we read everything that Dickens had written. I loved *A Tale of Two Cities* and *Bleak House*, but hated *Martin Chuzzlewit*. We read Edith Wharton and Henry James, Willa Cather and a young writer who had recently become very famous called F. Scott Fitzgerald. I was later saddened to hear the story of that young man's turbulent life. I felt a kinship with him because he had suffered so much. I felt a kinship with him because he had made so many bad choices.

Some of these books I did not entirely understand, but Pope, two years my senior, filled in the gaps. He would stop reading and explain slowly and carefully to me the ideas that I wasn't quite able to grasp, with all the benevolence of a true pope.

In the evenings, Doc quizzed us both—particularly in history, as this was his special passion. Nora told us stories from the Bible, but not in any way that I had heard told before. She told them, not as if they were bland and insipid platitudes, useful merely as ethical harnesses to keep us on the right moral road. They weren't fables to her. I began to see, as she told the stories of passion and failure, triumph and destruction, courage and cowardice, that they were definitely not stories about good little boys and girls; they were about bad little boys and girls and how a good God was able to use them for his good purposes. For this reason the Bible became significant to me. I knew quite well that I could be wicked; Nora's stories gave me hope that God could find a use for me anyway.

In November, I had my twelfth birthday and Pope turned fourteen. Our birthdays were only two days apart. Doc and Nora threw an enormous party and invited nearly everyone I knew. Their house was full and shook with music and loud laughter. It was my very best birthday. Reed, Ham, Thena and Adda all came, and I cried because I had missed them all so much. Adda sat and told me all the gossip and how they had passed the time at the Wilkins' and how much Ham had grown, and that her sons Gad and Asher had come to see her from her hometown, forty miles to the south. Gad and Asher had wives and families of their own by now and worked as farm hands. Adda's belly had become quite large and I couldn't help staring at it and wondering how Adda could have a baby without a marriage bed. She caught me staring and I blushed. She smiled and said that I could touch her belly if I wanted because the baby was kicking.

There was an enormous cake with rosettes made of pink and blue icing, and people brought us gifts. This was something of a milestone birthday for me, because I had never been given a birthday party and I had never received a birthday gift. On our birthday, no matter how big we got, Mama would pull us onto her lap and tell us the story of the day we were born. Then she would hug and kiss us, tell us how much she loved us, and send us on our way. It was a good way of doing birthdays.

Grandma Netta brought me a beautiful handmade quilt with every color I had ever seen in it—and a few I had not—and a chocolate pie, which she insisted I must eat entirely on my own. Nora gave me a beautiful ivory dress with green vines and red roses that I felt absurd wearing. I often caught myself thinking it would have looked much better on Thena. Doc and Pope each gave me a book. Doc gave me Mark Twain's *Puddin'head Wilson*, saying that I would laugh my head off when I read it. And Pope gave me *Little Women*. Mama gave me a beautiful winter coat of pale blue wool. It must have cost her dearly. No one but me seemed to have noticed the extravagance of the gesture, and I later realized that it was because most people who had seen how badly I was injured had not expected me to live. I didn't find out till I was about fifteen that I had not opened my eyes after Dan's beating for more than two weeks, and it was generally believed that I never would. This birthday was, therefore, a very real and actual celebration of my life.

In early December, Doc and Nora, determined that my injuries would not keep me from enjoying the season, took me to watch the first practice of the yearly Christmas pageant. This year it was to be left in the guiding hand of *Ms.* Adele Somersby, Pope's piano teacher, a good and faithful member of the Shady Grove United Methodist Church. This was a position relegated each year to some poor sucker who had evidently not heard about the previous year's Christmas travesty.

This year's poor sucker was Ms. Somersby. She swept into the nave on the first day of pageant practice, parting the tides of so many expectant children and their shiny-eyed, rapacious parents, like a big-breasted, big-bottomed Moses parting the Red Sea. She called the rehearsal to immediate order, standing on the stage like an ill-tempered dictator delivering a speech upon the marble steps of her palace.

"Childrennnnn!" she cried, with her shrieking hyena's soprano voice.

"You may consider this pageant practice as called to order. There is much work to be done and I need my workers to stand at the ready!"

The pitch and timbre of her voice were brain splitting. I suddenly felt the need to raise a hand to either ear, hoping to hold the sides of my head together.

At the sound of her voice, the children instantly stopped their pushing, whining, pinching, spitting, shoving and yelping, as a flood of divine fear swept over their small bodies. She proceeded on, conducting and superintending at the veritable speed of light.

Within moments, she had laid the foundations for a costume design team, a group of merry musicians, a band of golden cherubs, a herd of fetid animals and their considerably rumpled guardians, along with the holy family—with Reed Wilkins playing Joseph and Thena Kelley playing Mary—as well as establishing Pope Barrett as the narrator. There was a general murmur from the crowd; it was typical and certainly more diplomatic of each year's director of this tradition in Methodist pageantry to allow each child to audition for a part. But not so with Ms. Somersby and her gargantuan bosom. Both remained unmoved, with her bosom laced tight in the metal stays of her girdle, and her heart held firmly in place by the protective armor of both her sternum and her implacable disposition.

"I am certainly sorry at your disappointment, but this is the last year that Thena and Pope will be young enough to participate in our Christmas eventide traditions; therefore, it is essential that each have a significant role."

While this was the extent of her explanation regarding Thena, I suspect her reasoning was more involved than she stated. Thena was, of course, incontestably the most beautiful child in the parish—and everyone likes a beautiful Mary—though Ms. Somersby could hardly have made that admission to a roomful of mad-eyed, snarly-toothed parents.

"Moreover, *if* I had been given *my* way, we would have begun to practice in late October or, at the latest, early November. However, as such things are not my decision," here she looked markedly at Reverend

Davis, "we must do our best to make of a sow's ear a silken purse. There is simply no time for auditions, and one and all must trust the extent of my expertise after many years of musical involvement of all kinds."

She spoke these words, not boldly, but even blandly, without even the tiniest presentiment of what little help musical involvement of all kinds had been to the crushed and defeated pageant directors of Christmases Past.

And there had been a lot of defeats. There was the year that the Christ-child's mother's mother sent word on the day of the pageant to inform the minister that Lilly was terribly ill with a fever. That year—though it would be forever after remedied—there had been no understudy for the part of Mary, and the pageant aficionado herself, little old Elsie Denton, had arrived on the little girl's doorstep, begging that she come and perform just long enough to say her five lines. The mother relented. The wailing and less-than-half-lucid child was dressed in a ridiculous costume and hurried to the stage.

Lilly, looking pale and a little green around the gills, rode down the aisle on the back of a large donkey—which bore a stunning resemblance to four cranky and naughty little boys with grubby knees, covered in dyed burlap. As she was delivered onto the stage, she promptly projectile vomited a stream of greeny-yellow fluid onto the baby Jesus' face. Unfortunately, the baby Jesus was actually six-month-old Helen Jane Peters. Helen Jane's mother, of a slightly hysterical and fastidious nature, forced her way up on to the stage, took up her vomity progeny and tore, shrieking, from the church, leaving a long slimy trail of sick in her wake.

A second later, young father Joseph, disgusted by the propulsion of bodily fluids from Mary (and onto the face and open mouth of the she-child Jesus, no less), bent double and vomited on the heads of the unsuspecting sheep, two small twin boys of four who had never enjoyed the pleasure of pageantry performance, and who would forever after forgo it.

The little sheep threw up on the little donkey and the little donkey puked on three wise men and three wise men passed on this special Advent blessing to the angels, sweetly singing, and the angels turned and bestowed it upon the front row, containing the horrified minister, along with the bishop, the deacons and their wives. Through it all, the half-deaf pianist continued playing "Hark! the Herald Angels Sing." And how they did sing, and sing and sing, and the entire church was filled with the echoing sounds of their very special singing.

Then there was another year where the pageant was stopped about four minutes into the long expected presentation after an over-large and brutishly strong wise man found the need to strongly reprimand an errant sheep over the head with his staff. Jacob Alder/Sheep #2 was knocked out and received a dangerous concussion. He was unconscious for over an hour after the accident. The mothers of the two boys, out of good Christian love (and, indeed, after the true spirit of Christmas), stopped speaking to each other and never resumed even the most banal decorum. Here I should stop; these are but a few of many illustrious pageant stories, and if I shared all, I would have to write another book entirely.

At any rate, the afternoon passed with the self-satisfied Ms. Somersby directing this and overseeing that. She designed this costume and painted that backdrop and felt all the importance that the director of a Methodist Christmas pageant in an immensely small town could ever feel. And all was right with the world.

Now, it should be noted that Thena Kelley was thirteen years old during the year of her debut as Mary. A more reluctant Mary could not have been found. Because of her innate sense of dignity, she detested the pageant and looked at it as an opportunity for the adults, while their children were made to look absurd in not-very-accurate period costuming, to sit comfortably in their seats for an hour, throw back their heads and laugh.

She explained all of this at length to Mama. According to Thena, the adults were always laughing too hard at the stupidities of the children to be struck by the profundity of the coming of the Christ-child.

"Profundity?" said Mama.

"Yes, profundity." countered Thena, firmly.

This was a new word for her and she must have thought now as good a time as any to try it out. For just an instant, I thought I saw Mama's lip twitch, but I could not be sure. I still wonder if I imagined it there, or if our Mama actually had moments were she struggled not to laugh when disciplining us. This seems doubtful; and, yet, Mama was human, too.

Thena expressed these thoughts, though perhaps without eloquence, in what most certainly were no uncertain terms. Mama listened and then said that Thena would attend the rehearsal and take part in the practice and that *not one more word* was to be heard about it.

Thena knew this tone of voice, because of—not in spite of—the rarity of hearing it. She stomped from the house and stomped the two miles to Shady Grove United Methodist Church, hoping at every moment to be blown away forever on the icy winds of her distaste.

It was not the Christmas story itself that Thena disapproved of; I think that she loved the story of the angels singing the world's most beautiful songs to announce the coming of the world's most important child. But what to her seemed reverent and "just downright holy"—or so she said, though I never really felt that Thena knew the meaning of the word—seemed every year to be made into a spectacle in a new way. Mama was unrelenting; and for the sake of her dignity, I wish that she had not been quite so stubborn.

Thena, Reed and Pope began to plot. I was made a party to these plottings, but was unable to take an active part in their treachery and sabotage because of my immobility. Yet, I reveled in the inestimable wickedness of it all. I ate of it till my belly was full to bursting. I swam in it till my limbs cramped and my fingers and toes looked like fat raisins.

I don't think that I was really a bad child in most ways. In fact, I have heard Mama say that as a small girl I was the best behaved and the most tenderhearted of her children. But I had a penchant for mischief, and the embryo of Thena's plans for revenge wet my long-sleeping appetite for devilry.

It may seem, from the stories of our childhood, that Thena was a bad-natured girl, always looking for trouble; but that is not true. I think that Thena was a good-natured child and that trouble had the most mysterious way of finding her. I think that maybe it simply remembered where she lived. She was high-spirited, high-strung, strong-willed and maybe a little spoiled. These traits, along with her passionate, impulsive nature sometimes compelled her to think only of the shining glories of an action and never its likely pitfalls. In spite of these parts of her nature, which could and did produce both positive and negative outcomes, I am firmly convinced that, had our circumstances been different, and had we never met Dan Brown, her life would have been an unequivocal triumph filled with all of the joys of human life and probably very few of its sorrows. Thena was a loving sister and dutiful daughter. One story, in particular, reminds me of just how generous and loving my sweet sister was.

In January of my tenth year, I was suffering through a tremendous growth spurt. My shoes had been too small for some time, but I couldn't bring myself to burden Mama with the responsibility of another expense. So, for many months after I had begun to need new shoes, I said nothing, tramping to and from school in a pair of ante-diluvian saddle oxfords which had been Thena's before they were mine and had probably been the once proud possession of our great-great-grandmother's great-great-grandmother. After a while, my feet began to swell and blister. There were places on my toes that filled with puss and infection and oozed painfully, particularly at night, after I took my shoes off. But still I said nothing.

I was careful during this time to always wear socks, though up until then I was never seen with a pair of socks on, in summer or winter, unless Mama commanded it. By this method, I hoped to lengthen the utterly inevitable occurrence of Mama realizing that I needed new shoes. If Mama noticed this new habit, she never mentioned it. In fact, she probably gave a great sigh of relief at this change for the better—one tiny step away from my tomboyish ways; one tiny step toward becoming a lady. Maybe she just chalked it up to an adolescent oddity, thinking to herself that I was growing up and would probably begin to do things differently.

Whatever her reason, Mama never brought it up, and it was Thena who asked why I limped when I left the house. I carefully pulled off my socks and showed her the battleground of carnage on my feet. She filled a pan with water, heated it, added in some salt and for a long time I sat soaking my lame feet. The next morning, I awoke and hurried to get ready for school. I was surprised to see that Thena was not in the house. I opened the door and looked into the yard for her, but she was not there.

When it was time for me to go, I went reluctantly to the tiny bedroom that all the children shared—except for Jim and Ted, who shared the hayloft—and crouched beside the bed in search of my shoes. I mentally prepared myself for another bright and shining day of boundless tribulation. To my surprise, my shoes were missing, and in their place were Thena's shoes, two sizes larger than my own. I sat down on the bed. I wasn't sure what it meant. After a long time, I put the shoes on and walked to school.

If at that moment a young Fred Astaire had appeared before me and asked me for a dance, nobody would ever have heard of Ginger Rogers, because I would have danced circles around her, and Fred would have been forced to break the news to her that Grace Kelley was going to be his partner instead.

That is my name—Grace Kelley—although I don't believe I have mentioned it until now. No, I was not named after the beautiful movie star; she was not famous until nearly two decades after I was born. What's more, I didn't look a thing like her, although I would have sold my soul, and those of several family members, to do so. People have always thought it clever and seemingly original to tease me about my name—never seeming to note the difference in the spelling—but really, Grace Kelley is not an unusual name for an Irish girl, and she and I shared it with a thousand others.

In Thena's shoes, I felt that I would never know pain again. And though my feet had certainly not yet healed, I was so very happy that day that I never felt a moment's discomfort. To my horror, when I got to school I found that Thena had been sent home because she had not worn shoes. It was, of course, less than a day before Mama got wind of this indiscretion; Mama, exasperated and irate, confronted Thena, who refused to explain.

However, the cat was out of the bag when I arrived home wearing Thena's shoes.

"*Grace Canton Kelley, why* are you wearin' yer sister's shoes, and *where* are yer own?"

I looked confusedly from one to the other; not sure of Thena's plan, squirming and uncertain of what to divulge. Thena uncrossed her arms and stood from her seat. She walked to me, unlaced my shoes and gently pulled them off. Mama sat down on the floor beside me and started to cry.

"Why didn't you tell me?" Then, looking at Thena, she asked, "Why didn't *you* tell me?"

But Mama knew the answer.

I can think of countless other times when Thena's gentle heart and loving nature caused her to protect those she loved. When Thena was eleven, her body began to change. She grew tall, and started to develop hips and small rosebud breasts. Her face lost its childishness; the bones of her cheeks broadened and her chin became firmer and sharper. Her waistline curved in subtly and her hips and ribs flowed gently outward like a sweetly flowing stream. That was what she looked like when she moved: water. She was languid and still. Her touch and movements were light, weightless. Thena floated. She wafted like a summer scent on a quiet breath of wind. She hovered above the earth as she moved; wherever she went she left behind her the scent of hydrangea, vanilla and the warm, brown coniferous earth. Wherever my sister went, she also left behind her the smell of love and joy and sorrow.

As these changes in her body deepened and further widened the gap between us, Thena began the curse. When we were young, people didn't say much about such things. I had a school friend, Barbara, mention in passing, twenty years after the fact, that when we were teenagers her mother had miscarried in her sixth month. This confused me. I had no memory of that event taking place and I asked her about it.

"What do you mean?" I said. "I saw your Mama every day. I never knew she was expecting. No one ever said a word. Why did you never tell me?"

"I didn't tell you because I didn't know. Mama just told me last year."

Her mama had not told her because women did not talk about sex, conception, birth control, pregnancy or birth in those days, much less miscarriage. Consequently, when the time came for Thena's womanhood to begin, she was shocked by it. She had no idea what was taking place in her body. The bleeding and the dull insistent pain that coursed through her like a thick heat gave her a strong sense of foreboding. She was certain that there was something terribly wrong with her, and she was pretty sure that it involved a horrible death. She later told me that she lay awake at night, soaked in sweat, with her hands to her eyes, wondering what Mama would do without her. Wondering, when she was gone, who would protect us all from Dan?

She continued to wonder, because she refused to tell Mama. Mama had too much to worry over, to Thena's way of thinking, and she must not try to supply the vast fortune that would be necessary to save her dying daughter. This went on for some time—two years, in fact—until Thena suffered from some sort of female problem.

We knew so little about such things then, and the inconsistencies and complexities of women's bodies were still a boundless and, in many ways, unexplored territory. Moreover, most doctors were men and, understandably, a man cannot be expected to fully comprehend a woman's body. Regardless, something happened inside of Thena—probably relatively minor, but horribly painful—and I found her lying on the floor of the back room, curled tightly in a ball, sweating, with her fists clenched and her eyes closed. Tears coursed down her death-white cheeks and she groaned softly.

I had become nearly hysterical, but Thena with a word had silenced me. She would not allow me to go for help, because Mama would be worried sick, and so I sat on the floor and held her hand. I put her head in my lap, gently stroked her beautiful curls and cried with her. Mama found us in just this posture and, seeing the terror etched into both of our features, she raced across the room and gathered Thena up into her arms. At first she was terrified, but it didn't take her long to realize what was happening. She asked Thena where the pain came from and what were the other symptoms and how long had she had them.

"I guess a couple a' years."

"Two *years!*" shouted Mama.

"They come n' go," whispered Thena, still not opening her eyes.

"Come n' go?"

"Yeah, they come fer a week or so n' then I don't have 'em fer a while."

"How long's 'a while?'"

"Don't know. Four or five weeks, I reckon."

Then Mama knew. She laughed, as tears streamed down her face.

"Thena, gurl, why on earth haven't you told me this?" said Mama.

"I knew you couldn't afford to put me in the hospital," whispered Thena.

"Thena, honey, you don't need a hospital. You need a scaldin' bath n' some rest. This happens to every woman, everywhere, and it has since the beginnin' of women."

Thena sat up. "This happens to you?"

Mama knew then what Thena had been thinking and, sending me from the room, she set her straight. Neither Thena nor Mama ever told me much about that conversation, but I am sure that Mama kept the facts of life to the very threadbarest minimum.

This was Thena's true heart; this was her consideration for us. She could, as most children, be quite bad, but she was also often quite good. In fact, she was often splendidly good. It must seem strange to anyone hearing our story that we so protected Mama. Now, as a grown woman who has raised children of her own, it seems strange to me, as well, but then it seemed the most natural thing in the world and, in fact, the *only* thing to do. Mama was tiny, as I have mentioned. Not much over four and a half feet tall and not a bit more than eighty pounds at her very wettest and fattest. Her bones were so dainty and small that when she had married my Papa, he had had to buy a child-sized ring, because there wasn't a woman's ring small enough to fit her finger.

I think that part of our desire to protect Mama stemmed from the fragility of her little bones, her delicate physiognomy and the insubstantiality of her baby hands and feet. We wished to protect our Mama just as an adult wishes to protect the frail body of a child; although, of course, our desire to protect was without any sense of condescension, as the goodness and wisdom of Mama's nature demanded respect. But, in spite of our desire to protect her, life is life, and it will plague us all at times. And so it did Mama. And, occasionally, I am ashamed to admit, as in the case of the Christmas pageant of 1937, we proved to be that very plague.

I have sufficiently veered from my stories of "bad Thena" and, for now, must tell no more stories of "good Thena" or "brave Thena" (although perhaps Thena was bravest when she was "baddest"). Instead, I shall now finish the story of Thena's theatrical debut as the blessed Virgin.

As it turned out, Thena was wrong about the children being made spectacles of in the Christmas pageant. Ms. Somersby didn't like spectacles. She liked flawless, seamless professional-style productions, with big booming crescendos, gripping beginnings and epic endings. And she wouldn't settle for anything less. The hours of pageant practice were grueling, and she presided over them with all the pomp and self-importance of the Speaker of the Roman Senate. The only problem was, the children were neither senators nor Romans. They were more like the snotty-nosed, bleary-eyed, ill-educated and impoverished masses. They were the rabble. And so, at the beginning, there was a tremendous disparity between what Ms. Somersby wanted them to be and what they actually were. But I've got to hand it to her: the woman knew how to get results.

The weeks went on, and things began to happen that had never happened before. The angels began to look angelic, the cattle lowed, the shepherds became shepherds, and the wise men looked wise. And as I sat in the church pews, looking on, the scene I saw before me actually began to look like a holy night.

Finally, Christmas Eve arrived. The costumes were perfect. The actors knew their lines. The choir sang sweetly—and in tune. And by the end of the dress rehearsal, it looked as if nothing could go wrong. That night, Doc drove Nora and I to the church. It was one of the most beautiful nights I ever remember seeing; I can't imagine that the first Christmas could have been any prettier. The sky was lit up with a brilliant light, the air was cold and clear, but friendly, and I could almost see the heavenly hosts.

We entered the church to find it packed and completely, utterly silent. The room was filled with hundreds of candles and, from the highest rafters down to the old pine boards of the floor, there were sprigs of holly and the elegant boughs of evergreen trees. It was a room too beautiful not to be reverent in.

The pageant was perfect. The sheep bleated beautifully. Baby Jesus slept quietly in his manger. The holy family looked so innocent, so pious, and the North Star shone down as if into the very souls of the congregants. As the last strains of the last carol died away, I thought I heard a corporate sigh expelled from the relieved audience. Our church had a reputation…

After waiting a respectable length of time for the audience to applaud, Ms. Somersby mounted the steps of the platform, the black velvet train of her evening gown trailing along behind her. She cleared her throat. She smoothed her hair away from her face. Then she squared her shoulders and began.

"Ladies and gentlemen, Reverend Davis, Mrs. Davis, Bishop and Mrs. Wallace: we thank you all for adorning this blessed yuletide evening with the honor of your presence. It has been a long road with many wendings and unforeseen detours. But here we are, after much travail, arrived safely home. It has been, for us, and I hope for you, a glorious homecoming. We hope that our humble attempt at a re-telling of the blessed Christmas story has touched you and has helped you to worship. This evening will, for us, and we hope for you, remain as a precious and forever preserved gift in the treasure box of our memories."

For a moment, she bowed her head. Her dark brows furrowed.

"I have always believed that great things could be reaped from the ever-ripe harvest of this town's progeny. Tonight, I believe we have seen those great things."

And then it happened.

At that moment, I saw Thena reach up and tap the shoulder of the third wise man. After receiving her signal, the three wise men and their gold, frankincense and myrrh took an almost imperceptible step forward onto the train of Ms. Somersby's gown.

"Ladies and gentlemen," she cried, spreading her arms out wide in a gesture of magnanimity to the crowd, "let us never forget the great things we have seen here tonight!"

And then, bowing once, she took a step forward. As she did, I heard from where I sat in the fifth row the sound of fine velvet being torn. The dress ripped in one long tear down the front of her body, and was torn from the great tower of her shoulders. And there she stood, in the presence of the holy family, and all of the heavenly hosts, and the minister, and the bishop, and the great cloud of witnesses which was our town, in her sturdy black pumps and her underwear and her enormous girdle, with her gargantuan bosom standing out from her chest like two bowls of jelly.

It was the best Christmas pageant our town ever had.

IX.

In January of 1938, Adda gave birth to Harriet Tubman Sinclair. That same month, Doc decided that my body, though it would be years before I had fully recovered, had healed enough that I might go home to be with Thena and Mama. Three weeks after I moved home, Adda brought her new baby to see me.

Harriet Tubman was a fat, howling cherub of a baby who at birth had the startling baldness and corpulent waistline of an old man. In spite of these features, she was a marvelously cute baby, and from the moment she first curled her tiny fingers with their mother of pearl fingernails around my hand, I loved her. The birth was extremely difficult for Adda, and after a day and a half, despite her reservations about exposing us too early to the things of this world, Mama sent for Thena and I.

Although we were not allowed into the birthing room itself, Mama made us useful by ordering gallons of hot water and coffee and, occasionally, asking Thena and I to cook for she and Doc Barrett. The labor was far too long and Adda was too old—by several years—to have withstood its rigors. But somehow she did. With great determination, after the shrieks and sobs of many painful hours, Harriet Tubman Sinclair rode the freedom train on out of her mother's womb and told the world of her liberty with her brand new voice.

After the baby was delivered, Adda fell back, tears running their course along the lines of her face, and slept for many hours. Mama called us in after Adda and the baby had been cleaned. She allowed Thena and then me to hold and kiss baby Harriet Tubman (Adda's baby was always called by both of her names, just like my younger brother, Franklin Delano). We helped her clean up the room and throw open two windows and we sat and watched the morning give birth to the sun.

Several days passed and Adda grew stronger. She held and nursed her baby and sang sweet songs to her. Adda had a beautiful, mellow and very deep voice. Her voice was so low that it could have been a man's, save for its shattering sweetness. Mama was a soft alto, though much higher than Adda's. I remember them singing together often when I was a young girl. Adda's singing would often make me cry; though, as a child, I never understood why.

My whole life long I have loved to sing. I sang often when I was young, mostly when there was no one close by to hear. Though my voice may have been good, it lacked the intensity and fullness of Adda's.

In the first few days after her baby was born, Adda sang many lullabies to the little girl, and Harriet Tubman seemed to listen with great intensity.

She was a pretty baby; large and round. She had an insatiable appetite and virtually sucked the life out of her mama. Adda, who had always been a thin, well-muscled woman, lost a full ten pounds after she began to nurse.

After nine full days of rest, Mrs. Rachel requested that Adda bring the baby to her. Adda did as she was asked. No more than a moment after she entered Mrs. Rachel's room, she was sent out without her job. After twenty-five years of service, Mrs. Rachel had dismissed her. Harriet Tubman's hair was kinky curly and pale brown. Her skin was the color of deep caramel and her eyes were a startling and unflinching blue-green—the precise color of Reed's. Her features were small and thin, with a long, patrician nose.

With Ham there was adequate room for speculation. His beautiful, smooth skin was fairly—though not uncommonly—light brown. But both his hair and eyes were black. Therefore, his paternity couldn't be pinned on one man; certainly no one white man. However, Harriet Tubman certainly seemed to be the child of a white man. Although Mrs. Rachel had harbored suspicions even when Ham was born, ladies in those days didn't have the disrespectful natures that we emancipated women of today have. We no longer permit our husbands their playful lecheries. Also, while, with Ham, ambiguity had served as a sufficient barrier to Mrs. Rachel's dignity (because he was clearly black), Harriet Tubman made Mrs. Rachel a joke—or so Mrs. Rachel thought. With Adda's black son, Mrs. Rachel could preserve the illusion of respectability. With Adda's white daughter, illusion was shattered and the truth was ushered out into the town square in the broad light of the bustling noonday sun.

With no more words than were necessary, Adda told Mama what had happened. Mama helped her pack her few things. Plans and arrangements were made. Lives were changed. Empires rose and fell in an afternoon. Nothing was ever the same. I have tried on a number of occasions to muster a certain degree of compassion for the mayor—I can't imagine that the pleasures of the marriage bed would ever have been acknowledged as pleasures by Mrs. Rachel. So sour was her expression on even the most glorious sunlit fall afternoon that I can't imagine her to have enjoyed anything that went on after the sun had set. As an adult, when I understood the dynamics of conception, I rather marveled that the mayor had convinced her to lay with him the minimum of two times it would have taken to create their sons.

Who knows, perhaps he even loved Adda. I have to admit that, at forty-five (although still a very pretty woman who looked far younger), she wasn't exactly the young tarty type that the archetypal powerful, spoiled, narcissistic town lech would have gone for. Maybe there was more involved on his part than simple lust. At any rate, the way that I occasionally heard Adda speak of him, she did not return his feelings if, in fact, he had any.

I remember one afternoon, as a little girl of probably five, being sent to the butler's pantry to put away a tray of newly polished silver. I opened the door and switched on the light; inside stood Adda and the mayor. Mayor Wilkins' back was to me and Adda was backed against the counter. The two were struggling, with Adda pushing him away, but the mayor was a large man, and she was a small woman. I was not sure what was happening or why Adda and the mayor were in this tiny room with the lights off.

"Here, sugar, hand me that silver," said Adda, reaching around the mayor.

"Now, go o'an. Get."

She said it softly, but I realized—without realizing much—that I shouldn't stay and talk to Adda, as I would have normally done.

It wasn't until some years later, when I began to piece together the reasons why Adda and Ham were sent away so soon after Harriet Tubman was born, that I suddenly remembered that encounter with Adda and the mayor. I have wondered many times since then about the nature of their relationship. If those two children were not born out of love, then why did Adda never speak out? Why did she continue working for the mayor? But I think I have always known the answer.

It would have been a black woman saying "no" to a white man—her boss—just more than fifty years after the civil war, and in the heart of the south. Who would care if she did? The mayor outweighed her by a hundred pounds. He was a man. He was white. He was the mayor. Who would have believed charges against the mayor? Added to this was the problem of Adda's skin: she could only have offered a black woman's word against a white man's, in a southern world, where crimes against blacks went all but unpunished, and in a region where black people, although legally sanctioned, were not generally *permitted* to vote or testify in court.

This crime, if it was one (and I think that it probably was) would have taken place in a town containing a city hall (the office of the mayor), which didn't allow black people to use its restrooms, much less its judiciary services, and at the foot of which stood separate black and white water fountains. So, Adda drank from the water fountain for black people and said nothing. Not even to Mama, her best friend.

It took me many years to assimilate all of these things. But even as they were taking place, I knew that something lay beneath the surface of what was said, and I was also quite certain that Thena knew more than I did. She could see something that I couldn't see—that I was afraid to see. And, because I was afraid, I didn't ask.

I love the south; it is a part of me. You cannot escape who you are. But there are times when I shudder at us, at what we have done, at what we have left undone—allowing others to do—and I am ashamed.

New Yorkers love their home. They love the culture and the excitement, the bright life in a big city. They love the opera and the luxury of a well-spoken play. They love the park in its seasons—ice skating in winter and walks through great lakes of leaves in the fall, and long naps in the sunshine of the park on spring afternoons. But they hate the crowds. They hate the pollution. They hate the filth, the poverty, the crime, the racial tensions, the miles upon miles of concrete.

We both love and hate our homes—just as we love and hate our own bodies, our own natures. We know the best and worst parts of our homes and our cities just as we know the best and worst parts of our insides— they shine out like a beacon in the bleakest and loneliest of nights, and sometimes the light keeps us from sleeping.

Adda left one morning, when the cold stood thick on the windowpanes and the wind cried out like a woman deeply troubled. Her brother and her twin sons drove into town and packed her few belongings into the back of an old rusted wagon. Pope, Doc, Nora,

Mama, Thena, Reed and I all stood outside to watch them drive away. Everyone stood silently, dazed by the insipid banishment of this faithful and gentle servant—one who had quietly withstood years of eternal days, virtually non-existent pay, and general poor treatment. Everyone felt too much to cry; all of us had too much to say to be able to speak.

I once asked Mama, a number of years after Adda, Ham and Harriet Tubman had gone back to Adda's childhood home, how Mrs. Rachel could hate Adda so much after having lived together for so many years, and after Adda had nursed her through so many long nights of illness. Mama was still for a long time. Then she frowned and shook her head.

"She didn't hate her, child. She loved her."

"Mama, how can you say that?" I asked.

She continued ironing Dan's blue work shirt.

"She loved Adda, in her way, but she loved her pride more. Her dignity was more important to her than Adda's livelihood or friendship or love. It's sad, surely. But I suppose we cain't say that Mrs. Rachel is much diff'rent from most people. Besides, she didn't send Adda away to punish her. I don't reckon Adda ever figured into it at all."

"What do you mean?"

"She sent Adda away to punish *him*."

Impulsively, I reached toward Adda for one last hug before she left us. She held me tightly and close to her small, warm body and kissed the top of my hair.

"Don't you cry, baby girl. Things change, chile," she whispered, and then walked away.

Adda got into the wagon with Ham, Gad, Asher, her brother George and Harriet Tubman. She nodded to all of us. She did not cry. Ham did not cry. I glanced over my shoulder at Mrs. Rachel's window, and saw that the curtains were slightly parted. The mayor was nowhere to be seen. Slowly, they drove away.

Reed got onto his bike and raced after them. He followed them down

Main Street and through the town.

"Fine!" he screamed after her, "You leave me! Go o'an! Git! I never did love you no ways. You ain't no 'count! Ham, you ain't my friend and I don't want you here!"

He pelted the wagon with rocks and still neither Adda nor Ham looked back or acknowledged that they had heard. He screamed and shouted and the more he shouted the more furious he became. Tears began to run down his face and his shouts of anger became sobs of pain. As the wagon rounded the last corner, just at the end of town, Reed threw his bicycle down beside the road and lay down in the dust and wept as his mama drove away.

Just after Adda left, Mama walked away from the mayor's house without saying a word to any of us. She left and did not come back that day. Thena and I went into the house and washed dishes, swept and carefully dusted Mrs. Rachel's beautiful crystal and china. We quietly cleaned the carpets and polished the silver, tiptoeing through the house, uncertain of what needed to be done and, so, doing everything. We watered all the plants and changed all of the sheets and took all of Mrs. Rachel's meals quietly to her room—a job that we had never been allowed to do, but on this day, there was no one else to do it. As we entered and exited her room, Mrs. Rachel never said a word, but watched us quietly with her cool eyes.

Every couple of hours, Thena or I would go up to her room to take her tray away, and as far as I could tell the food was never touched. I have no idea where Mama went, or what she felt that afternoon. She never said a word about it and I never asked. As far as I know, this was the only time that Mama ever missed a day of work, other than the flood, the day after she had given birth to one of her babies, and, many years later, after the fire.

Thinking back on it, I see what Mama had lost. I think that Adda must have given her the listening ear that she needed to go on providing for seven children and to continue living with a no-good husband. I have so many memories of them standing or sitting close together, their backs bent over a task, their heads almost touching, quietly talking to each other. I remember watching from the shadows as Mama spoke in a small voice to Adda. Adda's eyes remained on what she was doing, and occasionally she would shake her head and sigh. Mostly she listened, with her lips pursed together a little and her head tilted to one side, and then she would nod. I think that Adda was the sister of Mama's heart. When she drove away that winter morning, I think a part of Mama's soul flew away after her on the bitter wind.

The spring and summer of 1938 passed quietly away. Occasionally, we heard rumors about Germany's new dictator and his bloodlust, but I must admit that we thought little of him. Mostly, we were concerned with what was there, before us. We kept our minds and eyes on the task at hand. Our thoughts were filled with keeping Mrs. Rachel's house just so and buying Franklin Delano his first pair of shoes and with planting and weeding our garden and studying for school. The summer was a hot one. I remember this summer—although it may have happened earlier—as the summer that Mama began to insist on keeping us fully dressed. Up until that time, when we were quite old, I don't believe that we thought much about the differences between our male and femaleness.

Mama was not silly about such things, and we were raised with a great many brothers around us. We often swam together naked, or nearly so, and I thought very little of it, noting without a great deal of interest that there were differences between girl and boy parts. But that summer, after realizing that Thena had started the curse and knowing that I wouldn't be far behind, Mama no longer permitted us to swim with the boys and we were much disturbed by this new (and, in our minds, silly) mandate of Mama's, although, for many years, we actually obeyed it.

It was also during this time that Mama decided that Thena and I should no longer be so very tomboyish. That most accursed time in the lives of all young girls had come. It was time for us to become ladies. For my part, I look back on the years before I was a lady with great nostalgia. I have always liked to be dirty and sweaty; really, the dirtier and sweatier I was, the better I liked it. I have always liked being loud—screaming and shouting whenever I chose to as a girl. Furthermore, boys' activities have always seemed a great deal more interesting to me. While I could play with a doll (Thena and I only owned one, which we shared—a pink gingham doll named Lollie) for perhaps an hour or two, I could play baseball all day long.

I was always chosen first when playing baseball with the boys, because I could hit the ball harder and farther than almost anyone else in our town—even farther than some of the big boys. It was my one and only claim to fame in childhood. In fact, it may have been the only one I ever had. I would still prefer to be known for prowess in baseball than to be known as a great lady. Mrs. Rachel was a great lady and I never liked her much.

X.

I very seldom thought of Dan in the two years that he was gone. In fact, I don't suppose that I thought of him consciously at all. Some nights I woke up shouting, my bedclothes and nightgown soaked in cold sweat and tears, but I never told Mama or even Thena what the nightmares were about. Even the scars that remained on my body did not remind me of him, because I did not allow them to; I never allowed myself to think of Dan Brown. Not even in moments of weakness. It was only in my dreams—when I had no control over it—that he came to mind.

I still walked with a cane when I returned to school that fall, but my ribs had healed and my legs were much stronger. The stitches, which had lain in livid rows of red across the side of my face, were gone; only the scars remained. The scars themselves had become quite small and it seemed that I could see them a little less every time I looked in a mirror.

To tell the truth, even after everything that had happened, I wasn't very frightened of Dan. My dreams, as dreams always do, made him powerful and terrifying. But when I was awake, he seemed little but pathetic to me. Except for the musty smell of sadness left behind in the wake of Adda's departure, a smell which saturated the mayor's chintz curtains and red velvet couches (and that could still be smelled more than thirty years later when I returned for the mayor's funeral), life had really smelled of sweet spring since Dan had gone.

Even so, even with the safety and peace of a Danless house, when

Adda left, she took away something that could never be replaced. Even in the happiest moments of that spring and summer, there was an abscence in Mama's smiling eyes and in the laugh that still burst forth from Thena—an absence that nothing but Adda, Ham and Harriet Tubman, back with us as they ought to have been, could have filled. If it had not been for that one icy morning in January, it would certainly have been the very best of all of our years together. It would have been a perfect year; a year when Mama could have slept soundly, dreaming the prettiest dreams. A year when she would not have cried.

No matter what Mrs. Rachel told herself, Adda would forever remain in that house. Her memory and her smell were always there. She was a sweet smelling presence. A specter. I could hear her jubilant laugh and deep contralto voice whenever I went into that house; and surely Mrs. Rachel must have heard it, too.

A year passed, and we slowly became accustomed to the void caused by Adda's absence. With Dan gone, we felt free for the first time in many years. We felt powerful, as if we were given a chance to change all the bad that had been done and make it into good. My two oldest brothers had become young men and both had taken jobs, which brought in a little money every week. Mrs. Rachel allowed Thena and me to take over the work that once belonged to Adda and, as a result, Mama received an extra dollar every week. In truth, this was nowhere near the amount that Mama should have been given for the work that we did, but she accepted the extra dollar without comment or complaint.

In November of 1939, just after my fourteenth birthday, the weather changed rapidly. I remember the months that followed as the coldest of my childhood. On one particularly long afternoon, Thena was sitting on the clean pine boards of the floor with a boy on each knee. Edwin sat facing her. With her arms around Franklin Delano and John and her eyes turned to Edwin, she was spinning a long and somewhat complicated story involving a pirate and a princess. (As I recall, the story ended with the princess taking all in a single hand of poker and seizing command of the pirate's ship. She then traveled to a system of caves in the Caribbean where the pirate's hoard was stashed. After robbing away every gold coin, ruby and pearl necklace, she sailed away into the sunset.)

I sat in a corner, absorbed in *Jane Eyre*. Mama had given up her Saturday to stay with Mrs. Rachel, and Ted and Jim were working for the day on Grandpa King's farm for two dollars apiece. Alternating bands of shadow and sunlight fell across the boards of the front room. It was peaceful and comforting. I smiled at the sound of the boys giggling, then tucked my legs comfortably up underneath my body and settled in for an afternoon of quiet reading. I sighed, utterly content.

Then the door opened, and in walked Dan Brown. He carried with him a coarse, brown potato sack filled with his belongings. He had grown a thick beard. His hair was longer and hung in black ringlets around his face. His clothes were worn and dirty. His skin was dark brown—nearly black—and he was painfully thin. He smiled as he stepped through the door and said, quietly,

"Howdy, childr'n. Where's yer Mama?"

No one answered.

No one moved.

Dan turned and gestured to someone standing on the porch. A woman passed through the door behind Dan. She was small and quite young—she seemed about my age. She wore a slouchy green velvet hat, which covered her permanent-waved hair, cut short in an uneven bob. From her scarlet painted lips hung a long, ashy cigarette. She stooped when she walked and her shoulders and back were hunched over, graceless and gawky. The girl wore a red print dress that showed much of her legs and her badly ripped silk stockings. Her nose was long and thin, and looked as if it might have been broken once. Her eyes were large and startlingly blue, her hands long and dirty and her fingernails were painted the same color as her lips. She looked surly and defiant, and with her eyes she flung across the room a look meant to be both bored and confident.

"This's Elsa," said Dan.

She said something in response, though I could not tell what it was.

Thena and I both nodded at her, but remained silent. Neither of us spoke to or even looked at Dan. I went back to my book, without the slightest understanding of a single one of Mr. Rochester's charming harangues at dear Jane. Thena went nervously back to her storytelling, the plot becoming increasingly befuddled with each sentence. Dan and Elsa sat silently at the kitchen table, watching all of us.

Elsa chewed at the bright red tips of her fingers and smoked one cigarette after the next, lighting a new one with the still live end of the last. Eventually, Dan laid his head on his arms and within minutes was snoring loudly. After a time, I cast a glance at Thena. Her eyes were closely watching me, their emerald fireworks brightly flashing. I bent my head in the direction of Elsa and raised my eyebrows. Thena clenched her fists and I could see the tiny muscles of her jaw as they expanded and contracted. She shook her head once, quickly. I studied her eyes for a moment and knew that there was nothing for us to do but wait for Mama.

Several hours passed and the door opened. Mama stepped quietly inside. She came through the door smiling. She stooped and held out her arms, bracing her body for the blow of the two small boys who always rushed to her. Her cheeks were flushed with the cold November wind. Her eyes laughed and long curls had escaped from her bun and hung around her thin face. I realized just then how young our Mama was, and I think that this was the first time I realized that she was pretty. With Dan in the house, neither of the boys had flung themselves into her arms, as they usually would have done.

As she moved several steps into the room and her eyes began to adjust to the light, she stopped, unbuttoned her coat, and unwound the frayed scarf from around her neck. Her bright eyes lit up, her smile widened and she said,

"Why, I didn't know we had company."

Dan lifted his head from the table and stared at Mama, his eyes red and bloodshot with weariness. For an instant she looked confused, then her smile faded and her eyes died.

"Dan," she said quietly, her voice thick, "I hadn't heard it said you were back in these parts."

Dan nodded once, drumming dirty, cracked fingernails nervously on the table. I stared at his hands, perhaps for lack of a better place to look, noticing that the thumb and index fingers of his right hand had no nails. He ran a stained hand over his beard.

"Got back today. Been to Missoura," he said, and then fell silent, waiting for Mama to make a move.

Mama's gaze shifted to the young woman at the table. She studied the girl for a moment. Elsa stared defiantly back at her, her eyes flitting nervously to the door. Mama studied the flaming hair, the bob, and the cigarette hanging from Elsa's full mouth. Her eyes took in the garden of butts carelessly tossed aside and lying all over the table. Her eyes moved back to Dan.

"This's Elsa. She's from back home," said Dan.

He offered no other explanation, and Mama did not ask for one.

For just an instant Mama stood still and silent, assessing the situation. Her eyes moved from Elsa to Dan and back again. I saw something pass across her face, but I did not recognize the expression. Then her face softened and she stepped forward. Holding out her hand, she said,

"How d'you do, Elsa?"

There was a response—some sort of heedless mumble and a grunt that I could not comprehend. Mama seemed satisfied. She watched Elsa's face for a long moment. The girl returned her gaze, her expression coolly disdainful, but somewhere in her face I saw fear. Mama smiled and put a hand on Elsa's shoulder.

"You must be real hungry."

I watched Mama, stupefied. She was actually going to allow Dan Brown to stay in our house. She was going to cook him a meal. And this foundling creature he had brought with him? There was an unanswered question hovering somewhere in my mind. I knew that Dan's relationship to this girl was significant, but I couldn't have exactly identified its weight. I was pretty sure that she was Dan's woman, but was not exactly sure what that meant, or what it would mean for Mama, or how it would affect us all.

Mama made beans and ham and cornbread. Ted and Jim came back from King farm at sunset. Both stepped inside and stopped just over the threshold. Dan stood and offered a hand to both boys. Neither took it. They watched irascibly from the door. Both studied Elsa, neither nodding nor speaking to her. She returned their stares with a look which tried very hard to say that she did not care what they thought, and that she had a right to be here as much as anyone. She sat silently until dinner, looking frightened and belligerent, like a very young pugilist in a bad hat.

Dinner was quiet. Jim and Ted refused to eat and had gone out to the barn to "tend to chores." I was silent out of confusion, unable to eat, restless, picking at the hem of my dress, which had just begun to come loose. Thena was silent out of anger. She sat with her hands in her lap and neither ate nor drank. Mama waited for Dan to say why he had come and what he wanted. Elsa was silent because she was making light work of the food on her plate. She was too thin, and this was the only time that evening that I saw her look interested in anything. She must have eaten six or seven plates. I have never seen anyone eat that way; she had probably not eaten in many days. As she sat under the one light that hung above the dinner table, I noticed that she had purple rims beneath her eyes, and that the bones of her face jutted out, salient and sharp as razor blades. I also noticed a deep scar at her temple and wondered absent-mindedly if Dan or some other man had given it to her.

As I watched her, I felt that this little girl had dressed herself up and come with Dan Brown from Missouri to Tennessee in desperate hope that Tennessee had more food than the Ozarks did. She was starving, and that is a perfectly good reason to take up with a man—any old man. As I sat silently at the kitchen table, I found myself wondering where her mama and papa were and did she have any brothers or sisters. Suddenly I felt very sorry for her. She must have left a cheerless, hopeless past, hoping to prosper and have it good in the future—only to find that life with Dan was more of the same.

As if to prove to Mama that things would be different, Dan was fairly sober that evening, taking only an occasional swig from a silver flask, which he then returned to the inner pocket of his old, torn tweed coat. After dinner, Dan said something into Elsa's ear. She looked displeased and then nodded. Both stood up and moved toward the door. Just before he stepped out, Dan looked back to Mama and said,

"Mary, I'll be back later."

Mama didn't say anything. As soon as the door shut, Thena erupted.

"Mama, what's he doin' here? How could you let 'im stay here? How could you let that girl in yer house? How could you cook fer her n' pretend you didn't know what she is?"

My mother has always been a mystery to me. It must seem like terrible folly to anyone else that Mama would neither leave her husband nor kick him out, but she never did. Things were so different then. People in those days rarely separated and almost never divorced—at least good, church-going people didn't. It was never a consideration for Mama. I think that "'til death do us part" always rang out in her mind, and that its resonance moved all through her body and gave her no peace. She had given her word, and she meant to keep it, whatever the consequences. Mama always kept her word.

I don't mean to imply that I delighted in the fortitude that Mama showed by 'standing by her man.' In truth, I thought she was a fool regarding Dan. I still do. Had it been me, I would have left after the very first punch; I wished and cried and fought against her remaining with him. But it was a very different sort of world then.

When I was a girl, I asked hundreds of questions every day. It was important that I know and understand everything. It was important to me, as a small child, to be able to make sense of a world so very large. I was a nuisance to adults and big kids everywhere—relentlessly asking and, when a question had been answered, asking for more information. Mama was the only person I can remember who *always* answered my questions, as many as I had, anytime that I asked to be told, and never lost patience with me. She would spend as much time as was necessary explaining a thing to me.

But that night, Mama didn't say a word. She wouldn't answer our questions.

"Thena, Grace, will you do up the supper dishes n' watch over the boys for me?"

She put on her hat, coat and old worn scarf and stepped outside. I went to the window, listlessly wiping the fog away from the panes with the tips of my fingers, and watched as she crossed the yard and moved toward the woods to the northeast.

She was gone for a couple of hours. When she came back, she hung her things on their proper hooks, one at a time, without saying anything. She swept the floor, which Thena and I had already done, but neither of us spoke. I think she swept for reasons of her own that had nothing to do with dust on the floor. She quietly took both boys to bed, then came back and sat in her rocker, blinking at the heat of the flames as she stared into the brilliant colors of the fire.

After what seemed like a very long time, Dan returned. The door opened, he stepped in and, removing an old hat from his head, held it awkwardly in his hand, looking like a man unaccustomed to wearing hats—or, indeed, any of the common accoutrements of a civilized society—and faced Mama. He and Mama watched each other for a long time. If her face told him anything, I could not tell what it was.

"Mary, can I come in?"

Mama nodded, looking back to the fire.

Dan moved forward and sat on the wooden boards before the hearth. For a long while he looked at Mama without speaking. Mama never took her eyes from the flames. After several minutes, he sighed a long, plaintive sigh, then he leaned back on his elbows and stared into the fire. From my seat across the room, I studied his face. I noticed the lines of strain around his eyes and mouth. As I watched him, trying to seem as if I were engrossed in the inclemency of Jane Eyre, I noticed a long scar, probably four inches long and two inches wide, running from his temple down along his cheekbone. The scar passed into the edge of his beard, with one part of his cheek too badly scarred for his beard to grow over it. I recognized it as the scar I had given him on the evening I held the kettle against his cheek. Over the next few months, as I observed Dan closely— edgily waiting for any sign of his old lunacy—I noticed that, at moments of absent-mindedness or, perhaps, confusion, Dan gingerly stroked the scar.

He once caught me watching him touch that faintly purple place on the side of his face. He quickly jerked his hand away. I stood frozen to the spot, not knowing if I should speak or pretend not to have seen. Then, suddenly, he laughed, with a roguish grin on his face.

"Ain't very purty, is it, gurl?"

This was the one and only time that Dan and I acknowledged what had taken place between us. And, really, what could we say?

Mama continued slowly to rock, both hands folded in her lap. Stalemate. No one moved. No one spoke. There was no sound, save for the lonely talking of the wind, softly promising that a long, dark winter was coming. We all sat listening, watching the bright firelight, the faint bodies of the flames casting shadows upon the walls. We watched as they contorted and twisted. It was almost as if they were writhing in pain.

Dan's voice, quiet and uncertain, broke the silence.

"I beeyn down at my people's place, near o'an a year."

He glanced over at Mama. She did not turn her eyes to him, but nodded. He scratched his beard and ran two fingers over the scar.

"My people come from Missoura—nearly all 'em still'ere."

Dan's way of speaking was always indistinct. He spoke in a lazy, haphazard manner, shaving off the tender ends of verbs, dumping by the wayside the heaviness of words, making light his load as he went. He spoke as if his tongue were groggy and maybe sleep-deprived. In spite of this, I don't believe that Dan was a stupid man; perhaps not bright, but not, I think, stupid.

"Daddy still 'live. Mama run off when I was still a young'n. Daddy sez she got religion, but I never did think that preach'r wuz a preach'r. You ask me, he was too purty fer one. Mama wern't never worth no 'count. My people," here he waved his hand absently across the room, the shadow of his large, brown hand striking the wall, "none of 'em, never worth nothin'." Dan slowly traced the scar.

"Mary, yer people's good people. You got preach'rs 'n schoolteachers. Yer people had lernin'. Mine never did. Never did have nothin'."

Mama's eyes turned from the fire. These were more words than I had ever heard from Dan. I have to admit, though my will worked against it, I was riveted. Thena stared at the floor, never turning to see Dan's face. For a long moment, Dan was still, staring into the flames, stroking the scar.

"My Daddy wuz okay, I reck'n. He wuz strict, stricter'n people is now. But when I's a boy, nobody never said nothin' when a man lay a hand on his son to correct 'im. I reck'n he did hit me some, but I never thought much 'bout it—'ceptin' it hurt." Here he grinned a little.

"He wuz okay, my Daddy. Stayed with us, fed us when'er he could, tried'n keep us 'live. Don't guess you'd a called 'im a nice man, but I never did mind. Don't reck'n none a' my people wuz whatcha might call nice. Nah, Daddy, he wud'n no gennleman."

Dan sat up slowly and crossed one long leg over the other, stretching his feet toward the fire, then leaned back on his elbows. Mama's eyes went back to the fire, and she continued to rock. After a time, he spoke again.

"My granddaddy wud'n no good. He lived way up in th' hills. Took care 'a hisseff n' his brother. Don't 'member what happened to their ma n' pa, I only heard Granddaddy ever talk 'bout the two of 'em."

Dan paused and stood to stretch. Then he took a poker from the hearth and stirred the fire.

At that moment, Jim and Ted entered. Neither looked pleased to find that Dan was still there. Jim moved from the door to the back wall, with Ted following. Both remained standing, arms crossed, watching Dan, Jim occasionally turning to glance at Mama.

Dan added two logs to the fire and again sprawled out on the floor before the hearth. The house was quiet. The air was heavy and onerous; pregnant with sentiment and unspoken words. My heart felt full and heavy in my chest as if it were weighing into my organs. Everyone was waiting to see what would happen, what Dan would do. I begrudged Dan his space on the floor, wishing him three hundred miles away, still at his people's place. Long minutes passed. All I could hear was the weeping of the wind and the steady ticking of Mama's old mantle clock.

Still, I listened. After a time, I began to perceive other sounds: the creak of Mama's ancient rocker—a gift her father-in-law had made and presented to her as a wedding gift on the day she married my Papa, saying softly, "For all the gran'babies you're gonna give me." And the gentle sound of Mama's breathing, a sound I had fallen asleep to every night of my life. Even today, in the peaceful embrace of the twilight, if I tightly close my eyes and strain to shut out all else, I can hear that peaceful sound, the sweetest sound in the whole world—better than music; better than verse. On the very darkest nights, I sometimes think I can even hear the muffled sounds of her womb. Mama was the very peace of my life.

I was lost in these thoughts—thoughts of Mama, and my sweet granddaddy, who had died two years after I was born, and wondering what our lives would have been like if it were my Papa sitting in front of the fire that night instead of Dan. Then he began to speak again. He never raised his voice much above a whisper, but he spoke for a long time. This is the story Dan told, as I remember it:

In what must have been about the first quarter of the nineteenth century, Dan's great-grandfather, Hiram, and his young brother, Fenton, thirteen years his junior (the boys were born by two different mothers), stumbled out from the primordial darkness of the Ozark hills.

"They were real tough men. Fars I know, Hiram raised Fenton—an' Hiram wouldn'a been a real sweet Mama." Dan grinned.

"He wuz rough. Drank a lot. Hit a lot. Swore a lot. But I reck'n he cared 'bout his brother in 'is way. I 'member my great, great-uncle Fenton sayin' that when he wuz 'bout nine, Hiram used to take 'im out in the yard and beat 'im—with his fists, with a belt, with a tree limb— whatever he could find. He did it fer a long time. He'd beat 'im real bad, n' wait a spell for it to heal, then take 'im out to the yard and beat 'im again. This went on fer a long while. Then Fenton stopped cryin', and he jes' took it. Hiram kept at it. Finally, after months a' this, Fenton started hittin' back. Hiram stopped."

Dan pushed his long matted hair away from his face.

"Now, I don't reck'n Hiram stopped 'cause he'd met his match. He was a great big bear'uva man. Near six an'a half feet tall n' 'bout two hundred'n fifty pounds. I reck'n he stopped 'cause Fenton wud'n afraid no more, n' that wuz all he wanted. Jes' wanted to take the fear outta th' boy."

Dan continued with the story.

Down from the hills, the brothers passed into some small town, and whether they stayed there only for a time or made a home for themselves there was unclear. However, one evening, as the young Fenton joined his brother in a terrific bout of whiskey drinking, the two were ensnared in a horrible fight with what I can only think to refer to as some rather "rough riders." Dan wasn't sure of the number of men, but thought it was six or seven, nor was Dan certain of who began the fight.

"I reck'n it was prolly Hiram started it," said Dan.

"He wuz a real low man. Drank too much, with a real wick'd temper. My Daddy used'a say I wuz like 'im."

Here he glanced at Mama with a sad smile.

"I never much cared fer the comparis'n, though."

Regardless of the particulars and regardless of the blame, a fight broke out. As best as Dan knew, it began between Hiram and one other man. However, the fight between the two men began and ended at nearly the same moment.

"Hiram broke hisseff a whiskey bottle n' slit the man's throat, then had all his drunk buddies to reck'n with. Half a dozen rough, tough men fightin' Hiram, n' him not the least bit scaired. Now, Fenton joined in the fightin', maybe hopin' fer a chance to be the hero n' make Hiram proud. An' jest as things wuz 'bout to git messy fer him n' Fenton, Hiram pulled a nasty trick. Pulled a gun outta his boot'n shot all six of 'em dead."

The bar was stunned. The town was stunned. Where was this man's honor? The magistrate was called in to settle the matter, the townspeople demanding that both man and boy be hanged.

For reasons of his own—I suspect it had something to do with hanging a thirteen-year-old boy—the sheriff gave the two until sunrise to make a run for it. At sunrise, he would send out a posse to track them, and if they were ever found, they would be hanged on the spot. So, the two were sent to wander in the wilderness, and they did so for some time.

"After a couple a' years hidin' in the hills n' caves, they stumbled out. Posse'd gotten sick fer home, I reck'n. Decided they'd prolly die anyway—jes' leave 'em. So Hiram n' Fenton been alone with their thoughts n' each other n' those cold, empty hills fer more'n two years, n' they's powerful ready fer some company. So out they come, n' down into a town. By this time, Hiram wuz twenny-eight er so n' Fenton was 'bout fifteen. Hiram thought it wuz time to take 'im a wife, n' Fenton that he might should as not."

Marriage being the order of the day, two young brides were chosen. In a double wedding, Hiram married a twelve-year-old girl, while Fenton, preferring his women a little more mature, married a matron of thirteen. The brothers packed up their women and left the town in search of a place further away from the watchful eye of the townspeople. After a number of years—Dan believed it was no more than a decade—Hiram's wife died in childbirth, leaving him with nine children. Without missing a beat, he married again (his second bride chosen from the fine selection offered in the upstairs of a local saloon) and promptly fathered eleven more.

There were several other harrowing tales of knife fights and gunshot wounds told that night, and my general impression was much the same as Dan's: Hiram seems to have been a "real mean man." However, one story stands out in my mind above the others, indicating to me that the man was actually more like a monster:

After several years had passed and Missouri became increasingly populated, Hiram grew restless and began to wish for a farm without neighbors. Hiram and Fenton moved their families to the southwestern corner of Missouri, cleared a space of land, and set up housekeeping in a dense cropping of trees. One day, as Hiram passed through the forest on the way to his fields, he was shot with an arrow by an "Injun" perched in a tree. The wound, though painful, was not mortal. Hiram, always armed, shot the man from the tree, killing him. He then took the body back to the farmhouse, cut away a strip of skin from the man's back and stretched it across the face of his barn. When the skin hardened, he used the leather as a razor strap.

Dan talked on until the fire had burnt low. As he spoke, there was no other sound. I couldn't even hear Mama's breathing. After a time, he grew silent. Minutes passed, first a quarter and then a half hour. We all sat horror stricken. Thena sat on the floor with John's head on her knee and Edwin and Franklin Delano on her lap. Mama and I rocked in our rockers. Jim and Ted stood silently watching Dan, their backs against the wall. Then Dan spoke again.

"Yer people, Mary, they wuz good people. My people, they wuz nothin'—mean as th' devil—always been nothin', n' I don't 'spect they'll ever be anythang eltz."

He stood and moved to Mama's side. For a moment, he looked as if he might touch her. His hands stretched out for just an instant, his back slightly bent. Then he straightened, dropping his hands.

"If it's all right by you, I guess I'll get o'an to the back room'n sleep a while."

There was a faint question in his voice. Mama did not speak. She sat rocking, her eyes straight before her.

"Nite' Thena. Grace. Nite' boys." He nodded to each of us in turn.

I could have sworn his eyes rested on me for just a moment longer than the others, but I couldn't be sure. Then he left the room. We all turned to Mama. But she was far, far away.

I fell asleep sometime late into the night, lying uncovered on the floor of the front room, keeping watch over Mama. As the sun began to wake the world, I heard the roosters, and just for a moment I opened my eyes, startled, looking for Mama. As I turned my body toward her rocker, I felt the weight and warmth of a blanket. I saw her there, watching the dead ashes lying inert in the grave of the hearth, still rocking.

I have thought a thousand times of the story that Dan told that night. Why did he tell it? What was he trying to say? To accomplish?

I am not entirely sure; but I think that Dan was a fatalist. From very near his beginning, he was sure of what the end would be. He knew what it was to be born a man into his family. That night when he was telling Mama about his people, he was trying to say that he never had a chance. As Dan saw things, the jury was out before the crimes were committed.

I can't quite say that I agree with that. I think we always have a choice—some choice. But Dan didn't believe that; in his mind, there could be no choice. Or maybe he just felt that he could choose or not choose, but the outcome would be the same. Whether it was what his parents or grandparents had been, or if it was something else—lying dormant inside of him, unknown and unseen—I think he always felt that a force much greater than himself would overcome him at every turn. That this force would make bad anything that he wished to make good. He could fight if he wanted to, and I think that sometimes he did— though that desire blew in with the rarefied airs of spring and, being ephemeral, like the leaves, vanished with the colors of autumn—but he couldn't change what was written on the pages of time.

I think that maybe his storytelling that night, as he lay trying to warm his soul before the fire, was his way of asking Mama's forgiveness. It was an act of contrition. He sought solace for a long-damned soul. In truth, I believe he was asking forgiveness for the things that he *would* do, that he *must* do, because it was written that he should, long before those things ever came to be.

Dan was by no means all bad; though, at the time, I wasn't able to see that. Today, I think I see things a bit more clearly. There is even some part of me that feels a quiet compassion for him, as one might feel for any such piteous, wretched creature. But at the time, I saw him only as one who had caused my mama great pain; one who had caused us all great pain. Later, I saw him as the one who had brought about an end to it all—

to all of us, each in a different way. I saw him as the ultimate end of both Mama and Thena, in different ways and at different times; though perhaps that was not entirely fair.

I see, in hindsight, that both Mama and Thena had their own choices to make, and they both made them. I once saw Dan as an end to myself, having destroyed something good and pure in me, having taken away my dignity and made me low. But now I see that it was not Dan who is responsible for who and what I am, but it is I who made and allowed myself to become this very particular person, for better or for worse.

We should have heard it in his voice that night. We should have seen it in his face; in the way he walked and held himself. We should have known. Something ought to have told us.

We ought to have sent him away, marked like Cain, to wander the earth alone. We ought to have sent him in search—find it if he could—of some kind of redemption. But we didn't. No one spoke. The moment passed. The sun rose, and the world changed.

XI.

The months that followed were quiet. Dan was not exactly sober, but he wasn't exactly drunk, either, and he was certainly better behaved. There were times when he disappeared for a day or two, reappearing looking worn and dirty with bleary, blood-shot eyes and a troubled, care-worn countenance. Whenever he returned, he usually slept for a couple of days, his body hoping, I suppose, to recover from all that he had put it through. I can still faintly picture how Dan looked coming home on these early mornings, slack-jawed and heavy-hearted, from the delights of these late night revelries, and I am reminded of a somewhat bizarre saying of Campbell's.

Campbell generally had a nonsensical saying for every one of life's occasions: if he saw a man looking especially unwell, he would say that he looked as if he had been "beat through hell with a buzzard's gut." Though I have never understood most of Campbell's sayings, I have to admit that this seemed a perfect way of describing Dan after one of his binges. He did certainly look like a man who had been beat through hell with a buzzard's gut.

We heard little of Elsa in the months that passed. I heard the breath of a rumor that Elsa was living in one of the abandoned shacks at the river's edge—houses so dilapidated that even the poor had decided they deserved better and had withdrawn—and that she had managed to find a few odd jobs here and there. Someone from town told me that she had been seen moving in and out of a few houses, washing and ironing laundry and cleaning, but I don't think that there would have been much work for her in our poor town. I wasn't really sure how she lived, unless Dan did more for her than he ever had for us.

I hoped, rather than believed, that that was the case—feeling a strange sort of sorrow mingled with jealousy for this little girl who had given up what little she had for a life of what must have been even less with Dan Brown. Maybe she loved him. Her face never showed any sign of either joy or sorrow in his presence. And even later, when I came to know her, she spoke of her days with Dan only once. I surmised that she must have left home because she had to.

What little money Dan was able to find—whether begged, borrowed, or earned (even Dan had his limits and was not, I felt certain, a thief)—seemed to go toward the pleasures of loose living. I can't imagine that any of it went towards Elsa's maintenance.

Over time, I began to see some small changes in Dan. He seemed a little more interested in all of us. I won't say that he became a proper husband or father, because, of course, this would have been beyond his ken. But there were afternoons when he helped Jim and Ted mend fences and feed the horses and milk the cows. He spoke more softly to Mama. I think there may have been days where he didn't drink much, taking only an occasional swig. And there were times when he gave his attention to his three sons, attention that had never been given before. I think, though, that his efforts were too little, too late.

Jim and Ted didn't object when Dan offered help, but they certainly never invited it, nor did they converse with him or work together with him in the easy-going way that they did with Grandpa King. Edwin, John and Franklin Delano never rejected a kind word from their father, but seemed somewhat dazed by this change of heart; more dazed, probably, than they would have been if Dan had taken a hand to them. And I think they, like the rest of us, expected that the good weather would be short-lived, and that sooner or later an ill wind would blow in.

Even with these unsettling but pleasant changes in Dan's behavior, I was never pleased to see him or to know that he was in the house. I can't say, even in his most jocular and best-humored moments, that I ever came to like Dan. Eventually, I would dread him less and tolerate him more easily, but I was always glad for the hours when he was gone—to be with Elsa, I suppose, or to drink and carouse with his friends.

I was not quite sure how things stood between Mama and Dan. It seemed that Mama spoke very little to him; although, when she did, I never saw anger, fear or hate in her face, nor did I hear such in her voice. She spoke quietly, gently. She was patient and calm. They lived in the same house and slept in the same bed. It wasn't exactly as if they had come to an agreement, because there had never been any discussion. No questions asked, no answers given. Dan simply showed up one night and didn't leave.

Each morning took Mama and the smaller boys to the Wilkins', Thena, Edwin and me to school, and Jim and Ted to work. Dan was left to go or stay as he pleased. The dance continued; pieces were moved across the board and threads woven together. The snows fell and thawed, thawed and fell. And the end moved toward us. When at last it came, I don't think it caught any one of us off guard, even for a moment. Its promised arrival thundered over us, its merciless power and brilliance taking our breaths away like the floods that came every spring—washing, it seemed, the whole world away.

XII.

One February afternoon, on my after school trek to the mayor's house, I caught a glimpse of Elsa just as she rounded the corner of Main Street. I felt a strange curiosity about this girl who had become so inexplicably bound to us all. Feeling like a traitor, I moved along silently behind her. I stayed far back under the shadow of the ancient elms and watched as she moved toward the river. She was walking very slowly. There was something about the way that she moved that made me wonder if something was wrong.

After a few minutes, she stopped and sat under a tree in a grassy place alongside the dusty road. She leaned back against a poplar and, in spite of the cold February wind, unbuttoned the top two buttons of her blouse. Then she closed her eyes. I stood for long moments in the shadows behind a grouping of trees, biting the tips of my fingers and watching Elsa. She was motionless. After what seemed an eternity, I silently approached her. I stopped about ten yards from her, watching with uncertainty. Still her eyes were closed.

For a long time I studied the girl, noticing again how young she looked. Her face was naked; without makeup, she looked as small and delicate as a child. The sickness evident on her face and in the way she held her body further emphasized her delicacy. She was covered in sweat, her skin glistening and pallid. Her breathing was shallow and she trembled, shivering violently.

The shadows of the trees lengthened. Still I stood and still she lay, soundless and inert. I considered approaching and offering her my help, wondering if there was somewhere I could take her and if it was true that she lived by the river. *How would she respond to an offer of help from me, Dan's stepdaughter, Mama's daughter?* I felt sure that she would scorn it. Finally, I stepped forward, my feet stirring up tiny clouds of dust as I walked.

She did not move or open her eyes as I approached; I thought that she must have been sleeping soundly. I stopped just before her and, stooping in the grass, I watched as her chest moved weakly, up and down, up and down. I could see the faintly purple veins lying at crossroads beneath the skin of her neck. I noticed a large green vein that followed the curve of her cheekbone and a tiny pink starburst on the same cheek. I saw her gentle pulse in the hollow at the base of her throat, beating out the moments of her life. I noticed that she was much prettier without makeup, and I saw that her skin was covered in places with dark smudges of dirt, showing both that she lived in a dirty place and that she had not bathed in a long time. I was also struck by her extreme thinness, which had become even more acute than the last time I had seen her. Her body seemed made only of bone, ligament, muscle and skin, having none of the softness of a woman to it. Her face was more gaunt and skeletal than when first I had seen her, and the angles of her jawbones looked sharp enough to cut through flesh. I touched her hand and saw that her wrist-bone was no broader than the width of my second and third fingers.

I crouched beside her for several moments longer, closely watching her face for signs of wakefulness, apprehensively wondering what to do. She stirred a little and softly groaned, laying a hand to her belly. It is strange that one so accustomed to a life of poverty could be so struck by this girl's indigence, but I certainly was, and I unwillingly felt a lump rise in my throat. I realized in an instant that Elsa was dying of starvation, and I began to feel a horrible hatred for Dan, who was allowing it.

Fearfully, I laid a hand to her face. Her skin was burning. I wondered if, rather than sleeping, she might be unconscious. At my touch, her eyes opened and she groggily looked at me. She turned her head from side to side, her gaze moving from the sky to the road and away toward the river, looking as if she did not remember where she was. As her eyes focused, she seemed to recognize me. With a gasp, she sat and then stood up shakily, pushing me away.

"What're you doin' here? What d'you wont?"

"You looked sick," I said softly. "I thought you might need help."

"I'm jes' fine. You go o'an outta here—*GIT*! I don't need nothin'. I's jes' takin' a rest."

Stepping around me, she hurried away. Several yards down the road, she glanced back over her shoulder, her eyes dark and hollow. She stumbled on, taking the dirt road that led down to the river.

At first there seemed no other alternative but to head back to town, but my conscience plagued me. As much as I disliked the idea of giving help to Dan's girl, she had seemed too unwell to make it safely to whatever destination she was moving towards. What was more, it seemed to me that no one—regardless of their relationship to myself or to Dan—should ever have to go without food. Even I, despite how poor we had always been, rarely went hungry.

I turned back, annoyed with myself for not showing more strength and disgusted with myself for becoming an accessory to Dan's infidelity, and went in search of Elsa. I found her not far away, again lying under the shadows of a towering oak, either asleep or unconscious.

I ran back to town, the pain in my back and legs reminding me whom I was aiding, and knocked at Doc and Nora's door. Nora answered and welcomed me in. I hurriedly told her that I needed to speak to Doc. She took me to Doc's study, where he sat looking through a great stack of papers. I glimpsed through the French doors and saw several patients who sat in the adjoining room, waiting to be seen. I told him about Elsa.

Doc nodded to me and said,

"Nora, speak to my patients. Tell them all I'll stop 'round by their houses later."

He took up his black bag and I led the way to where I had last seen Elsa. We soon found that she was no longer there. Without stopping to discuss it, the two of us headed further down the road, near the water's edge, to a shabby, gray group of buildings. This was evidently where Elsa lived. I absently wondered how Doc had known how to find her, and if she had been ill before. Doc moved up the collapsing steps of the smallest of these buildings and, passing through the open door, disappeared. I stepped in, just behind Doc, and saw Elsa standing at the edge of the room, her pale hands tightly gripping the knob of a rotting door.

I glanced around the room and was startled to realize that this was Elsa's home. The room was small, with an uneven dirt floor. The doorframes and walls sagged so much that the tops of the walls didn't quite meet the bottom of the roof, leaving large cracks to let in whatever weather the skies chose to send. There was a crumbling fireplace that had not held a fire for many years and a collapsed table lying like a corpse in one corner of the room. Parts of the ceiling had fallen in and there were pieces of board and other detritus scattered all around us. The gray sky peeked through the slatted roof, which must have offered Elsa very little protection. On the fallen table there lay a single tin plate and a broken fork. In another corner there was a pile of molding straw and several bits of dirty rag, which appeared to be Elsa's bed. Wadded in a heap next to the bed was the dress she had worn on the first night I had seen her, cradling an opened tin of peaches. The dress was Elsa's only other article of clothing, and the tin contained all the food that she had.

I processed all of these things within seconds and turned to face Elsa. Her face was a mixture of surprise and indignation. Her troubled eyes looked suspiciously from Doc, to me, and then back.

"What in hell are you doin' here? I told you I didn' need nothin' from you and I don't."

She turned and pushed open the door to a second room. As she did, I saw her profile for just a moment. Then I saw, with astonishment, that this little girl was carrying a baby in her belly. Unbidden tears welled in my eyes. Best as I could tell, she didn't seem to be very far along; and though I still understood very little about sex, I was sure that the baby belonged to Dan. I felt my breath catch in my throat. A powerful feeling of sickness washed over me. The room swam. I turned and stumbled back out onto the crumbling porch and sat down with my head in my hands. I wasn't sure what I ought to feel. I tried to—and couldn't—understand why on earth Dan would need more than one wife, and why Dan would have another child when he didn't seem to care a stitch for his other seven.

I sat for a long time on the porch, waiting for Doc. Eventually, he passed back out into the fading sunshine and stood, studying me closely. His eyes searched mine for several seconds. I felt my face go red. Then he nodded and said quietly,

"You did a good thing to come and get me. I need you to go back into town and send Nora. Tell her to bring food. Plenty of food."

He leaned down and put a strong hand on my shoulder. His eyes searched mine again, and then he nodded. He gestured that I should set out after his wife. Glancing back once more at the crumbling house, I walked away from the river.

I gave Nora Doc's message without saying much else, and she nodded without looking surprised and said that she would go as soon as she could get some things together. I said goodbye and once again turned toward the Wilkins'. When I passed into the kitchen, Mama glanced up and said mildly,

"You're runnin' behind, Grace, girl. I needed you for bakin' the bread. Thena dudn' have the patience for it—hers comes out flat or lumpy."

"Elsa's sick," I blurted.

Mama carefully set aside a stack of clean china and wiped her hands on her apron before she spoke.

"What do you mean?" she asked softly, her face unreadable.

"I saw her on the street and she looked pretty sick so I followed her. I asked her if she needed help but she—she didn't want any. Then I think she fainted...anyway, I went after the Doc. We went to her house. She lives in a shed by the river. She's pretty sick and I think it's 'cause she doesn't have anything to eat."

Mama sat down at the kitchen table and folded her hands, her eyes never leaving my face. She didn't say anything for several minutes.

"She's gonna have a baby," I whispered breathlessly.

That was all I could think to say; I had nothing to offer in the way of explanation. For just an instant, Mama's face changed. I wasn't sure what I saw there, but I knew that there was something different. I think that it was both pain and surprise. Even after all that Dan had done to her and the rest of us, I think Mama honestly still never expected anything but good from Dan. She expected only good from everyone. Usually, she got it. I remember very clearly that the few times I got into trouble as a girl, the first emotion I saw on Mama's face was always one of surprise. She expected better. She always expected to find the best in the people she loved.

I felt a moment of remorse for having told her, but I knew that she would have found out one way or another, and I would rather have told her than have the news reach her through the town gossip chain. I heard the ticking of the clock and realized that minutes had passed without a word from Mama. She continued to gaze at me steadily, and I wondered what was passing through her mind.

I was startled by the sound of the back door slamming. Thena came in, her beautiful cheeks flushed red with the raw force of the wind. She was carrying a basket of Mrs. Rachel's whites. She glanced from Mama to me.

"You're late. Where you beeyn? I needed help. Bread's gonna be lumpy."

I didn't answer, but turned my eyes back to Mama, questioning her, wondering what I should say. Then Mama stood and moved toward the pantry, saying over her shoulder,

"We best go n' see what needs doin' and take the girl some food. Grace, what does she have?"

"Nothin', Mama. There's no food, no furniture, no blankets; there wasn't even a fire."

"Who needs food?" asked Thena.

"Elsa," I said.

Thena flinched as if she had been struck, putting one hand to her cheek. She opened her mouth as if to speak and then shut it again after a moment. Her face was white as milk.

"Mama, you can't be serious!" said Thena. "*He* brought her here. Let *him* take care of her."

Her eyes flashed and burned like live coals.

"I guess he's havin' trouble doin' that, Thena, and somebody's gotta take care a' the girl. We cain't let 'er starve."

"Oh, yes we can!" she said fiercely.

"*Thena!* It doesn't matter who she is or what she is to us, she has to eat, and if there idn' anybody else to feed 'er, then *we will.*"

Mama left the room and Thena turned to me, her eyes seething. Her cheeks were flushed, feverish and red, and her hands shook with her hatred of Dan. She stood ramrod straight, her beautiful body stiff with anger—looking like our very own Dempsey, fifteen rounds and still not winded, crouching and ready for another spar. Her look was accusing, as if I was responsible for what Mama intended to do.

"You're a fool," she said quietly.

"Maybe," I said, nodding.

"Why'd you tell 'er?"

"I knew she'd hear it sooner or later and I figured she'd hear it from somebody who's not as nice as me."

"What's wrong with her?"

"She's starvin'."

"There's a depression on." She tossed her hair.

"I didn't say hungry, I said starvin'. Besides, there's a baby."

"Elsa has a baby?"

"She's fixin' to."

Her mouth fell open. Her face flushed a darker shade of red. She understood.

"She's just a girl. Not any older'n you—not old 'nough to have a baby."

"She seems to be," I said softly.

Then Mama passed from the pantry back through the kitchen. She carried a wooden crate filled with food and said, as she passed through the door,

"Grace, I'm goin' home to get blankets. Come with me; I want you to show me where Elsa lives. Thena, can you finish washin' those dishes and keep your eye on the bread?"

Thena didn't respond.

We walked the three miles home. Mama gathered blankets, socks, a sweater, a soft pillow filled with down and an armload of firewood. She handed me a tall stack of blankets, the sweater and the pillow, and then we walked the four miles back to the turn in the river just outside of town where Elsa lived.

The door to the little shed was now closed. Mama sat the wood on the porch and, taking the bundle of blankets and clothes from me, passed up the rickety stairs, across the crumbling porch and into the front room, without knocking. Doc and Nora were still inside. I heard their voices, surprised, as they greeted Mama. I heard Mama say,

"Doc, I guess we best get a fire started."

Then the door closed and I remained on the porch, feeling out of place, not knowing whether I ought to go in, turn and walk home, or stay as I was, waiting to be called.

A long time passed, maybe and hour, maybe more. Finally, the door opened and Mama passed out of Elsa's house and into the cold winter darkness.

"Grace! You ought to have come inside," she said. "It's so cold out tonight."

"Mama?" I said. "Elsa gonna be alright?"

Mama nodded.

"I reckon she will, long as somebody makes sure she has somethin' to eat. She wasn't too happy to see me, and she's too proud fer her own good. Said she wouldn't take any food from any of us. But Doc told her that she dudn' have the luxury of being prideful, 'cause she has a baby to think of. That put an end to it; she didn't say anything else and she ate enough for all of us."

She was quiet for a time.

"Grace, I'm gonna send you with a basket of food for her every day—you can just leave it on the porch if you like, then you won't have to deal with that sharp tongue a' hers. That girl doesn't seem to care too much for talkin', but when she has somethin' to say, she sure isn't shy about sayin' it."

Mama and I walked home together in silence. The wind spoke in a soft, strange voice. It passed rapidly through the fingers of the trees, whipping over slender limbs, patiently waiting to fall and be buried in the rubble of the ages. It rushed on through our clothes, slapping our faces and causing tears of cold to run down my cheeks. I shivered, half-fearful, not knowing what I feared. We passed through the town, seeing clearly through the lit-up windows panes of warm, safe homes—families reading by fires, listening to radios or finishing up the evening meal, women washing supper dishes, children lying before the hearth working hurriedly through their textbooks. Mama and I walked quickly, close together, breathing in the sharp night, our heads turned down against the cold.

As I walked, I thought of all that Mama had said, and all the mysteries that day held. I lifted my face into the wind for a moment, turning to look at Mama. I hoped that studying the lines and planes of her profile might help me see what went on in her heart and mind. She was a woman who returned good for evil. She prayed for her enemies and did good to those who persecuted her. I felt sure that a person like Mama didn't belong here on this wicked earth with the rest of us.

I don't think that Mama ever felt shamed by Elsa. She never saw her as a rival; though maybe that had more to do with the worthlessness of the one they would have been contending for. If anything, it was Dan's disgrace. Instead of blaming him for it, I think Mama pitied him. Dan seemed unable to take a step forward for stumbling over his own feet, while Mama just walked right across the water.

After close to an hour of walking, we passed into the lamplight cast out from the windows of the house. We found Thena telling the three smallest boys one of their favorite stories.

I sighed with relief, happy to be home; happier still to find that Dan wasn't there. I sat down in front of the fire and unbuttoned my coat, drawing a hand over my tired face. I had worn the beautiful blue wool coat, the birthday gift from Mama, for two years, and by now the sleeves ended only three or four inches past my elbow. The brown tweed coat that I wore that night was once Thena's, and it had been Mama's before it was Thena's. Grandma King had given the brown tweed coat to Mama after she considered it too threadbare to be of any use—supposing, I'm sure, that Mama would cut it up and use it for quilt pieces. There were holes at both of the elbows. Through the two thin places at the shoulder blades you could see my old green dress. The hem was frayed and unraveled. It was horribly out of fashion, but I had never been very fashionable—none of us had—and so no one expected me to wear better.

It always amazed me that, though Thena's clothes were also old and worn, it never seemed to matter. No matter what she wore, even had it been bought on Savile Row, it would not have added to or taken from her beauty in any way. Whatever assistance good clothes could offer the average person (even a plain man looks handsome in a tuxedo), Thena did not need. Her beauty stood alone and was perfect, and perfection cannot be added to nor taken away from.

XIII.

It was March when the rain started. It fell in torrents. Streams of water fell from the sky in thick blankets of gray. Within a matter of days, the whole world began to smell clean.

Eventually, the earth vanished and all I could see as far as I looked in every direction was an immense ocean of water and waste. Ancient trees had been felled by the power of the water. The banks of the river swelled. We knew it was only a matter of time—a few days, at the most—before this splendid sea of rainfall would merge fully with the mightiness of the river.

One rainy night, Dan walked out the front door and waded away, the water up to his ankles, calling out over his shoulder,

"Back later, Mary."

He didn't come back for more than three weeks. I have no idea where he went or what he did. No one ever asked him. Maybe he passed some portion of those days with Elsa, but I think he probably he went off tramping somewhere in search of some mythical river of strong Irish whisky. He may have even floated away on it for a time.

Before long, we had word that the river people were fleeing from their homes. Barns, livestock, houses, automobiles, sheds, the Presbyterian church, fences and even, evidently, several people had been washed away, and the water was getting higher all the time.

The life of the river had spilt over into the life of our town. We saw folks paddle by in boats and canoes. At our house, a mile from the nearest part of the river, the water was only a few inches deep, but closer to the river, the water was more than two feet deep. All of us sat confined to the house on Saturday and Sunday, restless, watching the sky crash down onto the hapless earth below. Staring through the front room window, I began to wonder if this was what the world had looked like in the time before God separated the waters from the dry land. I thought that perhaps this would be a re-creation, a sequel to the first movie—a better show, with a better ending.

On Sunday night, Grandpa King and Pope paddled over to our place, which stood on a little rise too small to be called a hill. So far, the location of our house had kept it fairly dry, excepts for leaks in the roof, but the water had now almost risen up to the first step of the porch. Grandpa King stomped into the room, shaking water from his shoulders and beard, wiping his dripping face with a wet hand. Pope moved quietly inside, looking something like a drenched owl.

Mama's face shone. Always happy to have visitors, she bustled around looking for dry towels and blankets. Stopping for a moment, she hugged Pope hard.

"I'm so glad to see you, son," she said.

"They say some a' the river people're trapped," said Grandpa King. "Water rose s'fast, there wuz nothin' they could do. I guess some got out—people canoed in to pick up whoever they could, but they didn' get everybody."

He paused for a moment, looking embarrassed, one hand rubbing at his chin.

"Mary, I wonder'd 'bout that girl... Far's I can tell, nobody heard anythang about 'er. I knew she wuz livin' down on the river. I wondered if—if Dan planned to do anythang or if he'd already done got 'er."

He watched Mama's face carefully, his ears red.

"I—I hate bringin' it up. But I ain't been easy 'bout 'er in my mind. I thought that if you didn' know anythang about it, I best go see if she's needin' help. If she did, she don't know nobody 'round here, and I don't reck'n she'd ask fer it."

Mama let out a long breath, one hand resting on the kitchen table.

"Dan left four days ago. I don't know where he went to, but I doubt it was to Elsa."

Mama never revealed more to anyone about Dan than was absolutely necessary. Her face was blank. It was impossible to know what she was thinking or feeling.

"Tom, I guess somebody needs to go. I reckon you're right; nobody else would think to go if you don't."

"I'll go with you, Grandpa King. You might need some help, if there was to be trouble," said Jim from the hearth.

Ted nodded. "I better go, too."

Both boys looked at Mama. She looked tired and pale, and I think that she was very scared.

"Go," she said. "Get back as fast as you can."

Both boys put on tall boots, canvas coats and hats. Jim took up a lantern and an axe. Ted fetched a long coil of rope from the barn, and the four left.

We spent the rest of the evening restless and pacing, snapping at one another, short-tempered and low-spirited. The boys asked Thena to tell them a story, but she brushed them off.

Grandpa King and the boys left at just after eight o'clock. Nine, ten and eleven o'clock passed, and no word came. Midnight, one and two passed. We heard nothing. The little boys had fallen asleep on the floor of the front room, lying in a circle around Thena, their bodies wedged as close to her as possible. Though Edwin was now big enough to want to be treated like a man, he still allowed himself to be caudled by Thena. It wasn't that he needed the attention; he just loved Thena and wanted to please her.

At two in the morning, Thena sat quietly holding Franklin Delano's hand and stroking his brown-red curls as she softly sang to him.

"Down in the valley, the valley below,
Hang your head over, hear the wind blow.
Hear the wind blow, Love, hear the wind blow,
Hang your head over, hear the wind blow."

Mama sat in her rocker, a hand firmly gripping either arm. She studied her young sons as they slept, her ears straining to hear the sounds of her older sons coming home. I sat curled on the old wooden bench, my reading place, with cushions tucked around me and a book lying heedlessly on my lap. I had given up on even trying to read some hours earlier.

At just before three, the door was flung open. Streams of rain and brown river water poured in. We heard the mad-dog howl of the wind and saw for an instant the flash of lightning. Jim stood in the doorway, holding Elsa in his arms. Her eyes were closed, and her clothes were badly torn. Her right arm dangled down from her body. It was obvious, by the sickening angle at which it hung, that it was badly broken. Her dress was torn away from the same shoulder, and I gagged as I saw that it was out of the socket.

Jim carefully laid her next to the fire. Grandpa King, Pope and Ted followed quietly behind. As Pope stepped into the firelight, I saw that he was covered in blood from his forehead down to his shoulders. He had a scrap of Jim's shirt tightly wrapped around his head, clearly covering some sort of wound. With the amount of blood covering him, I felt sick with fear at how bad it might be.

I felt weak, my legs buckling, but I grasped the edge of the table and held on, telling myself that this was no time to faint. I moved toward him, my hands stretched up toward his face. He shook his head and pointed to where Elsa lay.

"See to her and then we'll take care of this," he said.

As soon as the door opened, Mama had come out of her chair and crossed the room. When she saw Elsa unconscious, she turned and swept to the back of the house.

"Thena, get the boys to bed."

Mama entered the front room again a moment later carrying all of her bedclothes. Jim was pale and stumbling with exhaustion. Grandpa looked tired and grim. Ted looked scared. Jim started to cover Elsa.

"No Jim. Leave 'er. Tom, you and the boys get o'an to the other room."

Grandpa King nodded and motioned for the boys to follow. Jim and Ted obeyed, but Pope stood still. He had wiped away most of the blood, and in the firelight, I saw the sick yellow color of his skin.

"I think I'd better stay. This is a bad break," he said, nodding toward Elsa.

"I've seen Daddy set enough to know. It will be days before we could get to him. Even if we could get her to town, there will be so many sick and maybe even dying—there's no telling when he could take care of that arm. Her arm's gonna to have to be set tonight. I think you're gonna need me to put that shoulder back in its socket, too."

"How are you gonna take care of this girl while you're bleedin' all over the place?" asked Mama.

"I guess I'd better stitch it up."

"Pope Barrett, you are not—"

He cut her off with a wave of his hand.

"I've seen Daddy do it a thousand times. What other choice do we have?"

Mama sent me for her scissors, then quickly but carefully cut away all of Elsa's clothes. Pope turned very red, and walked to the other side of the room. Her body was still tiny and bony, but she no longer looked emaciated. Mama's plan to fatten her up had worked a little. Her belly had become quite large and I wondered when her baby would be born, and if the flood could have harmed it. Mama dried her off, except for the right arm, and gently laid a mass of quilts over her. During all of this, Elsa neither moved nor made a sound.

"Gracie, I need a mirror, boiling water, the smallest needle you can find, and some sturdy thread. When the water boils, bring me a bowl with some soap," said Pope.

I put water on to boil and went to find the other things. The water was boiling by the time I found them. I poured a bowl and carried it and a clean rag to the table. With one hand Pope scrubbed at the crusted blood on his forehead, nose and cheeks, with the other hand he held the gash together.

"Gracie, thread the needle for me," he said softly. I put thread to the needle and handed it to him. He sat down at the kitchen table, stooping in front of Mama's little mirror and let out a deep breath. Then he lifted the needle to his forehead. His hands shook badly.

"Gracie, I need you. Hold it together for me—like this—while I sew."

For a moment I felt that I would be sick. He glanced at me through the mirror and grinned.

"Nothin' for it, Gracie. It needs doin' and you're gonna have to help me."

It had to be done. I swallowed down the bile in my throat and put a finger firmly on either side of the hole in his head. It was about four inches long and seemed to be about half an inch across. He was covered in sweat, and I thought he might faint before he got it done. He slid the needle in and out of his forehead. I saw tears come to his eyes. He sewed slow, uncertain stitches, in Mama's red quilting thread. After the third stitch, I stopped him to wipe the sweat away from his face. It ran down into his eyes. Mama walked away from the table, both hands to her face, mouthing the words of a prayer. Four stitches. Sweat and tears ran down his face and neck onto the bloody color of his shirt. He never made a sound. He stopped for a moment to let the pain pass, then finally added a fifth stitch.

"They're not as close together as they should be, but it's the best I can do." He laughed weakly. "If my hands would stop shaking, I could do better. But I guess that should about do it."

He cut the thread from the needle and neatly knotted it against his forehead several times.

"Gracie, clean it again—real gentle."

His face was green with pain and fear. I took Jim's shirt from the table and tore off the other sleeve. I handed it to Pope and he wrapped it tightly around his head. He sat shaking and pale at the table for several minutes. Mama made tea and he drank it. He didn't speak or cry or groan. Nobody made a sound.

Pope spent a long time scrubbing his hands in scalding water and then moved to Elsa.

"Ms. Mary, tell Grandpa and Jim and Ted that I need 'em. Gracie, get a wet rag and wipe her face."

Elsa was also soaked in sweat. She lay shivering under a stack of blankets. I touched her face and whispered that everything was going to be okay. I put one hand to her round belly. The baby gave me a strong kick. I sighed, deeply relieved. The baby was still alive. As I stood watching over her fevered sleep, I realized that, during all this time, none of us had ever asked what happened.

Grandpa King, Jim and Ted entered the front room. Pope nodded to the three of them.

"I need you to hold her down. Take it slow and easy, and leave the right arm alone."

Pope squatted and took the upper part of her right arm in his hand. He glanced up at Mama and then at me. I nodded, nervously. Then with one quick movement and a sickening sound, he popped the shoulder back into place. There was one faint groan from Elsa, but she seemed to remain unconscious.

"Jim, Ted, one of you find something to set this arm with."

Jim brought him a long, flat piece of whittling wood and I tore up long strips of an old sheet. The three men again held Elsa down and Pope, without breathing, carefully set the arm.

XIV.

I awoke, startled by the powerful morning silence. It had stopped raining. Looking around me, I realized that I had fallen asleep on the floor of the front room. I had stayed awake beside Elsa for most of the night. Pope sat at the kitchen table, face down and sound asleep. Mama slept in her rocker and Thena on the wooden bench. Ted, Jim and Grandpa King must have gone to the back room, and the younger boys were still dreaming in their bed. I rolled onto my side and watched Elsa's face. The fever was still with her, but she must have regained consciousness to some degree, because her face was contorted with pain. Every few moments the silence was broken as she gave a soft groan. I sat up and tucked the blankets carefully around her and touched her cheek. It seemed a little cooler than the night before, but the fever was still present.

I pulled my stiff body from the cold wood floor and went to cover Pope. His black hair fell down across his forehead and onto his glasses, which he must have been too tired to remove. I pushed his hair back from his face and covered him with my quilt. I took another from the chest by the front door and tucked it around Thena. Then I walked to the back door and noiselessly opened it, gazing out at the world before me.

The landscape was unrecognizable. As far as I could see there stretched an immense, dark ocean of muddy water. The sky was bleak and cold. The landscape looked tired and defeated, as if the last drop of lifeblood had been wrung from it.

Floating through the water were bits of houses, the limbs of trees, swollen bodies of cows, the decapitated carcass of a chicken, an outhouse. There were chairs; legs, arms and backs of chairs. There were mattresses and bed frames; feet, posts, and railings. An icebox floated by and was batted by the limbs of a giant oak. It finally halted against the butt of a chicken coop. On top of the coop stood two hens, angrily squawking at me, accusing me of stealing their fine, fat eggs. I watched as they floated away, staring in disbelief at the number of trees that had been pulled from the earth, like they were nothing; like they were blades of grass. I felt vaguely numb, staring out at the world that had been destroyed and cast aside, lying limp and broken at my feet.

I heard a quiet step behind me. Pope stood in the doorway. He rubbed his eyes and ran a hand over his hair. He looked tired, and the color still had not returned to his face.

"How's your head?"

"All right, I reckon. Not hurtin' as much."

"Elsa?" I said.

He shrugged. "I'm not a doctor."

"We need your daddy."

"I think she'll be okay, but I don't know if I set her arm properly. And I'm worried about her baby."

He shook his head and turned to gaze out at the wasteland, stretching out for miles in every direction.

We didn't see the sun that day or the next. On Tuesday morning, Grandpa King said he would risk the water and go home to his wife. He stayed with us for as long as he dared, knowing that she was safe in their house perched high on top of the hill. We watched Elsa in shifts, day and night. On Tuesday evening, she opened her eyes and looked around. I touched her forehead and found that the fever was nearly gone. I put a hand on her belly and the baby gave a kick. Elsa smiled weakly.

"Don't worry about him. Come fire, famine or flood, this baby'd be jes' fine right on through anythang. He's strong's an ox. The way he kicks, he needs to carry me around 'stead of me bein' the one to carry him."

"Are you in much pain?"

She shrugged. "Reck'n I beeyn hurt before. There's worse things'n a banged up arm."

Then she slept. She recovered slowly, very seldom waking. I was glad to see her sleep, hoping that the more rest she got, the safer the baby would be. Mama woke her only to feed her; the rest of the time we stayed as quiet as we could. Every day the waters receded a little. Every day we could see just a bit more of the mud and rubble beneath the water.

On Wednesday afternoon, Doc arrived in search of his son. He went pale when he saw the jagged, red-teethed stitches across Pope's forehead and temple.

"What's this?" asked Doc, his voice tense.

"I got into a fight with a fallin' oak tree," said Pope, grinning.

"Who won?"

"Not sure. I got knocked out, but the tree drowned, so I guess it was me."

"You do the stitches?"

"Yeah."

"They're a little crooked."

"Thanks, Daddy," said Pope, smiling wryly.

The Doc looked Elsa carefully over, grim faced and silent.

"Did you do this too, Pope?"

"Yessir."

"How many fractures?"

"The best I could tell there was one clean break. The shoulder was pulled clean out of the socket. Popped it back in."

Doc carefully examined Elsa's belly, gently touching and prodding.

"That baby's jes' fine," she said, smiling. "Had the best seat in the house. The rest of us wuz runnin' around wailin' n' shriekin' n' makin' like it wuz the judgment day, an' he jes' slept right thew it. Ever' now n' again it'd get too loud n' he'd wake up n' kick me real hard to tell me to keep it down."

Doc scowled at Elsa and said sternly,

"You ought to have gotten out of that place as soon as the water started rising."

"And jes' where wuz I to go? Ain't nobody 'round here fer me to go to. My people ain't here and nobody knows me, or wonts to. I reck'n I know why. I figur'd the best thang fer me to do wuz to stay right where I wuz n' wait it out. Didn' know it would come a flood. Jes' looked like a spring rain, far's I could tell."

"How did this happen?" said the Doc, turning to me.

We had been too preoccupied with our worries over Elsa to ask for the details of how both she and Pope been injured. I looked to Pope, my eyebrows raised, ready to be told.

"We found her on Sunday night, on the roof of her house, hanging onto her chimney. That shack was just about to float off. We couldn't see anything and the water was louder'n anything I've ever heard. It looked like the whole town was gonna go. The water was so strong. I've never seen anything like it. She was up there, just holdin' on. She never made a sound. She wasn't cryin' or screamin'. She looked mad enough to spit, though, and not a bit scared."

He grinned over at Elsa.

"Just as we got to the house, we heard this terrible cracking sound— like a mountain breaking into pieces. It was so dark, we couldn't see anything, 'cept when the lightning flashed, but as soon as I heard it, I knew what it was. The house was being torn to shreds. Next thing I knew, I saw Elsa crawlin' on all fours, except that she wasn't using her right arm. She sorta dragged it behind her and it was funny lookin'. You could tell from a mile away that it was broken. She climbed over to this oak tree with branches lyin' up against the roof. Just like that, she was in the tree. She took one leap and landed about half way down. She had seen us and was trying to make it down to the boat. As she fell toward us, that same arm caught in one of the branches of the tree and it pulled her arm clean outta the socket. I don't think the break would have been nearly so bad otherwise. I heard this sick scream and saw her go limp. Her fall had been broken by one great big branch, and she just lay there."

Pope shrugged, "I was the lightest weight and I didn't know how long that tree was gonna last. The water was taking everything. I knew Grandpa wouldn't be too happy about the idea, and I didn't wait around for him to tell me not to—I didn't want to have to disobey him. So I climbed up to get her, fast as I could. I carried her over my shoulder, and I was pretty sure that neither one of us was going to make it out of that tree alive. Then I heard this crackin' sound from up above. I looked up and, just as I did, the branch came down on me. I don't remember much after that."

"This great big dead branch broke off with the wind n' rain n' all, and it hit him square 'cross the forehead. We managed to get both of 'em in the boat, but we couldn't tell anythang," said Jim.

"We didn't know whether they were dead or alive, and with the world lookin' like it was about to end, we couldn't take th' time to find out. We were jest tryin' to make it home fast as we could. I knew Mama'd be worried sick. I noticed that Pope's head was bleedin' pretty bad, so I took off my shirt and tried to stop the blood as best I could."

"How did you stitch up that wound?" asked the Doc, his fingers carefully seeing whatever his eyes could not.

"Same way you always do," answered Pope.

Doc looked it over carefully, turning his head to one side and then to the other. Shaking his head, he whispered,

"Good job for a first time. What about the arm?"

"I've seen you set so many. I just did the best I could."

Doc undid the sling on Elsa's arm and very carefully examined the way it had been set. He looked baffled and said,

"Looks just as good as I could have done."

He looked over at Pope, smiling and proud. Pope smiled back, looking embarrassed.

XV.

This was the start of Elsa's life with us. In the beginning, she was too ill to move around. The Doc watched carefully for signs of trauma to her baby. He visited her every day. After some days had passed and the Doc saw that Elsa's belly was getting bigger every day and that the flesh on her arms and face had begun to fill out, he seemed satisfied with her rate of recovery. After that, his visits came only every few days.

Elsa was a good patient; though she was tentative with us, her old anger toward us was washed away on the night of the flood. I don't think her anger was ever based on dislike. She behaved with hostility toward us because of the treatment she expected to receive from Mama. When she found that Mama was only gentle and kind, she relaxed and retreated into a quiet, experimental sort of waiting.

The town's recovery from the flood was extremely slow. The damage to many areas was extensive, and in other parts the destruction was absolute, with whole streets having been washed away. Even the school was closed down until repairs could be made (though none of us seemed to show any sadness at this sweet interlude in the beautiful melody of our education).

After some time, Mama was able to go back to tend to Mrs. Rachel and her house; though, at first, she did not stay for as many hours as usual. Instead, she would leave time in the day to go out into the town and offer help in any way that she could. Most of the people of the town responded similarly. In spite of the hardship of our poor economy, no one went unclothed or hungry. Many people took entire families into their homes until new houses could be built for them. Poor folks took from their small stock and gave to those who had nothing.

From morning until night, the banging of hammers, the clanging of tools, and the thud of board against board could be heard for miles. Many of the river people decided to relocate to the town. Their small homes were built in concentric rectangles around the town square.

Every day the water receded further, leaving behind a bitter and fetid smelling mud about two feet deep. For many weeks, on every street and in nearly every yard we saw the rotting bodies of farm animals that had drowned. The air smelled of death for months after the flood. All the winter wheat had washed away. The ruin of all the farmers—and there were many—seemed imminent. The farms of the surrounding country-side were composed almost entirely of bottomland.

As Mama and Thena went back to work, I remained at home to tend to Elsa, who was still unable to do anything for herself. We moved her to Mama's bed and made her as comfortable as we could. The sun slowly grew warmer. Over the weeks that followed, the sky began to look confident again, as if it could see from way up there that better things were ahead. Slowly, we began to breathe again. Elsa and I spent many days together with all of the windows in the house thrown open. One afternoon, as Elsa lay resting, staring away into the blue shimmer of the sky, she glanced over at me. I lay on my belly on the floor, reading, ankles crossed, legs bent at the knees.

"What do those books you look at all the time have in 'em?" she asked.

"Stories," I said, glancing up.

Her question startled me. Elsa rarely spoke.

"What kinda stories are they?"

"This one is the story of a poor boy who falls in love with a beautiful girl. She treats him badly. She has been taught to hate men by her bitter guardian. The guardian's lover jilted her just before they were married, and she sits around in her weddin' dress and cries over losin' him."

Elsa snorted. "In love, huh?"

I nodded, my head tilted to one side, eyebrows raised. I waited curiously for Elsa's thoughts on love.

"I don't know that bein' in love's worth much. My mama wuz in love n' my daddy wuz never good to 'er. She wuz black n' blue near ev'ry day a' my life."

She was quiet for a long time. I returned to my book, shyly glancing up at her from time to time. She stared out through the burnished panes of glass, peacefully watching the journey of the clouds as they coursed their way across the afternoon sky.

"I don't reck'n you'd wanna read none a' them stories to me, wouldja?"

I glanced up, surprised, and it must have shown in my face. Hers became defensive.

"I had a grandmama who could read. I guess my mama may've been able to, but she drank too much to have much time fer teachin' me. Then she went'n died when I was still a young'un. After that, I was purty much own my own, and I didn' have the time fer lookin' at books er readin' stories. Mama always said I wuz too stupid to learn anythang anyways. I reck'n she's right, but if *you* know how, I don't guess I'm too stupid to listen, am I?"

I shook my head, uncertain of what to say. I turned back to the first page of my book, suddenly feeling very self-conscious, and began to read aloud. She listened, her eyes intently watching my face. I glanced up after a few minutes, wondering if she was interested. Her eyes were bright, and there was an intensity in them that I had never seen before. I read to her for a long time. I could see every page so clearly. I was transported over the ocean, into the filth of the crowded, mucky streets of nineteenth century London. I lost track of time and even forgot that she was watching me.

I read to Elsa every day after that, for many hours at a time. I read until the shadows had moved from one side of the room to the other, until the sun's brilliant light had grown too dim for reading, until my voice gave out. She listened with rapt attention, one hand on her belly and her eyes glued to my face. I think I read for so many hours because she looked at me as if I had given her a gift—a beautiful, costly gift. If I stopped reading, she might think that the gift had been reneged, and I was pretty sure that Elsa had not been given many gifts in her life to begin with. In a way that I could not quite understand, Elsa's trust in me was conceived in those hours spent together reading.

Before I was aware of it, something happened to my insides, causing me to feel more for her than merely pity. There was no longer condescension in what I felt for her. I was amazed at this little girl, this woman-child who had lived through so much and yet kept her soul alive. I was now able to see that Elsa was not devoid of thought or feeling. She was merely one who, out of necessity and self-preservation, played her hand very closely to her chest.

In our days of reading together, two things happened. First, Elsa and I became friends. This was something I never would have expected to take place, and that never really did take place between Elsa and Thena. Second, Elsa learned to read.

One morning, after she had listened to me reading for several weeks, she became curious about how I was able to discern words through the characters on the page.

"Grace, how can you see the stories on th' page?" she asked.

"What do you mean?"

"Where do the stories come from?"

"They come from the letters. When you put the letters together they make words, and words together make sentences. The sentences, all put together, turn into stories."

Elsa frowned.

I climbed up onto Mama's bed with her and taught her the alphabet. When she had memorized it, I taught her the physical letters that corresponded to the spoken letters. Next she learned the sounds; finally, she began to read words.

You cannot imagine the pride she displayed in this accomplishment. It was then that Elsa finally realized that she was not stupid. In fact, she was very bright; had her ability been nurtured from her childhood, her accomplishments might have been great. She picked up on things very quickly. She was perceptive and insightful, particularly in regard to human relationships. She carefully observed everything that went on. She understood what was under the surface of words, recognizing that people use their bodies to speak more often than their mouths. She was perfectly aware that Thena didn't like her, though the rest of the family came to accept and even enjoy her presence. She was very philosophical in her understanding of Thena's dislike. She understood where and why Thena's loyalties lay, and expected nothing else from her.

Elsa was infinitely patient with Thena; I have to admit, her treatment of Elsa was embarrassing to me. I don't think she was able to disassociate Elsa from Dan in her mind. She could never see her as an individual, a human being with a nature of her own—one that was entirely different from Dan's. To my shame, I quickly saw that Elsa never expected to be treated well. This saddened me.

It was during the time that Elsa spent with us that her treatment of strangers began to change. In fact, her whole demeanor changed. She liked our family and was probably the happiest she had ever been while she lived with us. Her belly was always full. She slept in a proper bed with other warm bodies. She was never alone unless she chose to be. She had, for all intents and purposes, a mother, brothers and sisters to love and take care of her. I don't think she had ever experienced any of these things. We were Elsa's first real experience of family.

After several weeks of reading together, just after Elsa had begun to sound out her first words, Dan returned. His homecoming was unexpected and unwelcome; strangely, when Dan wasn't with us, we almost forgot his existence. He stepped in one afternoon, clothed in a new suit, with his long hair carefully combed and held in place with some sort of pomade. He strode into Mama's room and gave his brightest, most convincing Cheshire cat grin.

"I heard it said yer mama had done this fool thang. All the town tongues been waggin' 'bout her takin' in my woman n' the baby in 'er belly," he said, nodding to Elsa.

He began to laugh.

"But I wouldn'a believed it, even'uv Mary. Gurl, what have you gone n' done to yerseff?" he asked, eyeing her bandaged arm and inert body.

"Never could take care a' herseff," he said as an aside. "Always has needed somebody to wipe 'er nose n' do every dad'gum thang for 'er. She's jes' a child n' here she is totin' one uv'er own 'round. How you thaink you ever gonna take care of a baby, gurl, when you cain't even take car'a yerseff? You gotta watch this gurl all the time, else she go and get 'erseff killt, dead, jes' to spite ya'. Yep, she'd jest as soon cut off yer nose to spite yer face."

He gave a great laugh at the ingenuity of his joke. Elsa watched him without speaking. The look of perpetual disappointment returned to her face. Dan was incapable of making anyone happy. Even himself.

"I reck'n I'll take m'seff off. I've no bidness in the recuperatin' chamber with a bunch a' women. Tell Mary I'll bunk up at th' barn; she don' need to look out fer me, I'll come n' go."

Dan left, and neither Elsa nor I moved or spoke for some minutes. My mind stuck on Dan's words. I thought about what he had said about hearing from the townspeople that Mama had taken Elsa in. They were talking about us. Absentmindedly, I wondered what people must think of us. In an instant I knew. They thought we were fools, and I understood why. But I also understood Mama's reason for doing what she had, and I couldn't help but feel that Mama possessed a nobility that other people should've had, and didn't.

I turned back to our book and pointed to where Elsa had left off. Pushing thoughts of Dan from our minds, we pressed on, Elsa's fair brow wrinkling in concentration, squinting down at each word, pronouncing carefully and then glancing back at me for my approval. I nodded and smiled when she sounded out a particularly difficult word. She often paused to ask a word's meaning. Her capacity for remembering words and definitions was astounding; I am sure that within a year of when she began to read, Elsa's vocabulary was better than my own.

After Dan returned, he wasn't around the house much. I don't think that even Dan had the impudence to live in the same house with his wife and mistress. When he was around at all, he slept in the barn. To everyone's surprise, he took to mucking out the horse stalls and cutting large stacks of wood. He tended to these and other chores as his sobriety permitted. He stayed near to the farm for two or three weeks at a time and then would disappear for a while. I remember from that period as little about his coming as I do about his going. And, except for Thena's increased displeasure, his presence brought little change to our happiness.

As days went by, Elsa's appearance began to change. The magenta-colored dye faded from her hair, revealing that her hair was a beautiful shade of deep brown, streaked with gold. Mama said that her hair was the color of the sun on honey. The cavernous bones of her face became less pronounced, and the deep green and purple circles around her eyes went away. She sometimes smiled, though it was many months before any of us became accustomed to it. Her smiles were like fireworks in the night sky. Elsa had become a fine-looking girl; but when she smiled, she was *beautiful*.

We had fun washing her and made parties of cutting and fixing her hair. At night, when we had seen Elsa to sleep, Mama and I worked many hours to make her a beautiful rose pink dress for after childbirth. We also made every pretty scrap of material that we could come by into beautiful clothes for her baby. Every time we gave her a new one, she was just as astonished and filled with wonder as she had been with the last. She often laid in her bed with the pretty clothes all around her, stroking the softness of the fabric and examining each detail of the little dresses, her eyes large and shining with childish delight.

Eventually, Elsa's body began to heal and she was anxious to leave the confinement of Mama's bed. She hated illness, but I think that more than anything she hated the incarceration of our house. The weather-worn boards may as well have been the impenetrable stone walls of the tallest tower, with Elsa trapped far above the earth. She had lived a good many of her years under only the shelter of the solitary trees, with the Ozark hills serving as the walls of her house. Unaccustomed to spending much time at rest, she became quite restless. She was ready to recover long before her body was ready or able to do the work. Occasionally, when she felt she could not stand to be shut in for even one more minute, her old fractiousness returned. Hoping to keep her peaceful and still, I suggested we spend our reading hours on the front porch, with her in a rocking chair and me lying across the old graying boards, the slanting arms of the aureate sun warming our backs.

One afternoon, I brought a lunch tray out to the porch where Elsa sat sleeping in her rocker. I watched her as she slept. Her skin was luminous—the color of an ocean-washed pearl. Her belly was round with life and her fine cheekbones flushed with the pretty pink of sleep. The gold in her hair shone and her hands gently rested on the mystery growing inside of her. The way she held her body seemed to say that she would protect the child even in her sleep.

I woke her with the clanking of the tray. She sat up straight and, stretching her body, said,

"Y'all always eat three times ev'ry day?"

I nodded, confused.

"We do if we have enough food for it. And with all of us working, we usually do."

"I never heard a' such a thang. My people always eat whenever we'n find food t' eat. Most times that wuz once a day, or nearly ev'ry day. We wuz always hungry. I guess you mostly git used to it, though. But *here*, I am gettin' downright fat!"

I smiled at her.

"You eat just as much as you can hold. You need to feed that baby."

She grinned, complacent and happy.

One morning, shortly after Doc had removed the splint and bandages from Elsa's arm, she called out that she intended to take a turn around the yard. I parted the curtain and watched as she circled, stooping to pick flowers as she walked. She stood for a long time in front of Mama's hydrangeas, her head bent in adoration, watching the breeze shift the blossoms from side to side. Her face was a mixture of concentration and purity, giving her the appearance of a ragamuffin saint, deeply engaged in some beatific act of piety. She had one hand held aloft, not quite touching the silent blossoms, as if in blessing. She straightened, putting one hand to her back and the other to her forehead, shading her face from the bright morning light. She looked to the east.

Curious, I craned my neck and saw that she was watching a shining silver dust cloud as it passed over the dirt road. The cloud moved on around the bend. At the base of the cloud there was a black truck, moving steadily along. In the back of the truck sat four men, lanky and ill kept. All wore hats pushed low over their faces, shading their eyes from view. The truck passed into the yard and stopped a dozen feet from the front porch. It was driven by a small, sun burnt man with a long yellow mustache. From the passenger side emerged a thin man, smoking a cigarette burnt low. He sauntered toward the porch, his eyes never leaving me as I stood at the open kitchen window. I wiped my hands on the damp kitchen towel and walked nervously from the kitchen to the front step.

"Can I help you gentlemen?" I asked, thinking with dismay that my voice sounded like a colicky billy goat.

The man walked right up to me, stopping no more than a foot away and blowing cigarette smoke out of the corner of his mouth. He watched me for a while without speaking.

"Can I do something for you, Mister?" I asked again.

He seemed in no hurry to speak. His posture was careless and he held a cigarette loosely in the tips of his fingers. He waved a hand in my direction, motioning to me to be silent and took one last lazy drag from his cigarette before tossing it onto the porch. Then he turned to look at Elsa, possessively eyeing her with the gaze of a sunrise charlatan. I felt fear wash over me and was struck by the sickening sensation that he was touching her body with his eyes. He watched her. I watched him.

"Mister. Is there a reason why you're here or did you just drive your truck into my yard so you could stand there n' smoke?"

He didn't respond.

I studied his impassive face. His greenish skin was stretched tight over the broad bones of his face. It had the appearance of being clothed in garments two sizes too small, like his boy skin had never grown quite enough to accommodate his man skeleton. In the hollows of his broad cheekbones were hundreds of tiny, faded pockmarks. His most prominent feature, seated on the throne of his face, was an oppressive hooked nose, which had been broken in at least three places. The lower half of his face was slightly obscured by the ashiness of a five o-clock shadow. He was a tall man—uncommonly tall, with an implacable gaze. His eyes, an indefinable color, were small, selfish, and deeply set in his large head, giving the impression that he might not have a soul. His teeth were badly disjointed and had grown haphazardly, without reason or foresight, through the wending road of his mouth. He opened his lips every few seconds to remove bits of tobacco from his tongue.

He wasn't well dressed, but was better dressed than most men during the Depression, and was certainly more dapper looking than his traveling companions. He wore a faded overcoat of green corduroy, the breast pocket of which showing a brightly colored handkerchief. His dirty trousers were sturdy brown wool, fraying at the hem. He wore large black work boots, his feet very slender for a man. His hands had that same deceptive air of frailty. They were bone thin and seemed to be several inches too long.

I was amazed by how well kept his hands were. They might have been a child's. He looked as if he had never done a day's work in his life—honest or otherwise. In a time and area of the country where even women had freckled and calloused hands, this man had the look of an imposter.

His body and clothes were worn and, except for his air of invincibility, he might have looked haggard; maybe even ill. His skin gave off a sickly sweet smell. It may have been the smell of evil.

Sensing that he was being watched, he turned his gaze back to me. As his eyes met mine, I was suddenly seized with terror. A chill passed over my body, its icy fingers brushing over my spine. Believe as you like—we must all believe according to the measure of our faith. But I believed then, and still do even now, that on that spring day, standing in the afternoon dust of our yard, I was looking at the devil.

Finally, he spoke.

"I'm lookin' fer Dan Brown."

I licked my lips, trying to wet my mouth enough to speak, and slowly shook my head.

"He hasn't been here for a long while. I reckon it's been about five days. When he's here we don't see him much." I waved vaguely toward the barn. "He sleeps out in the haymow."

The man chuckled.

"I don't blame yer mama. I wouldn't take that dirty basterd in'na my bed neither."

He looked salaciously at Elsa.

"I bet you go out to him, though. That's all a whore's good for."

Elsa didn't flinch. She didn't turn away. Her eyes never left his face. She watched him disdainfully, hands on her hips. She nodded once and, the old steeliness returning to her voice, she said,

"You heard the gurl. He's got better things to do'n take care a' his family. Y'all get o'an outta here. You ain't got no bidness with these good people and they don't wont no bidness with you. I hear there's a colored woman he has some dealins with over yonder side a' the river. You go o'an bother her a spell. I reck'n you bothered us enough fer one day."

He gave a long shout of a laugh, head thrown back, Adam's apple bobbing.

"How that man gits his women, I'll never understand. I reck'n I best take some lessons in love from Dan Brown."

He laughed again, the sound ringing with rancor. During all of this time, the other men had never moved. They all remained in the truck, standing like Neolithic statues, their faces glistening with afternoon sweat, browned by sun and dust. Then he turned and moved back to the truck, calling back over his shoulder,

"When he comes, tell 'im Lucius Elder wants to see 'im n' that it'd be better for him if I didn' have to come out here again n' git 'im."

Then, with a flourish and a wave of his hat, the black truck drove away and hell followed with it.

XVI.

The first day of June was hot and the air was thick with water. The earth had dried, the waters of the flood receding more quickly than we thought possible. Every day since the rain stopped had been hotter than the last. Elsa was now nearly nine months along. In spite of the heat, she had been unable to bear the idea of spending the last days of her waiting indoors.

She and I passed many hours of those last several weeks walking the pastures around our house and trailing the interminable dirt roads around the town. Most mornings, we walked to the cemetery that lay three-quarters of a mile to the southwest of our house and sat under the shade of an elm that was well over a hundred years old. Elsa seemed quite peaceful there. Nearly all of those buried were members of my family—women with names like Lenny Bea, Eliza, Georgia and Maybelle. One woman buried there, Saritha, was of fabled beauty. Hers was a face that launched a thousand wagons. Thena was said to have looked like her, except that Saritha had no wild red curl. This trait was Thena's alone.

The men were named Elihu, Lloyd, Niram and Burns and had been poets and farmers and schoolteachers—all three at once. Sometimes, at night, lying restless in bed, I imagine each of those men scribbling their poetry in the dark of night; I see them hunched over lamps of hazy glass quickly burning, wrapped in scratchy blankets of putty colored wool and praying silently—both for inspiration and that their wives wouldn't wake up. Southern men in that time were providers, farmers; not poets. Writing didn't put food on the table. This innate compulsion for the pen must have been just as great as their God-given desire for the provision of their families.

No more than a hundred yards from the cemetery lay the ruins of the original Shady Grove United Methodist Church, a church that had been founded by my great-great-grandmother, Corinne. Evidently, under the very tree where we now sat, she had begun a revival meeting. It had met every night for many months. More souls were added to their numbers daily, and from this great meeting arose the church itself, where, until a suitable minister could be found, Corinne herself had done the preaching.

"Where's all yer fam'ly now?" asked Elsa.

"What do you mean?"

"I mean, my people, they all live within 'bout a hundred yards a' one 'nother—aunts, uncles, cousins, brothers, sisters, grandfolks—all of 'em. They don't get along, always shootin' guns n' cussin' n' fightin'. They don't much like each other, and they cain't get along worth nothin', but they're all close by. Where'd all yer people go?"

"We saw my aunts and Grandmama and Granddaddy a lot, before—before Dan," I said, embarrassed to be discussing Dan with Elsa.

"It's been a long time since we've seen any of them, and I can't really remember them much anymore. My daddy's family, as far as I know, they're all gone. Gran and Grandan died just about the same time that Daddy did. Daddy had one sister, but Mama hasn't heard anything from her in a long time. I reckon that's everybody."

Elsa lay down, her head on my lap, her hands stripping apart long pieces of grass, her belly a strong mountain.

"What wuz yer daddy's Christian name?" she asked, putting a piece of grass between her teeth.

"It was Stephen. What about your daddy's?"

"Well, now, I never did know. Daddy was older'n God. He always seemed too old to've ever been called anythang but 'Daddy.' He never wuz much uva daddy, though—havin' the name don't make you one."

After this she was quiet for a while, tearing the grass into fine shreds with her teeth.

"Did you ever pertend anythang, when you's a gurl?"

I nodded.

"What thangs'd you pertend?"

"I used to pretend that my daddy was still alive and that Mama was happy and that—"

I stopped. She nodded.

"No Dan?"

"Yeah," I whispered. "What about you?"

"I used to pertend I never had no daddy n' that I only had a mama. That she loved me, n' would sit n' brush my hair, tellin' me stories at night 'fore I went off to sleep. I used to 'magine her sittin' next to me n' singin' ever' song that came into her head n' that she loved me more'n any other thang an' that she n' I cooked together n' had a little ol' house n' that she would sew me the finest dresses made'a silk n' that I looked like a queen when I wore 'em."

"What happened to your mama?"

"I found her one mornin' when I went out to milk the cow. She wuz hangin' from the rafter of the barn."

I paused for a long moment.

"How old were you?

"Seven."

"How old are you now?"

"Fourteen."

"Me, too."

"My daddy said she went straight to hell cuz she killt herseff. Do you thank yer sent to hell fer that?"

"I don't know."

Elsa sat up. She put one hand to her belly and gave a funny grunt, then screwed her eyes shut tight.

"Elsa, what is it?"

She waved away my question with one hand.

"Don't fuss."

She sat quiet for a few minutes, while I watched, holding my breath.

"I reck'n we best head o'an back to the house. I think this baby may just be thinkin' to come into the world today."

My stomach dropped out at the bottom and I felt all the blood drain from my head. She stood up quickly and I stood with her, putting an arm around her shoulders. She pulled impatiently away.

"Now, if yer gonna' fuss, I'm jes' gonna send you o'an home by yerseff! I have to be calm, so you have to, too!"

I nodded and swallowed back my tears. Of all the things I have seen in my lifetime, there is nothing more terrifying than seeing a woman give birth. Even death has never given me so much fear. I have since worked in a hospital for many years and have seen both births and deaths. So many go to meet death with a brow clothed in peace. So many go, delighted that they are going home, to a better place, on to tomorrow, on to find those who have already left. Death is often quiet; usually the dying could just as easily be falling asleep. But when a child is born there is such violence—like a great war fought on the delicate battlefield of the unfolded womb. There is such blaring sunlight-pain, like the pain of a thousand suns, burnishing, creating; such shadowy fear, such deep, black uncertainty. The sounds of joy and pain are so thickly woven together that you can't discern between the two threads, and the sounds of dying flesh giving way and living flesh breaking through are so similar that you can't tell which is the dying and which is the living. The cries of the mother and the cries of the babe mingle together until you can't tell which is which. And though I know that childbearing is a glorious thing, having given birth to children myself, I still fear it.

"Elsa, we have to hurry. I've gotta run for the Doc."

"No time fer that."

"Elsa, the baby just now started comin'. There'll be plenty of time. Don't you worry, I won't be gone long. I'll run the whole way."

"Nope. Not got time. Baby beeyn comin' all mornin'."

"What do you mean, comin' all mornin'?"

"Why you think we beeyn lyin' under that tree waitin'? What'd you think we wuz waitin' fer?"

A flood of icy sweat slid down my back and stomach. I felt a claw-like knot growing in my throat as I realized I would soon be delivering a baby on my own. I couldn't breathe. Elsa moved steadily on. She was so calm. She showed no sign of pain or even discomfort. For a moment I wondered if she was mistaken, until she bent down at the waist and wrapped her arms around her belly, waiting for the pain to pass. She never made a sound. Her expression never changed. After several seconds, she straightened and walked on.

"Elsa! I don't understand. Why didn't you tell me?"

"What's to tell? Women beeyn havin' babies fer longer'n anybody can count. I reck'n I can have me a baby jest about as well as the next gurl. 'Sides, I figured if I told you, you'd start this huffin' n' puffin', and I figured I'd be doin' enough a' that on my own."

"Elsa, I can't deliver a baby! I have no idea how it's done. I can't do it; we have got to have help. Elsa, I have to get the Doc!" I stammered as I helped her climb the steps of the porch and then turned to race toward town.

She put a hand to my shoulder.

"You cain't leave me. I got to have yer help. And I'm tellin' you there ain't no time fer the Doc. This baby is knockin' on the door and he ain't gonn' wait long 'fore he pushes it wide open. 'Sides, you ain't deliverin' no baby," she said with a sly grin. "I am."

We passed into the darkness of the front room.

"Leave that door open n' light ever' lamp you can find," Elsa ordered.

"I intend to see what I'm doin'. Git me yer mama's oldest blankets. I don't wont to mess up her fine stuff. I'm gonn' need scaldin' water, lots of it, an' yer mama's good sharp scissors. Bring me that soft wool blanket yer mama made to swaddle up the baby in."

She bent over again, her eyes tightly shut. She breathed slow and deep, one hand on her back. Fifteen, twenty, thirty, forty seconds passed and I began to see her body relax. Then she let out a long, slow breath. I raced to Mama's room, threw open the cupboard door and pulled out her oldest blankets. They were all old, so I didn't see that it mattered much; but, to Elsa, Mama's things were "fine."

Elsa stood in the doorway of the front room, one hand still to her back. When I came back in, she turned and pointed to a space about two yards from the door.

"Spread out her oldest there by the door. Bring me the water, those scissors n' that real strong twine yer mama used when she sewed up those tater sacks."

I did as I was told. When I moved back to Elsa's side, she quietly said,

"I wont you to get o'an 'cross the room. If I need you, I'm gonna holler and then you come runnin'. Till then, I'm gonn' do this thang my way. I have to have this baby. But if I'm gonn' do it, I'm gonn' do it the way I wont to."

I nodded, dumped all the items on the floor, and went back to the stove to wait for the water to boil. Elsa slid her dress of dust-colored flowers over her head and squatted on the blanket in her slip.

Her face was gray and she closed her eyes tightly. Her hands cupped her head, her knuckles white. She gave a funny groan, one that sounded as if it caught in her throat, and then a great rush of straw-colored liquid poured from her body, over her thighs and down her calves, rushing over the blanket and onto the floor.

She gave a second groan. Gripping her thighs, she gasped for air. Her face turned purple and a webbing of green veins spread across her cheeks and forehead. Tears filled her eyes and slid down her cheeks. The pain finally passed; she slumped forward, her head to the floor. Her shoulders shook with silent weeping. For several minutes, no more pains came. Then her back suddenly arched and she raised herself back up into a squatting position, gripping her thighs until they bruised and turned blue. Another pain. More ferocious breathing. Another trail of tears down her fine china cheekbones. Minutes passed, or maybe hours, or days. The sun changed its place in the sky, the wind blew, flowers grew taller, the globe spun, and only the room and the two of us remained unchanged. I'm not sure how long we waited, but it probably wasn't more than half an hour. Half an hour or not, watching Elsa give birth seemed longer to me than all the years of my childhood put together.

She began to push. I sat on the floor by the hearth, crying as quietly as I could.

"Grace," she whispered, "come n' hold my hand. I'm scaired."

I crawled across the floor and gripped her fingers, feeling secret delight that Elsa could comfort me even at a moment when she needed comforting. Another push. Another. Dark rivers of blood flowed from her. Sweat poured from my body and the room spun. Elsa clutched my fingers, her nails digging into the soft flesh of my palm. I felt the bones crunching together and being ground into a powder finer than store-bought flour. Another push. Then I heard a terrible scream. It was unearthly. Like the scream of a wounded animal. A sound never heard before the Fall of Man.

Then the earth shifted and I heard the sounds of ripping flesh. Elsa lowered her head and both hands and caught her tiny baby, tears streaming down her face, sobs and laughter rattling her body until I could hear the clunking of her bones.

She snatched up a rag and, wiping the brown and red matter from the little girl's body, she took her by her two feet, turned her upside down and hit her once between the two isosceles triangles of her shoulder blades. The baby gave a scream of wrath and fear. Elsa handed the little girl to me and then slumped to the floor. I cut the umbilical cord, tied it with twine, and hurriedly washed her off with hot water and a rag. Then, wrapping her tightly in the new wool blanket that Mama had knitted, I laid her gently by Elsa's side. I turned to tend to Elsa, but she was unconscious.

I rolled her onto her back and touched her cheek, pushing strands of her honeyed hair from her eyes. She was still bleeding badly. I took several bits of rag and packed the fabric up against her body, hoping that the blood would clot and dry. I wet another piece of rag and laid the cloth on her forehead. I wiped her throat and chest and arms and the dried blood from her legs.

Glancing over at her baby, I noticed how ugly a newborn baby is. The little girl's skin was purple and blue. There were strips of green in her arms and gray in her little legs and her flesh was wrinkled. So wrinkled, in fact, that her tiny features were indistinguishable. They were lost in the folds of her pruny skin.

Elsa gave a tight-throated wail and began to thrash around on the floor. Her eyes rolled back in her head. She gritted her teeth together until I was sure that they would crumble into pieces and roll from her mouth like smooth, white pebbles. Her slip clung to her body, soaked in pale sweat, and there were hundreds of tiny, red capillaries on her face and neck that had burst under the straining of her body. She rolled over onto her side, pulling her legs up to her chest.

"Grace! Grace! The pains, why ain't they stopped?"

"I don't know, honey."

I was terrified. I was going to have to leave her and go for help, but was afraid that if I left her alone something terrible would happen.

"Elsa, I don't know. Move your legs away from your belly. I need to see what's wrong."

I began to press on her abdomen, unsure of what I was feeling for. My mind raced with questions. I knew full well that this was beyond me, and that whatever was wrong with Elsa, I couldn't fix it.

"Elsa, I need to go for help. I don't know what I'm doing. If there is something wrong with you, I won't know what to do. You're still bleeding and I can't make it stop."

"Grace, you cain-not leave me! You cain't. You have to promise me that you'll stay. I cain't do this by myseff. Don't leave me alone here to die."

I began to cry again.

"Elsa you are not going to die. Don't say that again."

I was furious that she had said aloud what had been echoing inside my head. I continued to feel her belly. It seemed like it was still very hard, like there was still something inside of her. Then I felt a tiny, fist-like ball digging into the side of her belly, and I knew.

"Elsa, I need to reach my hand inside of you and see what's the matter."

I wiped the tears out of my eyes and very gently put my hand inside her flesh. My hands shook badly and I can't remember any moment of my life when I have been more scared. I felt sick. After a moment, I felt my hand touch something solid and alive—another tiny body. It was a second baby. I slid my hand along one side, until my fingers felt the baby's soft, slippery feet digging into Elsa's side, as if it were holding on for dear life to the safety and warmth of her womb. The baby was turned sideways. I had seen her first baby leave her body headfirst. This must be what was wrong. Reaching my hand up to the baby's shoulder, I closed my fingers tightly around it and gave a firm pull. Then a second, and a third. I felt the body shifting slightly, but not enough.

Elsa screamed and I began to sob again. For several seconds, I couldn't go on because I was crying too hard. Then I gave another pull on the leg. The baby shifted again. Finally, I managed to slide my hand up to where the baby's shoulder lay and, with both hands, I gave a violent yank. Elsa screamed a second time, and then she lay silent, her eyes closed.

At that moment, I felt the tiny life sliding down the birth canal, and then I pulled the little baby out into the fading sunlight of the afternoon. He was tiny—so small that he looked like a miniature newborn. He was less than half the weight of the first baby. He couldn't have weighed any more than two and a half or three pounds. He was so weak that when he cried, though tears slid down his swollen cheeks, all I could hear were his weak breathing and a horrible wheezing sound. With each breath, his little chest looked as if it might cave in. The lower half of his body was badly bruised. I could see the bleeding under his fine, transparent skin and on his little face was a look of profound unhappiness and pain. His skin was gray and cool and he did not have a single hair on his head.

This must be what I looked like when I was born, I thought to myself, remembering the story of my birth.

I washed him very carefully and wrapped him in two of the blankets that I had knit for Elsa's baby. I held him close to me, against my chest, against my heart. I could feel his heart beating, just as he must have been able to feel mine. I heard and felt him breath. I studied the tiny road map of green veins that covered his eyelids, and I saw that he had the same strong green vein running around the rim of his orbital bone as his mama. He also had Elsa's tiny starburst on his left cheek. Both of his fists were knotted tightly together and held against his face. His little lips were ashy and blue and my insides trembled as I looked at him.

I lay him very softly on the floor and turned back to Elsa. She hadn't stirred and the bleeding hadn't abated. Moments after I laid her son beside her, her body passed the second placenta, but the bleeding continued. It was then that I knew with complete certainty that unless I left Elsa to go after help, she was going to die. I lay a great heap of quilts over her silent body and, taking a baby in each arm, I ran up the hill to

King Farm. I burst through the front door of the house without knocking and stood in front of Mae King and Grandpa. They sat at the kitchen table, just beginning to eat, Grandpa having just come in from his fields. Both looked up, then stood, neither of them speaking.

"Grandpa, go after the Doc. Mae King, Elsa's bleeding. I need your help."

Grandpa crossed the room in four strides, took his hat from the nail and, without asking questions or looking surprised, he was gone. Mae King took the little girl and passed out the front door. Neither of us spoke as we raced down the winding gravel road to the base of the hill where our little house stood. She went into the front room, handed the baby girl back to me, knelt on the floor and pulled the blankets back to examine Elsa.

"Grace, make out a pallet fer those babies 'n' take a bucket out to th' crick bed. Bring back as much sand as you'n carry."

I made a bed for the babies and took a tall tin from the back porch, running toward the creek that ran through the woods behind our house. When I carried the heavy bucket back into the house, Grandma King had taken charge. All of the blankets were pulled away from Elsa. Mae had placed cloths inside of her to clot the blood. Taking the pail from me, she poured a great heap of sand over the floor to soak up the blood, packing it tightly around Elsa's small body. She asked for a pail of cool water and soap. Washing Elsa very gently, she cleaned her skin with the cold water and wiped away the sweat and dirt from her deathly pale face. Then she carefully covered her with a single wool blanket and sat beside her, tightly holding her hand and softly singing.

About half an hour passed. I held both babies to my chest.

"Grace," she said softly, "those babies need to eat."

At that moment, Doc's old car rattled into the yard. He ran from the yard and into the front room, out of breath. His face was flushed with worry.

"Grace, what happened? When did she deliver?"

"It might be two hours, maybe not so long."

"How long ago did it start?"

"This morning, but she didn't tell me. About three or four hours ago she said we needed to come back to the house so she could have her baby. We walked back to the house and she squatted on the floor and pushed. The pain was real bad. The first baby came, but then the second wouldn't. She just kept bleedin'. Then I realized that the baby was turned the wrong way and I had to pull it out myself. She passed out and hasn't woken up since."

"The baby was turned? Are you sure? Which way did it come out?

"Feet first."

He nodded and, turning to Elsa, began to work.

"Well, it's not good," said Doc. "But, Mae King, I think between us we might keep her alive, yet."

"Yeah," said Grandma King, "the bleeding slowed down about thirty minutes back. I don't think she's too far gone."

Grandma looked after Elsa's baby girl. Grandpa King sat on the front porch and I held the little boy. I let him suck milk from my fingers. I sang lullabies into his ear as we sat in the rocking chair. Every few minutes, I unwrapped him from his blankets and massaged his little body, hoping that if I kept his circulation going, I might keep him alive. I touched his fingers and toes and marveled at their sophistication and simplicity. I whispered stories to him and told him all about his mama and all of us and how happy we would be when he felt better. He held my pinky finger inside his perfect, waxen hand. He looked unreal. I studied the tiny crevices at the joints of his fingers and the minute pearls of his nails, so small that they were nearly invisible. I saw a hang nail on the thumb of his left hand. I watched his little mouth suckle as he slept.

It is odd, but until the very last moment, I thought he would live. There was never any question in my mind. It was impossible to me that any life could end just as it was beginning. I held him all night. Mama and Thena came home and tended to Elsa. By this time, the bleeding had stopped completely; and though she hadn't regained consciousness, Doc still believed that Elsa might make it.

Doc Barrett tried to save the little boy, or at least made an attempt for my sake, but I don't think there was ever anything that could have been done. Long after there was any help to be given, Doc sat beside me as I rocked the baby. Just before dawn, he stopped breathing. Doc pushed on his tiny chest and breathed into his mouth. The baby took several more breaths. Then he stopped. The Doc repeated the procedure. Again, it was successful for a few seconds. The baby boy's chest heaved up and down with great thrusts, and tears streamed from his eyes. He was silent. He was still. There was no more breathing.

Doc tried a third time. The little boy took two breaths. I held him close to me, crying so hard my body shook. I whispered to him how much we loved him. I told him how much we wanted him, how much we had looked forward to his coming. I traced the lines of his cheeks, wiping his tears away. I kissed his beautiful, perfect head. I ran a finger over the rim of his right ear. I kissed the green vein and then the pink starburst on his left cheek. Then his heart stopped and he left us.

I carried him out on the front porch just as the sun arrived to wake up the world. The sky was pale orange, the color of melting sherbet. The sun burned fuchsia, emblazoning its shape on my corneas. I stared straight at it, refusing to turn my eyes away. The air was purple and hazy and the grass was the sleepy blue-green color of the early morning. The earth smelt hopeful, like pine trees.

The sun glided away from the ground and the grass was lit up like a billion torches, the sunlight reflecting off of the sweetly diminishing dew.

"Hey little, boy. Can you hear me? Your name is Stephen. That was my daddy's name. He was Stephen, too. He's in heaven now, and maybe you'll meet him there. If you do, will you tell him hello for me? Tell him I love him."

I sat with Stephen on the steps of the porch and listened as the sky and trees and plants and animals and all of heaven and earth began to wake up and he lay in my arms, eternally sleeping.

That afternoon, I carried Stephen to the graveyard where Elsa and I had sat on the morning that she went into labor. Jim built a tiny pine box to lay him in. I washed and dressed him in a beautiful white linen suit with blue piping. Refusing to let anyone come with me, I buried him under the oak, right next to my daddy, Stephen.

The morning after I buried Stephen, I awoke with my eyes and nose raw and nearly swollen shut. My eyelids were purple. My voice was so hoarse that I couldn't speak and my lips were torn to ribbons as if in the night, in my sleep, I had bitten back sobs of pain and powerlessness. Strangely, I hadn't shed a single tear since the moment of Stephen's last breath, and it seemed as if, because I couldn't mourn, my body, out of respect for the dead, had at least displayed the signs of mourning. Someone once told me that the body weeps the tears the eyes refuse to shed.

Elsa didn't wake up until the third day after Stephen's death—whether because of the trauma to her body or the trauma to her soul, I don't know. When she first awoke, she asked for her little girl. When I brought her, she put the baby to her breast and fed her.

During those first days, she stayed awake just long enough to feed her daughter, and when she was awake, she was silent. Her tired body lay quiet and still in Mama's bed. She held her baby, touching her face and smiling, kissing her soft curls. To Elsa, during those first days, there were only the two of them; it was because she didn't acknowledge the rest of us that I knew she remembered the birth of her son.

The little girl grew rapidly and was healthy and strong. After several days, she no longer looked like an old woman. I marveled as I watched her change. She became quite pretty. Her skin was pale and pure, like a piece of perfect ivory. It was softer than silk and flushed pink. Her head was covered in a mass of honey-colored curls. The third morning after she was born—the same day that her mama woke up—she opened her eyes. They were the startling green of the Irish countryside. Now, nearly always, when a child is born, her eyes are blue; whatever color they will later become, they begin as blue. But not Elsa's baby. Hers were green from the moment she was born. Elsa called her Lilliana Grace.

XVII.

It was not until the third week after Lilliana and Stephen's birth that Dan returned. He took note of Elsa's baby without comment. He never asked after Elsa's health, and Elsa offered no information about herself or their baby. Nor did she ever, I am certain, tell him about the second child born to them—a child who was so clearly his father's son, complete with a dimple on each cheek.

Around this time, we received a letter from Mama's mother, Isabel. Mama was accustomed to receiving somewhat businesslike letters from her mother several times each year. It was not at all that the letters were unkind; they certainly weren't. It was more that the letters were cautious, as if written by one unfamiliar with the language. There was a certain degree of awkwardness in these letters that had to do with Dan. Isabel had begged Mama not to marry him. She had seen from the start the trouble Dan would cause Mama. In Isabel's defense, Mama was primarily responsible for the formality in their letter writing. It was not from ill-will or bad blood; it was just that Isabel had been right about Dan, and Mama felt like she shouldn't burden Isabel with her troubles—or at least that's how Mama saw it.

Mama always wrote back to Isabel, telling her as many good things about each of us and of our life together as she could think of. The letters told her how we had grown, what we had accomplished (this, except with regards to Thena, must have been the shortest paragraph in each of her letters), what we were all doing, the crops, the weather. Mama told Grandma Isabel the town news and stories of life with the Wilkins. I'm sure she told her about all of the destruction that the flood brought, and that the town was still slowly recovering from the menace. I am also certain that in her deliberate, careful letters she never referred to Dan or her life with him.

A few weeks after Lilliana's birth, Mama received a short letter from Isabel asking for her grandchildren to come and stay with her for a while. Mama was very surprised and was happy to receive the invitation. I attempted to recall any memory that I could of Grandma Isabel. Though I must have seen her quite often before my father's death, I could only remember one other time when I had gone to visit her.

I have a vague memory of that visit. I remember standing behind Isabel one dark, cold morning, brushing her shiny black hair. I must have been about five years old. Isabel had thick, fine hair, perfectly straight and perfectly abundant. Her hair was like a living thing when unbound. The quantity of it, when it was down—and it almost never was—gave her a look of power, awe and sternness. With her hair down her back, falling away beyond her waist, there was something wild about her appearance. When I picture her this way, I see her, or something hidden away inside of her, as being almost savage and utterly free.

I remember very clearly how she looked that morning. After I brushed her smooth satin hair, she had me divide it into two braids. Then she coiled the braids around her head.

There was an air of militancy to my Grandmother at all times, hair up or down. She would have made an excellent soldier. She was demanding and impervious, liberated and ladylike—Isabel the warrior princess. I have never known another woman like her.

When silent, Isabel had such an air of nobility. But when she opened her mouth, the idyll was immediately dashed on the razor sharp rocks of reality. Isabel never minced words—though her words could very well mince you. Her sentences were sharp, severe and clipped short. And she always spoke with complete authority. She could have been a queen. Maybe she was.

She was very tall and angular, flat chested, with a regal hulk of a Roman nose. Her eyes were snapping, jigging and black as hell at night. Her cheekbones were salient, incisive and looked like they could have been used as implements for cutting. Her teeth were smooth and brilliantly white. And when she smiled, which was rare, my heart skipped a beat.

Her skin was both brown and perfectly smooth. I caught her late one night sneaking into the kitchen to wash her face in a quart jug of rich cream mixed with honey from her own hives. She must have done this to ward off sun damage and old age, and it worked. Her skin was certainly smooth as honey cream. I don't think Isabel could have been called beautiful; but she was, at the very least, one of the most striking women that I have ever seen.

As I brushed her hair, I stood behind the velvet stool at her dressing table mirror, proud to be treated as Grandma's pet, surprised that it was me, and not Thena, that she had invited to brush and braid her hair. I brushed patiently, silently counting out a hundred strokes, and then began to braid. As I did, she told me what I believe is the story of her life; it is a story I have never forgotten.

I relayed the account to Mama once and she insisted that the story couldn't be true because Isabel had never told it to her. Be that as it may, I have the most acute memory of it, even down to the large, square ruby ring that Isabel wore on the ring finger of her right hand. I remember that the beautiful ring looked out of place on her large, brown hands. They were ugly and might have been a man's. When Isabel touched me, it felt like being scrubbed with sandpaper; her fingernails were broken and split, permanently stained the color of dry river earth.

Isabel told me that her father, Sean Canton, was an Irishman who fled the devastation of the potato famine after seeing more than a million of his countrymen fade noiselessly away into the oblivion of starvation. Her aging father once told her a story about the priest of his parish. (Sean had come to America a Roman Catholic, but soon became a Protestant, quickly learning that maintaining his papal ties would make his life more complicated. So, he became a Methodist and learned to interpret the word "Catholic" as "catholic," meaning "universal.")

Evidently, his priest had been forced to pass over the rites of Christian burial for many of the hundreds of men, women and children in his parish who had very slowly died under the patient, reliable fury of the blight. The village was small; the demands were great and the priest had very limited church funds to work with. In the end, he was forced to pick between buying coffins for the dead and buying bread for the living. He chose the bread or, rather, the living. As a result, many bodies were left above ground to rot, St. Peter preserve us. Those who were buried were laid in the ground coffinless, with only a foot and a half of dirt and the ragged remains of their clothes to cover their poor, emaciated bodies. The good priest grieved, but knew that God would forgive him. He stretched the pence as far as it would go to feed as many of the hungry as he could.

Sean Canton managed to remain alive, and alive, managed to journey across an ocean and a continent to start a new life; a life that did not involve potatoes, and that did involve food—as much of it as he could get. Sean left in '49, when all hope was lost, after fighting a four-year losing battle with hunger and sickness. He lost every member of his family. But the Irish are stubborn. Bloody stubborn. Somehow, Sean lived.

The tired, war-torn mick stepped off the boat on the eastern coast of America to find it a bit overpopulated for his tastes. So, he moved to the Tennessee woods, struck up a friendship with a Cherokee Indian chief and eventually fell in love with his beautiful daughter, Saritha. I have heard from many people that Saritha was considered the most beautiful woman who ever lived in the state of Tennessee, and maybe the most beautiful woman south of the Mason-Dixon. The redheaded Irishman married the free-spirited, black-eyed Indian princess. She died several years later of scarlet fever, the same fever that would blind my grandmother, Isabel.

Saritha lived long enough to give birth to six babies. Isabel was the eldest, and when she recovered from the fever—recovered, that is, all but her vision—she found herself mama to five babies. She married at thirteen and took her five brothers and sisters to live with her. Isabel had eleven babies of her own in twelve years; by age twenty-five she had been a mother sixteen times over, counting her five siblings. Three of Isabel's babies died in infancy, four died in early childhood, and four lived to be adults—Mama, her two sisters and a brother.

Isabel's husband and the father of her eleven children was Jacob Butler. He was a schoolteacher and farmer—very good at the former; not so good at the latter. Jacob owned many books for such a poor man and read at times when he ought to have been doing farm work. The farm was successful because Isabel made it so. Isabel and Jacob loved each other wholly and passionately, and when Jacob snuck away from the fields into the woods so that he could read, Isabel did his work without complaint or malice. After fifteen happy years of marriage, Jacob was kicked in the chest by a horse. After the accident, he pulled himself up, dusted straw and horse muck from his clothes and said he was fine, refusing to see a doctor. He died two days later from internal bleeding.

Isabel, stalwart and grim, moved on with life and somehow managed to feed siblings and children, blind and on her own. I think this may have been when she lost that look of freedom that burned in her eyes—the light I only saw when her hair was down. Mama says it was out of Isabel's sheer force of will that they all survived. She commanded that the cows give milk and quit their bellyaching, that the corn grow to at least the height of an elephant's eye by the fourth of July, and that the peach trees give not only peaches, but also cream. They obeyed.

Mama used to say that she remembered Isabel as an implacable sort of person—maybe not the best memory to have of one's mother. But Isabel was doing her best to play the hand that life had dealt her. This required all of her strength, thought and energy, leaving her with neither the time nor the animation for playfulness. I guess you might say she wasn't a lighthearted mother. She was quiet and hardworking. She told her children to stand up straight, mind their manners, be respectful, keep all their ducks in a row, their chins up and their noses clean, change their underwear, say their prayers and work hard.

Mama also claims that she presided over kitchen table studies with the iron fist and stony countenance of a Tennessean Machiavelli. In spite of Isabel's sternness and no-nonsense approach to life, Mary idolized her. Isabel made sure they had clothes on their backs and food in their bellies and insisted their suffering gave them solidarity.

She was not an awfully religious person—although she could quote Psalms, Proverbs and the New Testament almost verbatim—but she did require her children to attend their town's United Methodist Church.

While I think she did have faith, it was certainly unconventional. In fact, by the time that I knew her, she didn't bother to relegate her swearing to the privacy of her home, but swore wherever she damn well pleased. Moreover, she openly smoked, in front of God and everybody. Neither of these things was permissible for a southern lady of the church. Both were permissible for Isabel.

In addition to her other admirable qualities was added the one most important to the southern woman: she could cook like nobody's business. Mama said that Isabel was the best cook she ever knew. Maybe this was due, in some measure, to her blindness. The absence of one sense forced her to lean more heavily on the others. Her senses of smell and taste were far more acute than most people's.

Mama remembers that, before Jacob died, her mother laughed a lot and smiled while she held his hand. She sang in a sweet, clear soprano voice and played her papa's Irish folk tunes and jigs on her fiddle. After Jacob's death, Isabel put the fiddle away. She never played it again. I found it a few days after she died in a box with her wedding dress.

I have wondered many times if Mama's nature was a reaction to Isabel's. They were absolutely dissimilar in every way. Looking back so many years later, it is easy for me to see that the characters of Mama and Thena were also, in so many ways, diametrically opposed. It was as if the characteristics of Isabel's temperament skipped a generation and were given to her granddaughter. Interestingly enough, whenever Thena spoke of Grandma Isabel, which wasn't that often, she referred to her as "the old bat." And while this label was somewhat unkind, it wasn't completely off course. Isabel wasn't easy. She couldn't have been, or she and her children wouldn't have survived.

Thena inherited that same merciless determination and unrepentant fearlessness from her Grandmother. There was also that alarming attachment to freedom, which could be seen in every look, movement and feature—an element that Isabel had hidden away somewhere, perhaps out of a sense of duty or desperation. I suspect that Thena's devoutly irreverent spirit was also Isabel's gift. On the very rare occasions when the two of them were together (this only happened several times in my life), it was like a performance of a wildly popular Broadway spectacular entitled something like "The Parody of the Sacred."

We did go and spend three months with Grandma Isabel; but, because Elsa's recovery was long and slow, it wasn't until the following year. The summer we left Mama to see Isabel, I was fifteen. Mama wouldn't leave Mrs. Rachel, but sent Thena, Lilliana (who was just over a year old and had lately begun to walk and fall, alternately), Elsa, the three smallest boys and I all to stay with Isabel. They were wild, clamorous months and I'm not sure how Isabel lived through them. There were quite a few aunts hanging around Isabel's farm to try and keep us in check—I don't recall them being very successful at it. We certainly weren't intentionally bad. "Bad" is such a strong word. We were... Spirited. Energetic.

Isabel's farm was a four-hour drive from Shady Grove. On the first morning after our long trip, the boys woke up shouting and didn't stop for more than three weeks. Each morning when the sun came up, I watched them as they flew away, slowly melting into the pink fog. I watched until they were little brown dots on the purple and green horizon of the pasture. They mostly stayed out of sight until just after nightfall, but sometimes I heard them in the distance, shouting to one another and shrieking with laughter. No matter how many times they got into trouble and no matter which aunt took it upon herself to attempt the correction, they never remembered to come home for the noonday meal, which was always the biggest of the day. Dinner (never "lunch") was a celebration of work done well in the morning (the hired hands having begun work by five-thirty to beat the heat of the sun), and a prelude to work still waiting for the brown, steady strength of the worker's hands. Breakfast at Isabel's was wheat or corn bread with butter and honey and strong, black coffee. Supper was beans and maybe a piece of pork, with more bread. And because of the simplicity of the morning and evening meals, dinner was something of a fete. Though the boys missed out on this wonderful midday feast every day and came home at night to eat many thick slices of bread, I don't think that they were disappointed.

I always marveled at my grandmother and her magical relationship to bread. Isabel's supply of bread was never-ending; like the woman in the story who went every morning to her grain bin, expecting to find it empty, and always found enough for just one more loaf. Her kitchen was filled with loaf after loaf—streets and rivers and mountains of bread—yet, I never saw her make it. Her house stank of the overpowering sweet smell of her fresh bread. Even her skin and her sweat smelled like it.

One evening at sunset, after the day's work was done and all the workers had gone home, we sat on the porch, watching the night coming on. Isabel sat in her rocking chair, carefully rolling her own cigarettes. Even without the use of her eyes, this endeavor was always perfectly, meticulously carried out. She never did anything unless she did it well. I lay at Isabel's feet, reading, Elsa held Lilliana, the aunts had gone home to their own families, and the boys were with Thena in the barnyard. I heard Thena, from a distance, explaining the stomachs of the cow. The boys were giggling over any creature needing more than one stomach. I lay my book aside and rolled over onto my back, tucking my hands behind my head. I closed my eyes and took in a deep breath of the cool dusk. I lay there, listening to the familiar squeak of Isabel's chair as she rocked and to the sounds of Elsa whispering to her daughter. Eventually, Thena wandered over to the porch and sat down beside me, jabbing me once in the ribs and chucking me under the chin. She always thought I was too serious and did whatever she could to breathe more life into me.

For just a moment, the barnyard was completely quiet. I couldn't hear any sound from the boys. Then, suddenly, we heard a loud squeal of fury from an animal—a goat—and shouts of wild laughter from the boys, then the fence boards rattling and a final crash. Franklin Delano began to scream and sob.

Thena and I were off the porch and running in an instant. Elsa followed more slowly, Lilliana on her hip. Isabel followed close behind Elsa, her body straining to see what her eyes could not. It may seem strange, but I think Isabel could see better without the use of her eyes than any of the rest of us could.

There was a strange kind of prescience in Isabel. She knew a lot, and a lot of what she knew wasn't within the normal range of human knowing. She had the strangest ability to meet a person and, after examining them with her hands, fully understand their character. Her hands even seemed able to see what had happened in a person's past. The night she met Elsa, before Elsa had ever spoken a word, Isabel looked her over with her long, arthritic fingers. Taking the skittish Elsa's face in her old hands, she said,

"Things hadn't been so good for you girl, but they're gonna be better now. You're gonna have a happy life. You'll have a husband and another son, a healthy son, who'll live a long life. Don't you ever doubt that yer life'll be blessed. Things don't always end as they began." Then she hugged her and ushered her up the front steps and into the house.

It may have been that, through Isabel's special sight, she already knew what we would find. We rounded the corner of the barn and met Franklin Delano coming towards us, his hands covering his eyes. His pants, which were too short for him again, were dusty, his face was covered in brown grime, and tiny rivers made their way down over his sun burnt, muddy cheeks. He stumbled over his fat little feet in his hurry to get to me, and lay there in the dirt, crying as if his heart or entire body was broken.

I scooped him up and, tearing his little shirt away from him, I began to examine his chest and back, neck, head and arms, but could not find any injury. Gasping for breath, he wrapped his arms tightly around me.

"Grace, him's dead! Dead, Grace! Hep 'im, please hep 'im."

My body went cold. I stopped mid-stride, unable to move or speak. Images of John and Edwin toppling from the roof of the barn filled my mind.

"What is it, honey—who's dead? Who needs help?"

He was crying too hard to answer. I carried him to the barn and saw both boys standing on the boards of the fence, peering down at a creature lying still in the dust. I handed Franklin Delano to Thena and looked over the fence. It was one of Isabel's goats, shrouded in a potato sack.

"Edwin! John Michael Kelley! *What have you done?*" I growled, mostly mad to have been scared so badly.

Neither boy spoke. Both looked at me fearfully, their little faces grim and pale. I felt Isabel's strong, patient hand on my shoulder.

"Grace, what've those children done now?"

"I don't know. There's a goat lying in the dust, covered in a piece of tarp. I don't think it's alive, Grandmama. You boys had better explain to me what happened, *right now*."

"Grace, it was an accident, I swear it was."

"Don't swear anything."

"Fine then, I promise it was an accident."

"What have you done to him?"

"We was just playin' with him. We was kinda eggin' him on. He kept buttin' his head against the fence. Anytime we moved, he'd follow and butt, like he was trying to git at us. I thought it'd be funny to throw that blanket over his head, just to see what he'd do. He jes' went crazy— squealin' and screechin' and runnin' all over. He was runnin' into everythang he could find cuz he was spittin' mad, and I guess he just ran into that fence one too many times. On the last time, he got a real good runnin' start n' ran all the way from one side of the pen to th' other, and he butted into the side jes' as hard as he could. Then he jes' fell over. I reckon he's dead, Grace, but I sure didn' mean to kill 'im."

"You boys beat all I've ever seen. John, you are old enough to know better. Your mama taught you better than to be cruel to an animal."

"I wud'n bein' cruel, Gracie. That goat's just got a real mean temper."

"Who do you think it was that made him so mad, John?"

Squeezing my shoulder once, Isabel let out a low, rumbling chuckle. She moved to the gate, a smile touching the corners of her mouth, and said quietly over her shoulder,

"For affliction cometh not from the dust, neither doth trouble spring forth from the ground; yet man is born to trouble, even as the spark flies upward."

Her words puzzled me then. Later, I discovered that the words were from the book of Job, a story about a man who lost his whole life in an afternoon. I knew not how well acquainted Isabel was with their meaning—nor, in fact, how well acquainted I would become with their meaning. But I thought of those words, years later, when understanding dawned and filled the horizon of my mind. I still often think of them; occasionally, when I do, I smile to myself just a little.

Isabel moved into the pen, passing to the southern side of the fence. When her foot brushed against the animal, she knelt down and pulled the blanket away. The animal was clearly still breathing. She gently examined its body, testing each limb for broken bones. She passed a hand over its eyes. The lids were shut. Stroking the animal's belly she called out,

"There's nothin' wrong with this animal, other'n that you made 'im knock his senses out. He's unconscious. He'll come to. Just give 'im time. In the meantime, if you boys can't behave better, you'll have to sit in the house n' play with yer mama's old baby dolls."

≈ ≈ ≈

I have many memories of our weeks with Isabel, though one evening has remained in my mind all these years and stands out above all the others. It was a night when Isabel and I sat together on the porch, listening to the bullfrogs and screech owls. A hot wind swept under the branches of the two poplar trees standing ancient and immovable just in front of the house, barely, just barely, giving us some relief. Isabel hummed quietly to herself and worked at keeping cool with an old hand-painted fan covered in swans. The night smelled like stale heat and honeysuckle and lavender. I could hear Thena inside, tucking the boys in for the night. I could hear the crinkling of the straw ticking as they settled into bed.

My whole life I have loved nighttime. I have loved it for different reasons at different stages. And, I admit, I especially love the fiery heat of southern summer nights. They are eternal. It sometimes feels as if I have been living one my whole life long. As a girl, I loved the night because it was the only time our boys were ever clean. Every night they said their prayers with Thena (a delicious irony), which, after their baths, gave their insides a good cleaning out, as well. In return, they were offered the blessing of one of Thena's stories.

Elsa had taken Lilliana to bed early and had stayed with her, just as she did every night. Elsa belonged to the age-old race that slept and rose with the sun. Occasionally, lightning flashed across the sky. The ferocious heat of the day had left the overthrown atmosphere on its knees, begging for rain. It had been a devilishly hot summer and all of us were perpetually covered in sweat. I remember many nights when I couldn't sleep because the atomic power of the heat, long hours after the sun had set, still wouldn't allow it.

"Yer mama says you work hard in school. She says you have a good head, like yer daddy, and yer granddaddy," Isabel said.

I wasn't sure what to say. I continued rocking in my chair, which stood opposite Isabel's.

"You like school, then?"

"Yes, Grandmama."

"Maybe you'll make a teacher."

"Maybe."

"You don't say much, do you, child? It seems to me that them that says the least oftentimes has the most to say. My daddy always said that deep waters is good fer fishin'."

She was silent for a long time. Waiting for her to speak again, my mind edged away and finally stood and leapt over the porch rail, into the yard, racing away after a stream of light cast out by the orange moon. From far away I heard the faint murmur of Thena's voice and the low, droning hum of the wind. So many minutes passed that I thought Grandma Isabel might have fallen asleep.

"Your mama doin' okay?"

"Yes, ma'am."

"How's that little house of yer daddy's holdin' up?"

"I reckon it's okay."

"And Jim and Ted?"

"They're good, I guess. They both work as farm hands, and when they aren't working, they're usually hunting. I think Jim has a sweetheart, but he won't say so if he does. When I ask him his ears turn red. I guess that means yes."

Isabel smiled faintly and nodded. She went back to humming and fanning. She rocked steadily and slowly, the old wood of the chair squeaking time to her rocking.

"What about Elsa? Where did she come from?"

"I don't rightly know. Missouri somewhere, I think."

"How'd yer mama come to let her stay with y'all?"

"I guess Mama figured she needed a place to stay. Hers was washed away in the flood."

"How'd the girl come to be leavin' all her people?"

"I'm not sure. I never asked her."

"And Dan?"

"I guess he's alright."

"Has he been able to find work lately?"

"I don't guess he has."

"He still at the bottle?"

"A fair amount."

"Yer mama…okay?"

"We take care of 'er."

"Did Dan bring that girl from Missoura?"

"I believe he did."

More rocking. More fanning. No humming.

"Where's that baby's daddy?"

"I don't think that baby has a daddy."

"All babies have daddies, child."

"Lilli doesn't. She has Elsa and Mama and Thena and all of us, but no daddy, and I don't think she knows the difference."

Low-burning lights began to appear all over the sky. When I was a little girl, I thought that stars were angels. I used to lie on my back in the grass and gaze up at them. Lying there on the warm earth, I would kiss and then stretch out my fingers, thinking that if I reached out far enough, I could touch one of them. I distinctly remember comforting myself with the promise that next year my arms would be longer, and I would finally be able to reach the sky and give the angels a kiss.

Isabel rocked. I rocked. My body began to feel heavy. All of my muscles were uncomfortable, taut, as if the bones were too long or the muscles too short. My fingers and toes were curled tightly closed and I realized that I had been holding my breath for a long time. My lungs burned and I felt sure that any second my chest would burst and spill out all over the porch.

In my mind I begged Isabel not to ask me any more questions. I was torn between wanting to protect Mama's dignity, which kept me from speaking too ill of Dan, and veracity, which kept me from speaking too well of him. I also knew enough to know that I didn't understand the relationship between Elsa and Dan, or the relationship between Mama and Dan—or between Dan and anybody, for that matter—and I didn't want Isabel to ask questions about so many things that I couldn't fathom. But she didn't ask anything more. I have a feeling that she pretty well understood the situation.

"Girl, I guess you best get o'an to bed—it's gettin' late an' those younguns'll be up early callin' yer name n' wantin' to be fed n' dressed, so's they can go n' git into Lord knows what kinda trouble."

"Yes, Grandmama."

"Goodnight to you, Gracie."

"Night."

I went into the cool, white room that Thena and I shared, pulled back the covers and my dress over my head and, still wearing my slip, climbed into bed. Thena was there already.

Thena always possessed the most remarkable ability to fall asleep under any circumstances, in no more than one minute's time. She rarely lay down—the wellspring of her energy ran deep. But when she did, she was gone. This was a characteristic of hers—like so many others—that I never could comprehend. I spent hours every night trying desperately to shut down my mind for long enough to sleep.

Today, in my very old age, it is much worse than it was then. Now I sleep only a couple of hours a night. A great deal of thinking—and wondering—can be done when the rest of the world lies quiet. But even then, that summer, there were many hours between when I slid into bed next to Thena and when I finally journeyed to whatever land we go to when we sleep. Thena just as often slept out of doors as in. In my whole life, I have fallen asleep outside only once. The outside world has always seemed too wild and uncontrollable to sleep in. I have always felt too vulnerable to sleep in the open.

Even now, each night after I finally lay aside my book and just before I shut off the light, I walk to the bedroom door and lock it. Now, of course, if a person really wanted to get into my bedroom, the inadequate lock on my door wouldn't suffice to keep anyone out for long. One good shove and the door would give. But this ceremonial door locking is essential to the illusion of safety, and only my illusions allow me to sleep.

≈ ≈ ≈

Summer days on Isabel's farm were not for sleeping. We always woke up early. There were always things that needed doing, and if you couldn't find anything, Isabel found it for you. Many years ago, when my children were still young, they would occasionally come to me complaining that they were bored. They would knock on the door of my study and say,

"Mama, I'm bored. There's nothing to do."

"Well, let me find something for you to do," I would say.

Then I would hear the scuttling sound of running feet, and they were gone. I learned this trick from Mama and Isabel. It was delightfully effective.

In spite of the constant and demanding work of the farm, there were many times for playing. We occasionally convinced Isabel to come with us. She liked to show off her farm; not for vanity's sake, but because it was a part of her very being, indistinguishable from herself. It kept her alive and sustained her. If it had died, she would have died with it. Evidently, the land felt the same way. There was a peach tree on the crest of the hill where her house sat, which she tended to every summer day for more than thirty years. She touched it and spoke to it and it seemed to live for her. On the day she died, the tree began to wither; within a month, it was dead.

At times, we would convince Isabel to go with us on our adventures. The girls would walk through the tall, shining wheat, Elsa or I with Lilliana on a hip. The boys would run ahead with Isabel's hounds, brandishing giant sword-sticks and fighting bloody battles. At the end of these skirmishes at least one, and usually all three boys lay dead on the field of glory.

Isabel often took us to The Desert, a beautiful place named by Mama when she was a very little girl. Mama was right—it certainly looked like a desert. At the edge of one field, on a plateau ending in a cliff, we stood looking down into a deep canyon. Its walls were made of loose sandstone and the floor was covered in white sand more than two feet deep. There was a single promontory rising up toward the clouds in the center of the basin. It reached as high as the surrounding walls and was a dangerous climb. We named it Dead Man's Climb, and then promptly climbed it.

The very top of this obstacle, which was more than twenty feet high and no more than four or five feet across, was crowned by a single spruce that had somehow taken root and thrived in the sandy soil. Whoever could climb to the top first, boy or girl, was given the auspicious title of King of the Desert.

On one afternoon, Isabel took us to see the house where she was born. It was a misshapen, rotting structure that couldn't have been more than twelve feet long by eight feet deep. The house had no windows and would have been more convincing as a second-rate poultry shed than as home to a family of seven. They had slept, lived, worked and ate in a single room, boys, girls and man, all together. The floors were smoothly packed dirt. Birds had built nests in three corners of the ceiling, and there were cracks between the boards of the walls that were wide enough to slide my hand through.

In the front of the house, on either side of the weary-looking door, stood two enormous rosebushes covered in hundreds of fuchsia-colored flowers. Saritha planted the two bushes the day after she was married. In my mind's eye I could see her so clearly, standing in the doorway, her black hair hanging down her back, her black eyes laughing as she watched her freckled, copper-haired Sean dig the holes for the bushes.

The weeks passed quickly. As much as I wanted to stay with Isabel, worries for Mama were lingering in the back of my mind. Where was Dan, I asked myself, and was he plaguing Mama? On the morning that we left, Uncle Tobin (Mama's brother-in-law) packed us into his truck and made the long drive to take us back home to Mama, to our town, to the river. Our aunts and cousins stood on the porch to see us off. The last of our bags were packed into the truck, and Isabel came through the screen door, wiping her wet, dishwashing hands on the hem of her apron. She stood tall and straight as a great tree, her black hair knotted tightly at the nape of her neck.

Even in 1940, Isabel wore skirts down to the very dust of the ground for the sake of modesty. She also wore two petticoats, even in the heat of August. She was beyond the time of life when one worries about what other people think. Being there now, myself, I have to tell you, it is bliss. To her, wearing long skirts was both modest and proper. It was what a lady should wear, and Isabel was a lady. Cigarettes, plain-spokenness and all.

Thena, Elsa and I worked in the truck bed to arrange the boys in a way that would keep them from falling or leaping out.

"Grace Canton Kelley."

"Yes, Grandmama?"

I stepped away from the truck and moved back across the yard. Isabel met me and put one hand on my shoulder. She took my hand in her other and pressed into my palm a fifty-dollar bill. I had never seen so much money.

"You take care of 'em—all of 'em—'specially yer mama."
Then pointing to the money she said, "Give it to yer mama. Tell 'er to put it away fer a rainy day."

She wrapped her arms around me and held me so tightly that I felt my ribs beginning to give.

"All the aunts have buzzed and squawked about how beautiful Thena is. That may be, but I see beauty in your soul. One day, you'll get to be an old woman. Yer bones'll creak and yer skin'll wrinkle and you might not be much worth lookin' at. Beauty fades and when it does, what matters is what's left on yer insides. I've never seen yer face, but yer insides're made a' gold. I'd take one woman with a golden heart over all the beautiful girls in the world."

She touched my cheek and looked straight into my eyes and I knew that she saw me.

XVIII.

It was when we arrived home that everything began to change. We pulled into the drive, leapt from the truck and fell across the yard to get to Mama. The door swung open and she stepped slowly out onto the porch, spreading her arms wide. When she did, I saw the slight curve of her belly. My heart rose into my throat and tears flooded my eyes. I felt betrayed, but didn't know by whom.

She stood waiting, pale and thin, one hand shielding her face. Her eyes were sad and guarded, her head turned to one side.

"Mama!" cried the baby. He wrenched himself from my arms and raced away to her. As he ran up the steps, she turned her whole body to face us. I saw that the left side of her face was black and badly disfigured. Her left eye was swollen shut and her nose had been broken. It wasn't until he reached up for her that Franklin noticed her face. Mama gasped and swept him up into her arms. The little boy put his soft, fat hand to her right cheek and, laying his head on her shoulder, he began to cry.

"Ma-ma!" I cried out, running to her.

Thena and the boys pushed forward, carefully hugging and kissing her.

"What's this? What happened?" Thena whispered, her face white.

"Nothin', child, nothin' at all, just a silly scuffle. It looks worse than it is. Don't hurt a'tall."

She touched and examined each of us, carefully wiping tears away from her swollen cheeks. Kissing Franklin Delano over and over again, she ushered us into the house. Neither Dan nor my older brothers were at home.

"Your brothers are still workin' out at King farm. They been workin' late ev'ry night this summer and I reckon they won't be home 'til dark."

She sat down in her rocker and pulled Franklin Delano into her lap. He snuggled close to her body and carefully laid his hand against her cheek.

"Mama fall down?" he asked softly.

Mama looked strangely at Franklin Delano, as if startled by his question. She was quiet for a long moment.

"Yeah, baby, I reckon Mama did fall down. I reckon I fell down a long time ago."

Then she straightened up and looked over at the rest of us.

"John! Edwin! You boys are so big and brown! I just cain't believe how much you're growed! Your britches is already too short and I'm gonna have to hem you up an old pair a' the boys' long pants."

"Where's Dan?" I asked.

"Haven't seen him too much lately. He comes n' goes and I've spent most of my time up at the Mayor's. Mrs. Rachel hadn't been doin' too well—in fact, she's gettin' worse, I think; and since my younguns weren't around, I tried to spend as much time with 'er as I could. I stayed with her most evenin's and read to 'er. That seems to keep 'er peaceful n' still. Reed n' Pope sure have missed you. Those two've been thick as thieves this summer. I think Reed Wilkins has asked me every day when Thena would be gettin' home! Grace, Pope says he has some books he wonts you to read n' said when you got back into town that Doc n' Nora wanna see you."

≈ ≈ ≈

A week after we came home, one of my teachers asked if I wanted a job at Shady Grove Public Library. I took the job immediately, both because I loved books and because I loved Mama, knowing that there would soon be another mouth to feed.

I spent every afternoon after school and all day long on Saturday at the library. In spite of the unpromising size of our country library, I was busy for many hours every day for the first month of working there. This was because of Shady Grove Public Library's one librarian and director, Ms. Martha Hampton. Ms. Martha had at one time been one of the country's most meticulous and erudite librarians, but had—so slowly that few had even noticed it—begun to lose her mind.

Ms. Martha's malady was a complicated one, and difficult to understand. Oftentimes, she seemed quite lucid, sometimes even for days at a time. At other times, I wasn't able to get a single sensible word out of her. Each morning was different from the one before; I never knew in what state I would find her.

However, after working with her for a while, I did notice some kind of slight pattern to her illness. For one thing, she was particularly coherent whenever patrons were present in the library. In fact, I had remained unaware of her true condition until I began to work with her, though I had spent many happy hours in the library since childhood. I had noticed for several years that Ms. Martha was becoming increasingly eccentric, but it was necessary for one to be with her for a number of hours to become familiar with the subtleties of her dimentia. If the library was empty, her mind would begin to slip. I began to realize that the more I talked to her, the longer I could keep her mind from darting away to wherever it was that it went.

As we talked, I began to learn many things about Ms. Martha and her life. She had never married. It was said that she had lost her love only days before their wedding, though she never specifically told me this herself. I suspect that this young man must have been called "Richard," because she quite often spoke to this "Richard," rather coquettishly, during the course of our working hours together. I also learned that she had lived in Saint Louis for several years and had earned a college degree—a fairly unusual thing for a young woman to do before the turn of the twentieth century.

It occurred to me several days after I had begun working that my real job must have been to watch over Ms. Martha, as much as anything else. She had been Shady Grove's librarian for a great many years and had certainly given the better part of her life to our town. Someone must have felt that it would have been disloyal and even inhuman to relieve her of her position.

Martha Hampton was a small woman, just five feet tall, quite plump and very pretty. She had masses of thick, prematurely white hair that she wore in a loose bun at the top of her head. She had very pink, round cheeks and soft white skin, without a single wrinkle, freckle or blemish. Her face and neck were covered in a fine white down that reminded me of a baby chick. She had a large dimple on either side of her mouth and displayed them charmingly each time she smiled, which was often. She smelled of face powder and underwear drawer potpourri. She had a wide, friendly mouth, a little bird's sing-song voice and small, busy hands. Her eyes were dark and sparkling. No matter the season, she wore light cotton dresses in girlish colors, accompanied by large hats covered in a profusion of brightly colored paper flowers, and shoes with tall, tottering heels. Every single day, she wore a small gold Victorian watch-broach, pinned to the collar of her dress.

On my first morning as assistant librarian, I entered the library to find Ms. Martha watering her plants with a pot of boiling black coffee, to "give them a kick," as she explained it. I was certainly surprised by this oddity, but it didn't seem wise to question my supervisor on the first day of a new job, so I pushed the strange scene from my mind and set to work. Ms. Martha began every morning with this odd routine; consequently, each one of her potted plants—and there must have been more than twenty—was very, very dead. Once I very gently asked her if scalding coffee was quite good for plants, and if, perhaps, hers were dead because of this strange method of watering.

"But, my dear child!" she chirped, sweetly smiling, hopping from one foot to the other and clapping her mouse hands. "They are not dead, they are sleeping! Osmosis is such very hard work, you see."

I said nothing. Maybe she was right—maybe they were only sleeping. I have heard of creatures in the wild that lie perfectly limp when in the presence of a predator, pretending to be dead, hoping to escape attack through deception and cunning. And maybe this was the method that Ms. Martha's plants chose as their best defense against their guardian. In any case, this method didn't seem to have been working out very well for them.

One morning, after I had worked at the library for several weeks, I gathered up an armload of books to be reshelved. I was startled to find that a number of them were very much out of place. After several minutes, I realized that all of the books on several rows had been misplaced; in fact, all of the books on the entire bookshelf had been painstakingly misarranged. I spent a long time trying to discover the reason for this. Eventually, I began to see what I thought was some sort of system—odd though it was. Confused, I moved on to the next shelf, and to the next, across the length and breadth of the room, astonished to find that, seemingly overnight, every single book had been taken from its proper place and rearranged by some strange new classification. Apparently, Ms. Martha had been constructing a system over the months that she found to be far more useful than Dewey's.

"Ms. Martha?"

"Yes, dear?"

"There seems to be something strange about the way this library is arranged."

"How do you mean, dear?"

"The books are all out of order."

"No, dear. Not out of order. They are very precisely *in* order; it merely happens to be a *new* order."

"New?"

"Yes. I found the old classification system to be outdated and awkward, not to mention unimaginative."

As it turned out, her system involved dividing the books into categories by publisher. Then each book was arranged on the shelf first in order of the number of pages contained within the book—greatest number of pages to least. These were then arranged in order of most to least importance, according to Ms. Martha. Books with forwards, prefaces and appendices were separated and given their own special shelf. These she regarded with particular delight, although I always felt that the books themselves must have bristled under this discriminatory separation, this literary apartheid.

I tried for months to return the books to their proper order. So many, in those days, cowered before what Dewey had created, I not the least among them. But as time passed, I saw the futility in this struggle of wills. Every morning I saw that Ms. Martha had corrected the "mistake" and returned the book to the appropriate inappropriate shelf, by publisher, page count, then importance.

Of course, this made every book in the building virtually impossible to find. Neither Ms. Martha nor myself had the foggiest idea which publisher had published which book. What was more, the books were no longer arranged by category (fiction, non-fiction, poetry, reference, etc.); so, a book on child rearing might now share shelf space with a book of physics, provided that the same publisher published both books.

A happy pandemonium ensued. Patrons were sent off to search for books in our belletristic wilderness, and there was no way of knowing what sort of book or beast they would meet with along the way.

"Ms. Martha?" I said sheepishly one afternoon, after dealing with a particularly exasperated patron, "I have noticed that people looking for books often seem frustrated and confused with the new system."

"Confusion and frustration are very good for the moral fiber, my dear."

"Yes, ma'am. But are they good in a library, do you think?"

"What's good for the soul is always good for the library."

"Yes ma'am, but the patrons come in to find a book, and when they can't find it, they go home without it."

"Those are only the weak at heart, Grace. The wise emerge triumphant from a glorious adventure and the foolish leave, hopefully having learned something about themselves."

Ms. Martha was delighted with the success of her classification system. So, learning that gentle reasoning did no good, I kept my opinions to myself and tried to keep the library as neat and orderly as I could.

This went on for quite a while. I went to the library every day and tried to keep everything and everyone from harm; although, from the start, the sleeping plants were on their own. I spent long hours talking with Ms. Martha. I think I was one of the only people she spent much time with. She always had a lot to say. She had many stories to tell and questions to ask, which she mostly answered herself. However, unpredictable as those times were, there were days when Ms. Martha did seem to wait for a reply, her pretty head cocked to one side. It was at those times that I answered with great patience, and even interest, feeling quite sorry for this strange lady. To tell the truth, I really rather liked her. She smelt faintly of happiness or something like it.

As she told me stories from her strange half-life, she often walked back and forth across the wooden boards of the library, carefully balancing some large tome on her head, practicing a strange art she mysteriously referred to as "etiquette." Often saying more to herself than

AS THE SPARK FLIES UPWARD

to me as she paced, she would whisper, "A lady can never be too careful."

I have often admired the wisdom of this statement and have taken it as one to live by, adding, in later years, "as gentlemen are scarce."

"Grace, dear?" she asked one morning as we stood side by side, arranging books by publisher.

"Yes, Ms. Martha?"

"I suppose you have a handsome young man somewhere who is courting you." She said it matter-of-factly.

"No, Ms. Martha, I don't suppose I do."

"What *do* you suppose, Grace?"

"Beg pardon?"

"Well, it has always been my experience that it is the young lady who does the supposing and the young man who follows after."

"I don't believe I understand you."

"My dear girl, you do not think a young man would actually come up with the idea of courting on his own? You have to think of it for him. If left to himself, a gentlemen will generally think of an idea forty or fifty years after it first occurs to a lady, and even that's only the very bright ones. Men aren't very creative thinkers, dear. They're rather limited, poor things. They need women to think for them. Men can *act*; women can *think*. It has been that way since the world was born. Women have always ruled the world with their brains and men with their bodies. Which do you think is the greater sort of power, Grace?

"For the last century there have been a great many accomplished and otherwise very bright authoresses who have written bitterly about the plight of women everywhere. I have never quite understood that tack. To write such things seems to me to say to the men, 'You have lorded it over us for centuries and we're tired of it. Now! Help us fix it!' But, my dear Grace, we have never needed their help. We have had the power all along, if only we had the good sense to use it.

"It is certainly true that women are not generally as physically strong as men. But a woman can deal with more relational, philosophical, emotional and spatial messes in an afternoon than most men will in a lifetime. My mother always had our family and a goodly portion of this town whipped into shape in the time it took to drink her afternoon tea. A woman is only as limited as her resources and her will. Men may very well rule the world, my girl. But it is women who rule men." She put a pretty pink hand to her face, laughed, and then winked.

"Why did you never marry, Ms. Martha?"

"I was married—in my heart, dear girl."

"How do you mean?"

"My young man was killed in the Great War. But I have been married to him in my heart and mind this last thirty years, every bit as much as if the minister had said the words."

"You loved him."

"Oh, yes. And he had the good sense and impeccable taste to love me back. But it was more than that, Grace. It was more than love or even friendship. It was partnership. It was someone to watch and guard and participate in my life and to say that it was good. And I was the same to him. We were really something. I took over where he left off and vice versa. Anything less is not a marriage. In fact, I consider myself to have had a better marriage than most women married for fifty or sixty years."

This conversation, as did most that I had with Ms. Martha, left me with a great deal to think about.

XIX.

I was never a woman capable of many great things. I have lived almost my whole life quietly. There have been moments, certainly, when I have desired greatness. But there have been few when I have known it.

Certainly, in the dark of night, lying still and soul-soft in my husband's arms, those were great moments, even by the standards of the great. I remember his bare body against mine, feeling his muscles and sinews and the smoothness of his skin. I remember the curve of his back and the power and valor of his thighs and, though he died twenty years ago, I can still taste him. I remember the feeling of the sorrowful fullness of his lower lip as I kissed him. I remember the gentleness of his sleepy green eyes. His eyes were the color of hope. I could see them in the night when he loved me, looking straight into my soul. And, oh God, I can still smell him in my clothes, my sheets, my hair. When he went, my soul went with him; I have held my breath continually since he breathed his last.

There is a special place inside the brain where memories are held. It just touches the lobe of the brain responsible for processing smells. When a person says the word "orange," you can distinctly smell that great, wet, sensual scent. For this same reason, whenever I hear my husband's name, or when I sit silently staring into the fire, thinking of him, I can smell him so intensely that he might even be in the room. His smell washes over me and gags me with its power and makes me weep.

I can still feel his hands on me. I can feel him underneath my fingernails and clinging to my skin. He was the one great passion of my life. There was not one before him and there has not been one since. There was never even anyone else in the running. Who could have challenged such a world-class record? What contender, what fool would have tried?

The moments of each of my children's births were also moments of greatness. Almost every day of my life, I have felt my body an encumbrance; an awkward mass of flesh, tissue, organs, muscles, bones, ligaments, tendons. Childbirth was the only time I can remember glorying in my body. Only in childbirth did I feel a sense of partnership and intimacy and beauty between my physical and spiritual selves. I remember the horrible, thrashing, quaking pains inside of me. I felt inside my swollen womb an earthquake and an avalanche and a train wreck all at once. And, though I wept like a child at those moments, it was almost with a sense of relief—I felt in those pains, rolling over me like the waves of a dark, violent, resolute sea, a great sense of purpose. Though I felt a great, surging, choking fear, the pains were leading me somewhere, taking my hand and walking me onward, and I closed my eyes and allowed myself to be led, surrendering to that terrible agony. It was a pain that felt like God was near, burning into my body and soul and leaving me weak and irrevocably changed.

When it was over, I looked back at the terror and horror and splendor, and could see that what I had done was great. It was good. But, as I said, those moments were few and precious as diamonds or pearls found in an ordinary, sometimes ugly and squalid life. In my years there has been much coal, but few diamonds. I think it is because the diamonds of life are so rare that they shine so brilliantly.

It is for this reason—the very ordinariness of my life—that I don't understand that wild, sweeping power that rushed through me when my mother needed me. When I sit sifting through the muddled dust of my insides, I don't find anything inside of me that should have made me able to withstand the pain of leaving the safety of myself and stepping out into the beautiful terror of that world.

Looking back, I am also shocked by the carnality and baseness of those actions. There was something very bestial in my confrontations with Dan, and that part of me—that explosive, insentient part of my insides—was one that I didn't know well, didn't want to know and hoped to destroy. It was a part of me that I had convinced myself, in between times, didn't exist.

Dan and I, since the time of our first violent altercation, had very little to do with one another. As I have said before, I have very few memories of him, and this forgetting was intentional. However, there was a night during that fall when I was unable to avoid Dan.

Pope and I had returned from a walk, just as the sun was setting. Pope had walked me to the bottom of the hill and turned to walk again the mile to his grandparents' house. I entered the front room of our house and saw that the old square kitchen table had been overthrown. There were three overturned chairs and a fourth that lay in broken pieces against the wall.

From the back room, I heard sounds of scuffling. I passed through the second room, where John and Edwin and Franklin Delano lay in their small bed. Franklin lay weeping quietly with his thumb in his mouth, holding tightly to the frayed edge of an old brown quilt. Edwin held hands with John and Franklin, looking at me with eyes dark and somber as the moon. Neither Thena nor Elsa seemed to be in the house. Thena must have been with Reed, and Elsa often took Lilliana for a walk just before they went to bed. I heard a sound of pain and fear and moved to the door of Mama's room. I stood for a moment, unsure of what to do, knowing full well that when my mother's door was shut, we weren't to enter. I heard the thunderclap of an open hand against flesh and a quiet sob from my mother.

There is a dark fog in my mind when I try to remember the moments that came next. When I close my eyes to see it all again, I see it through a blaring, wine-colored haze. I turned and walked to the front room, removed the rifle from the wall and took off the safety. I walked to the door of Mama's room, flung it open and stepped inside. It was at that instant, when that dark, boiling fire rose up from inside of me, that I realized with cold clarity that all men and women are murderers—whether in their minds, or with their hands.

I saw Dan and Mama on the bed, Dan's body pressed against her round belly, holding her wrists so tightly that her hands had turned white. Her eyes were closed and tears ran down her face, which was turned away from Dan's mouth. There were two red handprints on either side of her neck.

Without thought or decision, I turned the rifle to the ceiling and fired once, twice, three times. A scream tore from my chest that bore down on the night and squelched it. I walked across the room and took Dan by the hair. I drug him from the bed and across the floor. Small as I was, I dragged him, kicking and bellowing, punching and scratching me with his hands, tearing to shreds the thin fabric of my dress, across the second and first rooms and out into the front yard. I dropped him in the dust and aimed the rifle at his head, bracing it against my shoulder, a finger closed around the trigger. I remember full well that I hoped he would give me a reason to pull it.

"You dirty, weak bastard. You are nothing." My voice was low and quiet. "Get up. Get up and start walkin'. You get off this land and don't come back. Don't you ever touch her again. Take your filth, and your foul, stinkin' carcass away from here and leave us alone."

These last words tore from me with a howl. He turned toward me and I saw in his face both fear and hatred. His teeth were bared and he looked wild and deadly.

"You dirty lil' whore! She's my wife! I have a right to—"

"Yeah, you have a right to, just like I have a right to stick this gun up your hind-end and expel all that shit you've been storin' in there my whole life. I'm just about to pull this trigger, Dan Brown. And unless you want to take yer chances and see where the bullet lands, I reckon you had better be movin' on."

Inside of me, in the very innermost part of me, there was a childish glee at finally being able to use all of the words I had been hearing Dan utter for years—words I knew that I was expressly forbidden to use—words Mama abhorred.

They were the only words worth using on such a man.

Dan stood and turned to move away. I ought to have known better, but my thoughts were on Mama and her baby. I should have stayed to watch him walk away, but I was impatient to know that she was okay. I turned and moved up the steps of the porch. Just as I stepped into the front room, I felt the terrible strength of Dan's arm around my neck. My neck was being crushed. It felt as if it would soon be snapped in half and ripped from the throne of my small shoulders. I struggled against him with all of my might, clawing at his face with my fingernails, feeling the skin of his cheeks slide away, but he outweighed me by nearly a hundred pounds. I felt the world going gray, the rifle slid from my fingers and I watched as it fell to the ground with a thud. A strange peace came over me and I thought bemusedly that dying was not so very bad. Then I heard a shout and the sound of gunfire.

"Dan Brown! Take your hands away from her and get on out from here."

Dan's grip did not loosen.

"I'd do it Dan. I've never liked you much and I won't feel bad about putting a few peepholes in your gut. I'm a pretty good aim, too. I'm used to shootin' smaller game, but I'm not against the idea of takin' on bigger."

It was Pope. Dan's arms dropped and he stepped away. I fell to the porch and crawled inside the front room. I met Mama as she stepped through the doorway of the second room. Her face was white and her hands trembled as she buttoned the few buttons left on her faded dress. I lay face down on the floor and everything turned black.

Some time later I sat crouched in the doorframe, my legs pulled up to my chest, my head resting on the sharp bones of my knees. Pope sat beside me, his back to the front wall of the house, staring out into the darkness.

"Pope, how come you showed up—I mean when Dan and I were—how did you know we needed you?" I whispered.

"I had made it about halfway to Grandmama and Granddaddy's house when I heard the shots go off. I knew it was coming from your place and I figured it either meant that Dan was shootin' at somebody or somebody was shootin' at Dan. I have to admit though, Gracie, it didn't come into my mind that you were the one doing the shootin'."

He grinned.

"When are you gonna learn to leave that man alone—why are you always pickin' fights?"

I smiled back weakly, but didn't speak.

"I ran back into the yard and saw that he had his hands around your throat."

He was silent for a moment, one hand to his face.

"For just a second, Gracie, I thought I was gonna kill him."

He glanced over at me.

"I thought, if I just pulled that trigger all of this…" he waved his hand over the yard and house, "all of this mess that y'all have been livin' through would be done and gone and you could get back to the way things were before Dan. There was this part of me that knew it would be justified. There was this part of me that—Gracie, when I saw him, I hated him. I felt like the hatred would drown me; choke me. I just went cold and stopped breathing. I was afraid that I would kill him just because I was so angry, you know what I mean?"

He turned toward me and his eyes searched my face, looking for something, wanting me to say or do something, but I couldn't tell what it was.

"Not because I was acting as his judge and had found him guilty, but because he was lowdown. Just 'cause he was mean. 'Cause he was scum, and I wanted him dead. And I actually wanted him dead enough to kill him." His voice shook.

"I was so scared that I was gonna pull that trigger that I started to shake and I felt like I was gonna be sick. He was hurtin' you, Gracie, and I could have killed him. I would have."

He stayed with us that night, on the steps of the porch, the rifle lain over his knees, his back straight and his long legs stretched out before him. It was that night, I think, when something inside of me woke up and I realized that, somewhere along the way, while I had been absorbed in my own worries and joys, Pope had become a man. He was now seventeen and well over six feet tall. It had been several years since his eyes had outgrown the need for glasses. I think it was about this time that I began to feel shy around him occasionally. There were moments, after we hadn't seen each other for a spell, when I felt a strangeness in my stomach at that first moment of seeing him again. I had also acquired the habit of knocking things and people over when in his presence. If he noticed this change, he said nothing of it.

"Gracie?"

"Hmm?"

"He'll be back, won't he?"

I nodded.

"How long?"

"I don't know, Pope. I guess you gave him a good scare. I kind of think it'll be a while. Weeks, months, maybe."

"Why won't he just go?"

"I don't know. I reckon 'cause he knows Mama will never make him. She would never tell him to go. He's her husband, or at least she thinks he is."

"Gracie, how can she let him stay when he hurts you? He hurts her. And Elsa, and they say there's another woman, at least one, over across the river. How can she..."

I shook my head and said softly,

"I don't know what it is. I can't understand her. Sometimes I think it's because she made a vow. She gave her word and she said 'forever—'til death do us part.' I think maybe she feels like she can't break the promise now, just 'cause she doesn't like what it means for her. I think...I think, in her mind, that's the idea. I mean, that's kind of the whole idea behind it—you say, 'No matter what, I am with this man or this woman and we're together 'til the wheels fall off, 'cause we said we would be and we told each other and ourselves and the minister and God and all the witnesses.' Sure, it's bad, but she tells herself that she didn't say 'unless things get bad.' She said 'for better or worse'—and at the beginning, when she first took him, things were for better. Now. This—this is for worse. And, if she's willing to take the one, how can she say no to the other? Better or worse, worse or better, it dudn' matter much, it's 'til death comes and takes one or the other away. Even if that means that one will bring death *upon* the other."

"Gracie, I love your Mama and I respect her, but that's horseshit."

He took my hand in his. His large fingers wrapped completely around mine so that, when I looked down, my hand was no longer visible.

"I don't mean to hurt you, and I don't mean to disrespect your Mama, but I just don't believe that's what God meant by it. And you know what else? It's not just 'for worse' for your Mama. It's the baby in her belly and you and Thena and Jim and Ted and the little'uns. It's Elsa and her baby. If she took 'the worse' all by herself, that would be one thing, I reckon. But all of you take it right along with her."

"I know. I've never agreed with her. I think she has a right and probably a duty to make him go. But she doesn't see it that way. Sometimes…Pope, you remember that one time in school, when we were really little? It was the fall right after you and Reed became friends—and Anne Marie Palmer snitched on me to the teacher 'cause I had brought that turtle to school and hid him in my desk, and for some reason I just got so angry. I didn't even really know why, but I was just so mad and, after school, out in the yard, I marched up to her and took her by the hair and pulled just as hard as I could. And I pulled until I had knocked her right over, into the dust. Do you remember? And afterwards, Ms. Summers whipped me. She said I had the worst temper she had ever seen and that that was my greatest weakness. That was my biggest flaw and she said it would get me into trouble and she was right," I said, nodding toward the rifle.

"And Thena's—she never forgets a wrong. She cain't forget. She never forgives. You know? That's her greatest weakness. And Reed always acts or speaks before he thinks… Those are all of our weaknesses."

He nodded, his eyes questioning.

"All my life, for years and years, I thought Mama was perfect. I thought she never did the wrong thing or made a mistake…but do you know what I think, Pope? I think Dan's her weakness. He's her one big weakness. He's the one thing that's gonna get her into trouble."

He nodded and turned to look out at the sky.

I began to be sleepy and felt like I couldn't sit up any longer. I must have laid my head down on his lap, because at some point in the night, I woke up with my head on his knee, his arm loosely draped around me, and his coat tucked over my shoulders. When I woke in the morning, he was gone.

After that night I was vaguely cognizant of something having changed between us. There was a difference in the way that we related to each other. At times, I found myself flinching under his shrewd gaze. When I spoke to him, I found it difficult to look into his eyes and found myself intently studying the ground as I spoke. But I was uncertain of what had brought about the change, and I refused to allow myself the luxury of trying to figure it out. For a couple of years, I was fairly successful at preserving this paper-fine illusion. Although I rarely thought of him consciously, he was always in the periphery of my mind.

His sweet shadow fell across everything that I did; in all of my actions, I felt his movement; in bearing burdens, I felt his weight. I would have gladly borne him across the world and back. He kept me company when no one else could. When he chanced to brush against me, I could feel his touch days later. When I was quiet and still and my guard slipped down for one tired moment, I could most distinctly hear the exact timbre of his voice, all of its shades and rhythms and the soft velvet smoothness of its safety. It was not until the war changed the world and all of our lives that I would fully realize how I felt about my best and dearest friend.

XX.

One night in early November, I sat on the porch, wrapped in an old sweater, my bare feet digging patterns in the dust of the yard. Lilliana, fat and sleepy and sweet, sat on my knee, making me feel as if my body had been crowned with some bright jewel. We were reading a book of Grimm's fairy tales. Her warm hands were tangled in my messy curls, tugging, hoping to detach them so that she might get a better look at this new toy. Elsa sat rocking and singing softly to herself a sweet hymn, strange and lovely, her voice dark, deep and pure,

"Rock of Ages, cleft for me,
Let me hide myself in Thee."

Thena came from the house, having tucked the boys into bed for the night. Mama had not returned home, which meant that Mrs. Rachel wasn't well. Jim and Ted had gone into town, and I was pretty sure that they went in the company of two young ladies, though I kept my own council and asked no questions.

Thena wandered around the yard, restless, her hands clasped behind her back and her face toward the road. I followed her gaze. After a few seconds, my eyes adjusted to the dark and I began to see the faint outline of two figures in the distance. Thena seemed to spot them at just the same moment and gave a wild war whoop, tossing her shining black hair and clapping her hands. Then she extended one arm to the sky and waved to the two figures down the road. The smaller of the two waved back. She turned to me and said,

"Come o'an, Grace, it's time to go."

"Go where, Thena?"

"Pope and Reed have come to take us for a walk."

I strained my eyes, gazing down the length of the road, and recognized Pope, tall and lean, his hands shoved carelessly in his pockets, his walk ambling and his head bent toward the red dust. Reed danced along beside him, racing from one side of the road to the other, back to Pope's side to snatch his hat from his head; then he leapt onto his back and returned the hat back to its proper place. He remained perched there with Pope carrying him along, almost without noticing. Thena glanced back at me.

"Grace, go git yerseff some shoes. It's too cold for you to be wand'rin' around halfway naked. It's November, gurl, and yer still barefoot."

I reluctantly handed Lilliana to Elsa and passed into the house in search of shoes, thinking to myself that Thena was certainly up to no good, and that I was about to be dragged into it. Again. It is odd, but I never refused to attend Thena in her mischief. I believe that Pope and I had similar reasons for going: we went along to keep the other two out of trouble—and alive. Generally, we weren't successful at keeping either of them out of trouble, although maybe we were successful in curtailing the amount of trouble that they would have gotten into without us. At any rate, we had thus far succeeded in keeping them alive. And that was something to be proud of.

I took up my worn leather shoes and pushed them hurriedly onto my feet, then raced out into the yard. Reed held Thena's hand and stood gazing into her face, his smile dazzling, even under cover of darkness. Pope leaned against the porch railing, hands in his pockets, his face inert and calm, his eyes studying my face.

"Elsa, we're goin' for a walk. If Mama should get back, be sure and tell 'er. The boys should be okay and we won't be gone long," Thena said.

Elsa nodded and stood.

"Lilli n' I are goin' on to sleep. See you folks later," she said.

It is strange, the freedom we felt in those days. It is strange, the power that both Thena and Reed had over life and death. Not a power, I believe, that allowed them to control either life or death, but the power to be oblivious to either, to both. When they were together, there was Thena and there was Reed; everything else was unsubstantial—an apparition. Thena hooked her arm through Reed's and the two of them floated away into the pale November night. I almost thought that I could see a faint halo of light spreading out from them—a vague, burning intensity emanating from their hands and faces. They walked on ahead of us, their laughing voices clinking like china. I fell into step with Pope and watched the cool mystery of their levitation. We walked quietly behind them, passing into the woods toward the river, hands behind our backs, both feet on the ground.

"Has Dan shown up yet?"

I shook my head.

"Do you think he might be gone for good this time?"

"No. I wouldn't think so. Mama's too good a cook." I smiled.

"I heard word that he was stayin' with his woman across the river. They say there are several children."

I nodded. "Mama sends food to her."

"She does what?!"

"Yeah, she sends food to her—a whole basket, every week. You know Dan doesn't do anything for 'em. I guess Mama just figures they're gonna go hungry if she doesn't feed them herself. She never delivers it in person and she never sends word of who it's from. I guess Dan's woman thinks it's Dan sendin' it, and that'd be just as well."

"Gracie, maybe he's done messin' with y'all. Maybe he's gone for good this time."

I shook my head. "He'll come back when he takes a notion to. Sometimes he's gone for months, but he always shows back up. Dan Brown isn't strong enough to stay with us and he isn't strong enough to leave us. He can't do one or the other, so he does both." I shrugged. "It's his nature and a man's nature doesn't change—unless he wants it to. Even then, it takes work—hard work—and Dan's never been much of a worker, unless you count workin' his way through a whiskey bottle."

I grinned over at him. He smiled sadly and gave a troubled laugh.

"I wish you'd stop being so philosophical about him," he said. "You shouldn't just accept it; it's the same as sayin' 'let him do his worst.'"

"Pope, what is it that you wont me to do? It isn't my choice, it's Mama's. I can't make him leave. Mama has to. She knows he's bad news. She knows he had'n ever brought anything on us but trouble, and she still doesn't make him go. I reckon I might as well be philosophical about it—I don't have a say. Anyway, let's not talk about him anymore. It's too pretty a night to let him spoil it. He's gone for now, so why worry about 'im? There'll be plenty of worryin' to be done when he gets back."

Pope sighed.

We passed through the woods and began to climb uphill, both of us silent, Thena and Reed splitting the still night with their raucous laughter. As we reached the crest of the hill, I realized, with a quickening in my chest, that we had arrived at the old train bridge.

"Athena Kelley, what are we doin' here, and God please don't let it be what I think it is!"

"You're such a chicken," she said, dancing up to me. She threw her arms around me and stooped to kiss my forehead and nose. She took my hands and led me to the edge of the bridge and reached out to place her hand on the railing.

"No, Thena," I said, "this isn't bravery or courage, this is stupidity. This bridge is a hundred feet high if it's a foot and we don't know what could be down there in the river, just waitin' for us to land on and crack our heads wide open."

She did a little dance around me, pirouetting.

"Don't do this fool thing. If you wont mischief, let's look for it somewhere else. Why don't you go cover the minister's windows in cow patties, if you want—but don't do this."

"I've already done cover'd the minister's windows. What would be the fun in doin' it again? 'Sides, I'm perty sure he knows who did it the last time. Lately he's been lookin' at me like I'm a sinner."

"You are a sinner."

"Yeah, but not for decoratin' the preacher's house with cow pies. There's nothin' sinful about a little shit, Gracie-darlin'. I'm perty sure that the baby Jesus hisself must a let one in his swaddlin' clothes at some point."

I thought it better to pass over the second comment.

"It's not the cow pies that the minister minds. It's that you like adornin' his house with 'em."

She stripped off her dress and pulled off her shoes. Pope cleared his throat, embarrassed, and turned back into the trees. Reed chuckled and began to unbutton his shirt.

"Thena, you're a hypocrite and a fool. Not half an hour ago you got on to me for not havin' shoes on. Now you're runnin' around in yer birthday suit and about to jump into a freezin' cold river in November."

"Don't worry Grace, I promise I'll put my shoes back on soon as I get done swimmin'."

Reed howled with laughter.

"You jump off this bridge and into that freezing water, and *if* you live, and I'm not sayin' you will, you're gonna have pneumonia, or worse, and that'll just be one more thing for Mama to worry about."

"Grace, stop it. I've already got one mother and I don't need another. I need a sister. If you cain't be that then just go o'an home. You're always so busy tellin' people right from wrong and orchestratin' their lives that I'm wonderin' if you'll ever have one of yer own. I'm not gonna get sick or hurt and nothin' bad is gonna happen. Hell ain't gonna open up and swallow me whole—least not tonight," she said, grinning at Reed with her devil's grin.

"It's jes' a lil' jump off a lil' bridge, Grace, and then I'm gonna swim out and we'll go home. And that's it. It id'n that complicated and there are worse things we could be doin'."

She looked over at Reed with a salacious smirk and turned her back to me. She stood naked in the wind, her eyes closed and her head thrust back, both hands extended up over the water. Reed watched, immobile, unbreathing. For a long moment she stood motionless, breathing slowly, her long hair flying wild and free in the razor sharp wind. I shivered at the terror and holiness of her beauty. God himself had certainly made her. Fearful and angry, I stuck my hands deeper into the pockets of my sweater.

"Thena, stop this right now. It's not funny anymore. It never was funny. You put your knickers back on right this minute."

I picked up her dress and moved to her side, holding the dress out for her to take. Taking her arm, I pled with her with my eyes to step away from the edge. She looked over at me for a long moment and slowly, very slowly, she began to smile. Her lips parted and her white teeth flashed. She leaned toward me and, putting her face up close to mine and touching my cheek, she said,

"What is it you're so afraid of all the time? Dyin' cain't be any harder than living is, Grace Canton Kelley."

I grabbed her wrist.

"There's no way it can hurt any more. In fact, it might be just the easiest thing we ever do. This—" she said, gesturing down to the river below, "there's no more terror in this than gettin' married or carryin' a child. Mama—all women—do it over and over, and it makes them weaker every time, but they keep right o'an with it. Have you ever wondered why, Grace?" she whispered, her voice so low I wasn't sure that

I really heard what she said. "That act, of giving birth, it just might take yer life. But at that moment, that moment right before you fall, that's the most alive you're ever gonna be."

She gave me a wink, wrenched her wrist from my hand and jumped.

From a long way off I heard a woman's scream. It must have been my own. Pope rushed to the bridge railing and Reed stood looking white and frightened, as if, all along, he had thought Thena didn't mean to go. My limbs felt limp and bloodless. I turned to see Pope pull his shirt over his head and watched as he kicked his shoes away and pulled his trousers down.

"Pope Barrett, what are you doin'? No! I don't see how you goin' and getting' yourself killed is gonna help us."

"Gracie, climb down to the riverbank, quick as you can, only don't fall."

"Reed, go for help—my daddy if you can find 'im. Mrs. Simms is havin' a baby tonight, I reckon you'll find him there."

Reed turned and raced away, never looking back. Pope met my eyes and then jumped off the bridge. I watched him fall toward the water below.

I strained my eyes, hoping to see some sign of Pope as he fell toward the river. The night was so dark that everything below me was shut out. I listened to the faint rustling sound as he fell through the black night sky, isolated and alone, through the total darkness, down to the water below. It was a night too dark to sustain your belief in the moon.

I scooped Thena's dress up from the bridge and began to climb down the side of the river wall. Within seconds, I was covered in sweat and mud. When I reached the bottom of the steep hillside, my dress was torn, my legs, arms, and face cut and bleeding. My eyes scanned the banks for signs of life. I couldn't see anything. I walked along the bank, shivering and frightened, holding my breath. Tears filled my eyes and slid down my face. I wiped them angrily away with the grimy palms of my hands.

Then from the water I heard movement and, turning, I saw the vague shadow of a human body—a woman's body.

"I wuz wonderin' when you were gonna see fit to amble down here and bring me my dress. I've been paddlin' around here in this freezin' water for Lord knows how long."

I gulped back a sob and stumbled down the bank and into the water, holding Thena's slip up over her head so that she could slide into it.

"Have you seen Pope?"

"Yeah," Thena laughed, "he passed by a while ago. I didn't have any clothes on at th' time, so I didn't greet 'im."

"You didn't seem to mind not havin' clothes up there on the bridge."

" *I* wasn't worried, but I knew Pope Barrett would turn so red that I'd be able to see it even in the dark, so I didn't speak up. I cain't believe you let him jump in after me! What's wrong with you? I told you that nothin' was gonna to happen to me. I'm too young for dyin'."

"You are an idiot. There are lots of people younger'n you that are dead and gone, and for much better reasons than jumpin' off of bridges. If you're gonna die for something, you oughta choose what's well worth the risk. Why is it that you think you can do whatever you want, Thena Kelley? The laws of nature bind the rest of us, but not you?"

"What're you so mad about, Grace? It was just a little late night swimmin'. Once yer in for a while the water's not so bad."

"You're a fool."

I threw her dress at her and stormed off. I walked north along the river and met Pope running back.

"Gracie, I can't find her."

"She's just fine. Right as rain n' naked as the day she was born. I'm goin' home."

"Gracie, what is it?"

"I'm goin' home, Pope. 'Nite."

"Wait up a minute and I'll walk you." Pope followed and we walked southwest back through the woods toward home.

"She alright?"

"Is she ever otherwise?"

"I guess not. I better find Reed and Daddy. If they get to the river and don't find any of us, they'll probably be pretty scared."

I nodded and moved on without looking back.

"'Nite, Gracie. Gracie?"

XXI.

Not all of our days together were shot through with bright lights of horror, glory, sorrow or ecstasy. There were quiet days. I am sure that there were. Nearly seventy years later, they are difficult to recall. There are thousands of days between Then and Now, and we remember so very few of them, in spite of our best efforts. It is, of course, the fantastical moments that we remember best.

I remember the times that were lit up with brilliant colors, the days that were writ large across the sky, the moments of great passion and desire and terrible anger, the moments when I cried or when I laughed until I peed myself. I remember moments when I was at my very best and, with compunction and stillness inside of me, I still recall the moments when I was at my worst.

Time passes. The movement of days, months and years has always amazed me. They go by and our lives change. Often the changes are subtle, and we are unaware of them until the metamorphosis is complete. As a young woman, I was becoming old all along—completely unaware of the movement of time until it had already moved on, waiting for me to catch up with it.

I can still feel the great strength of my body as it was then, and I marvel at it, realizing that, if I were now faced with that same life, those same sorrows and joys, I wouldn't be able to live through it. I don't have the strength in me anymore. I look at my old-woman hands and remember when they were young and able. I remember days when I touched my babies with them, and my husband, and when I used their complete capability to go about the work of my life. They were once lovely, slim and slight and, for a farm girl, quite pretty. They tremble now. They are brown with the grime of the ages; scarred and calloused, their once smooth surface marred by the protrusion of strangely shaped and colored veins, like a mess of untrammeled ivy. I stare at them occasionally, unable to recollect how they passed from one to the other.

There were certainly days of utter ordinariness. There were days where I hung clean laundry on the line and took Lilliana on long walks or played with her in the shade of the yard for hours. There were, of course, many days of simple, hard work; days spent with Reed and Pope, with Netta and Campbell, with Mama. There were summer days of tromping through the woods and running along the river and sitting under the trees with a book in hand. There were days when Pope and I walked by the river, his hands in his pockets, head down; my hands behind my back, head to the sky. Of course there were. But, as hard as I try, I cannot picture many of them clearly.

I see through a mirror, dimly. When I think of those days, my mind sees them as taking place in the autumn. The colors of the fall seemed more brilliant then than they do now. I often wonder why this is. Perhaps because I was young and there was, in spite of all of our troubles, such a sense of possibility. Hope was thick in the air, and we breathed in the life and health of it and it gave us the gift of vitality. When I was young, fall was a prelude to and promise of the spring. Now it warns of the approaching end.

≈ ≈ ≈

Toward the end of November, I turned sixteen; Pope turned eighteen two days later. Two weeks after that, the Japanese bombed Pearl Harbor. The following day, Pope drove to the war office and volunteered. More than two weeks passed before he told me. I think I was the very last person in town to find out.

I was primarily concerned with the costumes for the Christmas pageant on that particular Sunday, worrying that Elsa and I were behind in our work. She had volunteered to do all of the sewing and had coaxed me into helping her, in spite of the fact that I secretly disliked the lady-likeness of this activity.

I had been up for several hours working on the costumes and left off for a time to go to church with Thena, Elsa, Lilliana and the boys. Mama had left some time before church to fix breakfast for Mrs. Rachel. After the service, we walked into the churchyard. I saw Pope and Reed standing by the red doors of the building. Pope nodded to us, nudged Reed on the shoulder, and moved in our direction.

"Have you heard what happened?"

His voice was soft and sad and angry all at once. My heart sank low as a stone. I shook my head.

"The Japanese have bombed a military base in Hawaii. Nobody had any idea it was comin'. We didn't stand a chance. Thousands dead, even women. The base was slaughtered. Now we're gonna have to enter the war."

I shivered.

"Will there be another draft?"

Pope studied my face for a long moment, and then he nodded.

"I think so," he said softly.

That was all; we didn't say anything else. We headed toward home. One cold, clear afternoon, about two weeks later, Pope strolled into the yard as I took down the cold, stiff clothes from the line. A laundry basket was balanced one on hip, Lilliana on the other.

"Go for a walk with me?"

I nodded. "Let me take in the clothes and the baby."

Pope held out his arms to Lilliana and walked me into the house.

"Get a coat. It's too cold for you to be dressed that way," he said, nodding to my cotton dress.

We walked down the gravel road toward Netta and Campbell's house.

"Gracie, I need to tell you something."

I waited without speaking. Looking back on it, I suppose I had known all along.

"I volunteered a little over two weeks ago. I leave for training in a week. In a month or two, I reckon I'll be somewhere in Europe. Daddy has a friend that works as a medic and he's asked that I be placed in his unit. Daddy told him that if I could stitch up my own head I could probably be of use to the soldiers."

He half-smiled grimly, looking at me out of the corner of one eye. I didn't respond. We walked to Netta and Campbell's house without speaking. I knew that if I spoke, I would cry; Pope must have known it, too.

Sweet Netta answered the door and, putting an arm around each of us, swept us into the cramped, over-heated front room, saying firmly,

"Well, I heard from yer Mama that you'll be leavin' soon. And I don't like it one bit, but since it's fixin' to happen anyway, I reckon we had better get some meat on yer bones afore you go. I jest don't think you'll find much to eat while yer off fightin', so's you might as well eat while there's eatin' to be done. I jest finished bakin' some coconut pies and was thinkin' I'd have Campbell drive me over, but here y'are. Grace is too thin anyways, and she oughta eat a whole pie on 'er own. After she's started off with that fer a snack, I'll cook y'uns up a *real* meal."

To the southern woman, food covers over a multitude of sins; if there is a problem, it can be fixed—but only with the right food. Evidently, coconut pies work well for war.

Campbell sat by the fire in his rocker, smoking a pipe and reading his newspaper. Pope sat down in the adjoining rocker and I sank onto the hearth. Campbell laid aside his paper, shaking his head.

"They're sayin' the woar'll be over in jest a few weeks, but I'll be dad-gummed if I buy into that line agin. Roosevelt's a good 'nough man, in some ways, though I'm not sure if you'n trust a democrat to tell the truth 'fore the Almighty Hisself. It's 'is wife I don't trust—runnin' around n' stickin' her nose into this n' that n' th' other." Here he waved his hand toward three corners of the room. "She's goin' hither n' yon, not worryin' a fiddler's fuck what she stirs up. Anyhow," he continued without taking a breath, "I think somebody in Washin'ton id'n tellin' the truth. I say we'll be in this woar for a year, if it's a day."

"Campbell, I think we best talk about somethin' else, darlin'," Netta said gently.

"Humppphh."

That moment was a remarkable one—one of the only funny moments of the war. During Campbell's evisceration of Eleanor Roosevelt, I mysteriously succumbed to a terrible fit of coughing and hurried out into the yard for a breath of fresh air. I have done a good bit of research into the meaning of the phrase about the fiddler, asking many old-timers for its definition—spelling the word, of course—and have never encountered another soul who knew what it meant. I once asked Grandma King about it, some years after Campbell had passed away. She turned very red and asked me where I had heard such filth.

"Campbell said it about Eleanor Roosevelt, of course."

"Girl, what an imagination you have! My daddy wuz a good, church-goin' man. He couldn't've said any such thang."

Whether he could have or not, he certainly did.

≈ ≈ ≈

Pope left on a Saturday morning. A sloppy, half-frozen sludge fell from the sky and the whole world was the color of soot. I walked with Doc, Nora and Pope to the station. I stood back as Nora and Doc whispered their good-byes to their only child. Tears streamed down Doc's face, but he didn't bother to wipe them away. Nora, distracted and half-frantic, listed off all of the things that Pope shouldn't forget. Doc handed Pope a leather-bound book of the poems of John Donne. Then the two of them stepped back, Nora reaching up to place her arm around Doc's shoulder, and Pope moved to stand before me.

"Gracie…"

I looked up, wanting to speak, wanting to say all of the things that needed saying. Incapable.

"Gracie…" He took my hand and held it tightly. "I—there are so many things to say—" He shook his head. "Things I meant to tell you."

His eyes were plaintive and I noticed for the first time the gauntness of his face and the dark smudges of sleeplessness underneath his eyes. His cheeks and jawbones jutted out from the solitary plains of his face.

"I kept thinkin' there would be time. I thought—I thought that there would be hours n' hours to say everything that needed sayin'. And then it passed by so quickly and I couldn't say it all, Gracie."

"Say it when you get back, Pope Barrett," I said softly, my voice full of weeping.

He nodded and put his arms around me. He held me so tightly. He was so full of life, so strong; yet his mortality clung to him like the broadcloth of his shirt. I clutched at him and tears slid out from my closed lids. I kissed his cheek and, just as I pulled away, he slid an envelope into my hand.

"I'll write you so many letters that you won't be able to keep up with 'em. And stay out of trouble." He smiled faintly. "This letter is the first. Write me back…oh, and Gracie, try and write legibly for once in your life. And you stay away from Dan, and tell him to stay away from you. And no more tusslin' in the yard. You're too old a girl to still be bullyin' the boys."

He winked, still looking sad, and turned. Just as he moved away, I called to him,

"Pope Barrett, you're the best friend I ever had."

And then he was gone. There was no looking back and no waving from the window of the train. Without waiting for it to pull out of the station, I walked away.

At home, I sat down on the top step of the porch, shivering in the December wind, tore open the envelope and unfolded the letter.

Dearest of All Graces Most Dear:

I am packing up my life into one small bag and preparing to travel to only God knows where. Mother has been racing around and has tried to enclose most of the contents of our house into my knapsack. She is scared, and when she is most scared she can only concentrate on practicalities, details. She can only do the things that don't ultimately matter because she can't stand to think of the things that do. Until I leave, she will be brusque and seemingly distant, and she won't realize what has happened until I am somewhere in the middle of the ocean. Daddy hasn't said anything for days. He sits in his armchair and stares out the window. He fought in the Great War and has never, in my whole life, said a word about it. He can't seem to say anything about this war, either, and that's okay. Daddy is Daddy and Mother is Mother and we will all get through this the best we can.

How will you get through it, Gracie? Your way of dealing with things is to act like they don't exist—and yet, silent though you generally are, you have never been so silent as you have since that day when I told you that I volunteered. You seem almost angry with me, yet I know that you aren't. You couldn't be. Or if some part of you is, you at least understand that I have to go. I can't very well stay here and you couldn't love me if I did. I have often found myself thinking lately that if you could, you would go, too.

I don't understand war. I never have and won't pretend to. But there are people, a great many of them, that are going to die if we don't fight—it looks as if there will be even more than if we do—and I can't stand the thought of keeping myself alive at the expense of standing idly by. How on earth could I let other people die just so I can live? And I if I did, what kind of life would that be?

Gracie, I will come back. I have loved you my whole life, even before we knew each other. I loved you when you were seven and I used to watch you and Thena walking home after school. I loved you when you were ten and I watched you give your lunch to John Michael every day so he could have more to eat. I loved you that day at the river. You were furious with those boys for picking on me. Your eyes were flashing, bright as lightning, and you had that deep line between your eyebrows—the one you only get when you're spitting mad. I have loved you every minute, every second for as far back as I can remember and never once have I said it out loud. I have to come back so that I can say it to you.

Pope

P.s. Take care of yourself while I am away and try not to jump off of any bridges. It really hurts when you hit the water. Write to me when you think of it.

XXII.

The first weeks and months after Pope left were quiet. I worked at the library, played with Lilliana, helped Mama, who was nearing the end of her term, and looked after the boys. I filled my days with work, both menial and physical, hoping not to think or remember. I looked forward to letters from Pope with both dread and delight. The delight was for obvious reasons; the dread came from the immanent place that he occupied in my mind and all of my thoughts for many days after the arrival of his letters. I preferred to think of him as little as possible, knowing that if I thought of him, it would be only to worry, and that if I worried I would drive myself mad.

I have always thought that the positions of those who go off to war and those who remain at home are essentially quite the opposite of one another. The soldier who goes off to war thinks constantly of home. Home is the promise of a life after war. It is the existence of home that allows—compels—him to stay alive. For the soldier's mother or sweetheart or wife, to think of the soldier is to admit that he is gone, and to admit that he is gone is to admit that he might not come back.

Shortly after Pope's departure, both Jim and Ted volunteered and left for training. It was a house of women; soon it would be a town of women and old men. Doc weakly joked that, with all of the young men away, he had nothing to do; they were off breaking bones and carrying out their thoughtless acts of restlessness and recklessness in other countries, rather than in the quiet of our small town. During the years of the war, years spent in mourning the departure of his beloved son and best friend, Doc looked like an old man, tired and sore.

It was during the years of the war that I became a serious student. Since the time of my accident, when I had gone to live with the Barrett's for a time, I had, of course, dabbled in my studies. I was interested enough, and my marks were above average, but I was not passionate. It was during the war years that I received the highest marks in the subjects I was traditionally worst at. I would literally spend hours pouring over one problem in calculus. This was representative of all the problems in the material world that I was struggling with. The difference was that I would eventually master calculus. I would solve it. Life, I never could solve. In fact, the longer I have lived, the less solving I have done.

As a girl, the world was straightforward to me. Right and wrong were self-evident; good and evil were easily identified. Now I marvel at my childish self-assuredness and moral audacity. I was so cock-sure, so knowing. How? Why? What happened? As an old woman, I now see that right and wrong are *not* always self-evident, and that good and evil are *not* so very dichotomized as they were to me then. I have finally learned that sometimes it is okay not to know—sometimes it is better to just shut up and wait and listen. But that lesson was a long time in coming.

At any rate, after Pope left and the U.S. entered into that terrible war, I studied the concepts of chemistry and physics and calculus until they were emblazoned in my mind. I can still remember the formulas and equations quite well. I worked until late at night, pulling the worn and weary oak table before the purple flames of the fire, my head in both hands, my back bent and body hunched forward, my eyes straining to see the letters on the page. Studying kept my mind engaged and worked to weary my body enough for dreamless sleeping. It was an adequate preoccupation for me; an insurmountable obstacle I was determined to surmount.

In February, Mama gave birth to a son. She named him Isaac, calling him the child of her old age. Isaac was her last baby, and she spent more time nursing and holding him than I remember her ever spending with the rest of us. I suppose that she must have known she wouldn't have any more. Sometimes I have wondered if she knew what was coming. Mama always did know a lot; I wouldn't be surprised.

I continued receiving occasional letters from Pope, usually several at once. I can't imagine that, amidst the chaos of war, a sophisticated system of correspondence was easy to design or implement. It seemed that he put pen to paper often enough, but it was not often that I received what he had written. So many years later, I still have his letters. They are distinctly carved onto the soft limestone tablets of my memory. Having read them so many times during the years of his absence, I can remember most of them word for word. I often marvel that I have difficulty remembering little things—where I put my glasses, or my birthday, or where SoHo is in relation to the apartment I lived in for so many years on the rim of Washington Square—and yet, I can still remember the exact color of Thena's hair and the sentences of nearly every conversation I ever had with Adda.

A few months after Pope left, I saw a beautiful gentlemen's toiletries set in the window of a shop in town and, with what little money Mama had forced me to tuck away for myself from my work at the library, I bought the set and mailed it to Europe, along with some chocolates wrapped in brightly colored paper. Many weeks later—in June, in fact—I received his letter.

May, 1942

Dearest:

After half a year of life in the army, you, my kind-hearted Gracie, have sent me an ivory and silver brush, comb and shaving set. I can see very clearly in my imagination that you must have seen it and, being struck by the "deprivations" that we soldiers are living through (and because you are truly one of the most thoughtful people in the world and the best of Graces), bought for me what have must have cost you very dearly—purchasing with meager funds this gift fit for a king, on the off chance that I might have a moment to brush my hair or trim my whiskers amidst the dropping of bombs and the flinging of hand grenades (I know, a bad joke).

Although, I must admit to you that I have been somewhat negligent of my toilet until this point, I can assure you that, with such beautiful accoutrements of good Christian tidiness, I will spend at least two minutes of every day beautifying myself for my comrades and fellow sufferers of the hardships of war. It seems the least we can do to comfort our wives, mothers, lady friends, etc.: we may not be entirely safe, but, by God, we shall be clean!

As for the chocolates: ah, the chocolates. They were smelt from the first instant they were brought into the camp and lasted only several minutes after I cut the string away from the package. For just a moment, I considered sprinting away to some quiet hiding place to save every last one of them for myself, until I opened the second part of the gift and it occurred to me that I would soon be the tidiest fat man ever to serve his country. That would not do.

In the end, I decided to share with the others and I tasted only one piece myself. But I swear to you, it tasted as if my Gracie her own, dear self had made it and sealed its perfection with a kiss. What's more, after the chocolates were passed around, honesty compels me to tell you, there were made to you several offers of marriage from handsome young soldiers! One particularly dashing soldier, with a fine mustache, eyes of cerulean blue and limitless charm implied that a large diamond ring would be included in the deal. I leave the matter entirely up to your discretion and would be quite happy to act as go-between to any interested parties. You can think of me as your telepathic transcontinental matchmaker.

I have heard often from Mother and Daddy. They have kept me informed of the town news. Mother says that she ran into Elsa and Lilliana the other day, and that Elsa looked so pretty and happy, and that Lilliana is quite grown and not at all a baby anymore, but a little lady. Mother claims that she floats through the streets of our dusty town on a cloud of angelic beauty and that her little elegant clothes are handmade by Elsa, and that they make her look like misplaced royalty. It is odd, the differences in how men and women communicate: Daddy would have written, "Saw Elsa and the little girl the other day. She's a pretty little thing and her mama is, too. They both seem healthy and well." And, really, man though I am, I prefer Mother's descriptions, because when she writes, I can see all of you so clearly and you don't seem nearly so far away.

I am not too lonely, and if I were there wouldn't be much time to think about it. Weeks pass so rapidly. We work all hours of the day and night, and as soon as we are done sewing one up there are three to replace him. There hasn't been much time for resting or letter writing. In between surgeries I mostly sit playing cards with the other medics. There is one in particular that I spend most of my free minutes with. His name is Adam Donovan O'Neill and he's from Tallulah, Louisiana. He has four freckle-faced sisters who send him letters by the truckload. We work together in surgery every day, sewing up and disinfecting wounds, taking care of fevers and dysentery. Sometimes we lose men, but oftentimes we don't.

After having done this work for five months, I am convinced that when this is all over and I come home, I want to go to medical school. I am good at this, Gracie, and I feel useful and as if I belong in the infirmary. When I am working on those injured men, I feel that my hands are finally touching what they have been aching for my whole life. Sometimes, late at night when I sit and watch them sleep, I feel that I could never do anything that mattered more. Some of them are seriously wounded. Most of the time just having somebody that cares whether or not you make it will make the difference between living and dying.

Does it seem strange to you, Gracie—the idea of Pope Barrett turning out like his old man? To tell you the truth, there isn't anyone in the whole world I'd rather be like—but you are sworn to absolute secrecy, or I'll never hear the end of it.

I am sitting at my small, cramped writing desk, which I estimate to be at least six inches too short for me. Next to me sits my brush, comb, shaving cup, razor and manicure instruments. It is a fine set, Gracie. Too fine for me. Some man on Fifth Avenue wearing wing-tips, gold cufflinks and a double breasted, pin-striped suit ought to be using it; not some scruffy, muddy soldier who can't even manage to smooth out his cow-licks and wouldn't know how to look good if he needed to.

My fine new silver brush speaks softly in my ear. It says that it thinks of you every day. Every single minute of every day. The comb whispers that it dreams of you at night. The soft hairs of the shaving brush miss your shining green eyes and your soft silvery moonlit laugh. Evidently, the manicure set most misses your soft, gentle hands. Don't ask me, Gracie—I'm just writing what I've been told to.

I think that, in celebration of my extravagant gift, I will go and have a shave. Take care of everyone for me, Gracie. Stop in and see Mother and Daddy from time to time. They think of you as their own child and, with one gone, the other is all the more important. Don't let Daddy overwork himself. Keep your temper in check and no more shooting at your relatives, you cheeky girl! I

*will write to you every free minute of the day and will think of you
a thousand times more often. If you have any to spare, love me a
little.*

   Pope

The letters were both a blessing and a curse. Whenever I received
one, I remember thinking, *he was still alive when he wrote this.* I grew
angry with myself for these thoughts. They were morbid and made me
feel weak. But the plain truth was that we were receiving word daily of
the death of a boy we had known. At times, it seemed that there was
more dying than living going on. We heard word every day of battles lost
and won, of tragedy and destruction, and our boys were so very far away
that their fate and the fate of so many others became sometimes lost or
jumbled together in our minds.

To tell the truth, I did not visit Doc and Nora nearly as often as Pope
would have wanted me to during those years; they were too sharp a
reminder of Pope. When I was in their house, I felt that I would choke.
There was too much of his soul floating through the atmosphere of the
pretty rooms. He was so thick on the air that I couldn't breathe.

It was easier during the times when no letters came. When I did
receive letters he seemed so close to me—close enough to reach out and
touch; except that, when I did reach out, my fingers found nothing at all
to hold on to. I reached out for the solidity of him, the bulk and safety of
his strong body, and my hands returned to me empty. Every time a letter
came, the end of the war seemed further away.

XXIII.

It was near the end of 1942 that the restlessness and unyieldingness of Thena's nature became all but unmanageable. That is not to say that Thena could not manage it, because I believe that she could have; rather, the rest of us couldn't. There were times when she would listen to me, or nearly so, but I believe that Mama's gentle persuasion was no longer effective on the power and irrepressibility of Thena's disposition, which had been let to run free for far too long. There were also moments when Reed, with his pretty cajoling and white-teethed, sparkly-eyed enticement, was able to steer Thena toward a second, less destructive, and sometimes less reprehensible course of action. I will say, in Thena's defense (if there is a defense), that I believe there were two primary events which caused this final break between Thena and her better judgment, between Thena and her self-control, and ultimately, between Thena and Mama.

There is undoubtedly a good deal of religious hypocrisy among the devout, but Mama's life was truly an act of sincerity. Her faith was simple, and maybe misguided—I have never been able to decide—but unquestionably profound. It was real and determined all of her actions and reactions. It wasn't a coat wrapped around her to be taken off and hung upon a brass hook; it was the substance of her being, the adhesive that held together all of the inconsistencies of her nature and the tattered places in her soul.

While I, and everyone who saw her, was dazzled and sometimes blinded by Thena's brilliant, fiery audacity, I respected the solidity and constancy of Mama's goodness. Thena had the appearance of wholesomeness; Mama had more than the appearance. I turned to Thena when I needed to laugh and Mama when I needed to cry, to Thena when I wanted to sparkle and to Mama when I wanted to shine. I went to Thena when I needed to wonder and Mama when I needed to know.

Mama's soul was sweet and gentle and precious. Thena's sang, shouted, cried out and echoed off the mountains. Mama's heart was tender and limitless in its capacity to love. Thena's was turbulent, voracious in its appetites and tossed back and forth between two blazing suns, love and hate. And she was only capable of one or the other. She could not hate an action, but love the individual. When she loved, she loved person and action, even at times when the action did not deserve love. When she hated, she hated person and action, even at times when the person did not deserve hatred.

And so, Thena's determination and fearlessness made her more like Isabel than Mary. Though, while Isabel's determination was bent toward goodness and her fearlessness applied to what needed doing, Thena's determination was given to whatever she desired to do, and her fearlessness was often given to whatever others were afraid of doing. But the bright light that surrounded her, the force and power of her laughter and the ground-shaking vigor of her smiles came neither from Mary nor Isabel. Ah, that was all her own. It was Thena's gift to herself and the world and came from no one else.

More than half a century later, I still try to understand who I was in all of this. I don't think I know. Maybe I was somewhere between the two of them. I wished to be both at once, and was able to be neither. I had neither Mama's goodness, nor Thena's beauty. I didn't possess Mama's slow and deliberate wisdom or Thena's rapid cleverness. I never possessed Mama's hope nor Thena's vision; I could never have seen what she saw. I never had Mama's ability to love, nor would I ever have Thena's ability to hate.

I am a simple soul, composed of a few uncomplicated parts. I am neither angel nor devil. Neither Mary the mother of our Lord, nor Herod, sacrificing all of the Hebrew babies on the altar of his pride; more like a smelly, bleating, but lovable sheep, knelt in all the world's refuse at the foot of a manger. I was always just average; mediocre, even; sweet, maybe, but also just a little stupid; unknowing and unextraordinary.

Those of us who are not welcomed into either of these worlds—the gold-paved streets of the celestial realm, or the reeking stench and loneliness of the dark places of the damned—live in the partly cloudy limbo in between. We have neither the fantastic heat of summer nor the paralyzing cold of winter, but live cool lives in cool places. We live quietly sad, or quietly happy…but quietly.

I watched in the years during the war as the gap between them broadened. The fissures grew between where Mama's feet stood still and solid and where Thena's danced and stomped. They became chasms. And the chasms brought about the breaking apart of their one world into two. They drifted away into separate galaxies, on and on, until a universe stood between them.

And neither would be with us long enough to retrace the distance.

The first event that began the descent happened in the fall of '42. At that time, Dan had been "missing" for nearly a year; although, perhaps "absent" is a more accurate, less theatrical word. We would later understand that he had been *hiding* for a year. There were times when I thought of him, in an absent-minded sort of way, never doubting that he was right as rain, causing trouble for someone, somewhere. But I thought of him rarely, and only to hope that he would never come back.

But there came a day when he was unable to stay away any longer. Even Dan had some strange, though certainly skewed sense of honor; one windy night at the end of October, this was provoked in a way that must have forced his hand. Dan could treat his family shamefully, but no one else was allowed to. In fact, I think that, in some strange way, he may have even loved us a little.

I remember first noticing a strange rustling sound; it was as if great bunches of leaves were being swept by the wind through the rooms of our house. The sound of this sweeping floated somewhere just outside the reach of the lamplight of my conscious mind, hovering somewhere in that indefinable world between sleeping and waking. It was a vague and bothersome noise, and kept me from finding the deepest caves of sleep. I rolled to my other side, hoping to drift away from it.

Another moment passed and to the rustling there was added a crackling sound. Thinking that a log may have fallen from the fire, I stirred myself awake, trying to gauge whether or not the room was warm enough for me to get up and check that a log hadn't rolled out onto the solitary rug that lay before the fire. The crackling continued and, realizing that it wasn't going to go away on its own, I opened my eyes. There was a strange glow coming from the front room. The glow was deeper and farther-reaching than what was usually produced by our small fire.

Then I knew what it was.

"Thena, wake up! The house is on fire! Wrap the boys in their blankets n' get 'em outside! Thena, go! Don't waste any time, get 'em out!"

I burst through Mama's door. Elsa and Mama sat up, and Mama's feet were on the floor before the door had swung all the way open.

"Elsa, get your blanket and get Lilli and get out! Fire! Go! Mama, get Isaac—we have to get out of here now!"

I rushed to the cupboard and, without really thinking about what I was doing, seized a large stack of quilts. Racing back to the second room, I saw Thena carrying a frightened, sleepy Franklin Delano on her shoulder and pushing John and Edwin out before her. Following close behind, I saw that the front room was engulfed in flames. Shoving Thena and the boys out the door, I rushed into the yard, dropping all of Mama's quilts on the October leaves. Taking a single blanket, I dipped it in the rain barrel, smashing the thin layer of ice that lay across the top, and raced back into the house. I met Mama, Isaac, Lilliana and Elsa coming out.

"Grace Canton Kelley, don't you go in there!" I heard Mama shout over my shoulder as I rushed back in.

I worked frantically, beating at the hungry mouths of flame. The oppressive heat roared through the house like a powerful wind. Thena and Elsa rushed back into the room. Elsa, carrying a second wet blanket, worked alongside me, while Thena passed into the second room. After several seconds she returned, her arms loaded down with clothes, shoes and pillows. It dawned on me that she must have decided the house was beyond saving.

For a moment I dropped my blanket and, grabbing two wooden chairs, I tossed them out the front door. Next went Mama's rocker, then the kitchen table. Turning to Elsa I shouted,

"The mattresses! I'll stay n' keep it away from the door. Get the mattresses!"

Several seconds passed and I saw Elsa pass back into the blazing front room fiercely dragging a mattress under each arm. Next, Thena entered and I shouted to her to get Mama's mattress. A moment later she returned, pulling it through the doorway.

As morning came we sat, huddled in a cold, broken circle, wrapped in soggy blankets and covered in grime and soot. The bits and pieces of our life lay in heaps around us, and in the faint light of day, the chairs and table looked like the broken and rotting leftovers of a misguided carpentry project run-amok, or the fossils of some ancient civilization. I was amazed that we had continued to use them through so many years.

Bits of ash clung to my hair and face. Looking down at my hands, I saw that even the tiniest cracks were caked in black. My dress was soaked with sweat, and the pattern was no longer distinguishable, but had been stained by the ash and smoke and was now the color of loss.

Grandpa King stood over Mama with a hand on her shoulder as she rocked Franklin on one knee and Isaac on the other. Mama's face was dusted in soot, with thin trails of clean skin running through at intervals where tears had slid silently down her cheeks, washing the filth down onto the front of her nightgown. The ground and sky, the trees and the debris of dead leaves, the chimney of King House, the hill that rose to the south of us—all of it—had turned a sodden, weeping gray in the night, as if some angel of death had been sent to lay to rest all the world's color in the passing of a few short hours. None of us spoke. There was no sound; even the wind mourned too deeply for speech.

Grandma King held Lilli on one hip, looking grim.

"There's ain't no point in sittin' 'round here in th' dust. Come o'an up the hill way, an' let us cook y'all some breakfast. Things look bad now, but I reck'n most things look better on a full belly. We'll have some Johnny cakes, n' then we'll work this thang out," she said.

Later that morning, leaving the others asleep on Grandma King's parlor floor, I walked restlessly down the hill, across the dirt road and into the clearing where our house had stood only the night before. Seeing the faint glimmer of metal, I stooped and retrieved a tiny pewter jewel box given to Mama by my papa many years before.

Crouching among the rubble, I began sorting through the remains, hoping to find some of our few things in a partially usable state, knowing full well that Mama would have no money to replace the things that had been lost. I stripped off my coat, unbuttoned the two top buttons and the cuffs of my dress, and rolled the sleeves up to my elbows. I sorted through what little was left of the house, carefully lifting bits of still smoking timber.

I saw several small pieces of blackened tin and recognized them as the remains of our dishes. Walking back and forth, hunched forward, my eyes to the ground, I searched for the precious pieces of our past; the tiny, frail life we had built together. I felt strangely as if that life were dead—as if it had been buried in the night, and could never be retrieved. No matter how hard I tried to salvage it, it had floated away. I wondered what had been left in its place.

Hours passed. I continued to sift through what was left of the house. I found the blackened bones of Mama's brass bed, the bed she had set-up housekeeping with. It was partially melted, but I thought it might still serve as a bed frame. I hefted it from the pile and carried it to the edge of the yard. As I worked, I saw from the corner of my eye a bit of bright color and some movement. Straightening, I turned my body, one hand to my face. I saw a tall, thin man standing at the edge of a line of trees to the north of where the house had stood. I continued to gaze in his direction, waiting, vaguely aware that I had seen the man before.

"Howdy do," said the man.

I nodded, but didn't speak.

"I reck'n you n' I have 'ready had the pleasure a' meetin'. Name's Lucius Elder. Looks's if you folks done had some trouble."

I gave a second nod, my eyes never leaving his face. As I studied him, I felt quite sure that he had become thinner and uglier than when I had last seen him. His image, seventy years later, remains seared in my memory. The worst of my nightmares reveals his grim, spare face and the greenish pallor of his skin.

He tossed the stub of a cigarette into the ash and removed his hat, wiping sweat and grime away from his forehead, and then replaced it. From the breast pocket of his old coat he pulled a slim hand-rolled cigarette. I saw that the whites of his eyes were yellow and that his face and hands were the gray-green color of a Tennessee sky before a tornado. The hand that pushed his hat back down over his protruding skull trembled badly and, for the first time, I saw that his body was fading. The deadly color of his skin and the sharp jutting of his bones through his flesh gave him the look of a corpse. I thought that surely death must have been coming for him soon.

A shiver went through me. I stooped to retrieve my coat, pulling it tightly around me. Then, with a feeling of unease, I stooped to pick up Grandpa King's shovel.

"Mr. Elder, s'there somethin' I can help you with? As you can see, there are things here that need doin'..."

"Yeah, I reck'n maybe there is."

I waited tensely, my back stiff and straight.

"You'n give that daddy a' yers a message fer me."

"My daddy is no longer livin'. He died when I was still a baby."

Elder chuckled.

"I reck'n Dan Brown'd be plum hurt to hear you say that."

"I doubt it."

"You'n tell 'im fer me that he can try n' cheat me if he wonts to, but he's hurtin' more'n just hisseff."

Taking a step in my direction, he nodded once toward the ruins of our home. I watched, feeling the blood drain from my face. He removed his hat and wiped sweat from his brow again and, flicking the remains of his second cigarette into the ash, he turned his body to face me. He studied me for a long moment, his eyes holding mine, as his hand reached for his next cigarette. His cold eyes were beautiful, mesmerizing, deadly. He took the third cigarette from the rag pocket of his worn coat and bent to light it; then he put a trembling hand to his lips and inhaled deeply. I watched him dully, my body feeling small and cold. His eyes never left my face. A slow smile spread over his broad white lips.

"You're a real spitfire, aren'tcha, gurl? I reck'n you're the one they say prett'near killed Ol' Dan. Hell, if I took a mind to kill 'im m'seff, you jes' might help me."

"I wouldn't count on it, mister."

"Why not?" His eyes burned, wicked, hypnotic, coaxing. "Wouldn't you like to have Dan over'n done with, so's he cain't make no more messes of anybody's life?"

"His life isn't mine to take, nor yours neither."

Lucius snorted and the snort became a laugh. The laugh became a cough and the cough grew. Sweat streamed down his face and, putting both hands to his chest, he bent and spat upon the ground a thick stream of fluid the color of blood.

"He's poison. He never brought you er yer perty lil' mama nothin' but bad n' he never will."

I nodded. "You're probably right. I've never been too sweet on Dan, and that's no secret. But you know what I think, mister? I'm pretty sure that standin' next to you, Dan'd look like Father Christmas and a fairy godmother all wrapped up together in one bright package. And would you like to know somethin' else? I'd rather spend an eternity walking arm in arm upon the streets o' gold with Dan than the briefest glimpse of a moment in old Sheol with you."

Lucius threw his cigarette onto the scorched grass and walked toward me. I stretched the shovel toward him, crouching. He was on me in a moment, wrenching the shovel from my grasp. With one hand, he bent my right arm tightly behind my back, the other hand closed around my throat. He pressed his body against mine. I could smell the sweat and alcohol on him, and the sickly sweet smell of disease.

"You got an awful smart mouth fer such a lil' thing. But yer not quite right. You think Dan's a bad man, but not as bad as me? Well, I could tell you thangs that would make you think otherwise. You ever wonder'd who that woman is you been keepin' at yer mama's house all this time? You ever asked y'seff where she come from? How she knowed Dan? Where'd that baby a' hers come from? I'm pert'sure if you looked into it, you'd find her name's Elsa Brown."

He smiled at me, slightly relaxing his hold on my neck.

"Brown?" I whispered.

"Ye-uh, Brown," he said.

I studied his face, terrified. Wondering if I should struggle, if I should try to run, if he would kill me, and if what he said was true.

"I don't understand," I whispered.

He put his lips to my ear and said softly, "She's Dan's sister—half sister." He smiled, pressing his body closer. "The lil' gurl's Dan's, sure 'nough, but the nature a' the relationship's somewhat muddled. What you think should the little gurl call 'im?"

He straightened and took his hand from my throat, dropping both hands to his side. Stepping back, he watched me, his eyes calm, his posture relaxed.

"You'n tell Dan somethin' fer me. Tell 'im I said he can pay what he owes me, or more accidents might be liable to happen. Tell 'im I'd hate fer anything to happen to his perty lil' gurls." He grinned and pointed a slim white finger toward the heap of ash.

"An' next time, I reck'n it'll be accidents on his person, er maybe yers, even."

He raised his hat in a gesture of mock gallantry and gave a wink.

"Mister," I rasped, a hand to my throat, "I'm not sure what Dan has done to you, and frankly, I don't much care; looks to me like you n' Dan deserve one another; but if you want to hurt him, don't come after me. You hurt me, Dan'll throw you a party and invite all your kin."

His features spread in a slow smile.

"You n' yer daddy ain't much friendly?"

"Again, he isn't my daddy, and no, we aren't much friendly."

"I don't blame you fer not likin' 'im. He id'n much 'count."

"Nah, he isn't, but I find it strange that you don't like 'im; I never would have counted you for much, either. I would'a thought he would be just about your type."

Elder's smile faded.

"Gurl, I ain't got no quarrel with you…yet. Jes' tell'm like I told you."

"I haven't seen Dan in almost a year. He doesn't live with us anymore. You can tell him yourself, and give him my best. I've got work to do."

I stooped and, retrieving my shovel with trembling hands, I returned to digging in the ash. Sweat streamed in small rivers down my back. My heart pounded in my ears. I was cold with fury and weak with fear. The hairs on the back of my neck stood on end. I continued to shovel. Elder stood for a long moment watching me, smiling.

He gave a low soft whistle.

He took one small step toward me, his eyes traveling over my body.

"Do's I say, gurl; I ain't a nice man," he said softly.

Then, tossing down his cigarette among the smoldering embers and laughing, he walked away.

XXIV.

Dearest Pope:

I saw your daddy some time back. He told me that he had received word of you, and that you were in Africa, somewhere up north. Doc said he thought you were there trying to clean up the mess the Fuhrer left behind. Now, it seems you are in Italy, near the mountains—and that's all he knows. I hear word of what happens on the radio and on the newsreels; although, of course, the news I am getting is several weeks old. By the time I hear of it, the wounded have died or are healed up. Their limbs are long-since set and bound and you have fixed their bodies and, like the good Pope that you are, you have moved on to worrying about their lonely souls.

I sit in the dark of the picture house watching the planes and ditches and bombs. It's funny, but all of the soldiers smile as the cameras pan across the ranks. I wonder what it is that they have to smile about. I reckon that they smile for their mamas and daddies and sweethearts, because I just don't see that they could smile from joy or peace or anything like it. Most of them give this sort of half-grin, holding their cigarettes in place with the unmoving side of their mouths. Many of them give a carefree wave or do a quick-stepping jig, and still there's that cigarette, hanging on for dear life.

I wonder if you have taken up smoking. They say it calms the soldiers. I hope that you haven't; I don't like it and I think it's smelly. I have always liked your old, everyday Pope-smell of soap and water and starch, of the sun and sweat and long hours of hard work and the faint smell of your mama's house. Sometimes there lies in your smell the faintest tinge of the future. You have always smelled to me like tomorrow.

On Saturday nights, I go to the picture house, praying that one of those smiling faces I see will be yours. Somehow, every soldier that I see is you, or could be you, or was patched up by you, or saw you once from a distance, or owes their life to your healing hands, or protected you from falling shells.

I watch the screen and find myself praying. I don't guess I've ever been much of a prayer. It always seemed like Mama did enough for all of us. And anytime I thought Mama just couldn't pray any more, she was on her way to pray over something else. Anyway, it never seemed like my prayers were needed when hers were floating up by the thousands—Mama's beautiful prayers, straight on into the hands of God. If I was God, and I had to chose between listening to Mama or to Grace, I'd choose Mama every time.

Lately, though, I pray because I have to, or I won't be able to sit in my seat another minute, or lace my shoes, or sweep the floor, or hold Lilliana, or sing her to sleep, or hug the boys, or wait up for Mama, or believe that anything will be good again. I pray to believe that someday soon, in the fall, when the leaves are crimson and gold (do you remember how the maples turn that strange pink-orange color, just before they fall?), and the pumpkins are ripe and frosty, and it's time to take out that old thick, dark blue sweater-coat of yours, you will be here again and I can walk with you through the fields, or we can race through the heaped up leaves, and I will beat you.

It is very late now and I must sleep. But don't you worry, Pope Barrett, I will see you in tomorrow.
With all the love that is in me,
  Gracie.

≈ ≈ ≈

The recovery from the fire (to whatever extent we would recover) was slow. It would be some weeks before Mama or the younger boys would venture down to the ruins. Thena, carrying Lilliana at her hip, marched down the hill several hours after Lucius had departed. She sat Lilliana on the ground, chucked her under the chin and, rolling up her sleeves, she went to work. Tears streamed down her lovely fairy face as she sorted through the cooling black ash.

"All this silly mournin' over a house that weren't much better'n a hole in the ground to begin with. We been needin' a better place for a long time now and this is just the kick in the pants we were all waitin' around for," she said.

"I reckon I always liked our hole in the ground."

"Nah, it leaked and the fireplace was always blowin' smoke all through the house and it was too crowded for all of us by more'n a few rooms. I say good riddance."

"And now what?" I asked.

"Now we build a better'un."

"With what?"

"I'll think'a somethin'."

"I hope you're a quick thinker, 'cause we can't stay on indefinitely at King Farm."

She grinned over at me. "Lucky for you I *am* a quick thinker. I always have been."

"What'll we do?"

"I don't know right this minute, but it won't take me long. I'll work it out. It ain't a problem 'less it has an answer."

Thena and I were there most every day, working from dawn until dusk. Often, after the sun had set, we worked on in silence by the light of a small fire. Few words were spoken during those first days after the fire, but much was felt. Grandpa King came and worked silently beside us for nearly a week. If he felt the loss of our home to be a tragedy, he kept his thoughts to himself.

In the end, there wasn't much that could be retrieved; in truth, there had been nothing of value in the house to begin with. And yet, valuable or not, it had been ours. The loss of it felt much like a death, and would stay with us through our lives in just the same way.

One afternoon, about a week after the fire, Thena knocked on the mayor's study door. She went in and stayed a long time. As I dusted the china in Mrs. Rachel's parlor, I could barely hear the sound of their voices, soft and low, carrying down the hall. After what seemed like half an hour or more, the mayor's door opened and Thena stepped out into the hall. She gave me a small smile and winked, then returned to the back porch to her Thursday afternoon laundering.

Several days later, Mayor Wilkins came forward and said he wished to have all of us move into a house of his in the town. It was to be Mama's, for all of her life, as repayment for everything she had done for him and his wife and boy. Mama flushed dark red and shook her head, refusing to allow the mayor this act of charity.

"Oh, Mama!" said Thena, her eyes flashing, "Now don't be a silly, dither-headed ol' fool! I thaink we're just about past the point of sayin' no to handouts. 'Sides which, the mayor's right—if he were to give you keys to every house in the city, he could never repay you for all you've done for 'im. I reckon it's been a long time comin'."

Mama looked deeply upset but said nothing. The mayor watched Thena with his deep-set ferret's eyes. His faced burned sullen and red, his expression half sycophantic, half enraged. Thena flashed him a brilliant, garish smile—dripping wet with insolence.

She put an arm around Mama. "Thank you, Mayor Wilkins. It's real big a' you. We'll take it."

Eventually, after some argument, Thena and I persuaded Mama that there wasn't any other alternative for us, beyond being separated and sent to the houses of friends and relatives. It was only after Mama was made to see this that she began to relent.

On the day that we walked to the mayor's office to get the keys to our new house, there was a bright silvery-light in the air. Though the rest of us laughed and nearly danced with expectation, Mama remained silent. In the mayor's office, we all stared as he unlocked and opened a mahogany desk drawer and, pulling out the key, stretched his hand out toward Mama. Looking down at the floor, she quietly thanked the mayor, yet seemed unwilling to move forward and take the key from him. As if on cue, Thena strode forward, took the key from his hand, gave him a satirical bow and, scooping up Lilliana, danced away. Mama, Thena, Elsa, Lilliana and I walked, slowly and silently, the half-mile to our new home.

It stood on 7th Street, only a few yards from the road. It was tall and narrow; a white clapboard house with black shutters. On either side of it stood similar houses, cramped closely together—looking stiff and uncomfortable, like overgrown children piled into the backseat of a sedan—but neatly built. In back there was a small garden, wild and thick with bracken. It was enclosed with a split-rail fence, which needed painting.

The garden floor was covered with rose bushes growing in a hundred directions. There must have been fifty of them. All around them on the garden floor and peeking through the rails grew hundreds of tall, grubby dahlias, standing gallant and proud like disheveled southern gentlemen who had seen better days. Their arms were stretched out toward the sun and their faces smiled with peace.

I stood on the back stoop for a long time, watching them. They stood still in the light, looking refined and self-important. I expected that, at any moment, one might whisk out a clean white handkerchief—untouched by the trouble of the times—and tidy up its purple or mauve or orange suit coat and ask for a waltz, or quote Longfellow in an intoxicating, seductive drawl.

Since that time, dahlias have always been my favorite flower. They remind me of the Depression and the war years. They look sort of crooked-toothed and down on their luck—yet somehow full of promise and vigor and fight. They are the underdogs. They filled the garden and spilled haphazardly into our neighbor's yard, looking like they might make their unlikely comeback at any moment. I still root for dahlias.

In spite of the war and the absence of so many that we loved, and the bleak remembrance of all we had loved and lost and might lose still, these months were some of the happiest of my life. When we first saw it, the house was livable, at best; in the end, it would become a thing of great beauty. It would also primarily be a house of women. And, really, red-blooded, male-appreciating woman that I am, I think life is often quite beautiful without men around to make things dirty.

The first thing to happen after word got out that Thena had forced the mayor's hand and that he had given us a house was that it became filled, from front to back, with all the people of the town who had known and loved Mama for so many years. They came in floods and droves. Day and night we made pots of coffee and sat in straight-backed chairs in the kitchen and talked and laughed. I don't remember ever laughing as much as we did around that time.

It is odd how people seem to shy away from the misfortune of others; yet, when all is well again, they come back. While Dan was present, and even when it seemed that Mama could make do, the townspeople felt that it wouldn't be proper to "interfere." But after the fire, with Mama raising a houseful of children and an infant on her own, all of that civic bashfulness just melted away, as if within the flames of the fire itself.

Not a day passed without the arrival of welcoming neighbors—old men, women and children bringing gifts, basket after basket of fruits and vegetables from their gardens, advice, and help of all sorts. Within two weeks, both front and back fences had been painted and repaired, the flower beds were weeded, the house was given a new coat of paint, curtains were hung, beds were made, floors were swept. Beautiful furniture, repaired, refurbished or newly made, was lovingly transplanted into each of the rooms.

One quiet, sunny afternoon, with the sky bright and glaring like glass, I came upon Elsa, sitting on the bed in the room she shared with Mama. She held a squirming Lilliana tightly against her. She stared absently out of the window with tears, unchecked, streaming silently down her face. Her eyes and mind were far away, somewhere over the sky.

"What is it, Elsa?" I asked softly, gently taking Lilliana from her.

"This place is real beautiful, id'n it?"

I nodded.

She sat up straighter on the bed, wiping tears from her face. I fiddled with the baby's hands, silently watching. Elsa's face was pale and her eyes were large in her face. She looked up at me suddenly and smiled. She gave a faint laugh.

"Look at this place, so beautiful, an' me here cryin' on the bed n' makin' a mess a' my face. Don't know what I was cryin' 'bout to begin with. I reck'n I was cryin' outta happiness. Can you do that, ya think? Can you cry cuz yer jes' plain happy?"

I smiled at her and nodded.

"Elsa, darlin'-girl, you can cry for whatever reason you like."

"I guess I was just sittin' here, thinkin' about how beautiful this lil' house is, with curtains n' flowers in the yard, and so many rooms— rooms for plenty'a people—and I was so plum happy, it jes' made my chest hurt 'til I was sure it'd burst. I ain't never had nothin' perty before, 'cept my perty girl, here," she said, nodding to Lilliana.

"Id'n she fat an' jes' beautiful—those pretty curls n' eyes as blue n' big as cornflowers, and her skin as pale as cream, with pink lights in 'er cheeks? She looks like she's jes' shinin' with light from the inside, dudn' she?"

I laughed and nodded, handing Lilliana back to her mama.

"Do you think that yer own vanity can be found in somebody else—like yer babies?"

I smiled, but said nothing.

"Sometimes I feel real bad about it. I know bein' vain ain't right, and I guess wrong's wrong, whether I'm pleasurin' in somebody else's glory 'er my own, don'tcha reckon?"

Again I smiled.

"I reck'n, though, all women think that about their younguns."

I nodded. "I guess they do, Elsa. Mama always has thought I was pretty—cane and limp and scars and all. And the way she goes on about Isaac—you'd think his birth was the second coming. Yeah, I don't guess a mama ever thinks her baby is anything but pretty. But only some of them are right. Lilliana is truly the prettiest child I have ever seen. I don't remember Thena much as a little girl, but I think Lilli might be just as pretty."

Elsa's eyes grew large.

"I'm not sure's I think that's a good thing."

"How do you mean?"

She was quiet for a moment, her lips pursed.

"Well now, I don't know, 'cept some people's jes' as pretty as they can be, and it's alright for 'em—it don't spoil 'em none. Other people—knowin' they're pretty makes 'em wicked n' vain. And then there's people so pretty they're jes' 'bout worshipped. And bein' worshipped, after 'while, makes you start to think yer God. And thinkin' yer God and bein' God id'n the same thing."

She sniffed.

"Thena sure's beautiful all right, but I don't think it's ever gonna mean anythang for her but trouble—an' trouble a' the worst kind. One a' these days, I'm afraid Thena's gonna find out that she id'n God and she's just as human as the rest of us."

She sniffed again.

"There's only one God, and I'm perty sure Thena id'n it."

I laughed, though I wasn't sure that I felt much like laughing.

The remaining days of fall and winter passed happily in the new house. We suffered no more misfortune; there was no sign of Dan and we heard nothing more from Lucius Elder. Mama continued to care for Mrs. Rachel and her house. I returned to my work at the library and my nighttime studies.

The rooms of the new house stretched before us and upward to the sky. We marveled. We wondered. We were dumbstruck with our good fortune. Besides the room that Thena and I shared, the younger boys had a room to themselves, in addition to a third room shared by Mama, Isaac, Elsa and Lilliana. We reveled in the luxury and decadence of being well fed and warm. We dipped our fingers and washed our faces in the deliciousness of plenty. We marveled at having excess, uncertain of what to do when a person has *more* than they need. I had also recently received a dress as a surprise gift from Mrs. Nora, who said she saw it in a shop and thought she had never seen a dress that would suit me so well. Two dresses were enough. What was I going to do with three? Mostly, that third dress hung on a nail in my room and waited for special occasions that rarely came. But, my God, wasn't it glorious to wake in the morning to see it gleaming white and clean?

Dearest Pope Barrett:

It has been two months now since I last heard word of you. Your daddy sometimes gets short, convoluted messages about you. He says you have been recruited for some sort of special assign-

ment. *Sounds dangerous, and I guess that may be why you're not allowed to write or send word, or maybe your letters are just not getting through. I don't guess that the roads in the mountains of Italy (or wherever you are now) can be that good, and there must be millions of letters from thousands of soldiers and their wives and families all trying to make their way over the mountains and across the sea, and vice versa.*

Regardless, you are always in my thoughts, hovering below the surface of whatever I am doing. School has begun again, and for the first time, I am not among the students. Did your Daddy tell you? I was valedictorian. Even up to the very end I thought it would go to Mary Nell Stanton. And what will I do now? No one seems to know, least of all me. Though I am not yet sure what I want to do with my life, I know one thing for certain: I can't leave Mama. She has another baby now. His name's Isaac and he's now almost a year old. He's fat and handsome and has the sweetest little disposition. He laughs more than any of the rest of us did as babies.

Dan has stayed away for more than a year, but of course he will come back at the very moment when we least wish it. Besides worrying over when Dan will show back up, there are other reasons why I need to stay. There are the boys to be taken care of, and Elsa and Lilli—and, if I were to leave, Thena would surely overthrow the municipal government and start a merciless, blood-sucking dictatorship with Reed as the captain of her guard.

Reed has grown so tall and strong and is more fine-looking now than he was even when you were here. He works at the sawmill, though I don't suppose he needs the work. I think he does it to pass the time, and for the feel of the work in his bones and the sun on his back. Sometimes I worry over him a little. Mama says that I shouldn't; she says his heart is gold. I think she's right, but I worry about him still. He and Thena are together day in and out, and Thena is gone until all hours. I don't know what they do, and I don't ask. If I did, she wouldn't tell me anyway.

You have just missed my seventeenth birthday, and I have missed your nineteenth. On your birthday, Doc and your Mama and I made a cake and put twenty candles on it and sang away to you at the very tip-top of our voices. I didn't stay long. I know that you would want me to, but somehow being in the papal palace without the Pope seems…irreverent.

Most days, I am well and make it through the day. I work and take care of the boys. I talk to Mama and laugh with Elsa. I sing songs to Lilli that I make up as I go and we play hully-gull on the floor with marbles and a piece of broken chalk.

My thoughts of you are rarely above the surface, and mostly when they are I push them away, or else I start to cry. But when I see your mama, I can't help but think of you. I see your green eyes and wide smile. And when I see your daddy, I see that faint purple vein running across the right side of your forehead, your too-long nose with its skinny bridge, and that hard, square jaw.

When your daddy hugs me, I feel that same hug that you have given your whole life—the one that feels as if the life is being hugged right out of you, and maybe your bones will just crack and fall away. When your mama laughs, I hear precisely the same music—melody and harmony—that I hear in yours. It makes me hurt so much to be at your house without you. Your mama is still as pretty as the prettiest picture; I think that she becomes handsomer all the time. She will have the much-blessed fate of becoming prettier as she gets older. When I am her age, I will probably be a scarecrow in somebody's melon patch. The spiders will build nests in my teeth and the blackbirds will build their homes in the trees of my hair.

I am in awe of Nora—when I am with her, I feel like I should sit still and quiet, like I am in church. She's better than the best stained glass window, prettier than a verse in the Psalms. What is it that she always smells of? Lavender, I think. She comes from out of the kitchen and, having just made the biggest dinner, still she looks perfect—shining clean and wholly good.

Your daddy looks well. He is strong still, and handsome, with silvery hair right around his ears and patches of salt in the pepper of his beard. Has he told you he has grown a beard? I think he looks handsomer and more distinguished, like a city doctor, rather than an over-worked, harried, underpaid country doctor. He told me that he isn't making many house calls these days—only if the patient is really ill. And I think it has been for the best. Doc's been much quieter since you left. He still smiles a lot—his eyes still become those little down-turned crescent moons—but he doesn't speak up much now. It's fine by me; I love to sit with him in silence, all warm and subdued. We wrap ourselves up in it.

Sometimes, for only a moment, I see some faint, gray shadow of cloud and sorrow in his clear blue eyes. It was not there before you left, and I suspect it will pass when you are home again. Is it wrong for me to tell a soldier halfway around the world that his daddy is sad without him? Maybe it is, but I was never much good at keeping things from you. Anyway, I suppose you must already imagine how much he misses you. He carries on, though, the same as all of us.

Most times, he and I sit arm in arm and listen to the night and the sky and the faintest sounds from the river. We sit on the front porch, in the dark. It is easier that way. In the dark, I can't see that you're not there. And, do you want to know a secret? Sometimes, I pretend that Doc is my daddy. I think that my daddy must have been like him. Is it bad that I wish your father were my own?

I felt all evening on your birthday as if I was being haunted by you—but only from a distance. If it had been more of a personal haunting, I wouldn't have minded. But even when you are a ghost, you seem far away.

Come home to us, Pope. We need you and nothing can be good as long as you are far from here.

I miss you. Come home.

 Gracie

P.s. Your mama is quite right. Lilli is the prettiest girl on this side of the river. She's a living, breathing Rembrandt, all pastels and pale sunlight. Elsa spends her evenings sewing Lilli these beautiful dresses, and when she wears them she looks as rich as the Queen of Sheba. Elsa dresses her only in pinks (for her skin) and blues (for her eyes), just the color of the sky before sunset on a cold fall day. Lilliana laughs and dances all day and recites poetry taught to her from one of Mama's few poetry books, which she calls "recitations," pronouncing the word with scrupulous care. She memorizes each poem carefully, one phrase at a time. Her favorite is a Robert Frost, something about walking through the woods on a snowy evening.

XXV.

On a quietly sunny winter afternoon, three months after the fire, Dan found his way home again. I sat on the kitchen floor playing with Lilli while Elsa was in back of the house hanging laundry. Lilli sat prettily in my lap, her blond curls tucked under my chin, her feet crossed at the ankles. I was teaching her a poem about a blacksmith. I spoke each phrase slowly, pausing for her to repeat them. She held my forefingers in each of her fists, occasionally reaching across to poke at one of the blue veins on my small hands.

There was an abrupt knock at the door, and it was thrown open. I heard footsteps through the front room and down the short hallway. Next there was a loud, "Anybody here?" I stood up, startled, and shoved Lilli behind me. The next moment, Dan passed through the kitchen door. We stood watching each other, Dan grinning, me scowling.

"Howdy, gurl. Ain't you done growed up?"

I remained silent, watching. He was brown, browner than any man I had ever seen, and his blue eyes shone out from the brown of his skin with an almost supernatural glow, sparking and gleaming as bright as blue flame. His curly black hair was unfashionably long, but somehow suited him. His beard hung a full foot from his chin, and was curly and matted with leaves and grime. His blue work shirt was stained and torn. He wore faded overalls, which must once have been blue, but had become brown with age, wear and filth. He smelled badly and there was dirt caked in the lines of his face and hands. And, yet, in spite of his dirty and disheveled appearance, he stood tall and seemed young—no older than the first time I saw him.

"I reck'n I look a mess. I hadn' had no perty home to live in, like you has. I been wand'rn for quite a long while."

He paused, then said, "Two months ago, I got word 'bout the house and that you folks'd lost all. I figured I oughta come o'an home, but I was in California, so it took me some time to make it back."

He shifted a worn and broken hat from one hand to the other.

"Yer mama makin' it alright?"

I nodded.

"She had the child? Boy?"

I nodded. He smiled.

"I figured."

"What name'd she give 'im?"

"Isaac."

He laughed.

"Well, he wuz born to 'er in 'er ol' age, I reck'n. But thurty-eight's a far cry from a hunderd. Elsa still livin' with yuns?"

I nodded. He laughed.

"That her little'un?"

I took a step away from Dan, pushing Lilli gently against the wall. She wrapped one hand around the fabric of my skirt and, placing the other thumb in her mouth, she peered cautiously from behind me.

"Grace, who's that man?"

"His name is Dan, Lilli. Now, hush."

"Now, I don' mean 'er no hoarm. She's pretty little thing, id'n she?"

He bent slightly toward the floor, placing a hand on each knee and eyed Lilli.

"Here, now, perty gurl, I jes' come to say hi. I ain't gonn' bite."

I pushed Lilli out of view behind my skirt.

"She doesn't like strangers and don't you make her cry," I said sharply.

Dan straightened and studied my face.

"Well, I guess you hadn' changed much. Yer tongue still sharper'n a scythe."

He watched me for a long moment, smiling faintly.

"Yeah, I reck'n yer jes' 'bout the same Grace, ceptin' yer older—growed up n' lookin' like a lady. Goin' to London to see the queen, ain't ya?"

He laughed, his mouth open wide, his throat tilted back and exposed, the lines around his eyes deepening. In spite of everything, muck and filthy beard and smelling like a dirty, bleating sheep, Dan Brown was dangerously handsome when he smiled. In fact, he was handsome even when he wasn't smiling.

"Yer mama workin' up th' mayor's, I reck'n."

He stepped toward the kitchen table and, pulling out a chair, he turned the seat to face him and sat down. I said nothing.

"Grace, I'm mighty hungry and sufferin' a powerf'l thirst. Anythang 'round the house you'n gimme fer my belly?"

I had no intention of leaving Dan alone in our house; and yet, I didn't want him within a hundred yards of Lilli.

"Lilli, I want you to go on outside with your mama now so I can cook this man a dinner."

"But it isn't dinner time, Grace."

"No, honey, but he's hungry. He forgot to eat breakfast and lunch. Elsa," I called, "I'm sendin' Lilli on out to you. I need to start gettin' supper together."

I saw her shadow from behind the white sheets, her arms extended as she pinned each corner. With her mouth full of clothes pins she called out, "Lilli, baby-doll, come see Mama. I need ya help hang the laundry. You'n hold the pins fer Mama."

I led Lilli out to the stoop and watched her run across the grass to Elsa. I stepped back in and closed the door. Dan sat with his chin and arms resting on the top of the straight-backed chair, his blue eyes following me around the kitchen.

"Sure's a right perty place, id'n it? Yer mama deserves's much."

"Yes, Dan," I said quietly, "it is a pretty place. And we don't need you around here make it a dirty one."

"Well, gurl, I reck'n I could jes' take m'seff a bath."

"That's not what I meant."

I turned from the stove, my arms wrapped tightly around the heavy cast-iron skillet. I watched him for a moment as a lazy grin spread across his face.

"Now, I don' know, but I thaink yer jes' 'bout the unfriendliest gurl I ever know'd. Cain't a hungry, tired man git a meal'n a shave?"

I nodded. "Just so long as it doesn't turn into anything else. I'll feed you and let you rest for just a while and then I want you to move along and leave us be. We've been doing pretty well without you, and we can't seem to do anything but the other when you're here. So I think you should go."

Dan chuckled, stroking his chin with a philosophical air.

"Gurl, you must be tired out with all that hatin' you do. I reck'n you must get right heavy with it—hate—now that's a real burd'n."

"Dan Brown, I don't hate you. I don't spend enough time thinkin' about you to hate you."

He slapped his knee and let out a long laugh.

"Truth to tell, I don't think much of you at all. And when I do it isn't more than thinkin' of you as a drunk and a fool. It's hard to hate a man who's a drunk and a fool and a bully. Can't do much for such a man except to pity him. And what's more, I don't reckon you can really even call such a person a man. A man's a man; a drunk's a drunk; a bully's a bully."

His face paled and his mouth became drawn and pinched.

"Gurl, you best not start a fight you cain't finish."

I felt cold. My dress had become wet with sweat.

"Dan Brown, I haven't started one yet that I couldn't finish."

He smiled. "All it takes's one time, gurl."

I heard the door open and turned to see Elsa standing just inside the kitchen, Lilli clasped tightly to her.

"Lilli said there's a brown, dirty man in the kitchen, and I could only thaink a' one 'round here that could fit that description. What do you wont, Dan? 'Cause I'm perty sure that whatever it is, we cain't help you with it."

Dan touched one finger to his nose.

"I'm not yet convinced that you cain't, woman."

"Dan, don't make me git the sheriff or the mayor. You've long-since outstayed yer welcome in this town, and nobody much likes you 'round here. I don't rightly know how it happened, but I think folks around here has gotten the impression that you aren't a real good, upstandin', God-fearin' person. I tried to correct the mistake, but you know how folks is, they believe what they wonts to."

He chuckled and shook his head. "I'm not leavin' 'til the bidness I came for's settled."

"Business!" Elsa snorted. "I wouldn't say hard drinkin' n' thievery is business, and I'm perty sure you'n do both of 'em up in the mountains jest as well as you'n do 'em down here."

"It id'n drinkin' that I'm here fer, woman. I'n do that anywhere, and though I'm many things, I've yet to add thievin' to the number."

"If you ain't here for drinkin' nor thievin', what're ya here for, then?"

"I'm looking for somebody," he said, slowly, his voice soft and steely.

I felt my blood go cold and shuddered involuntarily. The rapid movement of my body caught Dan's eye and he turned with a smile to face me.

"I reck'n you done met the man I'm after, gurl—that's what I heard, anyways."

I said nothing.

"Man of the name Lucius Elder. You seen 'im?"

I nodded once, slowly.

"Talkin' a' men who's neither upstandin' ner God-fearin'...speak 'a the devil," he smiled over at me, his expression at once lascivious and lazy, "id'n that right, Grace?"

His eyes, burning dim and low, shone into my face. I said nothing.

"What'd he say to you?" he asked.

I studied him for a moment.

"I don't know that I much recall, except that he was looking for you, and he wanted to know where to find you and said if I saw you, I was to tell you that he was lookin' for you."

"What'd you tell 'im?"

"That I hadn't seen you in a year and I hoped that I wouldn't see you again."

His eyes burned more brightly, the depth and heat of their light intensifying. He stood up and took a step closer to me. The stench of his body burned my nostrils.

"What else?"

I watched his face, somehow sure that he already knew what Lucius had said.

"He took credit for burnin' down our house, n' threatened to hurt us if you didn't give him what belonged to him."

Elsa cried out and turned pale. Pulling out a chair from the kitchen table, she said quietly, "What d'you mean? Where'd you see 'im? We ain't seen him since before..." here she nodded to Lilli, but couldn't finish the thought, refusing to speak of the births of Lilli and Stephen in front of Dan. "Why'd he talk to you? Why didn' you tell us? Did he hurt you? You shoulda told me. You had no right to keep that to yerself!"

In three months, I had never spoken of our meeting to anyone—not even to Pope. In fact, I had never even mentioned to Pope that we had lost our house, and often found myself praying that his parents would not see fit to do so, either.

"I don't know, Elsa. He was pale and sickly lookin' and I was pretty sure he wouldn't live long enough to carry out any threat. I'm not sure, but I think he might be consumptive. He came to the house on the morning after the fire. I couldn't sleep and went down early to sort through the ash. He stood there, lookin' grim and smokin' cigarettes. Said he was lookin' for Dan. Said if he didn't get what he wanted, he might take it out on me and I told him that if he hurt me, Dan would be tickled pink, and so he was wastin' his time. I didn't tell anybody because I didn't know what to say, and because I didn't want there to be any more worry than there already had been and 'cause I thought I had seen the last of him."

"Where'd he go when he left you?" Dan asked quietly.

"I don't know. Off through the trees—back toward town."

"Wuz he on foot?"

"Yeah, I reckon he was."

"Wuz there anybody with 'im?"

I shook my head. "Not that second time. The first time he came, a long time ago—about three years back, I guess—he was with a big bunch of men in a truck. They came from town-way and headed back the same way as they came."

"What'd he say the first time?"

"Same thing. 'Where's Dan, I want to see him, tell him Lucius Elder is lookin' for him.' That's about it. He was mean and disagreeable and generally menacing, but he didn't stay long and, when he was gone, we acted like it had never happened."

For a while no one spoke. I rose and reluctantly fried Dan three eggs and cut thick slices of Mama's bread. Then, passing the plate to him and gently taking Lilli from Elsa's lap, I sat back down.

Dan ate voraciously. For a moment, I almost felt sorry for him. Some minutes passed; the only sounds were of the ticking clock and the scraping of Dan's fork over his plate. As he ate, his face remained thoughtful. Elsa sat watching without moving, her arms wrapped tightly around her body.

After a time, Dan said quietly, shaking his head,

"Well, whether he looks dead or not, he id'n, an' I don't 'spect he ever will be. Folks say he's been dyin' fer thurdy years. They say he gets real bad n' looks like a corpse up walkin' 'round, n' he looks like that for a long spell, n'then one day you see 'im again'n he looks jes' fine."

"Who is he; who're his people?" Asked Elsa, her voice thick and flat.

"I don't reck'n nobody knows. He come from nowhere, jes' showed up in these parts, long, long time ago. Never said nothin' 'bout who he wuz or where he come from. Never said nothin' bout nothin', far's I know. People says he dudn' look a day older er younger'n he did thurdy years ago. An' I wonder…"

Then, pushing back his plate and wiping a hand across his mouth and beard, he stood and shoved both hands in his overall pockets. Elsa and I remained seated. He stood for a moment, looking from one of us to the other.

"Dan Brown, what've you done to that man, an' why, in God's name, have you dragged this family into it? They ain't never done nothin' but good to you. And alls you ever done back is evil."

His face revealed nothing. He stood still for a moment, closely watching Elsa, his eyes traveling from her to her little girl.

"Well, Elsa, I reck'n I can take care of it and he won't bring nothin' on this family again. Only one way t'fight with a durty man n' that's durty. It won't come near you er your mama," he said, nodding to me.

"Tell 'er I'll visit her sometime."

"I don't think that would be a good idea," I said. "If you come into this house with Thena in it, I can't vouch for what will happen to you."

Dan smiled wryly.

"I reck'n I been warned an' I'll come at my own risk."

"Please, Dan," I said, taking a step toward him, "if you have any goodness or love in you for Mama, please leave us alone. Don't come back here."

He took off his faded hat and bowed slightly.

"Afternoon, Ladies," he said.

Turning, he passed through the hall and out the front door. For long minutes, neither Elsa nor I moved or spoke. I glanced up absentmindedly to the clock hanging to the left of the back door, thinking that it must be near nightfall. It was only mid-afternoon, no more than half an hour since Dan entered the house. It was at that moment that I suddenly realized something: Dan had been sober.

Elsa and I said nothing to Mama, the boys or Thena of Dan's return. Thinking back on it now, it seems strange to me that we didn't tell Mama that her husband had returned. But at the time, we thought nothing of it.

≈ ≈ ≈

June, 1943

Dear Pope:

I saw your daddy today. He said he had heard word of you and that you are safe. I can't tell you how relieved I was or how happy it made me to hear some news—any news—of you. I think of you every day. Nearly every minute of the day. Although, I keep telling myself that I have to try and put you out of my mind. I hope that doesn't sound cruel to you, but when I think of you for very long, I suddenly find that my face and dress are wet with tears and I am distracted and worried and sad and can't think properly.

It has been too long since I have gotten a letter from you. Doc told me that letters are not getting through, and that oftentimes the soldiers are not allowed to write, for fear of giving everything away to the Germans. I worry about you and wish that I could hear from your own hand that you are safe and healthy. We get letters every so often from Ted and Jim. Both are okay, I suppose, or as okay as a soldier can be. Jim was sick for a while with what they thought was maybe dysentery, but they were able to help him and make him well again, and after he had rested for a while in an army hospital, they sent him back to the front. He and Ted are fighting somewhere in France. Your daddy told me that you have been moved to France as well, and I wonder if you will see my brothers. If you do, please do your best to keep them safe. Ted is quiet and steady and brave; Jim is wild and reckless like Thena. I wonder, which type makes a better soldier? Regardless, neither of them is invincible, and I would feel better knowing that the three of you could look out for one another.

The spring has passed and the days are hotter. The sun is bright as a mirror again and it burns my eyes to be out in the heat of the day. Did your daddy tell you that summer came late this year? There were heavy rains. Everyone said there would be a flood again, but somehow it never came. The river did get very high, around the middle of May, but never overflowed. I can't remember a year with so many flowers and so much green everywhere. I wonder if it is always this way and I am just now going to the trouble of noticing it, or if it really is prettier this year. The honeysuckles are blooming and the children are running around naked and splashing through the shallows. Even though it has only been hot for a short while, their skin is already turning brown. We are living in a house in the town now and are closer to the river. I can hear the children screaming and splashing when the wind is just right.

Do you remember when we were young and we used to swim in the river? It's strange to me that those days are gone forever. I *was thinking the other day of when you nearly drowned yourself that spring when the water was so high and threatening—you always were so much braver than me. Brave and strong as you were and are, trying to swim that river was a stupid thing to do. I think that sometimes boys confuse courage and recklessness. Pope, please don't do anything foolish over there. If you have a chance to be very brave or to come home alive, please just come home alive. You were brave enough to enlist and you have nothing left to prove.*

Sometimes, as I lay in bed at night, I find myself wondering what Pope is doing, right now, at this moment. I try to imagine you in the operating room, stooped over a wounded soldier, calm and steady and patient, just as you were that night you found Elsa clinging to the chimney of her house. Your hands shook so badly while you stitched up your forehead, but your breath came slow and deep. I remember moments when you seemed frightened, but still you worked on, trying to save Elsa and her baby.

I lay in bed last night for a long time trying to picture you. I wondered what you were doing. I tried to decide if you were sleeping or at work in the surgery or lying in the sun or walking in the cold. Do you talk to the soldiers as you work on them? Do you pray for them? Do you cry? Do you ever get sick? I know I would. I sometimes wonder if you sleep beside their cots, in case they need anything in the night.

It is strange to have a person be close enough to you that they are mostly just an extension of yourself—so close that you aren't sure where you end and the other person begins—and yet, for more than a year, to know almost nothing about their lives, what they are doing, or who they have become. It is strange that you are so close, and yet so remote.

Thena and Reed are thick as thieves these days. They are

together night and day and without you here to help keep them out of trouble, they make me nervous. The other night as I was coming home from the library, I passed by the river and heard giggling and splashing in the dark. It was Thena and Reed fighting and doing their best to drown one another. I left them to it, as usual. Most times, after Reed gets done working at the sawmill, they hop into his little car and drive off like the devil is after them. They come home all sparkly-eyed and tight-lipped and even Mama can't get much out of Thena.

Things are a bit better in the past couple of years between Thena and Elsa. They like each other more and maybe even understand one another a little; although, for some reason, Elsa doesn't care for Reed. I find that quite funny; without Thena, Reed is pretty harmless. Maybe Elsa feels loyalty to Thena and, because she can't quite like the way they traipse around together, she takes it out on the only other available party.

Can you remember how very beautiful Thena used to be? I don't imagine that anyone could ever forget. She is getting prettier every day of her life, and when I look at her my eyes hurt. My heart does, too. I wonder if that's how Michelangelo felt after he had carved his David, knowing that he would go through his whole life and never see anything more perfect, more complete, more beautiful. I sometimes wonder if that's how Mama felt too, after she made Thena.

Edwin and John are quite grown up and strong and they do a good job of taking care of all of us. Franklin Delano is five—nearly six—and he won't let me kiss him anymore or tuck him into bed. With brothers so much older than himself he is anxious to become a little man. Sometimes, at night, after he is sound asleep, I creep up to the boys' room and sit beside his bed and hold his little hand. Sometimes I even kiss him.

Isaac is almost a year and a half old now and still lets me carry him around on my hip sometimes. He hasn't started talking, but it doesn't seem to worry Mama at all. She says he'll start talking when he's ready to and not a minute before. In spite of his silence, he's very smart. I think he's biding his time. He watches all of us; once he has it all figured out, I'm sure he'll start talking like it's going out of style.

We miss you—I miss you, dearest Pope. I want to hear from you. If there is anyway that you can get a letter to me, please, please do. Even a letter to Doc and Nora would make me so happy; I just need to know that you are okay and healthy and that they are not working you to death and that you still think of us sometimes and that maybe, sometime in the midst of your busy days, you love us just a little.

Love,
Your Gracie

XXVI.

It would be several months before Dan entered our lives again. For one of the first times in my life, I lived in dread every moment, lest he should walk through the door. It happened on a Sunday afternoon in November.

For once, all of us were at home, sitting around the kitchen table. Mama, Elsa and I had cooked a huge lunch spread. We had just finished eating and were still sitting around the table, sleepy and fat with Sunday lunch. Reed sat next to Thena, leaning back contentedly in his chair, his long arms stretched up and hands clasped behind his head. He sat in a brilliant ray of sunlight, his eyes closed, his body relaxed, occasionally letting out a long, low sigh of contentment. The golden light shone on his handsome face. He reminded me of the story of the angels at the tomb of Christ. Mama had told us that their beauty and splendor had been so glorious that the Roman soldiers fainted dead away. The soldiers couldn't stand to look on the gold-shine and glory of the angels and, because of it, missed out on the Resurrection. I studied him for a long moment and then, feeling pretty sure that staring at Reed could have that same effect, I turned away.

I scooped up an armload of plates and carried them to the sink. Turning back to the table, I stacked up several more. Thena rose and said,

"If Mama keeps cookin' like that, I'm gonna git fat."

"I hope you do," said Reed. "You're too bony. I'd like to see you get a little bit fat."

Thena shook her shining curls. "Nope, skinny suits me best."

She patted her flat stomach and reached across Reed, gesturing for him to hand her his dishes. For a moment after he collected them, he held them aloft, just out of her reach, smiling into her laughing eyes. She played along until, becoming impatient, she slapped him once on his golden head. Reed, surrendering the plates and silver, reached up with a groan to touch the place where her blow had landed. I watched as Thena straightened to carry them to the sink. And then I saw her face turn gray. Her mouth fell open. My eyes followed her gaze, knowing already what I would see; then the plates fell from Thena's hands and shattered on the floor. Mama stood instantly, her back to the door. Slowly, she turned to follow Thena's gaze. Dan stood in the doorway. For a moment, no one moved.

He had shaved his long beard and trimmed his hair; though, in spite of the haircut, it still hung in thick curls around his neck. He wore a new blue work shirt and brown trousers. On his feet there were tall, black work boots. They were new and bright and hardly broken in. I noticed that, beneath his tan, there was a strange, sickly color to his skin. His face was strained and his eyes burned with fever. Both his hands were pressed to his stomach and were nearly black with blood, which flowed from a wound in his shoulder and another, larger wound in his stomach.

Franklin Delano screamed. John and Edwin stood stiffly, hands gripping the back of their chairs. Isaac ran from his chair into my arms and began to cry. Elsa was the only one who remained seated, her hand gently holding Lilli's head against her shoulder. Thena still had not moved. Reed pushed himself slowly upright. He placed an arm tightly around Thena's shoulders, his expression grim.

"Mary, I wouldn'a come, but I didn' thaink there wuz any other house in town that'd take me," Dan whispered, trying to smile.

He paused. A deep cough seized him, shaking his body. He rocked on his heels, and for moment it seemed that he would fall. Taking one hand from his stomach, exposing part of the gaping hole and torn flesh, he caught himself on the doorframe. Mama moved forward to catch him, wrapping her arms around his middle.

"You did right to come here," she said softly. "John, Edwin, go get Doc Barrett. Go! Run! Go o'an, git! Reed, I could use some help. Thena, clear that table, now! Help me lift 'im up."

Reed and I moved to help Mama lift Dan onto the kitchen table. As soon as we laid him on it, he lost consciousness.

"Grace, I need my scissors. There's a bottle a' bourbon in the cupboard in my room. Bring it. Elsa, hot water. Thena, I need some clean rags."

Thena remained motionless in shock, her mouth hanging open, her hands limp at her sides.

"Thena! Now! Or Dan'll die on our kitchen table—do it!"

Thena, seeming to recover, went in search of bandages. Elsa took Lilli's coat from its nail by the door and gently pushed her out the back door, instructing her to go and play in the flower garden. I hurried after the bourbon. Mama took it from me, ripped open Dan's shirt and poured it all over his belly and shoulder. She poured the whole bottle over his body, gently wiping the liquor away with a clean kitchen cloth as she poured. Thena returned, ripping up a sheet as she came. Mama took the strips from her and held the cloth tightly against Dan's belly.

"Grace, you take another and hold it there," she said, gesturing to his shoulder.

I reached across her and pressed the worn strip of sheet across the wound. Dan groaned and stirred but did not open his eyes. The front door opened and Doc and the boys entered the kitchen. Doc dropped his black bag on the table and opened it, quickly ordering,

"Mary, stay. The rest of you, out, now."

For two days, Dan hovered between life and death. At about midnight of the first night, Mama stepped out on to the front porch, looking tired and pale. Her hair had slipped from her bun in places, and the strands she had pushed away from her face so that she could work were caked with blood. The front of her dress was also blood-soaked; in the faint light of the moon it shimmered, slippery and black. She held one hand to her eyes.

"Mama," I said softly, "come and rest for a minute."

"I cain't rest, girl, I have to go back in to the Doc. He cain't take care a' Dan alone."

"Has he spoken?"

"He's delirious—says a few things here'n there—it's all just garbled nonsense. Just cryin' out from the black, an' I cain't make sense of it."

She paced the porch.

"Is he gonna make it?"

"Doc thinks no; we'll see. Dan comes from fightin' stock. They didn't survive all those years up there alone in the mountains by chance. Where's Isaac n' Thena n' Reed…the others?" she asked, gesturing out into the yard.

"Gone to Nora's house, Mama. She walked over a couple of hours ago and said she would make hot cocoa if they'd come stay with her a while."

"Why didn't you go?"

"Didn't know if you might need me."

"Go o'an to Nora's then—nothin' you'n do here. Nothin' anybody can do. We jes' have to wait."

"I could stay with the Doc for a while and you could rest."

She shook her head, her lips pressed in a hard line.

"I couldn't rest even if I wanted to. Might's well stay n' make m'self useful to the Doc."

"Are you sure, Mama? You look awful tired."

She nodded.

"Go see about Lilli n' the boys."

"Alright, Mama."

I stood, stretched out my cramped limbs and moved into the yard, then turned south toward Pope's house. I glanced back and saw Mama still pacing the porch, her head down and her lips moving. I stopped to watch. She was praying. She looked small; I noticed for the first time that, at thirty-nine, she still looked like a girl. After what seemed like a long time, she turned and moved back into the house—back to Dan.

≈ ≈ ≈

Late one afternoon, about a week after Dan returned to us, after not having heard from Pope in 18 months, I received a large bundle of envelopes sent from France. I never learned how it came to be that I received them all at once, or why they had been delayed for so long; perhaps they had been misplaced for a time. Whatever the reason, now that I had them—now that I had Pope—it didn't matter much. All I wanted was to hear from him, to know his thoughts, to sit and hold in my hand a letter that his hands had touched. I took the bundle from the postman and walked slowly to the river. I sat in the sunshine, by the water, and read and re-read the precious letters. Over and over I read them; when I had read them all to my heart's content, I realized that the sun had set and I had been straining for some time in the darkness to see their pages.

August, 1942

Gracie Canton Kelley:

I have traveled halfway around the world and am now stationed in the mountains of Europe. The farther I travel away, the closer you seem to me. When I close my eyes, I see your face—I see your clear, wide green eyes, which shine with some soft light that could only come from the best places of your insides. Did you know that you and Thena have almost exactly the same eyes, except that hers turn up a little at the corners, burning with some strange fire, while your eyes are all lit up with peace and joy, just like your mama's?

Do you know how much you look like her, your mama? It is uncanny. It isn't only the way you carry yourselves, or the way you tilt your head when you want to know or understand someone; it isn't just your crooked half-smile, or that great big laugh that shakes the ground when you are really tickled by something; nor is it only the diffidence that both of you always carry with you, like an old brown rag coat, or your inimitable desire to love, even strangers—especially strangers. I am sure that, if we could open you both up and look at your souls, they would be made of just the same stuff, and they would be of just the same quality. I have always felt that your mama must be the friend of God. As you have grown older, I have begun to think of you in the same way. Just like hers, your eyes are like two great, shimmering lights, leading all of us on the way Home.

Did you know that even from five thousand miles away, I can clearly see the light dusting of freckles on your cheeks that you have never been able to get rid of? For years you have been saying that they are going away, but do you want to know a secret? They aren't. They look exactly as they did when you were nine years old; they remain in exactly the same places, and they shine from the sky of your face like the glow of constellations in the night. Did you know that if you lost those freckles, I would mourn them, just as I would the loss of the stars? Maybe more.

From a distance of five thousand miles, I can plainly see your small nose and broad cheekbones. I remember the exact shape of your mouth: the way it is not quite broad enough for your face, and the way that your lips are soft and full and look like a piece of ripe fruit. When I see you in my mind, I remember perfectly the *way your hair is just the color of leaves in the fall, and the way it looked in the winter sunshine with the wind blowing through your tangled curls. Every day that I spend away from you is a day wasted. Every hour without you in it is one that might just as well never have been.*

Gracie, did you know that when I was a young boy my mama used to tell me stories about God? She said that he loved me with this great big, untouchable love. For some reason, I was never so sure; not until I knew you. In all the years since you were injured and came to live with us for a time, I have known that he does. I know that he must, because you do.

Goodnight, my strange, sweet girl, full of Grace. You are my dream, both sleeping and waking.

Thomas Pope Barrett

≈ ≈ ≈

Dan continued to improve as the weeks went on. Doc began to say, cautiously, that he might live. For nearly a week after the night Dan came to us, he was unconscious. He tossed and turned in pain and cried out both night and day. Mama sat with him almost unceasingly. Thena was rarely at home during the time of Dan's illness; most days, she worked for Mrs. Rachel so that Mama could stay close to Dan. Thena's nights were spent elsewhere. Mama, distracted and worried, didn't seem to notice and never asked where Thena had been. Thena was grim and uncommunicative and, because I felt sure that she was safe with Reed, I left the matter alone. During those days, I helped Mama in whatever way I could. This usually meant that I took care of the boys.

On the sixth night after Dan's appearance, he stirred and gave Mama a faint smile. The boys had gone to bed and I sat with her beside Dan's bed on a straight-backed chair, reading.

"Do you need a drink?" Mama asked.

He nodded and lifted his head several inches from his pillow. He took a short sip and, giving a faint nod of thanks, he was asleep again.

The next morning, he awoke for the second time, and was fed by Mama. After several days of sleeping and waking for short moments, he began to be awake for longer periods. One afternoon, Mama had gone to clean Mrs. Rachel's house and I sat reading at the kitchen table. I heard Dan stirring in Mama's bed and, thinking he might need water, went in to check on him. His eyes were open, his skin pale and glistening with sweat.

"You alright?"

"Don' know 'bout 'alright'," he said faintly. "I reck'n 'alive' is a better way of charact'rizin' it."

"You need water?"

He nodded. I poured him a glass from the pitcher by Mama's bed and held his head up while he drank.

"Your belly still hurtin' pretty bad?"

"Bad 'nough."

"Is it keepin' you awake?"

"Yeah, I reck'n it is."

"I'll ask the Doc to give you somethin' to help you sleep when he comes. If you don't rest, you won't heal."

"This house's awful quiet these days. It always so?"

"During the day it's pretty quiet. Right now it's quiet 'cause you're sick and the Doc wants it that way."

"Feels unnat'ral."

"Nothin' much is natural about this situation."

"No, I don't reck'n it is."

"You wanna tell me what happened to you?"

"Not really."

"I think you better, 'cause if it comes near us, I'm gonna to need to know what to do about it."

"It won' come to yer mama."

"You thought as much before; and yet, there's a man sleepin' in Mama's bed with a hole in his gut the size of Alaska."

He was quiet for a long time, and I thought he must have fallen asleep. Finally he said,

"I went over'n check on Lucius Elder. I thought with all the time he done had to anticipate th' situation, he'd be real glad t' see me." He smiled up at me weakly. "I thought he'd make such a fuss o'er me n' slaughter the fatted calf. But you know, Grace? I don't think he wuz glad to see me t'all. I was plum hurt. Sometimes, I feel jes' like I hadn' a friend in the woarld."

He tried to laugh, but quickly stopped as he put his hands to his belly.

"You don't deserve friends, and the ones you got, you don't know what to do with."

"How's that?"

"Mama's been a friend to you for more than fifteen years. And in all that time, I don't think you've been good to her as many as fifteen days."

His face darkened.

"You're so young, gurl. Too young to've made much mistakes. An' jes' 'bout spillin' over with yer own rightness n' virtue."

"No, Dan. You're wrong about that. I don't have any illusions about my virtue. But I do think that those who know right from wrong ought to go about tryin' to do it. You're no fool, and yet I've never seen you try to do right. In fact, seems that you try n' do as much of the other as you can. Most folks spend their lives tryin' to stay the hell away from wrongdoin'. You grab at it with both hands."

We were quiet for a while. I sat watching Dan's profile, wondering if I was too quick to judge him, pretty sure that I wasn't. Dan lay pale and still.

"So, Lucius wasn't glad to see the prodigal?"

"Well, it wudn' the homecomin' I'd hoped fer. I thaink he wanted me t' stay away for a spell longer, eatin' pig scraps n' muckin' out pens. I thought we might break bread n' chew the cud n' so forth. But that wudn' his incl'nation."

"What was?"

"Best I can make out, I reck'n he wanted to keep the calf n' slaughter me. Maybe he thought the calf wuz worth more." He smiled.

"There's no question that it was." I nodded to his belly. "Elder did that?"

"Yeah, but I reck'n I did more hoarm to him'n he did to me."

"How so?"

"I had me a rifle, too."

"How many?

"Two, maybe three."

"Dear God, Dan, he'll be comin' here."

"He don' wont y'all. He'll wont me. An' with me layin' two blocks from the county seat, it'll take a while 'fore he gits up the gall to come fer me. By then, my gut'll be healed up n' I'll be somewheres warm n' dry."

"Like where? A pine box in the ground?"

"No, temptin's that sounds, I wuz thinkin' somewhere far down south, er maybe out west. I wuz in New Mexico fer a few weeks. Sure's a perty place."

"In the meantime, how am I supposed to keep Lucius away from Mama and Elsa and the little ones?"

"You let me worry 'bout that."

"Lettin' you worry about that is what worries me."

Dan lifted a hand slowly, painfully to his face and wiped the sweat away from his forehead.

"You need more water?"

He nodded. He took a long drink and then closed his eyes. I sat with him for a while. His breathing became deeper. His voice heavy with sleep and pain, he said,

"Th' boy looks like me, dudn'ee?"

"Which?" I asked.

"Isaac."

"Dan, they all look like you, for better or worse. If they didn't, who else would they look like?"

"The little'un looks more like me than the rest."

"If that's so, Lord help him."

"I know—handsome devil, idn'ee?"

"That wasn't exactly what I was referring to."

"Grace, you're the somb'rest gurl I ever done met with."

"With good reason."

His eyes opened. He nodded once, his face bloodless. Then he closed them again and fell asleep. I couldn't tell if the pain on his face was from the wounds he had received or the ones he had given. I watched him for a long time and realized something. Dan was sober, yet again. For just a few seconds, I had seen some of the charm Mama had once referred to a long time ago.

XXVII.

Pope Barrett:

Today I took Lilli to see Grandmamma and Granddaddy King, and then on to see Campbell and Netta. Elsa had fretted over Lilli's little dress and hair; she looked as if she was going to a formal reception at the White House. Somehow, Lilli never seems to mind. I believe she half expects to be fussed over. To tell the truth, even with all of the attention, I don't think she has been spoiled one little bit.

I can't understand that sort of purity, and have known for a very long time that I could never have it. Isn't it odd that some people are born with such a great capacity for mischief, and even flat-out wrongdoing, and other people are born with their insides all clean? I don't mean to say that Lilli is perfect or that she has never done anything wrong; in fact, I sometimes see glimpses of her wicked temper—only glimpses, mind you. I guess I just mean that she is mostly good, and I often wonder if I am mostly bad. Does everyone feel that way, do you think?

Can you believe that she will be four years old next June? She is such a little lady, with perfect manners, and Elsa has been very careful to teach her to read and write already. Every night, for months, the two of them have sat before the fire, with Lilli on Elsa's lap, their backs hunched, the firelight casting shadows over their faces. Lilli's little face strains with the effort.

Elsa has taught her proper grammar, and won't allow her to speak in the imprecise, provincial way that the rest of us do. She's a funny little thing; yet, for all her pretty ways, I think there is still some secret wildness to her that is all her own.

She walks with me everywhere, small and quiet, holding my hand. We walk through the leaves together, and she always picks out the prettiest to take home to her Mama. You ought to have seen the fuss that Netta and Campbell made over her. They filled her up with moon pies and milk from Campbell's cows, and she fairly waddled her way home and couldn't eat dinner because of her bellyache.

Here it is nearly wintertime; the sunlight is silvery instead of golden, the way it is in summer. The wind is starting to feel unfriendly. It seems angry; and yet, somehow I can never be angry back. I love the winter. I always have. I love that in winter the sky gets dark earlier. And in the spring and summer when the sunset comes later and later, I always find that I long for the early evening peace of those dark winter nights. I was thinking, tonight, as I stood in the crowded kitchen, that winter is really the only time when the entire family is together. I love that feeling, when I am standing over the stove at night and I hear everyone talking at once and stirring and everything seems to be moving towards that final nighttime settle-down. As I work, I listen to the boys run and crash through the house; they fight and wrestle and slap at one another, as if working to get out every last bit of energy. I love the way they suddenly become gentle if they happen upon Lilli.

I have often thought of the earth as being suspended in winter: waiting and silent and still and so utterly patient, like it's waiting to be made new again; taking a rest-time before moving on to something better—moving on to spring. I wish that humans had a time like that. *Don't you wish that we had a winter and a spring every year in our own minds or hearts or souls or whatever it is that makes up our insides? Whenever I see the first flowers in the spring, I find myself wishing that I could do just that same thing— wishing that I could blossom, filling up with light and sound and fire and burning with goodness.*

I ran into your daddy yesterday. He looked so good and rested and happy. He said that he had just written to you. I wish he hadn't told you about Dan being back. I don't mean that I wish he had been dishonest, but I wish that he hadn't given you cause to worry when you are away fighting in a war with worries of your own. I hate that you'll be afraid for us when there isn't a thing in the world that you can do about it. You shouldn't let your mind be troubled over him or us—we haven't seen too much of him. He seems to have gotten into some kind of scuffle and gotten himself shot. Anyway, he's been really ill. Too ill to talk or cause trouble. I guess Dan is what made me think of winter and spring. I am not sure that I would have ever known how black and barren insides are if I had not known him. When I think of Dan, I wish for a spring all my own.

Did you know that there's a young man come to court Elsa? Or at least I think he is. She doesn't seem to pay him much mind, though. He shows up just about every night after supper. He sits by the fire, watching. He smiles a lot and doesn't say much. Sometimes I see Elsa watching him, studying his face whenever he isn't looking, but mostly she ignores him. She's not rude, exactly, but she isn't very encouraging, either. I don't think it's him that she's averse to; I think the idea of having a man around doesn't seem very appealing to her.

To be honest, I think I like him. His eyes are kind. He's very tall—I would think he must be six-four—and handsome, I think, or he would be, if he had a wife to see to him. He has nice, clear gray eyes and his skin is very brown and sort of rough looking. His hands are far too big for the rest of him and they are always caked with dirt that won't come off. Every night he comes to the house smelling like soap, but somehow his hands never come clean. Several of his nails are split clean down the middle and the index fingernail of his right hand is missing. He's been coming for months and that nail has never grown back. Each time he comes and Mama answers the door, he stands there with his hair gleaming, wet and combed. It is a bit too long and is very dark brown and it curls around his ears in a nice kind of way that somehow makes him seem friendly.

Whether Elsa does or not, Lilli likes him. She sits on his lap and rubs the bristles on his cheek. Tonight she has taught him to play Cat's Cradle. When he comes, he brings a guitar and he and Elsa sing old songs. Their voices together are clear and beautiful.

This is just the perfect night for one of our walks. It's a little chilly, but cloudless, and the moon is a soft orange, glowing color with the sky all lit up like the world is on fire. It looks just like the first night on earth. I wonder what the moon looks like where you are, and if the sky is just the same.

I wish that you were here right now and could tell me all about what your life has been for the last two years. We would walk through the trees and down to the river and watch the moon glowing dark and low on the still water. I can't imagine what life must be like for those who don't live near water. I know that I wouldn't like it. I love how the river has such a lazy look at this time every year, like it's napping. I could never leave the river. It is part of me, just as you are part of me.

Come home to us, Pope. Come home.

> *Gracie*

P.s. Today Ms. Martha had Eleanor Roosevelt to afternoon tea at the library. Apparently, Eleanor wore a lumpy tweed hat, gray woolen coat and scuffed navy pumps and carried a large, awkward black leather handbag that seems to have been "rather drab." Ms. Martha took it somewhat hard. She was disappointed that the President's wife wasn't more "smart," as she put it. However, Ms. Martha did say that her manners were charming and refined, and she swore that, whatever people might say, Mrs. Roosevelt, in addition to being very clever, was a "real nice woman." She also mentioned that she thought Mrs. Roosevelt's sociological ideas—as well as her ideas concerning domestic and foreign policy—were very progressive. Unfortunately, I was in the cellar searching for the library's fall decorations and missed the whole thing. However, Ms. Martha said that Mrs. Roosevelt sent her warmest regards. And so, Pope Barrett, in the spirit of Eleanor Roosevelt, and from a woman who holds firmly to progressive domestic and foreign policy, Grace Canton Kelley sends you her warmest regards.

Things were quiet for several weeks. Dan recovered a little every day. Without a word or coming to any kind of agreement, we all took care of him, except Thena, who was never at home. I think Dan's return was the second and final blow that drove Thena over the edge of that great sea we all swam in, into oblivion.

I suppose I knew all along that it would happen. It was like standing onboard a ship, watching a hurricane coming in. But I couldn't stop it any more than I could have stopped a storm. I think that, from that time forward, there was no doubt in Thena's mind that it *must* end for one of them. Her or him—I'm not sure if it even mattered to her. I have tortured myself over the years, wondering if she ever could have guessed that what would destroy one would, in the end, destroy both.

The weeks of late autumn passed and time moved on into winter.

Christmas and the New Year came and went. Dan began to get out of bed and move slowly around the house. Mama, Elsa and the two little ones had moved in to share my bedroom—the room Thena never slept in anymore. Mama, of course, knew that Thena was sleeping elsewhere, but I think she knew just as surely as I did that she didn't possess the power to compel Thena home. I missed her. But I never worried. I knew that she was with Reed and that he loved her and would keep her safe. I think Mama knew it, too.

One afternoon in January, as I was closing up the library, I could tell that Ms. Martha had something in particular to say. She stood with her back to me, sliding stray wisps of her gleaming white hair back into her bun. Buttoning her coat, she cleared her throat and very tentatively asked me about Dan.

"Grace, dear, I heard it said that your stepfather has returned home."

"Yes, Ms. Martha."

"It seems that he's been...ill?"

"Yes, ma'am, very."

"And he's mending?"

"Yes, ma'am, he will, in time. He's walkin' a little and eatin' more than he was. But, still, he's not strong."

"So then, he will make it?"

"Yes, I believe he will."

"Yes," she said softly, almost to herself, "it's usually the mean ones that are the strongest. So, then, he will stay awhile?"

"Yes, ma'am. I believe he will."

"Perhaps indefinitely?"

"Could be."

"More's the pity," she murmured.

We left the library, locking up the door as we went, and headed out onto Main Street.

"Grace, dear, have I ever told you that I grew up on a very lovely farm about ten miles from here? It was over there." She pointed across the fallow fields and away to the east.

"No, Ms. Martha, I don't think you have."

"It was nearly a thousand acres," she said in an impressive whisper.

"Your family must have been very proud."

"Oh, yes," she said, staring away across the fields toward where their farm must have lain.

Pulling herself back from her reflections she said,

"Grace, my daddy once had a bull."

I nodded, thinking this a strange turn to the conversation.

"It was a beautiful, powerful bull and must have weighed over three thousand pounds. My father was so proud of that creature. It was sired and raised on our farm and my father looked at it as one of his special accomplishments. Yet, in spite of its power and beauty, the bull had one very obvious fault. You see it…wouldn't leave the cows alone. Now, I don't mean that he wanted to procreate—for, of course, Daddy wouldn't have objected to that. I mean that he simply wouldn't let the cows be, night or day. He seemed entirely incapable of containing himself. He went from one cow immediately on to the next."

She paused, straightening her hat. I watched her face intently, utterly bewildered and thoroughly embarrassed.

"My daddy was flabbergasted by this problem and tried everything he could think of to get the bull to desist. He even called in a specialist. A bull specialist! Now, can you believe that there is such a thing?"

She glanced over at me, her eyes sparkling with wicked mischief and delight.

"At any rate, the specialist could not make out what was wrong any better than my daddy, and so he sent the man home, deciding that he would have to take care of the problem himself. And, Grace, do you know what my daddy finally did to his bull?"

"No, Ms. Martha."

"He cut his balls off."

My face burned with shame. I couldn't speak.

Ms. Martha winked and turned right onto her street, Idlewild Road, calling back over her shoulder as she went,

"It's something to think about, isn't it, Grace, dear?"

XXVIII.

With Dan ill, Mama now spent most of her evenings at home. Under different circumstances, I would have been completely delighted, but with Dan in the house and a pricking in my thumbs, I sometimes found myself wishing that she would go back to her old schedule of spending evenings with Mrs. Rachel. The new house, which had once been filled with laughter both day and night, had now become very quiet. Dan spent long hours staring into the fire, unmoving, silent. We all left him alone.

During the day, he tossed and turned, trying to sleep. Occasionally, he walked slowly from one room to another, fingering the pretty things that the townspeople had filled the house with. The weeks marched slowly by. Winter passed into spring with a sigh of relief. I began to breathe again.

Toward the middle of April it began to rain. It poured every day and the river rose higher and higher. The earth became soggy and thick with red mud and the dirt roads around our town became like little streams whose courses were arranged in neat city blocks. The mayor (who, to my great surprise, had now been mayor of our town for nearly twenty years) ordered that sandbags be set up around the banks of the river. Everyone waited and watched.

One morning, during the first week of May, I walked through the pouring rain toward the library. I saw in the distance an old truck parked in front of the whitewashed building. It was not yet seven o'clock; knowing that Ms. Martha always walked or rode her bicycle, I was a bit surprised to see the vehicle. About half a block from the library, I recognized the truck and saw through the downpour the dim outline of the owner standing on the other side of it. My heart began pounding like a snare drum inside my chest—I knew instantly who the man was. For just a second, I thought about racing home. I wasn't sure if he had seen me. Then I remembered that Ms. Martha arrived every morning at seven-thirty on the dot to scald her plants, and I realized, with a catch in my throat and beads of sweat beginning to slide down my stomach, that I couldn't leave her alone.

A few more seconds and Lucius heard my footfall. Lifting his hat, he swept onto the sidewalk and took my elbow. I tried to pull away, but his hands were stronger than any man or beast's ought to have been.

"Good mornin', yer Grace," he said with a chuckle. "I's thinkin' las' night that it'd been entirely too long since we last met. I thought you must be gettin' lonely, so I says to m'seff I'd come down to the library first thing this mornin' so not another day would pass without our bein' reunited. It's a nasty mornin', but I thought it might be made jes' a mite better by my comin' to see you."

"That was thoughtful of you, Lucius," I said, swallowing, "but it's a favor I could just as well have done without. I don't generally get lonely, and when I do, nearly any other creature that God ever did make would suit me better than you. I'd rather take a nap with a snappin' turtle and a bobcat than to exchange even 'good mornings' with yourself."

"Now that's hurtful, Grace—I thought we wuz friends."

"No Lucius, that's not the way I'd go about describin' our relationship. I'm fairly certain that, in order for that appellation to apply, both parties would need to like one another."

"I do like ya, Grace. But, I do have to admit, my motives're not altogether selfless. As it turns out, I came more fer what you can do fer me than the other way 'round."

"I don't guess I'm real surprised to hear it."

His hand closed more tightly around the flesh of my arm, his nails digging in. I might have cried out, but I wouldn't give him the satisfaction. He propelled me on toward the door and whispered, his hot breath in my ear,

"Open it, gurl. I've always loved a library n' feel strongly that it's the place to go when a man wants to edgicate hisseff."

I unlocked the door and we stepped in. It was dark and still and smelt of coffee and dust and paper and age. I sat down anxiously behind my desk, my eyes never leaving Lucius. He walked once around the large room and then lit a cigarette. As he paced, I realized that he didn't appear to be as sickly as when I had last seen him. In fact, apart from his extreme thinness, he looked pretty healthy. He wore a new green corduroy jacket and a sorrel-colored scarf and had his hat tilted jauntily over one eye. His hair, which was longer than I remembered it, curled from beneath the back brim of his hat. I was struck again by the neat and slim appearance of his hands and feet.

"I notice you're steadier on your legs than at our last meeting. The last time I had the pleasure, your health appeared to be…failin'."

"Yeah, I'd been under the weather for quite a while. N'fact, I been near dead fer the better part'a my life, but I always had unfinished bidness to see to, an' it wouldn't do to leave this earth without all my ducks lined up in a row, so to speak. I'd hate to go to the judgment seat without havin' er'thang accounted fer."

"I bet you must have a whole lot of accoutin' to do. How's your duck row so far?"

Elder looked at me sharply.

"We—all of us—is gonn' have a lot to reck'n fer, gurl. You'll realize that when you git older."

"I realize it now."

He smiled.

"With that temper'a yourn, I reck'n you would. At any rate, my sick spell's passed for the time bein', and now, as you can see, I'm fit as a fiddle."

He did a little jig on the old brick floor, rivulets of water running down from his coat and boots onto the floor. Then he turned his back to me and studied the rows of books, taking deep drags on his cigarette. Occasionally, he reached up to finger a title or to pull a book from the shelf. I sat and watched, silent as the grave. When his cigarette had burned low, he put it out in one of Ms. Martha's dead pots of Mother-in-Law's Tongues. He took another from his breast pocket and lit it. Then he dropped the match on the library floor and walked toward me, without bothering to put out the live flame. It burned for several seconds and then sputtered and died.

"Grace, I came to see ya this mornin' 'cause I got a proposition fer ya."

"You can't have anything to say to me that I would want to hear."

"You might be surprised."

He sat down in a chair in front of my desk.

"I been tryin' to have words with yer daddy for some months now."

"He isn't my daddy."

He smiled.

"Fine, yer step-daddy," he said, waving my words away with one long, thin hand. "At any rate, there's matters Dan n' I need to work out between oursevves. So far, on 'count a' his...convalescence, I had'n been able to see him. Which really has done broke m'heart. I wanted to go n' pay my respects n' see that he wuz doin' better, but I figur'd that, what with the mayor's house not ten steps away and all the neighbors in n' outta the house all hours, it'd be mighty crowded in there fer a person such as m'seff."

"Almost makes you wish you hadn't burned down our nice quiet house in the country."

"Why, Miss Grace, I don't altogether understand what yer implyin', but I git the distinct feelin' my honor's been impugned."

"I reckon you have to have some before anybody can impugn it."

For just a second his eyes burned like his discarded matchstick, then the light was gone. He laughed and slapped one knee.

"You got a wicked mouth on you, gurl. One a' these days, it'll be your undoin'."

"I thought it was gonna be my temper."

"Yeah, one 'r th'other should finish you off right good."

He looked at me for a long moment, his smile deepening the lines and pockmarks on his face. His eyes wandered over me and I suddenly felt naked and cold and very, very young.

"At any rate," he said, licking his dry lips, "I believe this conversation's digressin'. As I wuz tryin' to say, my inability to converse with yer daddy—stepdaddy, whatever—would make yer assistance all th' more useful. I was hopin' you could arrange fer me n' Dan Brown to have a reunion. It's been jes' too, too long."

I shifted my weight in my chair, uncomfortable, my mouth dry as dust.

"I don't follow."

He leaned back in his chair and put the tips of his fingers together, his long lean legs stretched out in front of him, crossed at the knees.

"I ain't an altogether subtle man, an' Dan certainly ain't, neither. Our...conversations are not generally quiet or tidy. Often, 'tween two such strong willed people, discussions'll escalate perty quick-like."

He studied my face.

"The location of yer house is an unfortunate one, an' I'd like yer help in gainin' unsupervised admitt'nce."

He propped his feet up on my desk, crossing them at the ankles, and reached up with one smooth hand to scratch his chin.

"And with the weather we've been havin' lately, the town's been quieter'n usual. I feel like it's a real good time for me to...be more sociable. I'm beginnin' to see that spendin' as much time alone as I been doin' fer all these years idn't good fer the soul. So, I'd like to be more neighborly; but I reck'n it's better fer Dan n' me to conversate without so many folks around. And now, with the rain, there's not so many house calls of an evenin' as there used to be—I reck'n it'd be better fer everyone involved if we were to meet 'fore the weather clears."

We sat quiet for a few minutes, steadily watching one another, dislike evident on both our faces. Elder smoked one cigarette after another. I sat afraid and silent, feeling streams of sweat running down my legs, under my slip and down my back.

After a while, he began to speak again. He talked for a long while, quietly unfolding his plan. I remained silent, my gaze never leaving his face. His mesmerizing eyes drew me in to their liquid depths. When he finished, he stood, saying,

"Well, I reck'n we've said enough fer the present."

"Lucius, I'm not sure that I'm interested in your plan," I said unsteadily.

"Well, I leave it entirely to yer discretion, yer Grace. Although, I will say, I think it'd be wise to comply. Yer family's seen firsthand what can happen to good, innocent people such as y'sevves when they git mixed up with ne'er-do-wells like Dan n' me."

"What's between you and Dan doesn't have anything to do with me and my family."

"Nah, I don' see it that way. Far's I can tell, yer unfinished bidness with Dan goes back a lot further'n mine does."

He looked at me significantly, his cold eyes faintly smiling. Then he tipped his hat and walked out of the front door of the library, shutting it softly behind him.

That morning was one of the longest I can remember. I heard Elder's words over and over in my mind. I felt sick with dread. As far as I could see, there wouldn't be a good outcome to this situation no matter what course I chose.

"Grace, dear," said Ms. Martha from her footstool as she reshelved books, "you seem distracted. You look a little unwell, dear. Would you like to go home early, my girl?"

"No, thank you, Ms. Martha. I'm all right. I guess I haven't been sleeping much lately."

"What is it, Grace? Is Dan not minding his manners?"

"No, it's not that, Ms. Martha. Dan Brown has been too sick to be at the bottle and, though I haven't had much experience with it, he seems to be better with his p's and q's when he isn't…I think I'm just real tired."

"You must be so exhausted with taking care of him all these weeks."

"Yes, ma'am, I guess so."

"Seems like an awful waste of energy. Doesn't much matter if the doctor patches him up for now. His liver's going to get him pretty soon anyway, if some underhanded dealings of his own don't catch up to him first."

Startled, I studied her face, and was pretty sure that I saw some sort of prescience there. I think she understood how close she was to the truth.

"Perhaps you should send him over to stay with Dr. and Mrs. Barrett for a while. It might be better—and safer—for everyone if he was there," she said, reaching down to place a large volume near the bottom of a case.

"No, ma'am, I think we'd better not. He'd be more trouble than they ever would have bargained for."

She must have heard something in my voice, because she glanced up at me quickly. Her clear, steady gaze held mine, and then she reached up and patted my cheek.

"Grace, you let me know if you need anything. You know where I live."

"Yes, ma'am."

"And, Grace?"

"Yes, ma'am?"

"Remember what I told you about the bull."

That night I walked home through the rain. The water stood three or four inches deep on Main Street. Soon it would be too high to walk through. I felt a tightening in my gut and throat. It looked like it would come a flood.

As I walked into the yard, I saw that Dan was sitting in his shirtsleeves in Mama's rocker. He gazed out into the sheets of water that poured down from the sodden sky. He had grown pretty strong again and the color had come back to his face. Mama had kept him clean and well fed for weeks and, though he was still too thin, he looked very handsome. I climbed the steps and sat down wearily in the rocker next to his.

"Afternoon, Grace," he said quietly. "Looks like this town jes' might wash away after all."

"It might be better for everyone involved if it did."

"How's that?"

"Lucius Elder came to see me this morning."

"That so? I thought he might."

He rocked on, seeming unsurprised. Looking at me out of the corner of his eye, he said,

"I hope he done conducted hisseff in a gentleman-like manner."

"His manners are good enough, but it's not them that concerns me."

"What does?"

"Well, best I can tell, Lucius wants to finish what he started, and he wants my help to do it."

"I see. An' how does he intend t' go about that?"

"He wants me to set a trap for you."

"You plan on doin' it?"

"Well I can't say I wasn't tempted. But Lucius seemed to think I needed time to think things over. He very graciously left it up to my discretion," I said dryly.

"I bet he did. Lucius's nothin' if not gracious," he said, grinning.

"I've been thinking on it all day."

"And?"

"I think I may know what needs doing."

"What's it needs doin'?"

"Well, that depends on you."

"How so?"

"I'm afraid I'm not able to like you much, Dan. But even with all that's happened, and all that you've done, it doesn't seem right to help Lucius kill you."

"Glad to hear it."

"But the way I see it, I don't have much choice."

He looked at me.

"Unless…"

"Unless what?"

"Unless I agree to help you outsmart him."

He fiddled with a splinter of wood breaking free from Mama's rocker.

"And jes' what would convince you t' do a thang like that?" he asked, looking at once hopeful and bemused.

"The way I figure it, you don't stand much chance against him."

"Sure 'nough?"

"You're gettin' stronger, but you're still banged up pretty good, Dan. You're not yet quick on your feet and you're no match for the five or six men he's sure to bring with him."

"So wha'dya propose?"

"I'm willin' to give you some very valuable information in return for a promise from you."

He laughed.

"Y'know what I've always liked 'bout you, Grace? 'Part from yer obvious charm n' disarmin'ly sweet nature..." At that moment, he looked directly into my eyes with a wide smile spreading over his features and grazed a hand over the long scar that ran across one side of his face. "You're a real smart gurl. Don't think I've yet met th' man that could pull one over on ya."

"We'll see," I said. "Be that as it may, you haven't told me if you're interested in my proposal."

"Innersted well 'nough to listen."

"Alright, then: I will tell you what I know in exchange for your promise that, after this is all over, you'll head out to New Mexico or wherever you like, and never come back as long as you live. You never come here again and we never see you or hear from you. Never. In fact, I want your word that you will never again set foot in the state of Tennessee. And if you ever go back on that word, I vow to ask Thena to put a rifle shot in your chest. Now, Dan, I have plenty of faults and weaknesses. But one good thing about me is that I'm dependable."

My eyes searched his face. I noticed for the first time that his crow's feet had deepened over the last few years and he had the beginnings of lines around his mouth and between his brows.

"If I say I'll do a thing, I will. And, Dan, if I asked Thena to do it, she'd be happy as a girl on Christmas morning."

His face was serious for a moment and he said softly,

"I believe it. Strange thing about Thena. I always knowed well 'nough that you'd never hurt nobody 'less'n there weren't no other way out. I never had no illusions 'bout the day you gave me this." He pointed to the long scar that ran faintly down one side of his face. "I don' remember much 'bout that day; I wuz dead drunk. But I knowed then n' I know now that you did what you did to protect Mary."

Those words were the closest Dan Brown ever came to an apology.

"But Thena, she dudn' hate what I done to yer Mama. She hates *me*.

An' I know if she ever got the chance, she'd kill me dead quicker'n she'd bat an eye, n' then she'd stomp on my corpse. After that, she'd throw a party n' two-step 'cross my grave. And that kinda hate dudn' go away. Someday, I'll be long gone, n' all that hatred'll still be trapped inside 'er, n' that's poison. Hatred'll kill ya quick as a gun."

I was surprised to hear those words from a man I'd always considered to be so wicked and thoughtless, so absent of feeling.

We sat quietly after that, rocking and staring out into the rain. The water was rising rapidly in the yard, and I realized with horror that it would only be a matter of time until the river overflowed its banks. My mind reeled. Everything was happening too fast. I wondered what to do—about all of it, any of it. I sat musing for a long time. The sky began to grow dark. Then Dan said softly,

"Alright. I'll do it."

I continued to stare out into the rain.

"Do I have your word?"

"You do."

"And you're certain?"

"Yeah."

"Dan?"

"What?"

"You better keep it."

"I reck'n so. When's Lucius comin'?"

"Sunday. Middle of the night. I'm to leave the doors unlocked and your window open."

"Can you git everybody outta th' house?"

"No. He said if I did, you'd suspect. If he gets here and the house is empty, he'll know I told you."

"You n' Elsa'll take the little ones into yer Mama's bedroom n' bolt the door. I'll give you a rifle. What time?"

"'Round three."

AS THE SPARK FLIES UPWARD

"His men comin' with 'im?"

"Yeah," I said softly. Then, glancing up into his weary, bloodshot eyes, I asked, "Dan, will he come after us, too?"

"No. Believe it er not, Elder's not an unreason'ble man. He's got no quarrel with you. If I kill 'im, then you've got nothin' to worry 'bout. If he kills me, then he's done what he done come to do, an' he'll leave."

I nodded. "He said as much, but I've never been inclined to trust him. Come to think of it, I'm not sure how inclined I am to trust you."

He chuckled. "Well, Grace, much's ya hate to, yer gonna have to trust one of us."

"Dan, what is it that you've done to Lucius? How did this whole thing get started?"

"It dudn' much matter anymore, Grace. I owe him money. A lotta money."

"And there's no chance of you payin' it back?"

"Not since I kilt three a' his men."

"No, I guess not."

"Sunday night?" he asked.

"Yeah."

He stood up and walked from the porch out into the rain, wading through the water. I watched him for a long time until he turned the corner onto Main Street. It was the first time he had left the house since he came to us.

XXIX.

Dan didn't return that night. I lay in bed for many hours, listening, waiting, straining my ears and body, half-hoping to hear the thud of his boots across the front porch, but I never did. The next morning, long before sunrise, I awoke with a start to the sound of pounding on the front door. To my surprise, it was the mayor. He stood in the pouring rain, hat in hand, water streaming down his face and clothes.

"Something the matter, Mayor?"

"Ask your mama if she can come see to Mrs. Rachel. She's not well."

Mama came quietly down the stairs as he spoke, pinning up her hair and buttoning the top buttons of her faded blouse.

"What is it, Mayor Wilkins? Mrs. Rachel feelin' ill?"

The mayor stood blinking at the bright light flooding out from our house. He looked sickly and pale, the skin of his face stretched too tightly over his bones, his thin lips colorless, and his eyes dark with worry. I hadn't realized until that moment that he was not a young man anymore.

"She's...at it again, I'm afraid."

"Well, come o'an in here outta the rain while I pull m'self together," said Mama.

She put an arm around his shoulders and pulled him gently inside. For just a second, I saw a look of relief flit across his face. He nodded and stepped across the threshold, shaking water from him as he came. It pooled in puddles around him and ran away across the hallway floor, finally settling between the cracks in the floorboards. He ran a hand over his pale face and let out a low groan, so soft I almost didn't hear it.

"How bad is she?"

"I've never seen her worse. She's hallucinatin'. I haven't gotten anything out of her all night that made any sense."

Mama watched his face for a moment, then nodded.

"How long?"

"Most of the night—two or three in the morning, I reckon."

"What's she had?"

The mayor's gaze shifted nervously from Mama's face to mine. He licked his thin lips and moved to stand before the fire. There was a long pause and then he said,

"I found two empty fifths underneath her bed, and she's finished off the last of the pain medicine."

"She took all of it?" said Mama, putting a hand to her heart.

I looked from one to the other, confused. The mayor nodded without turning away from the fire.

"Have you sent for the Doc?"

He turned to face Mama then.

"You know I can't do that."

"I know it's hard for you, Bentley." Mama's voice was soft and sorrowful.

I glanced over at her, startled. I had never heard her call him by his Christian name.

"But I don't thaink you have much choice this time. Mrs. Rachel's been bad for a long while now—months—and I'm not sure that she'll make it if you don't."

He turned back to the fire and stood looking into the flames. After a moment, he straightened his thick shoulders and nodded, putting his hat on his head.

"Mary, we best get back to her. She's been askin' for you all night. I didn't have the heart to come over here and wake you earlier, but she won't be able to rest until you're with her."

Mama pulled on tall boots and her threadbare coat and opened the front door. The sky was beginning to grow lighter, but there would be no sunrise. The rain poured down, the wind driving it sideways in pale, diaphanous ribbons. The drops fell thick and heavy, landing blows on the streams. I strained my eyes, trying to see out beyond the yard. As far as I could see, the earth was covered in water. I could no longer see where our yard ended and the sidewalk and street began.

"Grace," said Mama, "go after the Doc. Go as fast as you can, n' be careful."

She and the Mayor waded out into the yard and onto Seventh Street.

I climbed the stairs, thinking that I should check on the boys before I left. Franklin, John and Edwin lay quietly sleeping in their bed. Isaac slept in Mama's bed with Elsa and Lilliana. I glanced across the hall to my empty bed. Thena hadn't been home in several days. I sat down on her side of the bed, my hand touching the still, cool cotton of the sheets. I sat there for a long time.

After a while, I suddenly remembered what had brought me upstairs. I dressed hastily, pulled on boots and trudged toward Doc and Nora's. Their house was not a mile away, but it was half an hour before I made it. The water was about a foot deep and the current black and strong.

As I walked through the downpour, I noticed with surprise that many of the houses in the town were already lit. Occasionally, I saw a pale, uncertain face peak out toward the street from behind a muslin curtain. The town was already awake, and I realized it was because they were afraid; afraid of the water that continued to leap down from the sky, landing heavily on the waterlogged streets; afraid of what might be coming—afraid of the river.

I met Doc coming down the steps of their little white house. Light poured out from the windows; through the pale curtains I could see that

Nora was up and moving around the house.

"Grace! Dear Lord, what're you doin' out in weather like this?" asked Doc.

"Mama sent me."

He looked surprised.

"Dan?"

"No, sir. Not this time. It's Mrs. Wilkins. The mayor knocked on our door not an hour ago, saying there was something wrong with her."

"What is it?"

"I don't think I entirely understand it, Doc. But it must be bad—the mayor was pale as death."

He nodded, stepping down from the porch into the swirling water.

"Grace, I need to go down and check on the river people. The river's rising fast. If the rain keeps up, it won't hold for more than another day or two. Those people need to get out of there and move up to higher ground. I need you to go and tell Mary and the mayor that I'll be there as quick as I can, but until then they're going to have to do for Mrs. Rachel."

"Doc, I think she may have taken too much medicine."

"What?"

"The mayor said something about liquor and pills."

I saw a flash of understanding pass over the Doc's face. He nodded.

"I see."

He took a small translucent brown bottle from his leather bag and handed it to me.

"Tell your mama to give Rachel this. They need to give her all of it. Slowly. Tell Mary they have to make her drink. Even if they have to force it, she has to drink. This will make her sick," he said, pointing to the bottle, "very sick, but it may save her. They've got to flush it out of her. Give me two hours. I'll be there in less if I can. I hate to leave her, but down the river way there are dozens and dozens of families—women, children, babies. Somebody's got to get them out of there. Run, Grace."

Then he was gone.

I stayed with Mama and the mayor that day, although Mama, who must have sensed the mayor's humiliation, kept me out of the sick room. Doc arrived many hours later, looking worn and weary, his clothes and hair dripping with dirty brown river water. I filled him up with black coffee and cold meat and, though he was dead tired, he worked through the evening trying to save Mrs. Rachel. The hours passed and I sat at the kitchen table, reading a book from the mayor's library, not daring to leave in case Mama should need me.

At some point in the long evening I must have fallen asleep. I awoke in the dark kitchen to the sound of Thena and Reed's voices as they came through the front hall. They entered the room with Reed carrying Thena on his back.

"Gracie!" she said, leaping to the ground. "How long since you been out there? The water's up to my knees in places! I made Reed carry me the last mile or two. I couldn't think of any reason why we should both get worn out," she said, laughing.

She stepped over to the fire, shaking water from her hair and clothes.

"Why're you here?" she asked, looking around, as if it suddenly occurred to her that I shouldn't be there.

I glanced over at Reed, uncertain of what to say.

"Mrs. Rachel's not doing well."

"Oh, is that all? I'm sure she'll be feelin' better in the mornin'."

Thena touched Reed's shoulder and smiled at him—a smile I had never seen her give to anyone else. He stood in the doorway, watching my face for a moment. Without a word, he turned and went upstairs to his mother's room.

"Why'd you and Mama git out in this jes' fer one of Mrs. Wilkins' hangovers?"

"One of her what?"

She laughed.

"Gracie, you're a smart girl, but you aren't very worldly-wise, are you?"

"No, I guess not. Least not so much as you."

"No," she grinned. "Not so much as me."

"Did Reed tell you?"

"He didn't have to. Has it never seemed strange to you that Mama has spent the better part a' the last twenty years—her nights and weekends, and every minute a' time that she ought rightly to've had to herself—takin' care of Mrs. Rachel, without ever once mentioning the nature of her mysterious illness? What? Did you thaink she'd had a bad cold all this time?"

I shrugged.

"She'll sober up in a day or two n' be right as rain. Then she won't touch the bottle for a week or two or three an' then, one day, for no reason, she'll be at it again."

I was stunned. It suddenly seemed so obvious. How was it that, all this time, Thena had known, and I had never had any idea?

"I don't think she'll be right as rain in a day or two this time," I said slowly.

"What do you mean?"

"I think she poisoned herself—Doc called it alcohol poisoning."

"The Doc's here?"

"Has been since this afternoon."

Thena went white. Her green eyes shone from her pale face, surrounded by the halo of her black hair.

"Poisoned herself?"

"She took pills with the liquor."

She pulled out a chair and sank into it slowly.

"Will she make it?"

"Don't know. Doesn't look good."

"Oh, Lord," she said softly.

For a few minutes we listened to the sound of the falling rain. We both looked up as lightning split the sky. For an instant the town was lit up. In the strange light reflecting off the water, it looked beautiful and terrible.

"Ain't it strange that Mama's life seems fated for this?" Thena said, her eyes staring away into the drowning world outside the mayor's windows.

"How do you mean?"

"She spends all her time takin' care a' drunks."

"I reckon it seems to be all of our fates."

"Yeah," she said slowly, smiling strangely to herself, "I guess it does."

Then she began to laugh.

"What do you thaink, Grace?" she said, rubbing her eyes wearily. "With a mother n' a father unable to let the bottle alone, am I doomed to be a sot m'self?"

"A mother and a father? I don't follow. Dan's no blood kin of yours and Mama's never touched a drop in her life as far as I know."

"I didn't mean our mother."

"Didn't know a girl could have more than one."

"Sure she can," she said quietly. "Her own mother and her husband's mother."

Her eyes, snapping and sparking with mischief, bore into mine as a smile grew around the edges of her mouth. I felt the blood draining out of my face.

"Your husband's mother?" I said, my voice so soft I could barely hear it.

She shrugged.

"Last fall, soon as Reed turned eighteen, he got a letter from the war department saying he was going to be drafted. We had both known he would be n' we had it all planned out. The day he turned eighteen we packed a picnic, drove to Memphis n' got married. A week later, he left for Fort Campbell. He left on a Tuesday morning. We said goodbye, thinkin' we might not ever see each other again. By Thursday night, he was back. They wouldn't send him because of his lungs."

She watched me from across the table. For a while, I couldn't speak.

"You never told anyone?"

"No one." She smiled. "Not even our Grace."

"Why not?"

"Lotsa reasons. Everyone would've said we were too young—or at least that Reed was. Not to mention that I'm not exactly what the mayor n' Mrs. Rachel would have hoped for their only son. Imagine it—their son married to their servant's daughter! Both of 'em, though I'm sorry to speak ill of Mrs. Rachel when she's not well, are terrible snobs. An' if you wanna know what I thaink about it, they don't have much reason to be. Anyway, they would have been heartbroken n' humiliated into the very ground."

"That's not true Thena, and you know it. This whole town thinks you hung the moon."

"Maybe," she said, shaking her head with a half-grin. "Maybe most people do. But I don't know if the mayor n' his wife have ever noticed that there is a moon—I've never known either of 'em to notice anythang beyond their own selves. 'Sides, they wouldn't care if I had. Hangin' the moon's not the same as bein' rich or socially acceptable." She shrugged, looking impatient, as if the subject annoyed her.

"You're gonna have to tell them sometime or another."

She nodded.

"I'm not much lookin' forward to it, least for Reed's sake. 'Part from them," she said, glancing up to the ceiling toward the floor above us, "it didn't seem like much of a time fer celebratin', what with the war n' the fire. After the fire it didn't seem like any of us would ever smile again. Even after we moved into town, I couldn't look at Mama in the face. Her eyes jes' looked so dead, like he had finally beat 'er."

316

A deep line appeared between her eyes and she sat quiet for a minute, her jaws clenched.

"So, for weeks we didn't say a word. Every day it was drivin' us both crazy. Then, one Sunday, we just decided we couldn't keep it to ourselves no more. We figured everybody would be happy for us once they got used to the idea. So we thought we'd break the news after Sunday lunch."

Then suddenly I understood.

"But Dan came back that day."

She nodded, her face dark with hatred.

"After that, we didn't feel much like celebratin' either. And I knew I couldn't stay in that house with him one more day."

She stood and walked across the kitchen to stand before the window.

"Looks downright mournful out there," she said.

I nodded.

"The Doc went down this afternoon to get the river people out. He says the banks won't hold much longer."

"Doesn't look much like it. Did Doc get 'em all out?"

"No, he said most refused to go. They won't leave their homes."

"Poor ignorant wretches!" she said, half indignantly. "Don't they remember what happened last time?"

"I guess they remember that the last time they left, they lost everything they had—not that it was much."

"Better to lose their houses than their lives."

"I reckon they don't plan on losin' either."

"Things don't turn out the way we plan."

Thena took the kettle from the stove and filled it, then set it down to boil. The house was quiet; so quiet that it seemed like we were the only two people in the world.

"I'm cold. I've been cold for days. It's this rain. Keeps us wet through all the time. This town's beginnin' to look like the Atlantic."

She hugged her arms tightly to her body.

"You ain't ever seen the Atlantic," I said, smiling at her.

She smiled back.

"Sure I have." She nodded out the window. "And it's right out there."

The image of Dan wading away through the ocean of water sprang suddenly to my mind. I realized that, for many hours, I had not thought of him. I wondered where he was and if he had ever come home.

"Thena, I think you and Reed had better stay away from the house on Sunday night."

"Why's that?" she asked.

The kettle began to sing and I stood, pulling two hand painted, gold leaf trimmed china cups and saucers off the shelf. They looked too pretty to use, or at least like you would need to be pretty to drink out of them. Using them made me nervous. I filled both cups with boiling water and Thena added tea leaves. We stood side by side, stirring the steaming mugs. I looked over at her.

"Lucius Elder's comin' to finish off Dan."

"He's what?!" she exclaimed, her voice tight with fear.

I told her the story from beginning to end, starting from the morning after the fire. She listened without speaking, drinking from her mug, her eyes staring into the bright fire. When I finished she said,

"Grace, I hate to refer you to the obvious, but…don't you thaink it's past bein' time to take this to the sheriff?"

"We can't."

"I don't see there's anything else *to* do."

"Lucius told me that I would do well to leave the law out of it. He said as long as I do what he told me, nobody but Dan will get hurt. He said his fight's not with us unless we make it so. And he means it. Right now, I don't think he plans on hurtin' us, but I also don't think he'd have any qualms about changin' his plans. According to Elder, Dan Brown's a mean snake of a man and deserves what he gets, and I shouldn't let it trouble my conscience. Then he told me he would hate for anything to happen to our sweet mama or her little boys."

"Good God," she said, her voice weak.

Her face had become pale and her body shook with anger. I took the clattering china cup and saucer gently from her hand and sat them carefully on the table.

"Sit down, Thena."

I pulled a chair out for her and pushed her down into it.

"What will you do?"

"Well, much as I hate to say it, I can't let Elder murder a wounded, unarmed man. So I figure I'll make it a fair fight and then get out of the way."

"You're gonna help Dan?" she said, her voice trembling with wrath, her face incredulous.

"Thena, I couldn't have that fool's murder on my conscience for all eternity."

"I'm pretty sure the Lord would thank you for it."

"I think it'd be the devil."

"I'd rather be sleepin' in the devil's bed than be a friend to Dan Brown," she said, her voice quick and cold.

Her eyes burned into me. She thought I was a traitor.

"Be careful, Thena," I said softly. "The devil's bed might look like a good place for sleepin' from the outside, but once you're in it it's bound to be powerful hot."

I heard soft footsteps on the stairs and knew that it would be Mama.

"If Mrs. Rachel holds on, Mama should be out of the house," I whispered. "I'll send the little'uns with you. I'm hopin' Elder will be too busy to notice that they're gone. Elsa and I will stay in the house."

"No!" she said sharply. "I'm gonna be in that house. I'll keep the babies with me an' I'll keep 'em safe, but I'm gonna be there. I think I just might offer to help Elder."

"Speakin' of the devil, I think you'd be wise to stay about as far away from that man as you can. You'll keep on thinkin' Dan Brown's a real bad man until you know Elder."

She smiled at me then, her sharp white teeth flashing, her eyes feverish. Her face shone bold and brilliant with a fearsome beauty.

"Ya know, Grace," she said, "the devil always did scare you more'n me."

"I reckon that's true enough, but I don't think even you'd like to spend all your days with him."

"Oh, Grace, darlin', are you worryin' over my immortal soul?"

"Yeah, and mine, too."

"Well, if what you n' Mama say is true, an' my soul *is* immortal, I guess I'll have plenty a' time to contemplate it."

XXX.

Mama stumbled into the kitchen, looking exhausted. There were dark purple shadows under her eyes and the front of her dress was stained with vomit. I went to her, putting an arm around her thin shoulders. I took one of her tiny frail hands in mine.

"Mama, your hand's cold as ice. You need to rest and eat somethin'."

She pushed my hands away and sank down into a chair, pushing her hair out of her face with the back of her hand.

"No, Grace. I couldn't eat a bite. Jes' coffee. Black n' boilin' hot."

"How's Mrs. Rachel?" asked Thena.

Mama shook her head. "I don't know. It doesn't look good to me, but the Doc ain't ready to give up. I thaink he still has some hope."

"Is Reed in with her?"

"He n' the mayor both," said Mama, nodding wearily. "Grace?"

"Yes, Mama?"

"Has Dan come back?"

"I don't know Mama, I haven't been home today."

She sighed.

"I think you best go o'an home. Nothin' you can do here. The boys'll be hungry an' I don't want Elsa to have to feed n' put to bed all a' them younguns on her own. I know the water's high, but if it gets any higher, we'll both be stuck here 'til it's all over. I'd feel a lot better if you were there to see about the boys n' the baby."

"Alright Mama, I'll go."

"You should go with her, Thena."

"No, Mama. I'm staying here with you n' Reed. If you don't need me for anythang else, you might need me for company."

Mama sipped her coffee silently, looking too tired to argue.

Outside it was night, cold and black. I trudged home through water nearly up to my knees. The rain continued to fall, though it seemed a more gentle rain than we had seen for many days. Occasionally, the sky lit up with a great flash of light and I could see for a moment the underwater world our town had become. Houses seemed to float up through the water and the spire of the new Presbyterian church looked like a jagged tooth biting through the night sky.

At home, the house was quiet, the children subdued. Dan was home, sitting in Mama's rocker, pulled up close to the fire. Elsa stood over Mama's cast iron kettle, one of the few belongings that had survived the fire, cooking supper. She looked up as I came in.

"I'm glad you're home, Grace. I been worried sick 'bout you all day. Where on earth have you n' Mary beeyn?"

Isaac toddled over to me and reached up to be held. Lilliana came over and wrapped her sweet body around my leg.

"Up the mayor's," I said, picking Isaac up and holding his soft, clean smelling goodness to my chest. "Mrs. Rachel's real bad."

"I'm sorry to hear it, but I hate fer yer Mama to give up her evenin's rest over it. She spends more time in the mayor's house than she does her own, poor woman. You hungry?" she asked.

"Not much," I said.

"You're wet through to the skin. Run o'an up n' change."

I came back downstairs several minutes later, dry and warmer, and with the beginnings of hunger pains rumbling through my middle.

"Have you seen Thena?" Elsa asked.

"She stayed on at the mayor's house to be with Reed."

"Hmph," said Elsa, her face disapproving. "An' what does Reed need her fer?"

"Well, things with Mrs. Rachel don't look good," I said, wishing I could tell Elsa that Thena was now Reed's wife.

"Really?" said Elsa, pointing to the table and handing me a steaming plate of meat, vegetables and corn bread. "I had no idea thangs were's bad as that. I knew Mrs. Rachel'd been sickly fer years, but I never thought it wuz anythang serious."

"No, I don't think anybody did."

"What's wrong with 'er?"

"I'm not sure we'll ever really know," I said, feeling uncomfortable.

"Well, I have to admit, I never had the highest opinion a' the mayor or his wife, but I sure am sorry to hear 'bout anyone sufferin', and I hope that she'll recover n' live a long time."

"The water still risin'?" asked Dan from across the room.

"Not as fast. It's still deep, but I think the rain may quit yet."

I couldn't sleep that night. The day had held too much. My mind was tossed about on waves too big for me. I lay awake in my bed for many hours, listening to the lonely weeping of the rain and the sounds of the house. From time to time, I heard Dan stirring down below. I don't think he ever went to sleep.

Finally, a little while before sunrise, I went down the hall and climbed into bed with Elsa and the babies. The bed was warm and soft. For a few minutes, I lay listening to the sounds of their steady breathing. I kissed Isaac's soft, warm face, reached out a hand to touch Lilliana and fell asleep.

≈ ≈ ≈

I woke on Saturday morning to feel Isaac's little body pressed against mine. He lay on his stomach with his bottom stuck up in the air and his feet tucked under my ribs. I lay there for a long time without moving, watching him sleep. He was so beautiful and brown and fat. I touched the soft silk of his brown curls and the curves of his chubby cheeks. My mama, among her other gifts and talents, sure knew how to make beautiful babies. I have often wondered if it was because they were grown—in the face of terrible pain and poverty—with such fierce, immutable love.

Mama had not been home in three days and Mrs. Rachel continued to cling to life. In the meantime, I had taken to sleeping in Mama's place. In my whole life, I had never slept alone until the last few weeks. Without Thena, the bed was too empty to fall asleep in. I wondered when Mama would be home again, and when I would have to move back to my empty bed down the hall. The Doc had decided that if Mrs. Rachel didn't make a marked improvement by the next morning, she would have to be taken to Memphis somehow and admitted to the hospital there. In fact, if it hadn't been for the weather, he would have sent her already.

I lay there in the warmth of Mama's old worn blankets, reluctant to move or think about what the day would hold. I stared out the window into the gray, soulless morning. The rain had slowed to a trickle. The day was pale and unfriendly, and the flood had robbed the sky of its sunrise splendor. Though the barren sky was still clouded over, I thought it seemed a little lighter than the day before. I gazed out into the dreary half-light, thinking that the day looked forlorn.

As far as my eyes could see the earth was a wasteland; tree limbs and trash and leaves lay floating atop the sheen of the water. The dull light from above shone down onto the murkiness, which lay like a dirty blanket spread out across our once lovely town. The weak shimmer reflecting off the water was vaulted back onto the ceiling of Mama's bedroom. I lay watching as the reflection slithered and shimmered across the length of the ceiling and back, looking like a cool, pearly gray snake.

Elsa stirred and I looked over at her. Her body was wrapped tightly around Lilliana, a frown creasing her pretty forehead. Lilliana's plump white fist was curled around her Mama's slim forefinger and her blond head buried in Elsa's chest. I watched the tiny green vein throbbing just above Elsa's right cheekbone. There were dark circles under her eyes and she moaned quietly, as if in pain. I thought, with a pang of guilt, that perhaps she was dreaming about what I had told her the night before. About Dan. About Lucius Elder.

She opened her eyes.

"You sleep?"

"Not much, I guess."

"Me neither."

We lay there watching one another, each of us holding tightly to the sleeping babies. It was strange that, though I still thought of Lilliana as a baby, she would be starting school in the fall. I heard down below stairs the clumping of Dan's boots on the floorboards.

"I don' think he's slept in three nights."

I shook my head. "I don't blame him. You know, Elsa, I think, in some strange way, Dan feels responsible for us."

"He always has, honey. But the drink always got the better of 'im. Dan's a wicked, cruel drunk, sure 'nough. But when he's sober, he's not such a bad man."

"So I hear."

I remembered suddenly what Lucius had told me on the morning after the fire. My heart began to pound in my chest and I heard the whirring, booming sounds of my blood as it pumped up through my heart and rushed into my head and ears.

"Elsa? Can I ask you somethin' that's not really any of my business?"

She lay there beside me, studying my face, her eyes guarded.

"I reck'n."

"On the morning after the fire, Elder said somethin' to me that I don't quite understand. He said that Dan was Stephen and Lilli's father."

It was the first time I had ever mentioned her son's name to her. I saw a shadow flit over her face.

"I was already pretty sure that he was. But then he said that your name is Elsa Brown and that you and Dan are—brother and sister."

For an instant, her face flashed red hot with anger. Then she rolled over onto her back and put a hand up to her eyes. She began to laugh.

"Grace, do you know the one thang you'n trust a liar never to do?"

She glanced over at me. I looked at her with raised brows, embarrassed and yet inquisitive. She smiled softly, stroking Lilli's hair away from her pink face.

"Tell the truth."

She sat up and slid her feet over the side of the bed.

"Lilli n'…Stephen are Dan's children, but I ain't Dan's sister. My name *is* Elsa Brown. Dan's my first cousin. Our daddies were brothers. I'm my father's last child, conceived a' his third wife n' born to 'im on his seventieth birthday. One night, 'bout five years ago, in a drunken rage, my daddy kicked me outta the house. I wuz wanderin' 'round Missoura half-starvin' when Dan found me. He dudn' have many good qualities, but he didn' leave me sick n' hungry like everybody else did. Said he didn' know that he could do much fer me, but I wuz welcome to come with 'im. I never loved Dan—least I was never *in* love with 'im. But when he wudn' drunk, he wuz decent to me. And, in his way, he loved me n' took care a' me. I don' think real highly a' Dan fer what he done to yer Mama, but where I come from, he's not the worst man you could find by a long piece. As fer Lucius Elder, that man's doin' his damndest to mess with this family, and I reck'n he'll lie 'bout anythang that'll bring about a bad end."

I spent the day with Elsa and the little ones. They were tired of being cooped up inside and were restless and ill tempered. Edwin and Franklin Delano rolled around the floor wrestling with one another, kicking the table legs and knocking over chairs, until Edwin's leg knocked Isaac in the face and the game was put to a swift end.

I carried the bleeding Isaac over to the rocker and examined his rapidly swelling eye. Elsa took either boy by an ear and escorted them unceremoniously to the hearth. They sat pouting for a while and then asked if they could play again. Elsa said she didn't want any more trouble out of them, so she and I took turns telling stories until our voices were hoarse.

In the afternoon, Dan left for several hours. I decided to trek through the flowing, syrupy-thick water to the mayor's house to check on Mama and Thena. Mrs. Rachel had held on through another night. Doc said he thought her pulse was a little stronger and her breathing easier. I was deeply relieved, both for Thena and for Reed. Mrs. Rachel had never been a very good mama to Reed, but any mama at all was better than none. I sat for a long time with Mama and Thena and Reed in Mrs. Rachel's pale blue kitchen.

In the weak light, the dark room looked gray. Long shadows were cast over the floor and ceiling. Mama slept face down on the kitchen table. She had been up for nearly three days straight. Doc and Mayor Wilkins sat upstairs with Mrs. Rachel. The house was utterly silent; the only sound was the ticking of Mrs. Rachel's grandfather clock.

I set out for home mid-evening. Mama remained where she was at the table. I could not remember ever having seen her look so tired. Thena and Reed had fallen into an exhausted sleep stretched out on the uncomfortable horsehair settee in Mrs. Rachel's parlor. I walked to the front door and glanced back through the house, surprised, as I always was, by how unwelcoming it looked. It was a fine old house, but I don't believe it had ever really been a home.

That night, sunset came early. The day had been dark and unusually chilly for May, but the rain had stopped in the early afternoon. The town breathed a sigh of relief. Though much damage had been done, it looked for the moment as if, unless the rain began again, the riverbanks might hold; the worst might have been avoided.

I walked home through the cold, deep water just as it was beginning to grow dark. It was not yet seven o'clock. The night was coming on in shades of blue and gray and purple, the horizon just tinged with the faintest wisp of orange. I noticed that the current had weakened and absently wondered how long it would take for the waters to recede. I walked on through the town and saw not a single person. The flood had turned Shady Grove into a ghost town. It hit me, just then, that it was Saturday night. I shivered and hurried on toward Seventh Street.

Just about the time I made it home, another storm broke. The sky was ripped apart by dazzling flashes of light and the air filled with the popping and cracking of the bolts and the ominous rolls of thunder. The storm lasted for hours; the rain fell so hard that I could not see beyond the porch. Isaac sat on my lap, shaking, and I noticed that even Elsa and the older children looked nervous.

After dinner, I sent the children off to bed and, for once, they seemed relieved to go. The day had been too long for them. Elsa and I washed the supper dishes and decided we would also go to bed. Just before I climbed the stairs, I glanced over at Dan. He sat with his back to me, facing the fire. He sat still in Mama's rocker, one hand touching his rifle, which he had leaned against the fireplace.

"Dan. Maybe you should try and sleep a spell tonight. I don't guess you'll get the chance tomorrow night."

He nodded. "Maybe I will. I dunno. I reck'n I'm tired, but I don't feel's if I could sleep."

I still remember that night as if it happened today; five minutes ago; just now. I can see it as if it were in a movie. I have not yet been able to remove a single detail from my memory. Every second is etched in stone and blood. *Out, damned spot!* My mind still screams, decades later. But none of it has ever, ever washed away. The bloodstains in my mind have never turned to a dull, heavy, lifeless brown—the way an old bloodstain will. Every minute, every instant I still see in scarlet.

Somewhere far away I heard a tinkling, crashing sound. It couldn't have been the storm; it had stilled hours ago. I lay sleeping for another second, and then I knew, before I ever woke, what it was. Lucius had set me up. He had come tonight. Saturday. He had known that I would betray him. He was playing a game, and I was his pawn. I lay still for a moment and then heard a murmur that I thought might be Mama's voice. A shiver coursed over me and my body began to shake. I sat bolt upright, wide-awake and leapt from the bed. I tore out into the blackness of the hall, running as fast as I could. Sweat began to run in streams down my face. It slid down my cheeks and blended with the tears.

"MAMA!" I screamed. "MAMA! NO!"

A rifle shot tore through the silence of the night and I fell to the floor, sobbing. I crawled on my hands and knees down the rest of the hall, screaming to Elsa to keep the children upstairs. There was a second shot, then a third. Then a man's voice screamed into the darkness. I heard footsteps running across the wooden floor, then the front door opened and was slammed shut. I crawled past Edwin and John and Franklin's room. John opened the door a crack.

"Grace!" I heard Franklin scream.

I reached up and pulled their door closed. My voice choked with sobs, I screamed,

"John, you keep them in there! Don't come out!"

At the head of the stairway I looked down into the kitchen. The fire had burned out and the room was completely shuttered in darkness. I crawled down the stairs and thought I saw someone lying on the floor by the front door. I heard three more gunshots from outside the house and the sounds of men's voices shouting and cursing. I crawled up to the body on the floor and felt that the ground around it was warm and slippery with blood. The boards by the front door were covered in broken glass and it sliced through my hands and calves and feet. I knew then that Lucius had shot through the front door. I rolled the small form onto its back and saw that it was Mama. I remember hearing myself screaming, over and over, and the feeling of her blood all over me. Her body was still warm and she looked as if she might open her eyes at any moment and tell me not to cry.

But she couldn't. She never would again. She was gone.

I lay there on the floor with her, my body wrapped around her, and felt my mother's lifeblood flowing away over the floorboards. I watched the crimson river as it ran toward the fireplace. I saw an ember spark up in the lifeless ashes. I listened to the sounds of feet sloshing through the water. I heard the voices of the townspeople as they began to wake up. I knew that Doc and the sheriff would arrive soon. Things were happening around me and still I lay on the floor with Mama, rocking. As I lay kissing her face and brushing the hair from her eyes, the words of her favorite hymn flitted through my mind:

> *Are you washed in the blood,*
> *In the soul-cleansing blood of the Lamb?*
> *Are your garments spotless?*
> *Are they white as snow?*
> *Are you washed in the blood of the Lamb?*

I lay there for a long time. Her presence hung heavy in the room. It was peaceful and calm, somehow. I knew that she was happy, at rest. I lay there with her on the warm, sticky floor, my garments washed in the dark foam that streamed from the wound in her chest.

I still vividly remember the hours after she died. Doc and Nora were there, both of them stricken with pain and horror. I remember seeing Doc's body turned to the fire that someone had built and watching his back shake with sobs. I remember Sheriff Bridges' soft, patient voice as he questioned me. But I don't remember what he asked or what I said in return. He stayed for many hours, but after a time he, too, went away. There might be arrests in the coming days, but for now, there would be none. Dan had never seen Elder's face and, though he had shot into the darkness as the gunman retreated, he never hit anything, as far as he knew. Dan told the sheriff that he owed Elder a large sum of money and that he thought it had to do with that. The sheriff asked, his expression cautious, if there was anything else Dan could tell him. Dan said there wasn't.

Then Thena came in, her body held up by Reed's strong arms. She was silent and her eyes were dry. Mama's body lay on a pallet on the floor. Thena looked over at her. Then she walked slowly, painfully over to Dan. He sat crying quietly in Mama's rocker. She looked into his swollen eyes for a long time and then she struck him. He looked up at her, gasping, but stayed where he was. She slapped him again and again and again. Finally, the Doc pulled her away and she began to scream. I still remember the sound. For years after Mama's death I would sometimes hear those screams in the quietest part of the night. She fell to the floor, stretching her body out across Mama's and began to cry. Sobs rattled in her throat, low and dry. But tears never came.

Doc and Nora stayed with us all that night. At sunrise the next morning, Ms. Martha appeared. She sat with me the whole day, silent and still, her arm around my shoulder, my hand clasped tightly in hers. Her eyes were swollen and her face gray as ash. Occasionally, she shook her head or pulled out her handkerchief to wipe away silent tears as they fell. She stayed through the day and left at sundown. The rain continued through all of that day and the next and I heard, without much interest, that the river had begun to overflow its banks. The river people had been forced to leave their homes and, with the river just shy of a mile away, there was talk of evacuating the town soon.

Dan hadn't spoken a word for days. He sat in Mama's rocker, his favorite chair, staring away through the fire and beyond it. Sometimes he wept; sometimes he was silent. On the third day after Mama died, he left the house. Since Mama's death, Doc and Nora had stayed with us through most of the daylight hours, leaving only to go home at bedtime. On the evening after Dan left, Nora had pressed us to go home with them. But none of us wanted to leave the house where we had lived with Mama. Now I wish that we had. Her body had been taken away in the afternoon to be stored until the waters receded enough for burial. Her body was gone, but her sweet voice still echoed off the walls.

Dan came back late that night. He was very drunk; maybe the worst I had ever seen him. It was the first time he had been drunk in many weeks. He lay in the corner of the front room with his bottle for the rest of the night, crying and talking to himself, and though we didn't want to hear him, we could not have avoided it. Thena and Reed and Elsa and I sat in front of the fire long into the night.

"I ne'er thought Mary'd come home," he sobbed. "It was suppos'a be Sund'y night. She said she come home 'cuz Mrs. Rachel wuz better." He looked up at me. "It should've beeyn me."

Thena's face turned very white. Her knuckles were clenched tightly at her sides.

"She knew," he said. "I tol' 'er I wanted 'er take all a' y'uns n' run. I wanted y'uns git outta this God-forsak'n town Sund'y mornin'. I tol' 'er everythang, n' she jes' sat there holdin' my hand, tellin' me all'd be alright. She tol' me no place on earth is God-forsaken. She said we'd werk it out."

He took a long drink from his bourbon bottle and wiped the snot and tears from his face with the sleeve of his muddy shirt.

"Then we heard steps on th' porch n' she looked at me, her face wuz so white n' 'er eyes big's the moon n' she knew. She stood up n' ran to th' door, tryin' to git 'tween me n' Elder."

Thena began to sob and I heard a scream rise up from her throat.

"Elder couldn' see. He thought he wuz shootin' me. He shot 'er from not more'n four feet. He done thought all along he'd finally got me."

He laid his head down on the floor and wept again, his whole body shaking until I thought his bones would snap.

"Mary! Mary! Mary!" he cried over and over.

After a long time the sobs became quieter. Then, finally, they stopped. I felt numb and sick and cold all at the same time. The room was silent. I listened to the ticking of the clock. The minutes stretched out eternally before us. A long time passed and no one moved. We sat there, stunned, unable to speak for more than an hour. I must have fallen asleep eventually, because sometime later I heard from far away the sound of Thena and Reed whispering, their voices urgent and angry. I opened my eyes and scanned the room. Elsa lay asleep at the foot of the stairs. Thena and Reed stood over Dan.

"Take his arms," Thena whispered. "I got his feet."

I stood and crossed the room. I saw that Dan's hands and feet were tied.

"Athena Kelley, what in God's name are you doin'? Where are you takin' him?" I asked, my voice shaking.

She didn't answer. She looked up at me, straight into my eyes, but she never said a word.

She and Reed slowly carried Dan's dead weight across the room. Reed opened the door and a cool breeze glided into the stillness, whipping up the flames of the fire. I looked out at what had once been the yard and saw that the rain had stopped. Thena glanced back at me once and then she and Reed carried Dan out, shutting the door behind them.

I never said a word to stop them.

I sat in Mama's rocker for the rest of the night waiting for Reed and Thena to come back, but they never came. Sometime after midnight, I woke Elsa and sent her up to sleep with Lilli. I sat watching the hands of the clock move around the dial. The face of the clock stared down at me with accusing eyes. I stared defiantly back at it, listening to the soft falling of the rain, which had begun again. I didn't care anymore.

Just before sunrise, I wearily climbed the groaning stairs and wandered down the hall into the boys' room. For long moments, I sat watching the three of them sleep. John's eyelids were badly swollen and there were dark shadows under his eyes. He seemed to have spent most of the night crying. Franklin Delano lay in between his brothers, holding each of their hands as he slept. There was a deep crease between his brows and occasionally he moaned and stirred. He seemed to be having a bad dream. With a sigh, I finally decided to let him sleep. For the present, reality was worse than any nightmare could have been.

Edwin lay on his side, facing Franklin. His knees were brought up to his chest, both arms wrapped around them. His skin was flushed and sweaty and he had kicked all of the bedclothes down around his feet. I kissed each of the boys' soft brown faces and left the room, shutting their door behind me. I knew that something was coming, and that it would come soon. I hoped that the boys and Elsa would sleep through it—whatever it was. Though I never could have imagined what it would be.

I went back downstairs, put a kettle on to boil and stirred up the fire. Then I sat down with a cup of black coffee. I held the scorching hotness of the mug in my hand and stared down into its dark depths wishing for an instant that I could dive in and be carried away. I waited. For a moment, I thought I heard Elsa and Lilli whispering upstairs. Then everything became quiet again. I waited. After a time, I began to hear the sounds of the townspeople waking up. Minutes passed and I heard excited voices raised, then shouting. I waited. Finally, I heard a knock at the door. I walked across the room to open it, my body slow and heavy with reluctance. The morning sky looked bleak and the pitiful falling of the rain yet continued. On the porch steps stood Doc Barrett and Sheriff Bridges. Doc spoke first.

"Grace, the town is being evacuated. The river won't hold much longer. We've got to get everybody out. Get Elsa and Lilli and the boys together. The bridge is gone. We've got to get out of here. We're moving everybody further west."

I nodded, numb, insensible. Then the sheriff took off his hat and moved forward. He looked over nervously at the Doc, wiping a hand across his sweaty forehead.

"Grace?"

"Yes, sir?"

"When was the last time you seen your sister n' Reed Wilkins?"

I swallowed; my tongue felt thick and my mouth dry and scratchy as sandpaper.

"Last night," I said, my voice sticking in my throat.

I licked my lips, trying to unglue my tongue from the roof of my mouth.

"Do you remember what time?"

"No sir. I guess it was between eleven and midnight."

He nodded. "That's about what I thought."

"How's that?"

"Grace," he said, taking my icy hand is his large, warm one, "last night, my deputy, Tom Ferrell, was down at the river, tryin' to make sure the last of the river people was out. They're the stubbornest bunch a' fools I ever heard tell of. We was 'fraid some of 'em would've tried to sneak back to their houses, so I sent him back to make sure the area was clear. When he got there, the water was real high n' had already begun to wash over the bridge. He was there a couple a' hours, lookin' in all them shacks n' sheds, at least the ones he could still git to. Then he said he saw the headlights of a car comin' off in the distance."

He paused for a moment.

"Now, nobody had any business drivin' over the bridge with the water that high. And Ferrell was startled to see the car—he thought ever'body woulda had the sense to know that the bridge'd be impassible by now. Then he saw Reed Wilkins' car pull up to it. He said it sat there fer a long time. Then it began to cross over. Ferrell shouted out as loud as he could. He took off runnin' after the car, wavin' his hands n' screamin'. But either they didn't hear or they wouldn't listen."

"He said there was a woman in the passenger seat n' that he saw 'er turn n' look back at 'im. Ferrell says it was Thena. I asked him how sure he was and he said a hunderd percent. He told me that there'd be no mistakin' it; said nobody else in the world looks like 'er, and I reckon I know what he means. Ferrell said that when they got about halfway over the bridge, he saw this wall of water rush over it n' the bridge was washed away. Grace, honey, Reed's car went with it."

I felt a low burning beginning in my feet. It gushed up through my legs and the fire grew. I felt a tearing pain in my chest and pains like knives being driven into my lungs and brain. I slumped down onto the porch. I heard a strange whirring sound and remember continuing to watch the rain fall. Then I heard the Doc's voice in my ear.

"Grace, darlin', I know this is too much hurt for any one person. But we have got to get you and Lilli and Elsa and the boys out of here. We have got to go *now*. Grace? Grace Kelley!"

Merciless black washed over me and the world became still and quiet and, for the first time in many days, I could no longer hear the ceaseless falling of the rain.

XXXI.

The day Shady Grove was evacuated, we were sent to a tiny, musty town called McClellan, many miles to the west of us. We stayed for six weeks, living in attics and church basements, and, though they were good to us in McClellan, I am sure they were relieved to see us go. By the first week of July, the waters of the flood had finally receded. A great deal of damage had been done, though not as much as we had feared.

On July 8, the body of Dan Brown was recovered. It was found by townspeople as they dug through the rubble, well preserved in the packed, deep silt of the river. Sheriff Bridges drove me over to identify the body.

"Grace," he asked, his voice careful and guarded, as we drove through the bright sunshine, "can you think of any reason Dan would've been wanderin' 'round in the rain, with it comin' a flood like it was?"

I swallowed.

"No, sir. I don't know why he would've. But then, his doin's never did make much sense when he was drunk."

My heart beat in my chest with a great clanging that I could feel all the way down to my feet.

"So, Dan was drunk that night."

"Yes sir, as drunk as I've ever seen him."

"You think Elder could've finally gotten to 'im?"

"He could have, Sheriff, but I guess it'd be a difficult thing to prove."

He glanced at me out of the corner of his eye.

"Do you think Dan had any enemies 'sides Elder that mighta wanted to drown 'im?"

"Well, Sheriff, I think you could probably knock on just about every door in town and find somebody who did."

He glanced at me again, and then was quiet for a moment.

"Yeah, Grace," he said, his voice even, "I reck'n you could."

Dan's body had been badly battered and torn by the blind fury of the river—to tell the truth, there wasn't much left of him—but his long black curls and what remained of the scar down one side of his face made him unmistakable.

On the night that Thena and Reed carried Dan away into the darkness to his death—or, I will say it: *murder*—I convinced myself that they had simply sent him away. I swore to myself that Thena, with that implacable gaze of hers, had told him to leave and never come back. I told myself that he had seen it in her eyes and known that he must never return. I promised myself a hundred thousand times in the six weeks we stayed away from Shady Grove waiting for the flood waters to sink back into the earth that Dan was hundreds of miles away, safe and sound, roaming somewhere in the mountains or valleys of the west. I told myself that Dan must have seen the fervent half-mad light in Thena's eyes and known that she would never stop until he had left us for good—one way or another—and that, knowing only too well the depths of her sometimes brutal nature, he had decided that it would be better to go quietly away. I swore to myself every which-way to Sunday, with disquieting ardor, that Thena and Reed had succeeded in doing what no one else had ever been able to. That they had somehow roused Dan from the alcoholic muddle of his mind and convinced him to leave, to disappear; to liberate himself and us.

But I knew. I knew every second, every minute, every hour of every day. From the instant I woke up that night and saw them standing over

Dan, I knew how it would end. I always did. Maybe even from the first time I met him. I knew the instant that my eyes met Thena's. I knew when the door closed behind them. I knew as I listened to the thudding of their feet on the porch as they carried Dan away, down the stairs, into the cold, dark water.

But I lied so effectively to myself for twenty years or more after his death that I pretty well had myself convinced otherwise. It was a quarter of a century before I could whisper the truth to myself in the dark. It would be thirty years before I could say it out loud and, until today, I have never told another soul—not even my husband, my dearest and most faithful friend. For more than sixty years, I have never said a word.

Not even to God.

Vengeance is mine; I will repay, saith the Lord. I knew that. I understood it. I believed it. But whenever I thought of Mama's broken body, her broken spirit, her broken heart; when I thought of the evil Dan had done to her, both the scars we could see and those we never would; when I thought of the evil he had done to every one of us, I could not speak the truth. When I had wished him dead a thousand times in my mind, how could I stop Thena from making him so?

But I knew. I always knew that no matter what it cost me or what the consequences were, I should have stopped her. I knew what she and Reed had done and I knew that I never should have let them do it. But I sat still in Mama's rocker, without saying a word, and I became one of his murderers. I let the evil and the lies continue. They continue to this day.

A week after we returned from McClellan, Reed Wilkins' beautiful golden body was found. It was untouched and perfect. There was not a scratch on him, no discoloration, no broken bones, no bruises, no swelling. He was as beautiful as the day he was born. On the morning they laid him to rest in the warm earth, Reed looked like a sleeping angel. We buried Mama just a few days later on the hill, under the old oak, next to both of the Stephens. They lie there still—my mama and daddy—and I know with complete certainty that they are peaceful there, happy to be together again. They watch the sun rise and set and the seasons change together the way they did when they were young.

The weeks passed and Thena's body was still not recovered. No word was ever heard from Lucius Elder and as far as I know he was never seen in our town again. Maybe he went back to hell.

For months, I sat silent in my agony. I looked after and loved the boys; I was now their mama. Elsa and I took care of the house. I worked at the library. But the taste of loss never left my mouth. My eyes burned and watered with it, my belly ached with it, the earth smelled of it and the food I ate tasted like it—all of it, everything, was lost.

The summer passed and the fall came on. The wind blew from the northeast and the air became cool. I watched the leaves begin to change—from orange to crimson to rust and finally to brown. In October we celebrated John's thirteenth birthday. Doc and Nora invited us over and Nora made a beautiful dinner. She baked John a tall towering chocolate cake, sprinkled with powdered sugar and insisted, laughing, that he eat half of it by himself. Without any trouble, he obliged her. The next month, I turned nineteen, and Pope, still far away in France, turned twenty-one.

In December, the postman walked into the library and handed me a certified letter. The address on the outside of the envelope bore my name and it was postmarked Everett, Washington. I went and sat in the cold, clear sunshine on the steps of the library and opened the letter. It read:

Ms. Grace C. Kelley:

Last month, on the fourteenth of November, a young woman gave birth in our hospital. She was originally registered under the name of Mary Canton, though we now know this was not her real name. The young woman had a quick, easy labor and gave birth to a baby girl. She named the child Hope. Within hours, both mother and child seemed fully recovered from the labor and we left the mother to rest for the night.

At about four in the morning, one of our nurses entered the young woman's room to take her vitals and found that her bed was empty and her few belongings had been removed. On her bed we found a slip of paper with your name and address, saying that she wished for the child to be given to you. She declared herself an unfit mother and stated that she wished for you to raise the baby. She named you as her sister. The note was quite straightforward and very short and was signed Athena Kelley. As soon as the note was found, we informed the police and a search for the mother ensued. After several days, we did hear word that a woman of her description had been seen hitchhiking north on Hwy 9. Nothing further was heard of the young woman, but authorities assume she must have traveled up into Canada.

We thought it best to inform you of these events, thinking that if Athena Kelley—we presume this to be her legal name—is your sister and the child is your niece, you would wish to be made aware both of the young woman's whereabouts and of the birth of her child. The child has been turned over to state services and the state has been made aware of the mother's wishes. Please contact us if you would like to receive further information, or if you would like to proceed with the adoption of Athena Kelley's child. We would also be grateful to receive any information you are able to give on this subject.

Best Regards,

William Constance

Director, Everett Municipal Hospital

I sat in the sunshine, its warmth washing over me, feeling the bite of the wind on my face for the rest of the afternoon. Tears washed over my face and hands and clothes. They fell down on to the dusty porch steps and onto my scuffed shoes. Finally, close to sunset, I walked home, the wind whipping the hem of my coat. I packed a bag and kissed the boys and Elsa and Lilli goodbye and walked to the bus stop holding a ticket purchased by Doc and Nora. One week later, I signed the papers and brought Hope home to Shady Grove. I never saw or heard from Thena again.

XXXII.

May 11, 1945

Gracie:

Three days ago, the Germans surrendered and victory was declared in Europe. O'Neill and I were granted our first leave of absence in months and we caught a ride into Paris on a farm truck. When we came to the outskirts of the city the truck was stopped. There was no getting through. For miles and miles, as far as we could see, people were out dancing in the streets. Hugging and kissing—men passionately kissing women they'd never seen before, and the other way around. We stood and watched couples waltzing down the avenues and through the fountains. I have never heard anything like that noise. It was louder than any battle I fought in during this war. The people were shouting and singing, crying and laughing. Champagne flowed down the streets, under the doors of houses, away through the cramped, crooked alleys and down into the Seine. The celebrating lasted for two days.

I'm coming home, Gracie. I'm coming home. I can't undo what's been done. I can never take it away. I can't bring back what you've lost. And I know that I can never remove the past from your mind. But I can help you build a future, a good one filled with promise and happiness and, if it's alright with you, that's what I intend to do.

Pope

≈ ≈ ≈

One hot afternoon in July, I held Hope on my hip with one hand as I pinned laundry up on the line. The air was hot and smelt of burning honeysuckle and newborn roses. The wind blew through Hope's hair and she batted at it with her dimpled hands. She began to laugh, smiling up at me with her dazzling green eyes, deep and bright as the lazy green river. She reached up and patted my cheek and chuckled. It was a deep, throaty, merry sound and I laughed back. I shivered with pleasure and joy and pulled her body tighter to me, breathing in the heat and smell of her. I pushed the black curls back out of her face and fingered her one scarlet lock of hair. I smiled at her and kissed her fat, slobbery cheeks. And we stood in the blinding heat and light smiling foolishly at one another.

Out of the corner of one eye I saw a shadow and glanced up. There was a man walking down the dusty gravel track that ran behind our house. I put one hand to my eyes, squinting, and watched him as he came closer. He was tall, very tall, and thin. My eyes focused in the bright glare of the blaring July sunshine and I saw the khaki-green of his uniform. He smiled. I smiled back and moved across the yard and out on to the dusty street. He walked up and took my hand.

"Come on, Gracie," he said softly. "Let's go see Mother and Daddy."

I tossed down my laundry, shifted Hope to my other hip, and we walked away, he and Hope and I.

Jenna-Clare Allen is a Tennessee native, though she has lived the life of a gypsy princess. She holds undergraduate and graduate degrees in theological studies. She, her husband and son live in Cleveland, Ohio, a city that they are completely nuts about. Though she has written for as long as she can remember, *As the Spark Flies Upward* is Ms. Allen's first novel. She also writes poetry, non-fiction and children's stories.

CPSIA information can be obtained
at www.ICGtesting.com
Printed in the USA
LVOW12s1444071216
516239LV00001B/260/P

9 780984 430208